MW01133094

A Season in Pluto

Matt Stevens

© 2017 Matt Stevens
All rights reserved.

ISBN: 1545593671
ISBN 13: 9781545593677

Forward

MIKE PAGE STOOD on the top step of the dugout. He was calm, though his left hand gripped the green railing a little tighter than it had in the sixth inning, when his team was cruising, 5-2. Now it was 5-4 in the top of the seventh after a bases-loaded single had scored two and left runners at first and third with one out. His right hand lifted his cap and scratched his head with the royal blue bill. It wasn't a sign to his defense or a display of confusion. It was simply a scratch, a natural reaction to an itch—a logical part of a sequence that would soon end with the cap back on his head.

Mike would have taken great comfort from that, considering all the illogical and out-of-sequence events he'd witnessed in the previous sixty days, except that his mind was otherwise occupied. He was trying to win the state softball championship on May 31 with a program that had been a hot mess on March 31.

His view from Firestone Stadium's third base dugout included a glorious blue sky and an ancient, steel-beamed grandstand jammed with screaming fans from Pluto and Warren Champion high schools. Mike could have been staring at that sky, daydreaming about his accomplishments—the 27-0 record and the conference and regional titles in his first season as a high school coach—but he wasn't. Nor was he paying very close attention, just then, to the situation on the field.

Instead, he was staring at his second baseman, Bree Fenner, and marveling at her tenacity and strength. He was thinking how easily she could have quit—and not just softball. It was no less than miraculous that she'd survived the past six years.

"Coach! Hey, coach!" his assistant shouted, finally attracting his attention. "You might want to make a trip and talk defense."

"Yeah. You're right," Mike agreed, shaking his head and replacing his cap. "Time!"

The umpire threw up his hands to stop the game as Mike walked to the pitcher's circle feeling confident and somehow in control of a volatile situation. *Failure is the result of ignoring the need for preparation.* His father used to say that— usually after Mike had failed at something.

The worst of the failure speeches had come after Mike's team lost the district title in 1974 when he threw an 0-2 fastball down the middle to Washington High's best hitter. It was the last inning of a 1-1 championship game. Benji Williams hit a walk-off home run that ended Mike's senior season.

"What the hell were you thinking?" His father wanted to know. Forty years later, Mike's answer popped into his mind as he stood in the pitcher's circle. *'I wasn't.' Everybody fails from time to time,* he thought—*but my players will never say they weren't thinking.* Of that, he was certain.

Still, Mike was who he was—and that meant he was seconds from launching into a two-minute speech covering every possible scenario—just in case his group of teenage girls had lost focus. But first, he stopped and stared into the bleachers above his dugout. *His* focus had shifted to a beautiful blonde woman in her fifties. She stared back and waved. He started to raise his hand, but quickly shoved it into his pocket.

As he turned to greet his infielders, he realized that this moment wasn't just about a game. It was about his past and his future and all the things he'd learned about them during a strange and deadly spring in a rural Ohio town called Pluto.

Chapter I

Tuesday, March 25

MIKE GRIPPED THE wheel tighter as a line of cars passed in the pouring rain. His disdain for funerals was forty years old. Serving at dozens of them as an altar boy had filled his memory with the odor of incense and old lady perfume. A stack of five dollar bills and some mythical grace couldn't mitigate the trauma from those childhood encounters with mortality. He was damaged. He knew it. The light turned green, but the procession continued. He sighed. His mind leaped decades. It had been three months since his wife of thirty years had died of breast cancer. The ache came and went, but wouldn't disappear. It was a parasite eating his stomach.

At least it's a good day for it, he thought, turning the wipers a notch higher. The procession ended. The hearse passed, its black flag flapping in the wind. The final car cleared the intersection as the light turned red for a third time. He wondered if the deceased had departed with regrets. *We all have a few*, he thought. He turned onto the I-77 southbound ramp. After twenty minutes, his cell phone's ring tone interrupted his better judgment's effort to turn the car back north.

"Hello?"

"Mr. Page? This is Janice from Hewett Dental. We've been trying to reach your wife. She's overdue for her checkup."

He pointed his Buick at the Route 21 fork. "I'm sorry," he said. "She passed away in December."

His heart ached at the thought of Peggy's struggle and his own loss. There seemed to be no cure now for his emptiness. Whenever it left his consciousness for a moment, something would send it back—a call from her dentist, a song on the radio, even the empty passenger seat. His GPS sent him onto a country road. Tilled corn fields, muddy from melted snow filled his eyes in all directions for the next thirteen miles. "One mile to Pluto," he announced after passing a sign. "I could have sworn it was three billion."

The rain stopped. He lowered his window to the unmistakable scent of rural Ohio. He turned left on North Main Street. On his right stood a dark brown, one-story log cabin with a white silo next to it. Pluto Feed & Supply had appeared on cue. Across the road, a light fog fell on forty acres of crop residue. Mike wondered about the process, about what farmers did with those shards of beige cornstalk.

He turned left on First Avenue. He saw a smallish red-brick fire house with a single-truck garage. The truck wasn't there. On either side of the fire house, there were empty lots dotted with dozens of plump green trash bags twist-tied at the top. There were hundreds of loose bricks, too, some stacked by kids probably playing war games; some scattered; all from a hardware store and a bicycle shop that used to be part of the pulse of Pluto.

Mike figured there wasn't enough money to complete the demolition. It reminded him of north Philly during his years as an editor with The Philadelphia Inquirer. On the other side of the street, a theater marquee advertised *Friday Night Bingo*. He turned right on School Drive. After the Dairy Freeze, which was boarded shut, a building simply marked, *School Administration* stood on the right, guarding another tilled corn field.

"This must be the place," he muttered. He parked in the space marked, *VISITOR* and locked his navy blue, six-year-old Lucerne. He walked toward the front entrance, straightening the pants to his black Adidas track suit. He stood in the lobby for nearly a minute before announcing himself to the secretary. He noticed several small plaques on the walls. Two referenced community service. The others were awards for scholastic or 4-H excellence.

"Mike?" The man extended a small, pudgy hand.

Mike shook it firmly. "Mike Page," he said.

"I'm Walt McKee, athletic director for the Pluto schools." His body matched his hand.

"Glad to meet you, Walt." Mike was blasted by the strong odor of Walt's after shave—self-defense *against the cow smell*, he thought.

"Let's talk outside," said the A.D. "I'll show you the facility. You'll love it."

They walked across the administration building's parking lot and the larger lot in front of the high school. They turned left and followed the sidewalk to the back of the building. The school had been built in the 1980s, when Pluto had transformed from two dozen farms into a bedroom community for commuters to Canton and Akron. Land developers had taken advantage of frustrated farmers desperate to make ends meet during a long drought.

Mike noticed the football field first. The home grandstand featured a press box with *Invaders* painted in royal blue from end to end. To the south, there were four tennis courts painted royal blue with white lines. The baseball field was directly north, its dugouts painted royal blue with *Invaders* written on top of each. Mike could see that the infield grass was still yellowish brown, dormant—*like my life*, Mike thought.

"There it is," declared the athletic director, pointing east to the softball field. "Home of the Invaders."

Mike stared for a few seconds. "Wow. That's impressive!" he said, truly impressed.

They walked through the gate leading to the home dugout. The floor was smooth concrete, painted royal blue. There were individual cubbies for helmets. The infield was made of the most expensive combination of materials. It had the same consistency and reddish orange color as most major league baseball infields. The outfield grass was still dormant and flat, cut as close as a country club fairway. On the outfield fence, eight large billboards were spaced equally from foul pole to foul pole, advertising Miller's Pub; Pluto Feed & Supply; Jackson-Graham Insurance; Boardman's Lawn & Garden; Pluto Chamber of Commerce; Riggins Veterinary Services; Grayson Optometry; and Dental Associates of Wayne County.

Behind the fifty-foot backstop screen, a concrete grandstand capable of seating two hundred fans gave the facility a stadium-like feel. Attached to the top of the grandstand was a press box with *Invaders* painted in royal blue on the back.

Beyond the center field fence stood a flag pole that held an American flag and a state softball championship flag.

"How old is this?" he asked.

"We built it in 2009, right after we won states," said Walt, welling with pride.

"Terrific," said Mike as they walked to the pitcher's circle. "Just terrific."

Walt stared at home plate for a few seconds. "Morgan Miller pitched the last game in the old circle. She threw a no-hitter for the district title. Then she threw two more at the regional at Akron U and a pair of one-hitters at states over at Firestone."

"Where'd she pitch in college?" asked Mike.

"She wanted to go big time," said Walt. "Tennessee. But it didn't work out. Started maybe three games her first two seasons, then transferred to a D-2 school in Kentucky. She did well there. Graduated." Walt pointed to the Miller's Pub sign in left center field. "Tending bar at her grandpa's place now."

Mike smiled. "Did she ever coach?"

"No. But I don't think anybody ever asked her. Coach Loop sure as hell didn't, even though she made him look like a genius."

"Yeah. Pretty tough to lose games when your pitcher's throwing no-hitters," Mike laughed. "Why didn't he like her?"

Walt paused to gather his thoughts. He wasn't sure how much he wanted to disclose. After all, he wanted Mike to take the job—and Morgan's little sister was a freshman pitcher with a lot of promise.

"It was an ugly, mostly behind-the-scenes thing involving Morgan and her dad."

"Does he work at the bar, too?" Mike interrupted.

"No. He's a real estate broker. But he played baseball at Kent State and made it to Double-A in the Padres' organization. So, he's been around—and he knows the game. Anyway, Morgan was a bit of a free spirit. She'd show up late for practice. She'd talk back to the coach."

"You mean, she acted like a teenage girl and diva ace pitcher?" Mike smiled.

"Yeah. Pretty much," Walt laughed. "Anyway, Larry Loop was a stickler for team rules and discipline. He suspended Morgan for two games after she mouthed off at practice one day. That meant she couldn't pitch the double-header they were playing at Grove City, down by Columbus. Coaches from OSU, OU, Miami, Kentucky and a few other schools had arranged to be there to watch Morgan pitch."

"And Loop stuck to his guns?"

"He left her home."

Mike kicked some dirt. "Jesus."

"Russ Miller drove to Loop's house the night before the trip and tried to reason with him. It didn't end well."

"What happened?"

Walt thought about his answer. "Loud voices. Pushing and shoving. Threats. The neighbors called the sheriff."

Mike put his hands on top of his head and sighed. "Man. That's a tough one. I see both sides of it."

"Yeah. Well, that pretty much crossed Morgan off those coaches' lists."

"What happened with the dad?"

"Not much. No charges. Loop banned him from home games, but he didn't take it out on Morgan. She pitched every game after that and won the state championship."

"What happened to Loop?"

Walt shrugged. "Oh, he coached two more seasons. He was 60 by then. He'd had enough and the team wasn't very good after Morgan graduated. We hired Maria Hernandez from Akron's pro team, the Racers, but she quit after one season. She didn't like the constant bitching from parents."

Walt mimicked a softball pitching motion. It was awkward and Mike winced as he watched it. "Maria especially didn't like it that some of the girls seemed more interested in their boyfriends and their farm animals than in softball. You don't make it through four years at Arizona and five in the pro league without being dedicated to the game. Right?"

Walt moved some dirt with his foot to fill the shallow ditch he'd just created in front of the rubber. Then he looked at Mike. "And last year? Well..."

"Yeah. Everybody knows about that," said Mike, taking the A.D. off the hook.

Walt was relieved. The memory of that nightmare was still fresh. He had taken the advice of a few players' parents and hired a club team coach named Darryl Sutton to replace Hernandez. Sutton's Summit County Pirates 16U team had won several tournaments and he had developed a solid reputation for teaching softball fundamentals. Pluto's top pitcher, Darby Belasco, had been the Pirates number one pitcher since her group started playing as ten-year-olds.

With Sutton at the helm, the Invaders' 2012 season began well. They won five or their first six games. Darby threw a no-hitter and two other shutouts. It seemed like they were headed back to state championship contention. Then, everything went wrong. Darby didn't show up for school one day. Her parents had no idea where she was. Seven hours later, she arrived at softball practice, as she often did, in coach Sutton's truck. Walt was there, along with Darby's mother and father. Darby broke down, claiming she'd been in love with Sutton since age thirteen, and that they'd been having sex since then.

Sutton was arrested. He cut a plea deal that sent him to prison for three years and branded him a sex offender for life. Darby's family moved out of the district. The Invaders finished the season with twelve wins and seventeen losses after that promising start. Pluto High School's reputation was severely damaged. The softball program was in ruins. Walt still wasn't sure why he hadn't been fired.

"So, what we need is someone who can put this thing back together. We need a great coach who's an even better person. And we think that's you."

"I'm flattered," said Mike. "I'm not without faults, but I think you're making a good choice." Then he paused and looked across the playing field, beyond the flagpole and the corn field, to the red barn at least half a mile in the distance. Could he stand the cow smell? Did he need the aggravation? Was this the direction he wanted his life to travel? He turned back to Walt. "Do we have any pitching?"

"As a matter of fact, we've got a couple of good ones," Walt grinned. Then he grew serious. "I guess I should mention that Morgan Miller's baby sister might be the better of the two. She's a freshman."

Mike smiled. "Minor detail?" He paused. Then, he sighed. "Where do we go for ice cream after a big win?"

"Well, the Dairy Freeze is closed," Walt began. Then, he stopped as he realized what Mike was saying. "You'll take it?"

"Yeah. I'll take it," said Mike.

"Whoo!" said Walt, throwing his hands in the air. "We've got a game in less than two weeks. It would have been really ugly if I had to coach."

Chapter 2

THE HOUSE WAS dark when Mike returned to Brecksville. Peggy had always turned on the porch light. A framed, eight-by-ten photo of his wife sat on the hall table. "I did it," he said. "I took the job. I guess you already know."

Peggy Page had looked and acted like a Peggy Page was supposed to look and act. She was petite, blond, blue-eyed and bursting with energy. She'd been a high school cheerleader and tennis player. She was also something of a daredevil. She loved water skiing and bungee jumping and driving too fast in cars and boats. Her father grounded her often for being reckless on the road and the water. She didn't care. She wasn't going to change.

It seemed a contradiction that she married the first boy she ever dated, but Mike Page was a catch. He was a handsome star athlete--the one all the other girls wanted. Peggy's appetite for adventure never extended to her love life. When she learned at age twenty-five that she couldn't bear children, she told Mike that he could divorce her and find someone who could. Mike laughed and cried at the same time, thinking how absurd and precious his wife had been at once. They had each other. That's all either would need to be happy.

At fifty-five, Peggy was managing the J.C. Penney store at Pioneer Mall when she was diagnosed with breast cancer so advanced that she lived only another two months. For years, she had joked about writing a book called "My Life in Retail." No one but her yellow lab, Valentine, knew that she had been doing just that in her spare time.

Mike discovered the files about a month after Peggy's death. He'd been reading her memoir a little at a time ever since. Now, he sat at the kitchen table drinking a Bud Light and scrolling to the spot where he'd stopped reading the night before.

I had to send Caroline home because she broke into tears while helping a young mother find flip flops for her five-year-old daughter. The inquisitive child wanted to know why the sales lady was crying. Caroline told her she'd just learned that her own little girl was a lying piece of trash who'd been sleeping with her mom's new boyfriend while her mom was out making minimum wage at J.C. Penney!

Later, an old woman—probably ninety—came in with a purse she'd purchased in 1999 at Macy's. She told me she wanted to take it back at Penney's. She handed me a receipt for a pair of pants she'd purchased at Penney's in 1994. When I tried to explain to her that she was in the wrong store, and that the receipt wasn't for the purse, and that 1999 was a really long time ago in terms of returns, she told me that my attitude was precisely the reason J.C. Penney was going to hell. I gave her a $19 refund for the pants and told her it was for the purse. I gave the purse to Goodwill.

Mike laughed out loud. He stared at the light fixture above the table. Tears filled his eyes. Peggy would have been overjoyed at the news that he'd accepted the coaching job at Pluto. She had told him a few months before being diagnosed that she'd never seen him so lost—not even when his baseball career ended.

Mike had never wanted to do anything but play ball, which is all he did until the Atlanta Braves organization released him at age twenty-seven. Suddenly, he was forced to find a job. He said he majored in Journalism at Purdue because the university insisted that ballplayers take classes and because he was mildly interested in sports writing. He figured if he didn't make millions playing in the big leagues, he might have fun writing about the guys who did. Unfortunately, the only job he was offered was for a *news* reporter at a daily paper in northern Georgia.

Mike covered city hall and the police beat for six months. He quickly learned to hate politics. He came to believe that just about every politician lied just about all the time. Crime stories were more interesting. Twice during those six months, he developed information that helped police solve high-profile cases. His reporting on the second of those cases, the suspicious death of a young school teacher, was honored by the Associated Press for outstanding investigative work. Soon after, the Atlanta Journal-Constitution hired him as a general assignment reporter.

After a distinguished fifteen years with the AJC, Mike accepted a job as an editor with the Philadelphia Inquirer. Five years later, the Cleveland Plain Dealer hired him away with a promise of job security at a time when newspapers were folding across the country. Eight years after that, the PD eliminated his job as a cost-cutting measure. Mike quickly learned that fifty-five-year-old newspaper guys were pretty much on the no-hire list.

He signed on with a local sports facility to give hitting lessons and was pleasantly surprised to learn that parents of mildly-talented children were anxious to pay $30 for a half-hour of instruction from a former minor league shortstop. Still, it was never lucrative. His calendar only averaged fifteen lessons per week—and the facility took half the money.

On top of that, Mike had a tendency to be honest with parents. If little Bobby or little Megan couldn't make their eyes and hands work as a team to hit a baseball or softball, Mike would advise their folks that soccer might be a better option. That was always bad for business, but he hated to see people wasting money on impossible dreams.

In the summer of 2011, he coached a 15U baseball team for the same facility. He led the boys to a couple of tournament wins. The players loved him because of his extensive knowledge of the game and because he didn't put pressure on them to win. He was only interested in teaching.

In 2012, he accepted the challenge of coaching a 16U softball team. He hadn't so much as spoken to a teenage girl since his college days, and he'd never tried to coach one. However, he had played fast pitch softball at the same time as he played baseball in high school and college. The men's fast pitch game was as popular in the summer then as bowling leagues were in the winter—and Mike truly enjoyed it.

So, when a friend suggested he take over the 16U Blue Jays, Mike decided to give it a try. Under his leadership, the Jays enjoyed a successful summer, finishing second in three of their seven tournaments and having a lot of fun as well.

He closed Peggy's laptop and placed it on the desk near the telephone. It had been a very long winter. He couldn't seem to escape the loneliness. In truth, even before Peggy's illness and death, there were times when he felt no interest in life. He had applied for at least thirty jobs without getting an offer. He was overqualified for most of them, but was called for only one interview—a copy editor's job at a weekly paper. The managing editor was twenty-five and thought Monica Lewinsky was a tennis player. It didn't go well.

Chapter 3

Thursday, March 27

MIKE AND WALT made arrangements to meet with the softball players and their parents at 7 p.m. Mike arrived at the school a little early—10 a.m. He used Walt's office to make calls to every other coach in the Heartland Conference. He reached all seven. He wanted to introduce himself and get a feel for their intensity levels. Were they passionate? Or just collecting a stipend? Were they life-long residents of their respective school districts? Or were they just passing through on the way to somewhere they actually wanted to be?

Four of the coaches were women. All were young, ex-college players with less than two years' experience. They were polite, enthusiastic and respectful on the phone. All had ambitions beyond the Heartland Conference. They spoke of "paying dues" so they could make it to the college coaching ranks. Mike was looking forward to helping them gain experience—the hard way.

The men were veterans. They'd been with their respective schools five years or more. One of them, Jake Moffitt, had been the head coach at Wyoming High for 25 years. He'd won three Division III state championships and four Division III "Coach of the Year" awards. Moffitt was the kind of coach that sports writers call "legendary." He had already heard about Pluto's new hire—and he acted put off by Mike's call.

"This is a pretty small pond," Moffitt told him. "But it's deep enough to drown. You've got your work cut out over there. Good luck." Mike thought Moffitt seemed like the kind of guy who'd have his players steal bases with a big lead in the last inning.

He walked upstairs to the main floor of the high school just as the sixth period bell rang. He shuffled slowly down the long corridor toward the cafeteria, glancing from teenage face to teenage face. He decided they were all the same person despite their physical differences. They were all trying to answer the same question: Who am I? Funny. So was he—still.

"Mike?" He was greeted by a tall man in his fifties, wearing a royal blue hooded sweatshirt with "Invaders" on the front. His pants seemed to belong to a brown, pinstripe suit. His shoes were dark brown Wingtips.

"You're Mr. Richter," Mike declared, extending his hand. The cafeteria was a few steps away.

"Call me Paul. I've been a principal for 15 years, Mike. I've never had to deal with anything like the Darryl Sutton situation. I hope I never see anything like that again. I'm glad you're here."

"Thanks."

"Lunch?"

They grabbed plastic trays from the stack at the front of the cafeteria line. Mike chose a Cobb salad. Richter settled on a tuna sandwich and barbecue chips. They sat near the middle of the room, enveloped by the low roar that raging hormones produce.

"What do you think so far?" asked the Principal.

"I'm impressed," said Mike. "Great school. Minimal chaos," he smiled.

"That's our goal," Richter smiled back. "You're meeting the players and parents tonight?"

"Yeah. The sooner the better. We've got a game in less than two weeks."

Mike spent the rest of the afternoon meeting with counselors. He wanted to make sure that everyone on his roster was academically eligible to play. He didn't want surprises toward the end of the season. It was mostly good news. Lauren Phillips, his junior center fielder was the only one whose grades were near the borderline. The players had to maintain at least a 1.8 grade-point average per semester to be eligible.

"What's her worst class?" Mike asked Lauren's counselor.

"She's failing History," said Charlotte Simonson, an impatient fifty-something who'd been with the district for thirty years. "If we get her some help, she could turn it around."

"I'll tell her to come see you," said Mike.

"Yes. Please do," she said, smiling.

At seven o'clock, Mike stood alone on the school auditorium stage. The girls who'd been chosen for the JV and varsity teams, as well as most of their parents, sat in the front six rows. They looked as he expected they would—like they had driven tractors to the meeting after pitching hay and milking something. He was definitely not as curious about any of them as they all were about him. He gave them credit for simple values and basic desires. He gave them all a black mixed-breed dog, three ugly cats and a freezer full of deer meat. He knew they would love him.

"Good evening everyone," he began. "I'm Mike Page, your softball coach." He paused as one of the parents clapped to begin a round of applause that peaked at a smattering.

The teams had been selected in February after a three-day tryout conducted by Walt McKee and two club team coaches from Akron. The varsity squad consisted of four seniors, five juniors, three sophomores and one freshman.

"I've only been coaching fast pitch for about a year," he smiled. Some of the parents rustled a bit and raised their eyebrows. The last thing they wanted was a rookie coach.

"But, I played baseball all my life. I played fast pitch softball at the highest level while in high school and college. I played college baseball at Purdue and minor league ball with the Braves up to triple-A. After that, I was a newspaper reporter for over 25 years in Atlanta, Philadelphia and Cleveland.

"More recently, I've been a hitting instructor at the Home Team Dugout facility in Strongsville. They sort of conned me into coaching a 16U girls' team last summer. We had a good season and I learned a lot about teenage girls. I took this job anyway." He paused, waiting for laughter that didn't come.

"I don't know what our potential is here at Pluto because we haven't had a practice. I hear we've got some talent, though, so I'm excited about that. I will guarantee a couple of things. The girls will learn more about how to play this game in the next two weeks than they learned over the last five years put together; and they will win games they never thought they could."

He paused for another tepid round of applause. Mike couldn't think of anything else to say. He didn't want to talk about the past—his or theirs. "Questions?"

"I have one," said a forty-something woman wearing a Pluto High sweatshirt. "Why did you take this job?"

Mike smiled. "I'll have to get back to you on that one. Any others?"

One of the players raised her hand. "What time is practice tomorrow?

"Practice will always start at 2:45. That gives you plenty of time to change after 9th period," said Mike. He recognized the young lady from the team photo on the PHS website.

"You might be a little late tomorrow, though, Lauren. I want you to meet with Mrs. Simonson. She has some information for you."

Lauren looked startled. The room grew awkwardly quiet.

"Okay, Fine," she said, quietly. An awkward silence ensued.

"I believe in preparation," Mike finally said. "Our team will be in shape and we'll be fundamentally sound. Our team will know as much as possible about its opponents. Along the way, I hope we'll learn a lot more about ourselves."

"How do you feel about players who miss practice to attend 4-H events?" asked a woman built like a haystack. She tugged at one of the fatty skin flaps on her neck as she waited for an answer.

Mike considered his response carefully. "What's been the policy?" he asked.

"Miss a practice—sit out a game—even if it's for 4-H. But it don't seem fair since 4-H is like breathing for most of these girls, and they don't get to choose the dates and times for their meetings and events."

Mike put his hands in his pockets. Seventy-seven cents. He juggled three quarters and two pennies in his right pocket with the tips of his fingers. He thought about the time he interviewed a magician who entertained at minor league baseball games. Just as he was asking The Great Gregory about one of his tricks, the magician said, "Eighty-five cents." Mike remembered being confused. "That's how much change you have in your right pocket," The Great Gregory declared. He was correct—six dimes and one quarter. Mike remembered being amazed because the difference in the sound of six dimes and, say, five dimes or seven dimes jangling with each other and with one quarter was nearly impossible to discern.

15

The Great Gregory had explained only that keen senses were essential in his profession. He would not be coaxed into a repeat performance, so Mike always wondered if the magician had simply made one lucky guess. He decided that keen senses were essential to lucky guesses. Wasn't that the difference between winning and losing most ballgames? The coach who guesses best about when to bunt, when to steal, when to play the infield in, when to play the outfield back, etc., wins the game.

"I think hard and fast rules about anything can be dangerous," he began. "I'd much rather look at every case as unique and try to work out a solution that best serves the individual and the team. Part of that solution might be a team discussion. Great teams work together on and off the field. If we're going to be a great team, then we've got to do what great teams do."

Mike scanned the auditorium for reaction. Some nodded in agreement. Some looked confused. The haystack was definitely not satisfied.

"So, what is the policy?" she asked. "We need to know."

Mike took a deep breath. "I'm not going to sit a player if she has a legitimate excuse for missing a practice. I'll decide what excuses are legitimate. There's your answer. It's going to be like everything else--like deciding who bats where; when we bunt; when we steal. I'm the coach. I'll decide. Any other questions?" The haystack fell silent.

Chapter 4

Friday, March 28

WHACK! THUD. RICK Fenner sat on his couch watching Wheel of Fortune. The noise from the barn was so familiar by now that he barely heard it. Whack! Thud. The sounds, a fraction of a second apart, repeated every ten seconds. Bree Fenner's metal cleats scraped the hard, dirt floor as she shuffled forward and swung her bat, hitting the yellow ball dead center. It flew off the black, knee-high tee and shook one of the hay bales stacked against the wall twenty feet away. She grabbed another ball from a bucket and placed it on the tee. Whack! Thud.

Rick checked the pot on the stove and turned off the burner. He flipped the porch light on and off three times, signaling to Bree that dinner was ready. She whacked one last ball and shoved the purple and white bat into its slot in her equipment backpack. She walked from barn to the kitchen and plopped into a chair across from her father. She stared at her plate for about ten seconds.

"Eat, Bree," Rick demanded.

"I'm not that hungry," she said, grabbing her fork and stabbing a small piece of the chicken breast Rick had prepared on a George Foreman grill. "I had a big lunch."

"The soup is good. Try it," he pleaded. "Made with love at the Campbell's factory in Camden, New Jersey—one of the poorest cities in America. You wouldn't want Camden to go under because you didn't eat your soup. Would you?"

Bree looked up with a blank stare. "I'm not hungry, dad."

Rick was certain she was lying about the big lunch. He had questioned Bree's friends. They said she rarely ate more than a small salad.

"Bree, honey, you have to eat. This obsession you have with getting faster is going to make you sick. You can't starve yourself and stay healthy enough to play ball."

"I'm fine," she insisted.

"You're not fine," said her father sternly.

Bree dropped her fork on her plate. "What do you want me to do? Be fat? Waste my time with a boyfriend? Drink? Have sex? Because that's what a lot of my friends are doing. Would that be better?" She stabbed another piece of chicken and chewed it hard.

"No. No. Okay," he relented. "It's all relative, I guess. I'm thankful you've turned into such a great kid. I'm proud of you, Bree. I just worry."

"I know," she said. You know it hasn't been easy for me without mom, but I'm okay. I really am, dad. I'll get through it."

Rick nodded and stared past his daughter to the disorganized papers and photos on the refrigerator door. On a purple Post-It note, he could read the words: *Gone shopping. Back at 5.* His wife, Cheryl, had written that note on May 7, 2008—the day she disappeared without a trace.

It had been unusually warm and humid that day. The temperature reached ninety degrees. Everything else was normal. Bree, then a sixth grader, kissed her mom and dad goodbye and ran to her bus at 7:45 a.m. Rick left an hour later. He told his forty-three-year-old wife that he had a volunteer firefighter's meeting at the station in Pluto. He returned to an empty house at noon. He reported Cheryl missing the next day.

After a week had passed without any activity on Cheryl's cell phone or credit cards, Wayne County detectives started treating Rick like a murder suspect. They searched his house, his car, his office. They questioned his friends. Rick's only relatives were his brother and his wife and their two young children. They lived in Abilene, Texas.

Cheryl was an only child. All of her close relatives were deceased. Her grandfather was the last to go. He had died of kidney disease just a week before she went missing. Her mother had died of breast cancer the previous November. Her father was a Marine, killed in the 1983 barracks bombing in Beirut when Cheryl was just 12 years old.

The detectives were not subtle. They asked Bree if her father had been having an affair. They scrutinized Rick's finances and insurance policies. Newspaper and television reporters cited anonymous sources in stories that hinted at foul play. The lead detective, Arch Kimball, had been so convinced of Rick's guilt that he told Cheryl's friends and Rick's friends—simple folks who'd been raised to trust law enforcement—that it was just a matter of time before Rick confessed to Cheryl's murder. It never occurred to them that the cops could be wrong. Those friends soon stopped calling Rick to check on the investigation or to offer their help. They contacted Bree, but only to suggest that she might be better off living elsewhere until her mom's case was solved.

At first, Rick tried to convince everyone of his innocence, but he soon gave up and concentrated on his relationship with Bree, who never doubted her father. After five years, her belief in him was all she had left, except softball.

Mike heard the crunch of gravel and stones as the Buick's tires rolled onto the small, crowded lot at Miller's Pub. He parked between two pickups and walked inside. It was dim, but not dark, just light enough that customers could see the dozen or so framed photos on the walls. They included many of the iconic Cleveland athletes: Jim Brown, Paul Warfield and Bernie Kosar from the Browns; Bob Feller and Jim Thome from the Indians; and Bingo Smith, Austin Carr and Mark Price from the Cavaliers. Archie Griffin and James Laurinaitis represented Ohio State football; Ohio native Nick Swisher, who was in his second year with the Indians after playing for the A's, the White Sox and the Yankees, represented Ohio State baseball.

The largest frame in the bar, however, protected an autographed photo of Thurman Munson, the Yankees' catcher and captain from the late 1970s championship teams. *To my friend Bill Miller, who always has my back,* it read. Munson grew up in Canton and played college ball at Kent State. He was known for his toughness—a perfect representative of northeast Ohio. He died tragically in 1979 at the age of 32 when he crashed his Cessna while practicing takeoffs and landings at the Akron-Canton airport.

Families having dinner occupied four booths to the right of the bar. Couples eating chicken wings and other tavern standards made small talk at six round tables in the center of the room. Everything was made of pine because Bill

Miller loved the smell of pine. He'd grown up in northern Michigan, where pine forests covered more acres than houses, highways and parking lots combined. He missed the smell of it during his tours in Viet Nam, where he'd been sickened by the scent of jackfruit, jambu and raffesia trees.

There were two empty seats at the bar. Mike sat and waited for the bartender.

"What can I get for you?" asked the woman.

"Bud Light is fine," said Mike, certain at first glance that he was speaking to Morgan Miller. She stood nearly six feet tall and looked to be in excellent shape. Her blonde hair hung below her waist. She returned with a bottle and twisted off the cap.

"Two fifty. Wanna run a tab?"

Mike pushed a five-dollar bill toward her. "No. One's my limit," he smiled. She made change, left it in front of him and started to walk away."

"Jennie Finch could hit. Could you?" he called after her.

Morgan turned. "Are you saying I look like Jennie Finch?"

"A much younger Jennie Finch," Mike smiled. "I'm Mike Page—Pluto's new softball coach."

"Ah," she said sizing him up. Walt McKee had called the shot. He'd seen her earlier in the evening and predicted this visit. "I'm Morgan Miller. But, I guess you knew that."

Mike took a short drink. "Ya got me. I'm looking for some help."

"Yeah? What kind?"

Mike took another drink. "Assistant coach. Pitching coach."

Morgan wiped the bar and washed a glass in the trough in front of her. "Not interested. No time for that," she said. "Besides, my sister's on the team." She walked toward the other end of the bar. Mike wasn't ready to give up. He moved to another seat.

"What about something unofficial? Maybe you could work with our pitchers a couple of days a week."

Morgan stepped on Mike's words. "No. Thanks."

Mike twisted his bar stool toward the door.

"Nothing personal," Morgan called as he walked away.

Mike didn't turn. He just raised his right hand and waved. If she didn't want to get involved, he wasn't going to push it. Having a pitching coach in high school can cause a lot of problems anyway, he reasoned. Serious pitchers take private lessons. They don't need two people telling them how to do one thing.

Chapter 5

Monday, March 31

MIKE STARED AT the forty-inch Samsung mounted on the wall in front of his treadmill. The treadmill had been Peggy's idea. The TV had been his. Every morning, the irony bit him. Peggy had been worried about his health. She sent him to the doctor. The doctor told him to exercise. He felt better. Peggy died. "Go figure," he said aloud. "Go frigging figure." His hour of fast walking ended just as the new episode of Law & Order SVU began. Mike turned off the TV before the show hooked him. He grabbed his phone from the ledge on the treadmill. *Five hours until practice*, he thought. *Nothing wrong with being early.* He grabbed a hoodie.

Mike arrived at noon and found Walt eating a sandwich in the teacher's lounge. The athletic director stood up and introduced the new softball coach to all seventeen people in the room. Mike forgot their names immediately—except Ms. Leticia Cragmere (better known at Pluto High as Ms. Quagmire). She was seventy-three years old and her thin face was beginning to lose its battle with gravity. She wasn't jowly yet, but things had definitely moved in the wrong direction. Her legs were so thin they seemed on the verge of snapping as she walked. Yet, closer inspection revealed the muscles of a former distance runner who still spent time on a treadmill.

She always wore dresses or skirts—and they were always hemmed four inches above the knee. No one at Pluto High dared tell her that four inches *below* the knee would have been the better choice. They all feared her ferocious and fearless wit, the kind that could leave anyone red-faced. Most important, she had tenure and money—enough of each that she could say or do just about anything she wanted. She had something else, too: A mysterious past that had been the subject of rumor and innuendo in Pluto for decades.

"We've heard plenty of good things about you," she said, extending a boney hand. "We heard plenty of good things about the last guy, too," she added without regret for her tactlessness.

"It's a pleasure to meet you, Ms. Cragmere," Mike smiled. "I hope to prove myself worthy of your respect."

She struck him as a sort of female version of the gruff, but loveable, "Uncle Charlie" character on the old "My Three Sons" TV show. But while Mike was comparing her to William Demarest in *his* mind, Cragmere's mind was certain his eyes had drifted to check out her legs.

Mike had only come to ask Walt for a key to the equipment room so he could assess the inventory before practice. He accepted the key and smiled at all of them as he walked away. He did notice Cragmere's legs. *Why is this old woman wearing such a short skirt?* He thought.

Chapter 6

"DOES ANYONE HERE know why President Kennedy was so adamant about making the trip to Dallas?"

Mr. Willoughby's words floated to the back of the classroom where Lauren Phillips had just finished reading a text from her best friend, Rachael. She was smiling as Willoughby called her name.

"Huh? No. Well. I know it's pretty cold in D. C. around that time of year," she offered. "Maybe they just wanted to go south?"

"Excellent, Lauren!" Willoughby shouted. Lauren looked up from her phone as the wiry American History teacher walked toward her. "Incorrect! But excellent!" Barton Willoughby was a snob and a bully. He'd been extremely gangly and uncoordinated as a teenager. Everyone always wanted to know why a kid who was six-feet-seven didn't play basketball. Willoughby's answer came in two words: "I suck."

"You suck," Lauren muttered.

"Excuse me?" said Willoughby. "Did you say something?"

Lauren thought about the consequences of an honest answer. "No. I guess I was wrong."

"All right," said the bully. "Does anyone else have a guess? In other words, did anyone read chapter seven?" The room fell silent. "Fine. Read it now. You've got fifteen minutes. Then we'll have a quiz." Willoughby turned and walked to his desk. Lauren texted April: BW=DB. April texted back: MAJOR.

Mike opened the equipment shed with no expectations. He saw a pitching machine that looked fairly new. An orange extension cord that must have been a hundred feet long was plugged into it. He saw three white buckets. Two were brimming with yellow, regulation softballs. The other was filled with gray, soft rubber balls. He saw a large duffel bag and unzipped it to find two sets of catcher's gear. He saw three bases. He saw two nets for soft toss hitting. He saw a pitcher's screen. He saw five bats standing in the far-right corner. Three were Xeno models by Louisville Slugger. The others were DeMarini CF5's. He was satisfied with the equipment.

"Hi coach!" Mike turned to see a young lady standing in the doorway. She was slightly built and stood about five feet tall. She wore glasses with wide, black frames.

"Hi there," said Mike. "What can I do for you?"

The girl smiled. Then, she declared in a voice that seemed a bit loud for the snug space they occupied, "You can make me the team's manager."

Mike paused to consider the offer. He hadn't really thought about that position. He'd been worried about finding an assistant coach. He looked around at the equipment. His back was telling him not to carry any of it—ever.

"What's your name? What grade are you in?"

"Lana. Sophomore."

"Lana Turner?" Mike asked, figuring she wouldn't get the reference to the mid-twentieth century movie star.

The girl surprised him. "Do I look like Lana Turner to you?" she asked. "Maybe you should borrow these glasses." She held them out and shook the thick, dark brown hair from her eyes. "Lana Lewis is my name," she declared, replacing her glasses. "L-L for short. Nice to meet you."

Mike shook her tiny hand. "You're not very big. Do you think you can help carry all this stuff?"

"I'm strong," she declared. "I have muscles." She flexed her right biceps.

Mike leaned forward and strained his eyes to see the little bump in the middle of her arm. "Well, I'll need your social security number and your birth certificate."

"For what?"

"So you can be vetted. You'll have to be vetted," said Mike with a very serious face. He expected her to wonder if he thought she were some kind of farm animal needing a doctor.

She surprised him again. "I'm not a supreme court nominee. I just want to be team manager."

Mike smiled. "Well, I can't have any convicted felons or otherwise dishonest individuals associated with my team. Can I? Have you ever lied, cheated or stolen anything?"

Lana grabbed a softball from a bucket. "Yes," she replied.

"Which?" asked Mike.

"All," said Lana. "I've lied to my parents and my boyfriends. I've cheated on my boyfriends. I've stolen from my parents and my boyfriends." She paused. "So, who hasn't?"

Mike was a little shocked, but he wanted to laugh out loud at the same time. "It sounds like you're pretty rough on your boyfriends," he said. "What do they see in you?"

"Do I have the job?" she asked dryly.

"If it's okay with your poor parents, it's okay with me," said Mike.

"It's definitely okay with them," Lana smiled. "They want me to do something besides study all the time."

"Maybe they want you to have fewer boyfriends."

"Yeah. That, too."

The ninth-period bell rang as Lauren reached the front of the room with her quiz paper. "Don't forget to write your name on your paper or you will not receive credit!" shouted Mr. Willoughby. Lauren ducked his awful breath.

"Lauren. Stick around for a minute?"

"Sure."

"Your counselor came to see me this morning," Willoughby began. "She told me you've got an excellent chance to get a scholarship for softball."

Lauren didn't say anything. She knew Willoughby was up to something despicable.

"She said you really need to raise your grade in this class in order to ensure your eligibility to compete this spring."

Lauren couldn't help herself. "And you're here to tell me you'll do everything you can to help me?"

Willoughby sat. He stacked the quizzes as the last of the other students left the room. "I'm here to tell you, Lauren, that I will not be bullied into giving you a grade you don't deserve. You'll be treated the same as everyone else."

Lauren's phone vibrated in her purse. She grabbed it and read the text message: *He WANTS you.* She smiled.

"Care to share?" asked Willoughby.

"Definitely not," said Lauren. "I do appreciate that you've decided to treat me the same as everyone else from now on. So, thanks," she said, spinning quickly and disappearing into the crowded hallway before Willoughby could process what she'd said.

Chapter 7

MIKE SAT IN the third base dugout staring at his clipboard. The names of his varsity players were hand-written on a piece of note paper from a Holiday Inn Express. The logo took his mind back twenty-five years, but only for a moment. He shook his head and focused on the names:

PITCHERS: Jen Miller; Callie Stump
CATCHERS: Allie Parker; Maria Milanowski
OUTFIELDERS: Lauren Phillips; Maddie Marsh; Halle Kruger; Nikki LoPresti INFIELDERS: Bree Fenner; Darcy Lomax; Andrea Kendall; Dee Malloy; Rachel McKenzie.

He wondered how many of them could actually play. "Coach Page?" It was his senior catcher. "I'm Allie Parker."

Mike held out his right hand. "Good to see you, Allie. Ready for practice?"

"I am, but Rachel isn't," she said.

Mike looked at his roster. "Rachael McKenzie? Why?"

"She just texted me," Allie said, holding her iPhone so Mike could read the text: *Tell coach I might not make practice Sally bloated and I have to help with her*

Mike read it again, but didn't understand. "What's it mean?"

"Sally's her cow," Allie explained. "She's bloated. She could die if the vet can't get the gas out of her stomach."

"How's that happen?" Mike asked.

"They eat too much alfalfa or other stuff and they can't burp or fart for some reason. Then their stomachs get bloated and they can have a heart attack if the vet doesn't get there in time."

Mike shook his head. "That sounds awful. Tell her I said good luck."

Allie texted the message to Rachel. After a few seconds, her phone buzzed. "She says, 'sorry' and 'thanks'."

Rachel's dad was screaming her name when she sped up the drive in her '94 Chevy pickup.

"Dad! I'm here!" she screamed back.

"Grab that old fence gate and pin Sally against the barn with it while we shove this tube down her throat!"

Steve McKenzie held Sally's head, while the local vet, Dr. George Parrish, forced open the Holstein's mouth.

"Hold her bottom jaw!" said the straining vet.

"Hold that gate against her, Rachel! Don't let her move!" yelled Steve, as he watched the vet jam a slick, rubber hose all the way to the cow's stomach.

Rachel used all of her strength to pin Sally to the barn wall. She could feel her feet sliding in the mud as she pushed the gate with her shoulder.

Just then, she felt a low rumble from the cow's mid-section. The vibration rattled the gate and sent waves through Rachel's body. Then, a noisy blast of hot cow burp roared from Sally's mouth for five seconds, hitting both men directly in the face. At once, they reeled from the putrid smell of half-digested alfalfa— and God-knows-what-else. They rolled and retched in the mud like they'd each swallowed a can of drain cleaner.

"Oh my God!" Steve yelled. Just then, Sally's backside swung like a bucking horse. Rachel screamed as she lost her grip on the gate. It flew from her hands and missed the men by millimeters, crashing against the barn door. As the gate flew one way, Rachel flew the other, still screaming as she landed face first in mega-size pile of cow flop.

"Shit!" she screamed, jumping to her feet and running in place. "Shit! Shit! Shit!" She grabbed the bottom of her hoodie and wiped off the dung, shouting obscenities non-stop.

Her father and the vet, now recovered from inhaling the devil's last breath, sat up simultaneously, both laughing and pointing at Rachel. "It's not funny!" she shrieked, half-laughing, half-crying and sounding like she'd completely lost her mind.

Then they all lost sight of each other for a few seconds as Sally walked slowly between them. "Moo," said the cow, breaking into a trot toward the house.

"Moo yourself! Rachel screamed. "You Shit! You fat cow! You fat ass cow! I hate you! I love you!"

Chapter 8

AT 2:45 P.M., eleven of the twelve Pluto Invaders' softball players were on the field loosening their arms. Mike watched intently. He always told people he could tell if a girl could play ball just by watching her play catch. He liked most of what he saw. After five minutes, he called his team to the pitcher's circle.

"Hi, girls. We met the other night at the parents' meeting, but I'll introduce myself again. I'm Mike Page."

He told them he was still looking for an assistant coach, and that he wanted to work on fundamentals for the first few practices to see what their strengths and weaknesses were. He told them he was counting on them to help rebuild the program both on and off the field. They all paid attention. He was thankful for that.

"Some of you may already know that Rachel isn't here because she had to deal with a bloated cow," Mike said with a bit of a smile. A couple of the girls laughed. Others cringed. One stuck a finger in her mouth and pretended to vomit.

"Anyway, we've got a lot to accomplish over the next two weeks, so please do your very best to be here every day." The girls all nodded.

"I'd like to start by going over a few of the most important things about softball. I'm hoping that none of this will be new material for any of you. Based on what I saw while coaching my 16-U team last summer, however, I'm guessing that won't be the case. So, pay close attention. That means keeping an open mind. Some of you may have been taught different ways of doing things over the years. I'm going to offer you a chance to do those things the way I know is best.

You're teenage girls. You'll do what you want to do. Just know I'm not interested in failure. I don't like losing. In fact, I pretty much forbid it."

Mike told them to form a line at home plate, where he had placed a batting tee, a bat and a bucket of balls. "All I want you to do is put a ball on the tee, hit it and run to first base."

"Are you timing us?" Bree Fenner wanted to know.

"Nope," said Mike. "Just wanna see if you know how to run to first. Ready?"

Bree put a ball on the tee and grabbed a CF-5. She stood in the lefty batter's box and swung just like she did every night in her barn. The ball bounced twice toward the shortstop position before rolling into left-center field. Bree was a blur running through first base into short right field before jogging back to the plate.

"Well done, Bree," said Mike. "Next?"

Dee Malloy hit a line drive that landed on the grass behind second base and rolled toward the outfield fence. She ran as fast as she could through the first base bag. Then, she turned to rejoin the group.

"Okay," said Mike. "What did Dee do wrong?"

"She didn't round the base," said Allie.

"Right!" said Mike. "That's part of it." He spoke to the entire group. "I'm sure some of you were coached by someone at some time who told you not to watch the ball after you hit it. Right?" They all nodded.

"Well. That's just wrong. How can you know what to do on the bases if you don't know where the ball is?"

"Isn't the coach supposed to tell you?" asked Maria.

"Here's the thing," said Mike. "If you wait for a coach to tell you what to do on the bases, you could lose at least a step—and that could be the difference between being safe and out.

"When you hit the ball, I want you to watch where it goes. I also want you to run like hell while you're watching it. If you see that it's rolling toward an infielder, then I want you to keep watching it until the fielder picks it up. Then you can turn your eyes toward first base and make sure you run through the bag, touching the front of it with your toe.

"The reason you keep your eye on the ball until the fielder picks it up is that if the ball goes through the fielder's legs, or bounces off the fielder's glove and ricochets toward the dugout or something, you might be able to take an extra base. If you don't watch the ball, you'll be turning to the right after crossing first base while the fielders are still chasing the ball.

"Every time you hit a ball that goes through the infield or lands safely in the outfield, I want you to run from home to first as if you're going to go for extra bases. The exception would be hitting a hard one right at the right fielder. Then you have to run through the bag if she picks it up and tries to throw you out." Mike put a ball on the tee and whacked it into left field, then ran toward first.

"When you see that the ball is past the infield, you should start to run out to the right a little to make your path toward first base look like a question mark. That lets you make a tight turn while hitting the front left corner of the base with your right foot so you've got the shortest possible path to second. If they bobble the ball in the outfield, you have to decide whether you can make it to second. If they field it cleanly, then you put on the brakes and hustle back to first."

Just as Mike put on his own brakes, his feet slid out from under him and he fell hard on his backside. The girls roared with laughter. Mike jumped to his feet and continued talking as if nothing had happened.

"Yeah. Funny," he said. "The whole time, you keep your eye on the ball, except to look down briefly to make sure you hit first base. If you aren't watching the ball, you will not be able to make the right decision."

Mike limped back to the group. His tail bone was definitely bruised.

"You okay, coach?" The voice came from the first base dugout. It was Rachel, bending down to tie her cleats. Her hair was still wet from the most welcome shower of her life.

"Rachel! You made it! How's the cow?"

Rachel told the story and everyone had a good laugh. Mike was thankful for the shift of focus. He was hoping his unfortunate spill could be quickly forgotten.

"There are lots of little things about this game that you've probably never thought about," he continued. "But you will—and we're going to win games because you do.

"For instance," he continued. "Who can tell me what factors you should consider when deciding to go for second when you see a ball being bobbled in the outfield?"

"I have some thoughts," declared Allie.

"Let's hear them," said Mike

"Okay. Well, you should be thinking about how fast you are; how far the fielder will have to throw the ball; whether the fielder has a strong arm or not based on what you saw when she took infield practice; whether she might be throwing a wet ball if it has been raining—because it's hard to throw a wet ball accurately."

"Excellent!" said Mike. "Can anyone think of anything else? That seems like a lot to think about in a split second."

Hallie Kruger, a freshman outfielder spoke up. "My dad says if you're fast enough to steal second on the next pitch, you should never risk trying to take an extra base on your hit if you think there's a chance you could be thrown out."

"Your dad is a wise man, Hallie," said Mike. "So, let's consider the opposite. If you're *not* a base stealing threat, being able to take second because of an outfielder's bobble could help win us a game. Let's say Allie gets a hit with the game tied and nobody out in the seventh inning and the other team has a catcher who can really throw. We'll have to give away an out by bunting her to second because she's not going to be able to steal it. Right? But if Allie runs hard to first, makes a good turn and takes second when the outfielder bobbles the ball, we're in business with nobody out."

Mike liked what he was seeing and hearing. They were all engaged in a conversation about the mental aspects of the game. "Anyone else?" he asked.

Darcy raised her hand and spoke at the same time. "I think you have to know what the score is and how many outs there are and who is hitting behind you," she said quietly.

Mike said, "Go ahead and explain all that."

"Well," said Darcy. "If you're down by more than a run, you'd want to be more conservative than if you're only down one or tied. If there are no outs, you'd want to be more conservative, too, since a bunt can get you into scoring position with only one out. If there are two outs, it's not a bad gamble to go if it's early in the game and a good hitter is behind you. That way it's kind of a win-win because if you're safe at second, she might get a hit and drive you in; if you're out at second, we'll have a good hitter leading off the next inning."

Mike was impressed. "Good points, Darcy. Did everyone understand all of that?" Some nodded. Some shrugged. Mike smiled.

"The most important part of that exercise is that we're all thinking. You have to think for yourself in this game. It's my job to teach you the things you don't know. It's your job to be smart players, not robots."

Mike spent the rest of the practice learning as much as he could about each player's strengths and weaknesses. He learned that both of his catchers, Allie Parker and Maria Milanowski, had strong arms and were very good receivers. Catchers get banged up over the course of a season, so it's always a plus to have two good ones.

He also learned that most of his players were using a bunting technique that was ineffective. He stood in the right-hander's box and spent fifteen minutes explaining his favorite technique and why he believed it was best.

"Start in your normal batting stance up toward the front of the box," he began. "Hands up. Ready to hit. When the pitcher is about halfway through her wind up, simply open your hands far enough so the bat drops through them until you catch the barrel about halfway up with your right hand and about where the barrel begins with your left hand.

"Grip the bat by holding it tight with your left hand all the way around it, and with your right thumb and index finger in a V-shape behind it so you won't be hit by the ball when it makes contact with the barrel. By holding it on the barrel only, we take the entire handle of the bat, the skinny part, out of play. Any ball that hits the handle is likely to go straight back foul or straight into your facemask anyway, so we'll just eliminate those negatives.

"Keep looking at the ball through the whole process and don't turn when you drop the bat in your hands. That keeps the corner infielders from charging early and giving them a shot at forcing the lead runner. Then, as the pitcher is beginning her delivery, you pivot on the balls of your feet and point your belly button toward her. Keep your hands about chest high and angle your bat slightly so the top of it is pointing to about two o'clock. When the ball arrives, reach out and shake hands with the ball—as long as it's in the strike zone, preferably at the belt or lower. Don't bunt it right back to the pitcher unless we've got the suicide squeeze on, in which case all you're trying to do is get it down anywhere in fair territory.

"Standing in the front of the box helps you keep it fair. Maintaining the bat angle prevents pop ups." Mike told Jen Miller to throw a few pitches so he could demonstrate. She fired the first one high and tight at about sixty miles per hour. Mike moved his head back, but his feet stayed solid in the box.

"You don't throw hard enough yet to hit me, so don't try," he smiled. "But that's good thinking. If you know they're going to bunt, throw the first one up and in. Maybe she'll be anxious and pop it up. At the very least she'll give away her intentions for free."

Jen threw the next one down the middle and Mike pulled the bat back and swung. He hit a bullet that one-hopped the left field fence.

"Of course, if she figures you're going to put the one-nothing pitch on a tee for her, she might just swing away and hit a gapper," he smiled. The freshman pitcher had just learned something. All the girls were paying close attention now.

"Third basemen? That's why you'll hear me holler, 'Watch her hands!' when it's a bunt situation. You don't want to move too early. It can be hazardous to your health. Some coaches don't like to bunt at all. Some coaches don't like to bunt with their better hitters at the plate. Sometimes the batter will just miss the sign. So, you can't assume. You have to watch their hands."

Mike learned that center fielder (Lauren Phillips), second baseman (Bree Fenner) and shortstop (Darcy Lomax) all had exceptional speed. He was surprised that Walt hadn't mentioned it. Maybe he didn't know. Maybe he didn't care. This season was more about improving the program's performance off the field than on it. Still, Mike couldn't help but smile as he envisioned mayhem on the bases—lots of stealing, lots of aggression.

He ended his own daydream. "I think that's enough for today. I'm really impressed with all of you. With any kind of coaching, you should be a great, great team," he smiled.

Chapter 9

IT WAS AFTER nine o'clock by the time Mike had driven back to Brecksville and grabbed a couple of fish sandwiches at MacDonald's. He noticed the porch light was on when he pulled into his driveway. He thought of Peggy, but remembered he had left it on for himself. He was making progress, he thought. Later, he found himself sipping a Bud Light at the kitchen table again. He leaned over Peggy's laptop reading through the bottom of his glasses. Valentine was lying on the other side of the kitchen, her nose pressed against her empty food dish.

"Why didn't I know about this?" he muttered. "Val? Did you know this stuff?" The dog didn't react. Mike kept reading.

It was two o'clock. I'd been arguing with this Polish woman, Lilly Jadus, who'd been coming into the store just about every day since I'd been working. She was more of a complainer than a buyer. Obviously, she enjoyed the attention I gave her and didn't seem to mind that she was taking me away from my real work. Lilly was going on and on about how she hated the changes we'd made to the lower level of the store—how she couldn't find anything anymore, and how everything was too high or too low or the wrong color—when I received an urgent call on my walkie-talkie.

"Forty-eight to the first-floor women's fitting room. Red please."

Forty-eight was my code name and using the color, red, meant that it was urgent. I nodded and smiled and left Lilly waving her arms at a frightened mannequin. I rushed into the fitting room to find two co-workers bent over a young woman who'd passed out.

"Did someone call 911?" I asked. They looked at each other and then at me. "Do it!" I shouted.

I checked the woman's vitals. She wasn't breathing. I started CPR. After a minute or so, she started coming around. Jackie from the jewelry department held up the plastic bottle of painkillers she found under the woman's right arm. When the paramedics arrived about half an hour later, the first thing they wanted to know was why this woman would want to O.D. in the J. C. Penney fitting room. I told them to leave the questions to the detectives and get her to the damn hospital. I guess I was rude.

Mike looked over at the dog. "Val? Did you know about the woman who overdosed in the fitting room?" He thought the dog's left ear twitched a little as if to say, "Sure, everybody knew but you, Mike," but then again, Val tended to twitch and scratch regularly, so it could have been a coincidence. He kept reading.

Two days later, I received a call from a woman identifying herself as Amber David. She wanted to apologize for trying to kill herself in my store. I didn't know what to say to that ("No problem?"), but I wanted to know what had motivated her. Surely there was a tragic story behind it.

I paid her a visit at Parma hospital. She told me that she and her five-year-old son had moved in with her mother in Parma about six months before her J.C. Penney overdose; two months after her Macy's overdose; and four months after her Sears overdose (what person under 60 goes to Sears for anything?) That's right. It had happened twice before. Amber David appeared to be a serial department store fitting room overdoser. I'm not making light of it. I just don't know how else to say it.

She told me that her son's father was a married man who lived in a small town. They had met at a bar and started a relationship after having drunken sex the first night. Four months later, Amber broke the news that she was pregnant. It wasn't well received. In fact, Amber said the father was so furious that he threatened to kill her. He ended the relationship immediately and told her to get rid of the baby. She said she never saw him again.

All of that was five or six years ago. So, what made her want to kill herself now? I asked, but she changed the subject. I asked again, but she said only that she was deeply depressed about her life.

Mike closed the laptop and stared at Valentine. "This is incredible stuff," he said. "Where was I? Did Peggy try to talk to me about this and I just nodded my head without listening? No way! I would have listened to this! I would have remembered this!" Mike was flabbergasted. Why hadn't his wife told him about Amber?

Chapter 10

Friday, April 4

MORGAN MILLER LAY flat on her kitchen floor. The white ceiling turned slightly left, then right, then left. Her eyes followed. Her stomach ached. She turned her head just as vomit streamed from her mouth and formed a yellowish puddle near her right ear.

"God, help me," she groaned. She reached for the table leg, yanking it toward her until it stuck in the grout between the gray tiles. She grabbed it with two hands, twisting her body and pulling herself to her knees. Her stomach retched and she threw up again, liquid only this time. She reached for her cell phone, but her back pocket was empty.

"Somebody, help me!" she screamed. Her blonde hair was floating in vomit now, but the room was spinning fast and she didn't notice. She only saw the six blue canisters with red covers on the counter near the sink. Around they went, around and around until her eyes closed.

Only five years earlier, Morgan had accepted a scholarship from The University of Tennessee. In her mind, she was bound for stardom—a tall, pretty, flame-throwing pitcher who could make the softball world forget Jennie Finch. She would lead the Volunteers to the national championship four straight years and become rich from endorsements and personal appearance fees. She would marry a football star and live happily ever after.

In fact, Morgan was one of two "insurance policies" the program had signed in case its tall, unattractive, flame-throwing pitcher—who was better, and just a sophomore—hurt her arm. Morgan never had a chance. She pitched three games—all against weak, non-conference opponents—in two seasons.

She won them all, but never impressed the coaching staff enough to earn a meaningful start.

She certainly didn't win praise from the coaches during her freshman year when her name appeared on the list of people ticketed for underage drinking at a sorority party. It happened two weeks before the team's first game. She was suspended for ten games and required to attend weekly meetings for students with drinking problems. The suspension didn't mean much. She wasn't going to play anyway. The meetings, however, exposed her to some of the most undisciplined young men and women on campus—all in denial. She befriended a few of them and learned to drink without getting caught.

While Morgan was finding ways to fail, her father started laying groundwork for a transfer. He contacted at least two dozen coaches and finally found one who was desperate for a number one pitcher.

She transferred to the University of Northern Kentucky before her junior year and became the program's ace. She won fifty-seven games in two seasons and led the Norse to a pair of conference titles. She lost by a 1-0 score in the NCAA Division II regional finals both years. She graduated with a business degree, then moved back home to help manage her grandfather's bar and grill.

Five years later, she lay on the kitchen floor of her two-bedroom apartment passed out drunk for a third night in row. The breakup of her latest relationship—a three-month affair with a married divorce lawyer from Canton—had triggered her latest bender.

When the sun woke her, Morgan stumbled to her bed and collapsed. Her phone rang at noon.

"Hello? What is it?" she demanded.

"Morgan? It's grandpa. I need you at the bar."

"Shit. I'll be there in 15 minutes."

Chapter II

THIRTY-FIVE YEARS AFTER his discharge from the Army's Green Berets, sixty-five-year-old Bill Miller stood behind the bar filling beer glasses as fast as he could. All fifteen stools were occupied. It was just after noon. Ordinarily, that would mean the regular lunch crowd of twenty or thirty people would trickle in and out over a ninety-minute period. This was not an ordinary Friday. This was opening day for the Cleveland Indians at Progressive Field. Beer was two dollars for a twenty-ounce glass. He scowled as Morgan burst through the side door.

"Sorry, grandpa," she said, taking her place behind the bar. "I've got it."

Bill walked toward the office without saying a word. Apologies from Morgan meant little. They certainly didn't mean she was bound to repent. There wasn't much he could do about it. She was blood. His wife was dead. His only child, Morgan's dad, loved the real estate business.

Bill was torn between willing the pub to Morgan, and selling it so he could retire to Florida. He'd come close to selling it two years before, when Morgan was engaged to the son of a local car dealer. Phil Peck had promised to make Morgan the assistant to the chief financial officer of his dad's business. Bill figured Morgan would be all set, so he started looking for buyers. The plan died when Morgan spotted Phil and a forty-something divorcee who used to date her dad making out in his car. The car was in the parking lot at the pub—of all places.

Morgan's head throbbed. She massaged her temples and took three Tylenol with a swallow of Club Soda. Over the next four hours, she winced in pain whenever the baseball-watching customers cheered. She felt bad that she had overslept on such a busy day, leaving Bill in the lurch.

Chapter 12

MIKE WALKED INTO the athletic office at three o'clock. Walt was watching the Indians' game on the nineteen-inch flat screen on the wall above his desk.

"What's the score?" Mike asked

Walt swiveled his chair to face his visitor. "Indians just took the lead with three in the sixth. Up three to two," he announced.

"Guess I'd better watch the end of it," said Mike.

"How are the girls looking?" asked Walt.

"They're talented. They're smart. They execute. They seem to love the game. They pay attention. No complaints," Mike replied.

Mike grabbed two softball magazines and a red envelope from his mail cubby near the office door. He put the magazines back in the box and opened the envelope. He found a hand-written note: *We all need forgiveness. We all make mistakes.* That was all it read.

Mike examined the white paper for a few seconds. Then, he stared at the envelope, which was postmarked *Pluto*. There was no return address. The writing matched the writing on the note.

"What do you make of this, Walt?" He asked.

Walt took the note and held it close to his face so he could read it. "I don't know," he said. "Have you been tough on one of the girls for booting grounders or something?"

"Not that I remember," said Mike. "You never know about girls, though. Sometimes they interpret "Hello" as "You're fat, ugly and worthless." They both laughed.

"Well, it doesn't seem threatening," said Mike. "And whoever it is doesn't care if I know they mailed it in Pluto. Probably harmless." He tucked the note into the envelope and slipped it into his jacket pocket. "I'll keep you posted."

Mike was greeted at the softball field by a breathless team manager. The strangeness of this day was about to magnify.

"Coach Page! We've got major issues!" Lana shrieked.

Mike set his clipboard on top of the first base dugout. "What issues? You and me issues?"

"No. No. We're good," Lana assured him. "We've got issues with Lauren and Bree. You'd better sit down."

"Okay," said Mike, sitting on the dugout bench. "Let's hear it."

"Okay, Lauren first," said Lana. "She called Mr. Willoughby, May I swear?"

"What?"

"Is it okay if I swear?"

"Yes. If you have to," said Mike.

"She called Mr. Willoughby a fucking creep."

"Jesus," Mike sighed. "Was that the worst of it?"

"Ah. No. That was the best of it in my opinion."

"Oh God," said Mike, rubbing his eyes. "I don't want to make you uncomfortable, but would you mind telling the rest of it?"

"Sure," said Lana. "I don't mind. Well, she was mad because Willoughby, who can really push a girl's buttons by the way, was making fun of her even worse than usual."

Lana liked to practice modern dance or ballet steps when she told stories. She shuffled twice to her left. Then, she did a pirouette. Mike was getting annoyed.

"Lana? Tell me what she said, please."

"Okay," said Lana, now flat-footed. "She mentioned that his penis probably looked like one of those leaf-eating green worms."

"Oh, God," said Mike rubbing his forehead.

"It gets worse," said Lana.

"Worse than that?"

"Yeah," said Lana, shuffling the other way and stumbling a little on her pirouette. "She added that she'd rather get shot in the ass with a nail gun than listen to his stupid, squeaky little voice talking about lame shit."

"Oh God, oh God. No, no, no!" said Mike, grabbing his ears.

Lana walked over and sat next to him. "What do think we should do?" she asked.

"Oh God, oh God. No, no, no," said Mike.

"Coach, you said that already. It's time to make a plan."

Mike stared at her. "A plan? How do you plan for that? She's going to get suspended. Hell, I think she could get arrested."

"Not even close," Lana assured him. "It's America, coach. She didn't make any terroristic threats. She just called him a name, commented on his manhood and mentioned her preferred method of torture."

Mike sat in silence for about thirty seconds, massaging his temples. "I suppose we could have her apologize. Then, if the principal suspends her, or worse, we could suggest that her parents threaten to sue the district based upon her First Amendment rights," Mike offered.

"That's the spirit, coach!" Lana exclaimed, patting Mike on the back. "I particularly like the threatened lawsuit angle. This district has had quite enough negative publicity. Don't you think? Surely, the school board would work very hard to keep this quiet."

"Oh, that's a guarantee," Mike agreed. His plan was forming quite nicely now. Plan? Lana was right, he thought. Jesus. Who *was* this kid?"

"In addition," Lana added. "I think if the case went to a jury—and the jury was forced to sit through one of Willoughby's classes—the majority would favor a nail in the ass."

She performed a double pirouette and finished with her arms outstretched the way a Broadway star might end a song and dance number.

"Just sayin'."

"Okay, okay," said Mike. "So, tell me what happened. Was she sent to the office? What happened?"

Lana looked at her phone. "I really don't know. I just saw it in a tweet from a kid in the class."

"A tweet? Oh no!" yelled Mike. "How many followers do you suppose that kid has?"

Lana started dancing again. "Probably not more than a couple thousand," she said. "But after re-tweets and such, you're talking unlimited."

"Oh, God. We're screwed." Then Mike remembered the second issue. "All right, tell me about Bree."

Lana shuffled back to the dugout. "Oh. Yeah. The cops were at Bree's house all afternoon. Somebody said they had a search warrant."

"Her mom?" asked Mike.

"Well, that's what the tweet said," Lana replied.

"Again with the tweets," Mike sighed. "Anything else?"

"Not yet," said Lana. "I texted Bree, but she didn't answer—which is not like Bree, but she's probably going through a lot no matter what's happening. Right?"

"Yeah," Mike agreed. "Good point. I think we should cancel practice today so I can deal with this stuff.

"I'll wait around and tell the girls," said Lana.

"Thanks," said Mike. "Wish me luck."

"Yeah. "You're gonna need it."

Mike jogged back to the high school. He arrived just in time to see Paul Richter walk into Walt's office and close the door. He thought about letting the two of them hash it out, but decided against it. He knocked on the door. Then, he walked inside.

"Mike. Glad you're here," said Walt.

"Have you heard?" asked Paul.

"About Lauren?" asked Mike.

"No. No," said Walt. "Lauren will be fine. That guy Willoughby is a dick and he knows it."

"I'll get Lauren to apologize and that'll take care of it," said Paul. "If he causes trouble, I've got plenty of leverage. We're talking about Bree. The cops arrested her dad today. They're charging him with murder."

"Jesus Christ!" said Mike. "Did they find the body?"

"They must have. But no one has said a word to us," said Walt. "We've made calls. Nothing."

"What about Bree?" Mike asked.

"Well, she believes her dad is innocent." said Paul. "And she wants to stay home."

"Is she eighteen?" Mike asked.

"She turned eighteen last month," said Walt. "She can stay home alone if that's what she wants."

No one in the room thought that was the best choice for Bree. Mike volunteered to have a talk with her—in part because he was her coach—in part because the news reporter in him couldn't resist a compelling story.

Chapter 13

MIKE TURNED ONTO a dirt road that tested the suspension of his eight-year-old sedan. Through the dust cloud in his rear-view mirror, he could see another vehicle. It looked like a black or navy-blue van. After half a mile, he turned right onto CR 505. The van followed. The first house on the left was a small, white colonial built in the early sixties. The driveway was fifty yards long and unpaved. It ended at the sliding door of a red barn that served as a garage, a storage area and a hitting facility for Bree Fenner, senior center fielder of the Pluto Invaders varsity softball team.

The landscaping was sparse—a few knee-high shrubs and a couple of young, leafless maple trees. The trees stood on either side of a concrete walkway that led from the barn to the side door of the house. There was no sign of law enforcement. Bree's red Dodge pickup was the only vehicle in sight, at least until Mike looked into the mirror again as he parked.

"Excuse me? Are you a relative?" asked the pretty brunette, stumbling and barely saving herself from a fall as she stepped from the van.

Mike shut his car door and turned to feel the windscreen from the woman's wireless microphone brush his chin.

"Come on, please turn that off," he said calmly. The photographer immediately did as he was asked. The reporter persisted, however, unaware that her partner had abandoned the ambush interview.

"Sir, what can you tell us about the arrest of Rick Fenner for his wife's murder?" She was young, Mike thought. Not a reporter, but an intern or production assistant sent because the station was short-handed.

Mike smiled. "He's not rolling. You should make sure he's rolling before you ask a question?"

She turned to see the cameraman standing with his hands in his pockets and his gear on the ground.

"Bob? Why aren't you shooting?" she demanded to know.

"He asked me not to," said the white, middle-aged man who was probably against driving onto the Fenner property in the first place.

"Bob Holmstrom," he said, extending his hand to Mike.

Mike shook it. Then, he extended his hand to the young woman. "Mike Page. I used to write a column for the Plain Dealer. Now I coach softball at Pluto High."

"I'm Rebecca Greenwalt," said the woman. "I'm an intern at channel five. So, you're a softball coach?"

"That's why I'm here. I just learned about the arrest of one of my player's dads. I really don't know anything more than you do. Probably less."

"Does that mean you won't comment?" Asked the wannabe reporter.

"It's really not my place," said Mike, as nicely as he could. "I don't know who represents Rick Fenner, but that person should do the talking—if anyone talks at all. Now if you'll excuse me, I really just want to check on Bree and make sure she's all right."

Mike walked to the house without looking back to see if Bob had resumed shooting. He had, of course. Bree opened the door before Mike could ring the bell.

"They arrested my dad!" Bree cried. "They came in and took his shit and put him in handcuffs."

Mike gave her a hug. "I know. I'm sorry."

"He didn't do it! He didn't do it!" She pulled away and threw herself onto a beanbag chair in the next room.

Mike followed and sat on the floor. "They told you about your mom?"

"They said she was found in a vacant house in Cleveland. Dead for years—probably the day she disappeared," Bree said, crying softly.

The sheriff's detectives and crime scene investigators had been gone several hours. News of an arrest in the cold case disappearance of Cheryl Fenner was all over television, radio and internet.

"What do you want to do?" Mike asked. "Do you have anywhere else to stay?"

"I'm already packed. I'll be staying with Jen Miller's sister, Morgan, for a while."

Mike was surprised by that news. "Oh. Are you two friends?"

"Our dads are—and she used to pitch to me when I was first learning how to slap. She's nice. She listens when you talk to her."

She barely gave me the time of day, Mike thought. "All right. And you've got your truck, so you'll be driving there tonight?"

"Yes," said Bree.

Mike asked a few more questions to see how much Bree knew about her dad's situation. He learned that Rick Fenner was represented by the law firm Peavy, Mitchell & Kline. It was a large Cleveland firm known for handling criminal cases that couldn't be won. Recent clients included a serial killer, a cop killer and a sexual sadist ex-priest.

Rick Fenner didn't fit. The presumption of innocence wasn't just a formality in his case. It was actually viable. Plus, he owned property, had a job as a body shop manager and was apparently living a clean life while raising his daughter. He wasn't indigent like those other PMK clients. That was a problem. Mike figured Rick would be homeless and broke long before the case went to a jury if he didn't find cheaper representation. On the other hand, cheaper representation could cost him his life.

Bree zipped her duffel. "I'm set. Morgan should be here in a few minutes," she said.

"All right," said Mike. "Anything you need? Anything I can do?"

"I'm fine," she assured him. "I'm pretty tough. I'll see you at practice tomorrow."

Mike was surprised to hear that. "You don't have to..."

"I want to," she interrupted. "I need to."

Chapter 14

VALENTINE SLAPPED MIKE'S legs with her fast-wagging tail a half dozen times as he hung his hoodie on the closet door knob. He could almost hear Peggy's voice as he did: "Hang it *in* the closet, please." It was late and Mike was exhausted. He fed the dog and grabbed a beer from the fridge. He thought about going to bed, but Peggy's laptop was calling.

> *Her son was adorable—blonde hair, blue eyes, feisty personality. He was getting to the age where he'd need a father, or at least a father figure, in his life. Amber said she knew nothing about sports. She'd never been fishing. She'd never been camping. She had no father and no brothers, only an uncle she'd never met—her mom's brother.*
>
> *Her love life consisted of occasional one-night stands. She had given up on the notion of a white knight riding into Parma. She was always on edge because her mother was angry about the intrusion and intolerant of R.D.'s often rambunctious behavior. Amber felt trapped. She felt like there was no hope of improving her life. She said her conscience was always eating at her. She said the mistakes she made could never be undone. She was so desperate and pathetic that I couldn't resist the urge to help her. I asked what I could do. She said, "Nothing."*

Mike's eyes were heavy. As he closed the laptop, he looked at the ceiling. "Where *was* I?" he said.

Chapter 15

Saturday, April 5

DETECTIVE ARCH KIMBALL of the Wayne County Sheriff's Department sat across from Rick Fenner at a steel table in small room reserved for suspect and witness interviews. A video camera was visible, mounted on the wall facing Rick. Kimball was convinced that the man he was questioning was the only suspect—as well as the only witness—in the murder of Cheryl Fenner.

At six-foot-three and 270 pounds, Kimball was intimidating without saying a word, but when he stood over a suspect barking questions like a St. Bernard, he was terrifying. Rick was neither intimidated nor terrified. He was numb.

A squatter had found Cheryl Fenner's bones two weeks earlier in the basement of an abandoned house on the west side of Cleveland. The cops had kept the discovery quiet until the medical examiner's office could identify the remains. Dental records Rick had provided at the time of Cheryl's disappearance left no doubt. Rick wasn't told where the bones were found.

"You're aware that we're recording this interview. Correct?" Kimball asked.

"I am," said Rick.

"You've been advised of your rights and have declined to have counsel present for this interview. Correct?"

"Correct."

"All right, Mr. Fenner. Where were you on the morning of May 7, 2008?"

"I was home in the early hours. I left for a volunteer firefighters' meeting at 8:45."

"Was your wife home when you left for the meeting?" Kimball asked.

"She was," said Rick.

"Did she tell you about any plans she had made for the day?"

"No. She helped get our daughter ready for school and put her on the bus. When I left for my meeting, she said 'see ya later.' That's all I know."

"How long did the meeting last?"

"About an hour," Rick replied.

"So that makes it ten or ten-fifteen when it ended?"

"That sounds right."

"What time did you get home?"

"Noon. I remember looking at the clock in the kitchen after finding Cheryl's note. It was noon," Rick said, confidently.

"The note that said she was out shopping or something?"

"Gone shopping. Be back at five," said Rick.

"Right. It's about a fifteen-minute drive from the fire station to your house. But you didn't get home for ninety minutes. Can you explain that?"

Rick paused. As I recall, I went to Pettiti's Nursery to look for hanging flower baskets for the front porch. Cheryl had mentioned that we didn't have any flowers out there, so I figured I'd surprise her."

"Did you buy any flowers?"

"No."

"Why not?"

"I didn't like their selection of pansies and petunias," Rick said. "They looked a little picked over."

"Did you speak with anyone? Anyone who might remember you?"

"Not that I recall. I just looked at the flowers and left."

"Did you go anywhere else?" Kimball asked.

"No. I went home after that."

"So, you looked at flowers for, what, over an hour?"

"I looked at some other things."

"You said you only looked at flowers. Are you changing your story?"

"Yeah. Sue me," said Rick.

"No one saw you there?" asked Kimball.

"I have no idea who saw me," said Rick. "I wasn't there to make sure I'd be seen. I was there to look for flowers."

"So, you might have come and gone without anyone taking notice?"

"If no one took notice, then no one took notice," Rick said. "I'm not responsible for what other people do."

"Let's move on, Mr. Fenner." Kimball was confident that Rick's alibi was weak. He was much more interested in manipulating Rick into revealing his motive for murder. "Were you and your wife having any problems at the time of her disappearance?"

"None that I remember," Rick answered dryly.

"Everything was fine? Sex good?"

"As far as I remember. It was a long time ago."

"You're about to go on trial for your life, Mr. Fenner. I suggest you jog your memory," said Kimball, raising his voice.

"I suggest you kiss my ass," Rick said, looking Kimball in the eye and raising his voice as well. "I didn't do it, so I don't have to jog shit."

Kimball was losing patience. "I think you *did* do it," he shouted. "I think you killed her and drove her to Cleveland and dumped her body."

"And I think you're a fucking awful cop and a dumbass," Rick interrupted.

Kimball continued. "Now, if it was an accident or self-defense or something like that, then you need to tell us. You need to come clean on this, Rick. Get it off your conscience. Save your soul."

"I didn't do it. I loved my wife," Rick said quietly.

"Ever cheat on her?" Kimball asked.

"I didn't kill her," Rick insisted.

"That wasn't the question," Kimball said, staring at Rick's face like he wanted to see beneath the skin. Kimball had questioned hundreds of suspects. Rick was hiding something. "I asked if you ever cheated on her."

"Okay. Yeah. A couple of times. A few times. Nothing serious. Just one-nighters after getting drunk. That's it."

"That's it?" Kimball didn't like the answer. It was too probable, too believable. He knew how life happened—and it wasn't like that. Life was almost always improbable, unbelievable. Rick was definitely hiding something, but Kimball let it go—for the time being.

"That was a pretty nice insurance policy you collected on. What was it? Half a million?"

"I haven't spent a dime of it," said Rick. "But then, you know that by now."

The interrogation lasted four hours. Kimball wanted a confession, but Rick never wavered. At 4:00 A. M., Kimball pounded the table with his fist and called his suspect a lying son-of-a-bitch.

"Guard! Take this asshole back to his cell!"

Chapter 16

Monday, April 7

IT WAS TWO days before Pluto's first softball game. Mike wasn't ready. His team wasn't ready. Obviously, the discovery of Cheryl Fenner's remains and the arrest of Rick Fenner had shifted the focus. He wondered about the sensitivity of even suggesting that the girls show up for practice. At two o'clock, Mike walked into Walt's office seeking advice. He told him about his conversation with Bree.

"If she wants to keep playing, there's no decision to be made," said Walt.

Mike agreed. "Okay. Practice at two forty-five. I'll have an announcement made so they all get the word."

As he walked toward the school's main entrance, Mike saw Bree. She was flanked by Morgan Miller and Leticia Cragmere.

"Ladies," Mike said, tipping his Pluto Invaders ball cap.

"Coach Page, we were coming to find you," said Bree.

"What's up?" Mike asked.

"I think you know my great niece," said Ms. Cragmere, pointing to Morgan.

Mike would never have suspected that a statuesque beauty like Morgan was part of this Elmira Gulch lookalike's family tree.

"I didn't know you were related, but yes, I've had the pleasure," Mike smiled.

"She's here to ask for a job," said Ms. Cragmere.

"Oh?" said Mike, looking at Morgan, who was clearly embarrassed.

"She's right. I've had a change of heart. If you still need an assistant, I'd be happy to help," she said.

Mike was floored by this positive development, but he maintained his composure. "What do you think, Bree?"

"I think it's a great idea!" she said.

"Okay. Done deal," Mike said. "Practice is at two forty-five. See you there."

Mike started walking, but he stopped when he heard Cragmere's voice.

"Coach! We all need forgiveness. We all make mistakes."

Mike remembered the note and smiled. "I couldn't agree more, ma'am." Small towns, he thought. You have to love small towns.

Chapter 17

HALF AN HOUR later, Mike gathered the girls and introduced them to their new pitching coach.

"We just got a whole lot better," he told them. "As you know, Coach Miller led Pluto to a state championship. She pitched at a high level in college. She knows what she's talking about, so listen to her."

Morgan stepped forward. "I want all of you to know that I'm thrilled to have this opportunity. It's my first coaching experience, so I'll be learning from you as you learn from me. Let's have a great year!"

Everyone clapped. Mike clapped the loudest. Morgan had just made his job a lot easier. She'd handle the "girl" stuff that made him feel uneasy. She'd help the pitchers make adjustments during the games. She'd teach the catchers how to adjust to the strike zones of individual umpires—and how to call pitches. "Whew!" Mike thought. Things were falling into place.

Mike wanted to work with the outfielders, so he sent Callie Stump and Jen Miller to the bullpen area with Morgan and catchers Allie Parker and Maria Milanowski. He told the infielders and outfielders to take their positions. He told Lana to grab a glove and catch for him. She danced to the dugout and grabbed an old catcher's mitt, thrilled with the opportunity.

"I'm going to tell you what the situation is," said Mike. Then I'm going to hit the ball. I want you to throw to the correct place and tell me why it you made the decision you made. All right, here we go. We've got two outs and a runner at second. We're leading three to one in the bottom of the seventh inning."

Mike grabbed a ball from the bucket and whacked it into left field. Maddie Marsh fielded it on the run after two bounces and came up throwing. She fired it all the way home on the fly. Lana caught it like a pro and pretended to tag an invisible runner.

"Nice arm, Maddie!" Mike hollered. "But the runner was safe. Now tell us all why you threw home."

"I threw home to stop the runner from scoring," Maddie said with confidence.

"Well, you had good intentions. But you threw to the wrong base," said Mike loud enough for everyone to hear. "Remember what I said the score was? We were ahead by *two* runs. That means the runner at second didn't mean anything. The batter was the tying run. Unless we're absolutely certain we're going to get the runner out at home—which we can *never* be—we have to keep the tying run out of scoring position. So, when the ball was hit to our left fielder, she should have thrown to second base—even if her mom and her uncle and everybody else were yelling, 'HOME!'

"Now, let's talk about outfield positioning with two outs and the tying run at first base. Thoughts?"

Maddie spoke up. "Deep. So it takes more than one hit to score the run."

"Very good, Maddie," said Mike. "Unless there's a really weak hitter or a little slapper at the plate, we want to play extra deep in this situation so the runner can't score from first unless the ball goes over the fence. Ideally, we'd like to force them to get three hits to score a runner from first. I'll take those odds with our pitching every time."

Mike spent the next thirty minutes talking situational strategies. He told them how important it was to eliminate mental errors. "Everybody bobbles one from time to time," he said. "Everybody strikes out. Everybody drops the ball. Nobody's perfect—physically, that is. But mental errors? They're a different story. You *can* be perfect mentally. You *should* be perfect mentally."

Many of the girls were hearing this kind of information for the first time despite having played organized softball for years.

"That'll be the day," Lauren joked.

Mike laughed. "All right. *You* should probably try to be perfect *physically*."

Chapter 18

After practice, Mike and Morgan stood near their cars in the parking lot. Hers was a black, 2000 Ford Focus with well-worn tires and a few dents and scratches. Mike wanted to ask why her real estate mogul of a father hadn't fixed her up with a better car. Instead, he asked why she had changed her mind about coaching.

"Oh, let's just say I had an epiphany after a conversation with my grandfather."

"Yeah?"

"Yeah, well, he sort of mentioned that I was becoming a liability at the pub due to my excessive tardiness. Bad relationships and booze came up, too."

"And?"

"And he said if *I* didn't do something to change my lifestyle, *he* would."

"He threatened to fire you?"

"And to cut me out of his will," she laughed.

Mike paused. "So, you're here under duress?"

Morgan paused. "I'm here to help—both of us."

"How about Cragmere?"

"She's grandpa's older sister."

"Ah. Not much family resemblance. Thank goodness," said Mike.

"They're pretty close," Morgan continued. "I'm guessing she got involved. She's been hounding me to get out of my rut. She's the one who told me you were looking for help."

Mike smiled as he remembered meeting the old woman.

"She's loaded, you know," Morgan said.

"No. I didn't know," said Mike. "How loaded?"

Morgan sat on the hood of her Focus. "She inherited millions in real estate-
-farmland and other property; and a lot of stocks, bonds and cash from her dead
husband, Robert Cragmere. I think she even owned a minor league baseball
team for a few years. All of it came from the estate of Robert's first wife. Her
name was Wanda Shaw. She was heir to the Shaw department store fortune.
She died under mysterious circumstances in the early seventies at the age of
thirty-one."

Mike started to sit on the hood of his Lucerne, but thought better of it. He
leaned against the driver's side door panel instead. "Murdered?" he asked.

"They called it an accident," Morgan shrugged. "But there were fingers
pointing at Robert and Leti for a long time."

"Really?" Mike was intrigued.

"Yeah. It's a little tough to picture, but I've seen photos. Leti was a real
number back then. Sexy. Yeah, sexy!" she laughed. "I was told they met in
one of the Shaw stores—the young, kindergarten teacher and the married man
who'd lost interest in his rich, alcoholic wife. Robert was thirty-five. Leti was
twenty-five. The story goes that they were six months into a torrid affair when
the unsuspecting Wanda drowned in her swimming pool. She'd been drinking
the night before, as usual. Robert told the cops he woke up and found her floating face down."

"Wow!" said Mike. "That's right out of a movie! What do you think? Did
he kill her?"

"I heard Wanda was an excellent swimmer," Morgan said dryly.

"Have you ever asked your aunt about it?"

"Just once. She said it was an accident. Then she told me never to mention
it again," Morgan smiled.

Mike smiled, too. Then he changed the subject. "How was the night with
Bree?"

"Not terrible," said Morgan. "She cried a little, but I think she's more pissed
than sad. She really believes Rick is innocent."

"What do you think?"

"I have no idea," said Morgan. "I hope he is—for Bree's sake."

Chapter 19

MIKE'S PHONE RANG a few seconds after he left the school parking lot.

"Mike Page? It's Rick Fenner."

"Rick Fenner? What..."

"I need a favor."

"Okay. What can I do?" Mike had no idea why Rick Fenner would be calling him. He could only figure it had something to do with Bree, like making sure she kept her focus on school and softball. Maybe he objected to Bree moving in with Morgan. Maybe he wanted him to be Bree's guardian. No. Eighteen-year-olds don't need guardians. His head swam so fast with the possibilities that he barely heard Rick's answer.

"You were a crime reporter, right?"

"Huh? Yeah."

"I want you to help solve my case."

This was not on Mike's list of possible reasons for Rick's call.

"Rick, you have lawyers. They have investigators. I'm a softball coach. I don't..."

Rick cut him short. "I fired Peavy, Mitchell and Kline. They wanted my property as a retainer. That was *after* I told Wayne Mitchell himself to take a flying leap because the bastard said a manslaughter plea was the smart move."

Mike was stunned. "Rick, you need a lawyer."

"I know. I know. I have someone in mind," said Rick, calmly.

His voice was too calm, Mike thought. Why wasn't he out of his mind with grief and fear?

"Who?" Mike asked.

"Gail West. She's a former county prosecutor. She handled major cases for twenty years. She's perfect."

"You can afford *her*?"

"I'll find out tomorrow. If she takes the case, I'm hoping you can work with her."

Mike was dumbfounded. He'd never met Rick Fenner. He'd only known Rick's daughter for a couple of weeks. Now the man was asking him to save his life. That was just a tad presumptuous, he thought.

"Of course, I'll do what I can," Mike said, feeling like he'd just stepped into a Graham Greene novel.

"Thanks, Mike. I'll call you tomorrow morning."

Mike looked at his phone. He could see that Rick had hung up. "No problem," he said. "No problem."

Mike had been anxious to read Peggy's next chapter. The Amber David story was as intriguing as it was disturbing. He grabbed a beer and sat in his usual seat at the kitchen table intent on resuming *My Life in Retail*, but his mind wandered. It told him to Google Gail West first. Her name brought up more than two dozen articles from the *Akron Beacon Journal*, the *Canton Repository* and the *Cleveland Plain Dealer*. Most were connected to a single case in 1997.

She had been the lead prosecutor in the murder trial of a man named Phillip Dorsey. The Dorsey case drew national attention because he was accused of shooting three unarmed teenage burglars who'd broken into his car. The fifty-five-year-old Dorsey happened to be watching from the window of his home when the gangsters shattered the passenger side window with a rock.

The defense argued that Dorsey acted in self-defense after confronting the teens and trying to hold them at gunpoint for police. His attorney claimed the eldest suspect, a nineteen-year-old convicted felon named Melvin Cranbrook, pulled a knife and lunged at him. Dorsey told investigators that he panicked and shot them all.

Public opinion was on Dorsey's side. There was little sympathy in Cleveland for gangsters terrorizing inner city neighborhoods. Since everyone involved was black, no one played the race card. Only the dead teens' relatives cried foul, and most of them were of questionable character. West, however, was not interested in public opinion, only in the truth.

She dealt a major blow to the defense by proving that Dorsey had planted his own switchblade near Cranbrook's body. Dorsey took the stand to explain that he had panicked when he saw that Cranbrook's weapon was only a screw driver. He sobbed, claiming he hadn't slept a wink since being forced to take the lives of those young men. That seemed to weather the storm, but West was just getting started.

She couldn't prove who owned the screw driver, but she blew holes in the self-defense claim when she discovered that Dorsey had been holding a grudge against Cranbook and his cohorts. West learned that during a visit the previous summer, Dorsey's thirteen-year-old niece heard her uncle tell Cranbrook that if he ever got the chance, he'd kill him. Cranbrook had stolen tools from Dorsey's garage. The niece testified that Cranbrook had laughed when Dorsey called police.

West never wavered in her belief that Dorsey had planned the whole deadly incident. After the trial, she called it "obvious." On the night of the shootings, Dorsey's 1992 Cadillac Sedan Deville was parked on the street. His closest neighbors testified that Dorsey always parked inside his padlocked garage. In fact, they called him "paranoid." They quoted him as saying that anyone who parked on the street was "asking for trouble."

Investigators found a twenty-dollar bill and a new DeWalt power drill on the passenger seat of the Cadillac. West called it a "murderous plot." She told the jury that Dorsey used "a bill and a drill as an invitation to a kill." The defense called her theory "preposterous." The jury decided it was the truth.

Dorsey was sentenced to three life terms without the possibility of parole. On his way out of the courtroom, he told West that he was "proud to get that scum off the streets." Dorsey died of a heart attack three months later. West quit the prosecutor's office soon after that.

Mike did a photo search. He found thirty-two shots, most of them taken within the last few years. Gail West was fifty-four years old, but looked much younger. She had shoulder length blonde hair. She'd been a local beauty queen, Miss Summit County, in the early 1980s. She had reddish brown hair then.

There was one swimsuit photo. She wore a one-piece. Mike stared at her shapely legs. He arrowed to another photo and double clicked on it. She was standing on courthouse steps answering questions from at least a dozen TV and print reporters. The caption was interesting: *Defense attorney Gail West accuses investigators of railroading her client.*

Mike kept searching and found a companion article. It was published July 7th, 2012. Her client was a former Wayne County firefighter named Ron Parker. He'd been charged with murdering his wife. West told the reporters that police and prosecutors had ignored evidence pointing away from Parker. She claimed the real killer was a Cleveland cop named Jack Weatherby.

Mike found some articles published after the verdict. At trial, it was revealed that Melissa Parker had been having an affair with Weatherby in the months leading up to her death. Because Weatherby was also married, at least three people—Parker, Weatherby and Weatherby's wife, Jo Ann—potentially had a clear motive for murder.

Melissa had been found dead on her front lawn with a .32 caliber gunshot wound to her chest. Her husband had been asleep (so he said) in the house when a newspaper delivery man spotted the body and called authorities. The murder weapon was never found. It was determined that not one of the possible suspects could be linked in any way to such a weapon. Gail West had no trouble convincing the jury that being convinced of her client's guilt would be impossible. Had she helped Ron Parker get away with murder? Mike found an article published two years after the trial. The lead detective in the case was emphatic.

"He did it," declared Arch Kimball. "As far as I'm concerned, we proved it."

Mike bookmarked the photos and the articles. *Wow*, he thought. *I must have dropped off the face of the Earth after losing my job. How did I not know about this case?*

He turned his attention back to Peggy's story. He found the place where he'd left off and leaned forward while sipping a Bud Light.

I didn't believe her. There had to be something I could do. I looked at her face and saw despair that broke my heart. I kept pressing for information and learned that she had graduated from beauty college in 2010. She was a certified stylist and manicurist, but had lost two good jobs because of her addiction to pain killers. I offered to help get her hired at the J. C. Penney's salon. One of the girls there had just quit to open her own business. The timing could not have been better!

Amber just laughed. "They don't hire pill heads at J.C. Penney—especially the ones who try to kill themselves."

She was right, of course. I told her I'd think of something. She asked me for a hundred dollars. I gave her two.

Mike shook his head. Two hundred dollars? "Valentine!" he hollered, looking toward the front room. The dog walked into the kitchen after a few seconds and plopped on the floor at his feet.

"Did you know mom gave Amber David two hundred dollars?" Valentine looked away. "I think you did."

Chapter 20

Tuesday, April 8

MIKE'S PHONE RANG at 9:15 a.m. "She'll take it," said Rick.

"Gail West?"

"Just got off the phone with her. She wants the case. She'll do it for expenses."

"Great," said Mike, still shocked and confused by his sudden involvement in a high-profile murder case. "How'd you manage it?"

"I just laid it out for her," said Rick. "I told her I'm innocent and that the cops are lazy, good-for-nothing sons of bitches. Oh, and the lead detective on my case is a guy she tangled with on another big case. She proved this guy, Arch Kimball, tried to cover up evidence that would have exonerated her client. I also told her that you agreed to help in any way you can. So, she's waiting for your call. I can't thank you enough."

Mike shook his head as he processed Rick's rapid-fire delivery.

"Wait. Wait. Wait. What the hell!" He shouted when he realized Rick was gone. "Oh, what the hell," he repeated in a resigned tone. He Googled a phone number for Gail West, Attorney at Law. The secretary said his call was expected.

"Hello, Mike. I hear you've volunteered to help on the Rick Fenner case." Gail's voice was deeper than he imagined it would be.

"Well, I..."

"Let's have lunch today, if that's convenient. Noon at Miller's Pub? I hear you know the bartender."

Mike smiled. He liked her voice. "Okay. Noon at Miller's."

Morgan was behind the bar when Mike arrived half an hour early.

"Hi Coach," Morgan said.

"Hi Coach," Mike replied.

"Drink?"

"No. Thanks. Meeting someone for lunch."

"Anyone I know? Like, maybe Gail West?" Morgan asked.

"Exactly like Gail West," said Mike. "How'd you know?"

"Small town," Morgan smiled.

"Oh, yeah," said Mike, backing away and settling into the nearest open booth.

Rick Fenner's new attorney walked into the pub ten minutes later, fifteen minutes early. Mike recognized her immediately from the internet photos. She wore a navy suit with the skirt hemmed three inches above the knee. Her black pumps sported four-inch heels. Gail walked straight to the bar and spoke briefly with Morgan, who pointed a finger at Mike.

"Mike Page," said Mike, standing with his hand outstretched.

"Ah. Glad to meet you, Mike." She shook his hand firmly, slid into the booth on the opposite side and got right to the point.

"So, tell me why Rick Fenner thinks you should be my investigator on his case."

Mike laughed. "I'm cheap."

Gail opened her black briefcase and pulled out a stack of papers about an inch thick. "Cheap? I like cheap, but this guy's life is on the line. I need good, too. Are you good?"

Her tone seemed a bit blunt. Mike decided to soften her up with humor and charm. "Am I being interviewed for this job? Because I would never wear this outfit to a job interview," he said dryly, looking up and down at his orange golf shirt and black jogging pants.

"I'm glad to hear *that*," she smiled. "No. Sorry. It's not an interview. I just want you to know what we're up against. It's the whole Wayne County Sherriff's Department and the prosecutor's office against you and me."

Mike noticed the ring on her right hand. It was a thick, gold band with vertical rows of quarter-karat diamonds. The opposite ring finger was bare.

"That is one amazing ring," said Mike, purposely changing the subject.

"It was my Aunt Sally's," said Gail, without appearing to mind that he had done it. "She never had children and I was her favorite niece. I move it to my left hand if I want people to think I'm married."

"Does that mean you want me to know you're single?" He asked before realizing he was flirting.

She smiled. "It means I woke up with it on my right hand and didn't think about it."

"Sounds like a fair fight—you and me against them," Mike said, reverting to the original conversation. "Especially since you've already beaten them once by yourself."

"Ah," said Gail with a smile. "Then you know about my feud with detective Kimball?"

"I read a few articles," Mike said.

Gail smirked. "When he finds out I've taken this case, he's going to work twice as hard to put Fenner away."

Mike smiled. "Yeah, well, he shouldn't let his emotions get the best of him."

Gail handed Mike the stack of papers. "Here's all that's on the record in the Fenner case. Take some time and study it. I'm pretty sure there's a lot left to uncover. That's where you come in, Coach Mike."

"I guess this means I passed the interview?" Mike smiled.

"You didn't fail," she said.

They spent the next half hour talking strategy and getting to know each other. Mike was surprised to hear that Gail had never been married. She had been engaged once—to another University of Michigan law student when she was twenty-five. "He married someone else," she mentioned with a shrug.

Mike shared only a few things about Peggy and their thirty-five-year relationship—that she was unable to have children; that she was the most patient person he ever knew; and that she'd been writing a funny and interesting book about managing a J. C. Penney store. He did not mention that he broke into tears sometimes when he'd wake up and look at Peggy's side of the bed.

They parted with a plan to interview Rick together in the morning. Driving home, Mike thought about the crazy twist his life had taken. Wasn't it just a few weeks ago that he sat wondering if he'd ever break through the fog that enveloped his life when Peggy died? He remembered staring at the mountain of sympathy cards on the dining room table and wishing he could have gone with her. Loneliness and boredom are the co-conspirators of depression—and Mike had been housing them rent free for months.

Now he was up to his eyeballs in activity and intrigue. Now he could name three dozen people who were depending upon him for one thing or another. Pluto had brought him back to Earth. He actually felt burdened, like he used to feel when he was covering three hot stories at once for that little Georgia daily. Time wasn't grinding away with rusty gears now. It was running away with smooth strides. It felt good. He slept through the night for the first time in months.

Chapter 21

Wednesday, April 9

SHE STOOD ON the grass near a yellow maple that was still just green and gray. She spoke softly into her iPhone as if someone might overhear a national secret. There was no one close. Gail West wasn't paranoid, just careful—at least that's what she told people when they called her paranoid. Mike startled her when he said, "Good morning."

"Oh. God. Hi. I'm just dealing with some work issues," she said, clutching the phone to her chest.

"No problem," Mike said, backing away a little to give her a feeling of privacy."

Gail whispered into the phone for another thirty seconds, then said, "thank you" in a much louder voice, the way a mother might say "thank you" to a child who reluctantly agrees to empty the dishwasher.

"I have a new receptionist," she explained, as if an explanation were required. "It's been a little rough getting in sync."

She tucked her phone into her Coach bag and then smiled at Mike. "Are you ready?"

"I'm ready," he said.

The jail was a red brick one-story facility surrounded by a ten-foot fence topped with razor wire. Mike had seen many similar buildings during his years as a crime reporter. The deputies manning the metal detector both said, "Good morning, Miss West," as Gail set her briefcase onto the conveyor.

"Hi, Billy," she said to the taller of the two. "How's that baby?"

"Ornery," he replied with a smile. "But healthy. Thanks."

The detector beeped as Gail walked through it. She held her hands above her head and the other deputy gave her the once-over with a wand. It beeped as he waved it near the front left pocket of her suit jacket.

"Whatchagot?" he asked.

"Vibrator," Gail replied, dryly.

Both deputies chuckled. Gail pulled a lipstick from the pocket as she introduced her companion. "Paul and Billy, this is Mike Page. He's working on a case with me. Billy stared at Mike as he walked through the device.

"Mike Page. Mike Page," he repeated. "You're the new softball coach in Pluto. Right?"

"Word travels fast," said Mike. "Nice to meet you fellas."

"Yeah," said Billy. "My niece, Rachel, plays for you. She says you're a good coach."

Mike smiled. "I guess we'll find out next week. First game's on Tuesday."

"Well, good luck," said Billy.

"Yeah. Good luck!" said Paul, as Mike and Gail walked toward the intake area.

"Can't get over this small-town stuff," said Mike.

"Yeah," said Gail. "It never ends."

After signing a few papers, they were escorted to a large room with eight metal, picnic-style tables. Rick was sitting at one of them, with a guard standing about ten feet away, hands on hips.

"Welcome to my miserable life," Rick said, standing and shaking their hands.

After a minute or two of small talk, Gail looked at Rick and said, "I want to make something absolutely clear. If you lie to me, or if you hold anything back, you'll be looking for a new attorney."

"I understand," Rick said.

"All right," said Gail. "First question: Did you have anything to do with your wife's disappearance or death?"

Rick didn't hesitate. "No. I did not."

"Do you have any idea of what happened to her?"

"This time Rick hesitated. "I guess I could speculate."

"Great," said Gail. "Speculate away!"

Mike opened his notepad. Rick rustled in his seat.

"I wasn't faithful to her," Rick said. "There were a few women. I guess you could say there were a lot of women over the years. Maybe one of them got jealous. I don't know. Or maybe Cheryl found out about one of them and..."

"Remember," Gail interrupted. "Holding back is just like lying in my book."

"I know. I know. But the truth is that one guess is just as good as another. For all I know, she got carjacked at the mall."

"The biggest problem is motive," Mike said. "She was a stay at home mom who wasn't cheating and didn't seem to have any enemies. Outside of that random carjacking theory, you're pretty much it, Rick."

Rick gave Mike a look that said, "Kiss my ass." The look was followed by an awkward silence, with the two men locked in a stare down like a couple of twelve-year-olds with a crush on the same girl. Gail broke the silence with a suggestion.

"Do us a favor, Rick. Take a few minutes and write down as much information as possible about any of the women you've, uh, been intimate with. Whatever you can remember—names, addresses, husbands, children, workplaces, anything at all."

Rick grabbed the notepad Gail shoved across the table and started writing. Occasionally, he paused and tapped his front teeth with the top of the pen. His recollection was less than vivid. He finished in five minutes. There were four names on the pad. One was only a first name—Mary. Next to her name, Rick wrote "cocktail waitress at Wild Stallion, Cleveland."

The first name on the list was Patti Grant. Rick described her as the secretary at the State Farm insurance office in Marshallville, the town on Pluto's western border. He mentioned Patti's husband, Arnold, describing him as a deputy sheriff 'somewhere.'

The second name was Lisa Workman. Rick described her as the wife of Ronnie Workman, who was a fellow volunteer firefighter in Pluto. He also wrote, "Separated and lives in Pluto with mother."

Next to the other name, Grace Montrose, he wrote, "Divorced from Al Montrose. Works at Giant Eagle in North Canton."

Gail stared at the notepad for about thirty seconds. Then, she declared the meeting over. "If you can't think of anyone else, then we'll call it a night and get started," she said. "Remember what I said about lying," she admonished her client.

"It's all there—to the best of my recollection," Rick insisted. "If I think of anything else, I will let you know immediately."

"Screwing your friends' wives?" Gail asked as she stood to leave.

"Cheryl and I were going through some things. That's all I can say," Rick replied, apologetically.

Mike followed Gail. He said nothing until they were out of Rick's earshot. "I say we let him rot," he declared, dryly.

Gail smirked. "Not an option—unfortunately."

Chapter 22

MIKE SCROLLED PAST a few of Peggy's odd stories about her life as a J. C. Penney store manager. He skipped reading the one about the thirty-something woman who took five pairs of jeans and five T-shirts into a fitting room and came out carrying nothing, but walking like the Tin Man from The Wizard of Oz. "You're profiling me!" the woman screamed indignantly.

"Damn right, sweetie," I told her. "Everybody who gains twenty-five pounds from a five-minute visit to our fitting room gets arrested for shoplifting. No exceptions."

He skipped reading the one about the ninety-year-old man who thought he was attending his daughter's wedding.

He demanded to know why I wasn't wearing my wedding gown. I told him the tailor was making some last-minute alterations. We called social services. They sent someone four hours later. We had to entertain the poor guy until they showed up. Among other things, one of my associates, a college girl named Emma, took him over to Dick's Sporting Goods and watched him hit golf balls into a net. Apparently, he'd been a scratch player back when Ben Hogan was a teenager.

Mike was too anxious to find out what Peggy's next move had been regarding Amber David. He was desperate to know how much more he didn't know about his late wife—the person he lived with for thirty-seven years.

After giving her the two hundred dollars, I didn't see or hear from Amber for a couple of weeks. I was hoping she hadn't used the money to buy more drugs. People want to do the right thing, especially when it concerns their personal welfare. Don't they? Sure, they do—unless their addictions own them.

I drove to Amber's mom's house on a Saturday morning. Jean Swanson answered the door. She was a slight woman in her fifties with short hair dyed a shade of red that could never be mistaken for natural. She was dressed in a K-Mart uniform. She said she was waiting for a babysitter to arrive so she could go to work at the Brookpark Road store. Her grandson stood behind her, peeking around her right hip and sucking his thumb.

Jean told me that Amber had gone out one night more than a week before and hadn't returned. There had been no word from her. Nothing. Poof. I asked if she had reported Amber's disappearance to the police. She said she had, but that they were rude and dismissive after seeing all the drug-related issues on her record. Who could blame them? Amber was the perfect candidate for disappearance—voluntary or otherwise. They said if Jean couldn't provide information that suggested otherwise, they'd have to assume voluntary.

I stood there wondering how Amber's mother could bear a life so burdened. Did Jean Swanson ever have high hopes? Did she dream little-girl dreams about white knights and happily ever after? I so wanted to save her and her grandson, but as I looked at those tired, filmy, brown eyes, I realized there was nothing I could do. There were no white knights in Parma--not for her, not for her daughter—and there never would be. She had learned that the hard way and accepted it. I had to do the same. I walked away, taking a last look at the little boy's face as I turned. I cried all the way home.

Mike hit the down arrow key, scrolling for more about Amber David. He didn't see her name. He didn't see her mother's name. In a few seconds, he reached nothing but white space. He did some quick math and figured Peggy died about month after that visit to Parma. "What the hell," he muttered. "I guess that's it."

Mike closed the laptop and sighed. He was sure the rest of what she'd written was witty and wonderful. He just wasn't interested. Not now.

Chapter 23

Thursday, April 10

GAIL CALLED AT 7 a.m. "Mike? I'll take Patti Grant and Lisa Workman. You take Grace Montrose and Mary the cocktail waitress."

Mike was still half asleep. "Good morning to you, too," he mumbled. "I've got my first softball game today, so I'm tied up in the afternoon, but I'll make some calls this morning."

"Sounds good," said Gail. "Call me when you know something. And good luck with your game."

Mike smiled. "Okay. Yeah. Thanks," he said.

Grace Montrose was easy to find. Mike called the North Canton Giant Eagle store at nine and asked to speak with her. He was put on hold for about 15 seconds.

"This is Grace," said a stern voice.

Mike introduced himself and told her he was working as an investigator for Rick Fenner's defense team.

"I can't help you," she said. "I've told the cops and the prosecutor's office the same thing."

"I just have a few questions, Ms. Montrose. You never know what might help."

She paused for a few seconds. "Fine, but I'm working and they don't like us gabbing on the phone."

"Okay. Did you know Cheryl Fenner?"

"I said hello to her a few times at school functions and such. That's about it."

"Did your husband ever find out about your affair with Rick?"

"Not that I know of. We've been divorced three years. He remarried. She's twenty-five. We've both moved on."

"I understand," said Mike. "Did Rick ever say or do anything that made you think he harmed his wife?"

"You mean, do I think he did it?" she asked. "No. I don't."

"Why not?"

"He said he loved his wife. He said he missed her. He always said he was sorry about cheating on her."

"Were you?" Mike asked.

"What?"

"Sorry about cheating on her?"

Wrong question. Click. End of conversation. *No matter*, Mike thought. *She seemed like a dead end.*

Mike spent the next hour working on his starting lineup. After a few revisions, he finally settled on this one:

1. Bree Fenner 2B
2. Lauren Phillips CF
3. Darcy Lomax SS
4. Allie Parker C
5. Rachel McKenzie 3B
6. Andrea Kendall 1B
7. Halle Kruger RF
8. Maria Milanowski DP
9. Maddie Marsh LF
   Callie Stump P

Mike knew his decision to start Callie Stump in the circle over Jen Miller might cause some friction, but he figured the opposite might cause even more. In the end, friction wasn't a consideration. In Mike's mind, Jen Miller was the better pitcher. That's why he was saving her for the mid-week game against conference rival Austintown. Today's opponent, St. Thomas Academy, was not expected to provide a lot of competition.

His other big decision was batting Maddie Marsh ninth. He figured Maddie wouldn't like it because she was good enough to bat first, second or even third.

Still, Mike was confident he could make her understand the importance of having a good hitter with speed at the bottom of the order. If she didn't understand, he'd offer her a spot on the bench as an alternative. Players rarely chose that alternative. He spent thirty minutes on the treadmill, took a shower and headed for downtown Cleveland.

The Wild Stallion Saloon was one of three strip clubs in northeast Ohio owned by a former Cleveland city councilman named Max Markowski. The revelation that he'd been a silent partner in the clubs cost him re-election in 2010 after 16 years in office. Markowski managed the Wild Stallion himself because he still lived alone in a condo in the nearby "Flats" section of downtown—and because he liked to drink and stare at naked women.

There were only five cars in the parking lot when Mike arrived at 11:30. Three of them were the kind of older compacts owned by strippers who struggle to make ends meet. One was a new SUV leased by the ex-stripper bartender. The other was a red, 1966 Corvette recently purchased at auction for $47,000 by Max Markowski.

The beige, one-story building had a flat roof and it sat uncomfortably close to St. Clair Avenue. Mike wondered if St. Clair had been expanded to four lanes from two after the club was built. He pulled hard to open the heavy, oak door. His eyes weren't ready for the darkness inside, but they adjusted quickly and soon focused on an African American security guard in his forties. The man held a walkie-talkie with a cable attached to an earphone, much like Secret Service agents use. He stood at least six feet five inches and weighed more than three hundred pounds. Mike figured he must have played for the Browns at some point, but wasn't good enough to make the big money or blew out a knee before he could.

"Good morning, sir," said the guard. "Hold out your arms, please." He waved a metal-detecting wand over Mike from shoulders to shoes. "You're fine. Have a good time."

Mike walked into the club's main room. It was just as dark, but his eyes had adjusted. The bartender was an attractive forty-something blonde—skinny, with unnaturally white teeth. "Morning. Can I get you a drink?"

"Ice water and a menu, thanks," said Mike.

She produced both in less than fifteen seconds. Mike noticed her name tag. Patrice. "Everything's really good here."

Mike stared briefly at his menu, which featured salads, sandwiches and burgers in the $15 range. Then he looked up to the bartender's too-ample breasts, strangled by a white tube top.

"And expensive," he said with a smile. "I'll have the Wild Stallion burger medium rare with some fruit instead of the fries—if you've got it."

"Can do," said Patrice, taking his menu and turning to type the order into her computer.

Mike scanned the place. There were two other people at the bar—both young women wearing short, tight dresses and five-inch heels. Dancers. He turned to his right and saw a stage that looked to be twenty feet across and six feet deep. Two bronze poles about ten feet apart ran from floor to ceiling. On either side, there were smaller stages with one pole each. The only dancers in sight were the two sitting at the bar engrossed in a conversation with each other.

"Glad I didn't pay a cover charge," Mike muttered aloud. He turned back to face the wall of liquor bottles. Patrice was gone, replaced by a short, round man of about fifty.

"Max Markowski," said the man, extending his right hand. "I'm the owner."

"Ah. Councilman. Nice to see you. Mike Page," said Mike, shaking the hand.

Markowski leaned uncomfortably close. "That name sounds familiar. Why do I know it?"

"I used to write a column in the Plain Dealer," said Mike. "That could be it."

"Yes. Mike Page. Were you a friend or a foe to me in print?" Markowski asked with a smile.

"I'd like to think I was neither," said Mike. "In any event, I'm a softball coach now."

"Ha! Okay, coach. First time here?"

"First time," Mike said.

"To what do we owe the pleasure?"

"Well, I'm also an investigator," said Mike. "I'm working for an attorney who's defending a man accused of killing his wife. We think a cocktail waitress named Mary might be able to help our cause."

"Rick Fenner?" Markowski asked.

Mike raised his eyebrows. "Yes. You know the case?"

"I know Rick Fenner well enough to call him 'Farmer Rick.' Saw him every Saturday night for about two years. The guy spent a lot of money here. Very odd character."

"Odd how?" Mike asked.

"He seemed intent on starting a serious relationship with one of the girls here. And I don't mean a particular girl. I mean any one of the girls. He hit on all of them. He wanted a girlfriend. You know?"

Mike frowned. His opinion of Rick didn't need a big push to reach rock bottom. "Did he ever mention that he was married?"

"Said he was getting divorced—which made all the girls laugh like hell because they hear that shit three times a night. Like, of course, dumb ass, you're getting divorced as soon as your wife finds out you're trying to date strippers!"

If nothing else, Markowski was a straight shooter and Mike appreciated that in an ex-politician strip club owner. "All the dancers turned him down, so he settled for a cocktail waitress?"

"That sounds about right," said Markowski.

"Does she still work here?" Mike asked, knowing his luck never ran *that* good.

Markowski shook his head. "Got pregnant and quit."

"Pregnant? Rick's?" Mike's burger and fruit arrived. He ignored the bartender when she asked if he needed anything else.

"I can't say for sure. I only saw Amber once after that. She dropped by the club to show us the baby. Cute little guy."

Mike took a bite of the burger. It was better than good. It was fabulous. The bun was like a soft pretzel, only lighter. The meat was two inches thick and charbroiled to perfection. He started to tell Markowski how great it tasted, but stopped when he thought back to what he just heard.

"Did you say "Amber"? Fenner said her name was Mary."

"Her name was Mary Amber David. She went by Amber," said Markowski.

Mike took another bite and almost choked. "I'll be a son of a bitch," he said. "She from Parma?"

"I think so," said Markowski.

"Son of a *bitch*!" Mike mumbled. The coincidence was beyond belief. It soaked into his brain like bacon grease into a paper towel. *The woman from Peggy's laptop! How could it be?*

"What's so shocking?" Markowski wanted to know.

Mike took two more bites, tossed a twenty on the bar and headed for the door. "It's a long story," he said. "Nice meeting you."

Chapter 24

"He's got a son."

"What?"

Mike turned out of the parking lot onto Superior Avenue. "Rick. He's got a son. He got Mary the cocktail waitress, whose full name is Mary Amber David, pregnant six years ago—right about the time Cheryl went missing."

"Oh. My. God," said Gail, spacing her words a full second apart.

"Yeah," said Mike. "And here's the unbelievable, the *absolutely unbelievable* part: Remember I told you that my late wife was in the middle of writing a book about her experiences as manager of the Parma J. C. Penney store?"

"Yeah," I remember.

"Well, guess who overdosed in one of her fitting rooms?"

"No!"

"Yes! She wrote at least ten pages about Amber David. She even went to visit Amber and her little boy at her mother's house in Parma."

"Oh. My. God," Gail said a bit faster. "Where is she now?"

"Good question. The owner says he hasn't seen her in months. And listen to this: The last thing written in Peggy's computer about Amber was last October 17th, about two months before Peggy died. Peggy said she went to Parma to talk to Amber, but that Amber's mom said she hadn't been seen or heard from in over a week. The grandma's name is Swanson. Jean Swanson. She had the boy then, at least."

"This is completely crazy! Your wife never mentioned any of this?" Gail asked.

"Not a word," said Mike. "And I can't believe it because we were close. We talked about everything."

"Apparently not," said Gail. "So, why do you suppose your wife went to visit her?"

"She felt sorry for her, I guess. The Penney's O.D. was Amber's third suicide attempt."

"Her third?"

"Yeah. The other two were at Macy's and Sears."

"Jesus, Mike. Talk about weird!" said Gail.

"I know. I'm just in shock. And the little boy goes by the initials, R. D."

"As in Little Ricky? Priceless. Let's go visit granny together!"

"Sounds good. How about meeting me at the softball field? Game starts at four."

"Okay. I might be a little late. But I'll make it by four thirty or so."

"Deal," said Mike, as he veered onto the southbound I-77 ramp.

"I'll be the guy in the third base coaching box waving runners home like a maniac."

He was forty-five minutes from Pluto—and he used all of that time convincing himself that Peggy wasn't controlling these strange events from heaven.

Chapter 25

MIKE WALKED INTO the athletic office to make sure Walt had hired umpires and scheduled the maintenance crew to chalk the field and cut the outfield grass.

"Mike! I'm glad you're here early!" There was urgency in Walt's voice.

"What's up, Walt?"

"Your center fielder just had another dust up with her favorite teacher."

"Shit!" said Mike. "On opening day? How bad is it?"

"She's in the principal's office."

"All right. I'm going. Field ready? Got the umps lined up?"

"It's all good," said Walt. "Good luck."

Mike walked as quickly as he could, hoping his second meeting with Paul Richter would be as positive as his first. He announced himself to the secretary, who waived him through the open door. He saw Lauren first, sitting on the far end of a dark brown leather sofa to the left of Richter's desk. She wore her white softball uniform top and a pair of blue jeans. On the near end of the sofa sat Mr. Willoughby in a brown suit that was nearly the same color as the sofa. His bright orange bowtie stood out against a cream-colored shirt.

"Come in, Mike," said the principal, who leaned forward, bare elbows on the desk. Richter normally wore a suit to work. This day, however, he donned a navy-blue golf shirt with the *Pluto Invaders* logo and a pair of tan khakis. Richter loved to watch the school's teams compete, and he was dressed down to attend the first softball game in the Mike Page era. Mike sat in the chair opposite the sofa.

"Have you met Mr. Willoughby?" Richter asked.

"Never had the pleasure," said Mike, standing and extending his right hand. Willoughby did not stand. He shook Mike's hand politely and settled back into his spot on the sofa. Lauren sat nervously chewing on a fingernail.

"I've heard both sides of this story, Mike. I've also spoken with some of the students who witnessed this latest confrontation. My conclusion is that some people just can't get along in each other's company. These two are a prime example. So, what do we do about it? I'm against disrupting your team on opening day, but I'm also obligated to take action when a student is so extremely disrespectful to a teacher."

"I'm sorry," said Mike. "I haven't heard anything about this, so I don't know what happened."

"She called me a 'faggoty little prick,'" Willoughby interjected.

"Only after you called me a spoiled little bitch!" Lauren shouted.

"This is what I'm talking about, Mike," said Richter. "I must say, the word 'faggoty' is especially troubling because Mr. Willoughby is gay."

Lauren gasped. She honestly didn't know for sure.

"So, here's what I'm going to do," said Richter. "I'm going to suspend both of them for two days. As a member of the teachers' union, Mr. Willoughby will have the option of appealing his suspension."

Richter looked Willoughby in the eye. "Of course, that would require a full public hearing, which might prove awkward." Willoughby said nothing, but his posture did. He slumped, defeated. After twenty years with the district, he felt comfortable with his sexuality and with his under-the-radar lifestyle. A public "outing" would change everything.

"I'll take tomorrow and Monday," Willoughby said dryly.

"Ah. A four-day weekend. You'll do the same," Richter said to Lauren. "And I want your father to give me a call this evening."

"Fine," Lauren said.

"That's all," said Richter.

Willoughby walked out. Lauren followed without a word. Mike stayed.

"Think I should keep her out of the game?" Mike asked.

"It's up to you, but I'd prefer an ultimatum that sends her down the right path," said the principal.

"I think I know what to say," Mike smiled.

"Great. Now go win. We need to win something around here."

At 3:30, Mike sat in the dugout while his players loosened their arms and legs and hit balls into a net. He made out his formal lineup card and sent Lana to exchange information with the St. Thomas Academy scorekeeper. He hadn't said a word to Lauren.

"The book's ready to go, coach," Lana announced as she jumped down to sit beside him. "Want me to keep it?"

"Can you?" Mike asked.

"My dad taught me. I'm pretty good at it. I'll consult with you on the close ones if you like. You know, hit or error; passed ball or wild pitch; that sort of thing."

Mike laughed. "Sounds good, Lana. Thanks. Now go tell Lauren to come see me, please."

"Sure thing, skipper," Lana said.

Lauren stepped into the dugout a minute later. "Hi coach," she said with a weak smile.

"Sit down," he said with a stern glare. "Here's the deal: This is my team. I can do what I want. I can play who I want. I can sit who I want. I can kick any player off the team if I have a good reason. Do you understand those concepts?"

"I understand," said Lauren

"Good. If I ever hear about another issue with you and Mr. Willoughby, or you and anyone else for that matter, you're off this team. I won't have it. Keep your mouth shut and go to school. Keep your mouth shut and play ball. Any questions?"

"No sir," said Lauren.

"All right. That's the end of it. Get ready for infield practice."

The Invaders looked sharp in warm-ups. Bree, Darcy, Dee and Rachel fielded every grounder and put every throw on the money. Lauren, Maddie and Halle were accurate with their throws from the outfield. The St. Thomas squad was clearly impressed, watching wide-eyed in front of the first base dugout. The

Saints were not nearly as sharp when their turn came. Mike paid close attention to the strength of their outfielders' arms. The right fielder had a good one. The center and left fielders did not. He also noticed that the catcher's arm was strong, but inaccurate. She threw a little bit sidearm, which would cause the ball to tail into runners trying to steal second and third.

Mike felt butterflies in his stomach when the Callie threw her first pitch. "Strike!" yelled the umpire. Mike leaned back on the bench and let out the deep breath he'd been holding for at least thirty seconds. The Saints' leadoff hitter then lined the second pitch to right-center field. Lauren ran hard to her left. Halle ran hard to her right. They were on a collision course. Mike cringed. Suddenly, Halle went into a slide like she was stealing second base. Lauren stayed on course, stretched her left arm as far as she could and caught the ball. "One down!" she hollered, throwing the ball to Bree.

"Nice one, Lauren! Atta babe! Way to talk out there!" yelled Morgan from the edge of the dugout.

Mike had already moved on to the next hitter. "Forty-three! Forty-three!" he yelled to the infield. It was a defensive alignment designed to discourage the batter from bunting. First baseman Andrea Kendall positioned herself more than half way to home plate, about twenty-five feet from the batter. Third baseman Rachel McKenzie moved even closer.

Mike had received several emails from a person who seemed to know everything about the St. Thomas softball program. He figured it was the parent of a player or former player—somebody with an axe to grind. To Mike, that meant the information was solid. One of the things the tipster told him was that the Saints' number two hitter, a little lefty named Alexis Borden, always bunted—always.

"She's lightning fast, but she can't hit. She struck out 15 times to begin the season last year without so much as a foul ball," wrote the tipster. "So, the coach told her to bunt all the time. She's good at it, but if you play right down her throat on the corners, you'll get her out. There's no danger from playing too close. She won't swing. Even if she does, she won't make contact."

Borden stepped into the box with her bat held high. Mike was a little nervous. What if the email had been a ruse? What if Borden was a beast, who'd hit twenty homers last year? Mike hollered to his catcher, Allie Parker, and gave her a signal for a fastball high and inside. It would be an unhittable pitch if she tried to swing—and she'd probably shorten up on the bat and pull it back if she intended to bunt.

Callie fired the pitch on target. Borden moved her hands to the middle of the bat, revealing her intention to bunt, just before she ducked away from the high hard one. Mike felt better. He was not one of those control-freak coaches who had to call every pitch and direct every movement of every player. He was determined, however, to teach his players the finest points of the game. This was one of those "teaching moments" that he'd discuss with them in the after-game meeting.

Callie's second pitch was a belt-high screw ball that moved to the outer edge of the plate. Borden reached out and bunted it down the third base line. Rachel barely had to move her feet to field it. She threw the ball to Bree, who ran to cover first, for the second out of the inning.

Mike now felt confident in the anonymous scouting report, which warned that the Saints' third hitter, Megan Pearson, liked low pitches and could hit them out of the park. *She likes them low, but she's a sucker for the rise ball*, wrote the scout. Mike called time and walked to the circle, an unusual move in the first inning with two outs and no one on base.

"How's it going so far?" he asked Callie, as the rest of the infielders arrived for the meeting.

"Great, coach," Callie said.

"I just wanted to remind you that this girl can take you deep if you pitch her low down the middle or low inside. So, let's throw rise balls and try to strike her out or pop her up. If she walks, she walks. There's nothing too dangerous behind her."

Callie nodded her head. So did Allie. Mike walked back to the dugout and told Morgan about the meeting.

"In the big leagues, the pitching coach would have done that," she said.

"You're right," said Mike. "I should have sent you."

"I wouldn't have gone," said Morgan.

"Why?"

"No need. I went over the hitters with Callie and Allie before the game."

Mike gave her a surprised look. "You knew about the three hitter liking low balls?"

"I got the same scouting report you did."

Mike laughed. "He's thorough."

Morgan laughed. "Might be a she."

"Strike three!" They heard the umpire shout. Pearson had swung and missed on a third consecutive rise ball. Inning over.

Mike ran out to congratulate his defense. "All right! Nice job, girls! Now let's get some runs! Concentrate! Swing at good pitches and do the right thing on the bases! Be aggressive, but be smart! And have some fun!"

As he returned to his perch on the top step of the dugout, Mike stared into the grandstand and spotted Gail. He waved, but she wasn't looking. She was chatting with the woman sitting next to her—Leticia Cragmere. He made a mental note to ask her about that conversation.

Bree stepped into the left side of the box and stared at Mike, waiting for a sign. Mike flashed a few. Then, he swiped each arm from shoulder to wrist— which meant that all signs were nullified. Bree went into "slap" mode, running at the ball from the back of the box. She let the first two pitches go. Then, with a 1-1 count, she stroked a line drive over the third baseman's head. It rolled all the way to the fence in left field. Bree rounded second and stopped just as the fielder turned to throw the ball to third base. There were groans from the grandstand. Many thought she should have run to third. Mike hadn't signaled either way. He had taught them to make their own decisions on balls to left and center fields based on their speed, the strength of the fielder's arms and the game situation. Bree had decided to play it safe and not risk breaking the cardinal rule of not making the first out of an inning at third base.

Mike thought she could have made it to third, too, but he clapped his hands and yelled, "Nice hit, Bree. Nobody out. Don't run into a tag. Make it go through on this side. You don't have to run on a pop fly that drops, either, if you're not sure, just stay there. No force."

Lauren stepped into the box and looked for a sign. Mike grabbed both of his ears. Then, he touched each side of his face with his left hand before wringing his hands like they'd fallen asleep. Lauren wasn't familiar with any of that. She stepped out and gave him the signal to repeat the signs.

Mike hollered, "That means hit a two-run homer!" Lauren laughed. So did the umpire and the catcher.

Lauren walked on four pitches. That brought up Darcy Lomax, who fully expected to get the bunt sign. Last year's coach was a "little ball" advocate, meaning she always had her players bunting with runners on first or second or both with no outs—and sometimes with one out—to move them into scoring position. Her team was very good at scoring single runs. The problem was that her team's pitching and defense weren't good enough to win low-scoring games. When you score one and they score five, the game gets out of hand in a hurry.

Mike looked at her and clapped his hands. "Get a hit!" he yelled. Mike felt like he had the other team on the ropes already. He wasn't about to give up an out with a sacrifice bunt—especially with his best hitter at the plate in the first inning!

Darcy stepped into the box and eyed the pitcher. She took the first offering inside for a ball. Then, she looked at Mike. "Don't even look down here!" he shouted. "Pick one out and hit it!"

The second pitch was the one great hitters dream about. Straight, fast, belt high and right down the middle. Darcy didn't miss it. She swung hard and hit the ball just below center. The left fielder didn't even turn around as it flew high over her head. There was never a doubt that it was leaving the ballpark for a three-run homer.

As soon as Mike saw it go out, he ran from the coaching box to the top step of the dugout and held out his arms to block anyone from going out to greet Darcy at home plate. "Hey! No! No!" He yelled. "Let's give her the silent treatment! Everybody sit down. Don't even look at her. Straight faces. No expression until she's in the dugout."

The girls had never heard of "the silent treatment," but they were up for it. Mike ran back to the coaching box as Darcy crossed the plate. He watched his players treat her worse than if she'd struck out with the bases loaded. The look on Darcy's face was priceless, like she had turned the wrong way at home and wound up in the opponent's dugout. Finally, just as she was putting her helmet into its cubby, her teammates mobbed her and offered high fives. They all had a great laugh.

The Invaders played a nearly flawless game, winning 7-0. Callie threw a one-hitter. Allie and Rachel added home runs. Maddie had three hits, stole three bases and scored two runs batting ninth. Mike held only a brief meeting after the game. "I'd like to say that Lana did a terrific job of keeping score today," he said dryly. "The rest of you were almost as good. I'll make some notes tonight and we'll talk at practice tomorrow. Great game," he said with a big smile.

Chapter 26

HALF AN HOUR later, Mike sat in the passenger seat of Gail's white Mercedes Benz, heading for 255 Kline Avenue in Parma. She had followed him home to Brecksville so he could drop off his car and ride with her to Jean Swanson's house. They did not call ahead. Mike's experience as a reporter had taught him that people found it more difficult to decline an interview in person.

"You're quite entertaining on the field," Gail said.

"Oh. Thanks," said Mike. "I don't really plan anything."

"I especially liked the 'hit a two-run homer' sign," she smiled.

"That always gets a laugh."

"So, you *do* plan things."

"I have a repertoire," Mike grinned.

"Anything in it that might work on Jean Swanson?" Gail asked.

"We're about to find out," said Mike.

Gail turned onto Kline Avenue and parked in front of a small, white, one-story house that looked like every other house on the block. It needed paint. It needed roof repair. The two tiny patches of lawn on either side of the narrow concrete walkway were desperate for weed and feed. Mike knocked four times on the front door. It swung open after a few seconds to reveal the short, frail frame of Jean Swanson. Her grandson was not in sight.

"Yes?" said Amber's mother.

"I'm Mike Page. I'm an investigator. This is Gail West. She's an attorney representing a man named Rick Fenner. Do you know that name?"

"Yes. Of course," she said.

"He's in jail now, charged with killing his wife," said Mike.

"I watch the news," Swanson said. "I'm not surprised."

"Why is that?" asked Gail.

"Because he's no good," she said. "He comes here and plays with R.D. once in a while and gives me a few hundred dollars a month and thinks that's being a good guy."

"We're trying to find your daughter," said Gail. "Have you heard from her?"

Jean stared at her feet. "Not a word in months. Her little boy cries every night. The cops won't do a thing. They figure she ran off for good or finally killed herself."

Mike had to ask. "Do you remember Peggy Page?"

She paused to think. "Peggy? Peggy? Oh. Yes! The lady from Penney's! Such a nice lady! She tried so hard to help Amber—even gave her some money. Amber spent it all on Christmas presents for R.D. I haven't seen *her* in a long time either."

"She was my wife. She died of cancer about a month after you last saw her."

"Oh, dear Lord. I'm so sorry," said Jean.

She answered their questions for another twenty minutes. She gave them information about some of Amber's friends and former workplaces. When they left, Gail walked away first. Mike gave Jean a hug before following. It seemed like the thing to do.

"Do you think she's dead?" Gail asked, putting the Mercedes into gear.

"Maybe our boy killed them both," Mike speculated.

"I can't believe you just said that," said Gail. "I was thinking the same thing."

"Well, one thing's clear," Mike said. "Rick is a selective truth-teller."

"You mean he's a damn liar," said Gail.

Mike laughed. "That, too."

It was not quite 7:30 on a Friday night. Gail was hungry. They agreed on Mexican food. Mike directed her to take I-480 east to I-77 south to the Broadview Heights exit. In fifteen minutes, they arrived at Cozumel. The bar was just five feet from the front door. It stretched twenty feet, and there were dining rooms off both ends of it. The hostess led Gail and Mike to the right and she seated them in a booth with a view of the north end of the small shopping center. They ordered margaritas.

"Do you think the cops know about Amber?" Mike asked.

"Who knows with those guys?" Gail smirked. "She's reasonable doubt for us. I know *that*."

"True," Mike agreed. "The pregnant, gold-digging stripper girlfriend definitely had motive. I'll take what we got from Jean Swanson and run with it tomorrow."

"Maybe you'll get lucky like you did at the Wild Stallion," Gail smiled.

"Yeah. I'm just a lucky guy," said Mike.

Gail kept smiling and stared at her drink as the waitress arrived to take their orders. She wasn't sure if Mike knew she'd been flirting with him. *Maybe it was still too soon after his wife's death*, she thought. How long had it been? Barely four months? She stuck to business for the rest of the evening.

"We have to confront Rick about Amber," Mike said, cutting a two-inch section of burrito and turning his fork backward before bringing it to his mouth. His mother had taught him the backward turn when he was five. She explained that forks were curved for a reason. He still wasn't convinced that *her* reason was the *real* reason, but the habit was formed.

"Tomorrow morning?" Gail suggested, pinching a fish taco at the top and raising it for a less than dainty bite.

"Yeah. The sooner the better," said Mike. He pointed to a dot of sour cream on her cheek. "Maybe if he finally fesses up, he can save us some time and effort."

"You think he knows where she is?" Gail asked, dabbing her cheek and taking another big bite. "Sorry. I'm starving!" she said.

"I think he knows a hell of a lot more than he's saying," Mike said. "Mary? That's what he told us. Right? A cocktail waitress named Mary? Bull shit."

Chapter 27

Saturday, April 12

THE LOOK ON his attorney's face told Rick he'd better come clean.

"I'm sorry. I'm really sorry. I wasn't thinking," he lied.

"If you think I'm so stupid that I couldn't find out about Amber and your son, then why the hell would you want me to defend you?" asked Gail.

"Fair question," said Rick. "I want to protect my son," I guess.

"Protect your son?" Mike asked. "Yeah. Right."

"Screw you," Rick said, staring at his hands.

Mike wanted to punch him, but Gail intervened. "Boys! This is counter-productive. Rick, I want the whole story. Now! Last chance!"

"All right. All right," Rick said. "I met her at a strip club in Cleveland. We had an affair. She got pregnant."

"We know all that," give us more," said Gail.

"It lasted all of four months. When I found out she was pregnant, I ended it."

"Nice guy," said Mike.

"When was that?" Gail asked.

"April, 2008."

"Didn't your wife disappear the next month?" Mike asked.

"Yeah. So?"

"So, tell us about that last meeting," said Gail.

Rick sat up straight. "Okay. Amber just showed up at my house. It was eleven in the morning. I answered the door, but Cheryl was inside. I stepped out on the porch and asked her what the hell she was thinking. She said she needed to talk. She said she was four months pregnant with my son."

"Keep going," said Gail.

"She begged me to leave my wife. And I told her that was never going to happen," said Rick.

"Then what?" Gail asked.

"She started crying," said Rick. "Loud crying. I didn't want Cheryl to hear, so I grabbed Amber by the arm and walked her to her car."

"How did it end?" Gail asked.

"I think I said something like, 'Don't come here again.'"

"Nice," said Mike.

"How did she react?" Gail asked.

"She called me a few names and left," said Rick.

"How about threatening to tell your wife?" Mike asked.

"That didn't happen," said Rick indignantly.

"And you don't know where Amber is now?" Gail asked.

"Don't know. Don't care," he said.

"All right," said Gail. "Let me ask you this: Do you think it's possible that Amber could have killed your wife?"

"Amber? God, no! She's no killer. She's a drug addict. She's a slut. But she's no killer."

"It might be necessary to present alternative theories of the crime if we can't prove your innocence," said Gail.

"What about the prosecution having to prove my guilt?" Rick asked.

"Oh, don't worry. They'll be trying—really hard," said Gail.

Chapter 28

AN HOUR LATER, Mike walked into the Parma police station. A female officer in her twenties sat behind a bulletproof reception window. "May I help you?"

"I'm looking for detective Singer," said Mike.

"Up the stairs and to the right," she said, resuming the conversation she'd been having on her cell phone.

Mike followed the signs to the "Detective Bureau," which consisted of a small, corner office with three desks. One was occupied by an obese young man wearing a white shirt and a black tie. Except for the nine millimeter holstered on his left shoulder, he looked like a chubby kid from a prep school.

"Singer?"

"Mr. Page. Yes. Rob Singer. Sit down. How can I help you?"

Mike sat in the folding chair in front of Singer's desk. "I'm working for the attorney representing Rick Fenner. Have you heard about the case?"

"Sure," said the detective. "The guy who killed his wife."

"Allegedly," Mike cautioned.

"Yeah. And I allegedly eat too much," the detective laughed.

"Anyway, I'd appreciate anything you can tell me about your investigation into Amber David's disappearance," said Mike.

"Amber David? What's your interest?"

"Our client was cheating on his wife with her. He got her pregnant a few months before his wife went missing," Mike said.

"No shit? Well, Amber's in Vegas," said Singer.

"Really? You know that how?" Mike asked.

"Vegas P.D. talked to her after we got some hits on a credit card," Singer said. "They confirmed her identity. She was waitressing at one of the downtown casinos."

"Did you tell her mother?" Mike asked.

"Of course. Right away. She's the one who reported her missing."

"That's really odd."

"How so?" Singer asked.

"I talked to her mother last night. She said she hasn't heard from Amber in months."

"Maybe she hasn't."

"Bitch!" Mike said.

"Yup."

"Why?" Mike asked.

"I couldn't say. Maybe she's afraid you'll try to pin the murder on Amber," Singer speculated.

"Maybe we will," said Mike.

Singer checked his reports and gave Mike all the information he had on Amber David. She was living in a small rental house off Las Vegas Boulevard— about a ten-minute walk from her job at Binion's on Fremont Street. She had a female roommate. The reports indicated that Amber wasn't using drugs.

Mike drove back to Pluto to meet Gail for lunch at Miller's Pub. Morgan was tending bar. Gail was sitting at the bar wearing blue jeans, brown cowboy boots and a powder blue T-shirt.

"Cute outfit," said Mike, taking the stool next to Gail.

"Thanks. Just went for a ride."

"On a horse?" Mike asked.

"No. A camel," she smiled. "Yes. A horse. I used to rodeo in my younger days."

"Wow! Barrel racing?"

"Yes. What did Parma P.D. have?"

"She's alive. She's fine. She's living and working in Las Vegas," Mike said.

"Vegas?"

"Downtown. And Jean Swanson knew it."

"Bitch!" Gail shouted.

"That's what I said."

"Amber knows something," said Gail.

"Oh yeah," Mike said. We've got to get to her."

"I'll book you a ticket."

Morgan was pouring a couple of drafts nearby. Mike asked if she'd be able to handle practice alone on Monday and Tuesday.

"Not a problem, coach. We're game planning for Austintown on Wednesday. I'm going to watch them play tonight, so I won't be at practice."

"How about something that takes off from Hopkins at nine or so?" Mike said to Gail.

"I'll do what I can. Returning Tuesday night?"

"That's a plan," said Mike. "Hey. Do you know Leticia Cragmere? I saw you sitting with her at the game."

"You mean Morgan's great aunt?" Gail and Morgan looked at each other and smiled. "Everybody knows Aunt Letti."

"No, really," said Mike.

"She got robbed about 10 years ago. I prosecuted the guy who did it. I told Leti to stay calm on the stand and just answer the questions, but she went off. The bailiff had to restrain her. She jumped down and started after the guy, who happened to be about six-four and two-forty. Called him a scumbag and threatened to cut off his testicles."

"What? Cragmere?" Mike was astounded.

"She's a sweetheart," said Gail.

"As long as you don't cross her," Morgan laughed.

"I assume you won the case," Mike smiled.

"Oh. Yeah. He got the max. Twenty years."

Chapter 29

Sunday, April 13

MIKE'S ITINERARY BEGAN with a ninety-minute flight to Charlotte, N.C. After a forty-five-minute layover there, he was on his way to Las Vegas. He sat in the middle seat of row thirty-one. The woman in the window seat talked incessantly about her grandchildren, her medical problems and her fear of flying. She was in her sixties. She wore too much perfume. The scent was familiar, but Mike couldn't remember why.

The fat, thirty-something man in the aisle seat wore ear buds and slept most of the flight. Asleep and awake, he passed gas and poked Mike in the right arm with his left elbow. On top of it all, there was severe turbulence over the Rockies. It was a miserable flight.

Mike walked at least half a mile through McCarron airport before taking the tram to get his checked bag. He carried his laptop case over his shoulder. Outside, he spent $13 on a one-way shuttle ticket to downtown Las Vegas. Forty minutes later, he checked into the Golden Nugget Hotel just across Fremont Street from Binion's. He unpacked his bag and collapsed on the king size bed. He fell asleep watching a repeat of Sports Center on ESPN.

Monday, April 14

Mike's cell phone rang at 8 a.m. "How was the trip?" Gail asked.

"Awful. Middle seat. Annoying people on both sides of me."

"Sorry about that. I've got some news," Gail said.

"Let's hear it."

"I finally heard from Patti Grant. Remember? The State Farm secretary whose husband is a deputy? Apparently, Patti and Rick were meeting at the

Motel 6 in Canton every Monday morning. Cheryl Fenner disappeared on a Monday morning."

"Right," said Mike. "He went to a volunteer firefighters' meeting, then to Petitti's Nursery, where no one saw him because he wasn't there—because he was…"

"With Patti Grant at the Motel 6. Exactly!" Gail said. "She'll testify that he met her at 9:45 a.m. and didn't leave the room until 11:30 a.m. That means, according to the detectives' own theory of the case, Rick could not have done it."

"I don't suppose they paid with *his* credit card," said Mike.

"No. Cash. But Patti has no motive to lie. In fact, she'd be risking everything by telling the truth about the affair. She's still married with a kid in high school. I could definitely sell *that* to a jury," said Gail.

"So where does that leave us? What's *our* theory of the case?" Mike asked.

"I'm more confused about that than ever," Gail said. "We just keep digging, I think, until we find the truth—because it sure as hell doesn't look like we're going to hear it from our client."

Mike put on shorts, Dockers and a Callaway golf shirt. He took the Rush Tower elevator from his room on the 14th floor to the lobby. He wound his way past the swimming pool—featuring a giant aquarium filled with sharks and other sea creatures—and through the casino to an exit facing the five-block section of Fremont Street closed to motor vehicle traffic and enclosed by an LED canopy. He strolled past a couple of vendors hawking watches and T-shirts. He dropped a dollar into a cardboard box at the feet of a tall, ultra-thin young woman dressed only in devil horns, a red G-string and high heels to match. She held a plastic pitchfork and smiled, but didn't have an act—except that her tiny breasts were pierced through the nipples with silver rings that contained flashing lights.

He continued across the mall to the entrance of Binion's Horseshoe Casino. He walked past two craps tables manned by casino employees waiting for players. He followed signs that led to a counter where two young lovers were posing for a photo. They stood behind a plastic pyramid of hundred dollar bills in bundles totaling $1,000,000. An elderly man with a name tag stood behind the counter. He used a remote switch to snap a photo of the couple.

"Good morning," said Mike. "I'm looking for someone who might be able to tell me if this woman works here." Mike held a four-by-six photo of Amber.

"What does she do?" asked the man.

"Cocktail waitress, I think."

"Straight that way and next to the cashier's cage," said the man, pointing over Mike's shoulder. "Ask anyone with a name tag where you can find Brenda Shearer. She'll have your answer."

"Thanks."

Mike found Brenda Shearer standing near the first window of the cashier's cage talking with a woman half her age and twice her size. Shearer was sixty years old. She stood just less than five feet tall and weighed about ninety pounds. She wore glasses with square, black frames that were partially hidden by a Dolly Parton-like head of hair.

"Excuse me. Brenda? I was told you could help me," said Mike.

"Tell me how," said the tiny woman, whose voice was deep and full of gravel.

Mike handed her the photo. "I'm looking for this woman—Amber David— or Mary David. My name is Mike Page. I'm an investigator for an attorney in Ohio."

"What do you want with her?"

"She was having an affair with a married man back in 2008. She got pregnant. She had a son. The married man didn't want either one of them. But just before the baby was born, the man's wife went missing. She stayed missing until a couple of weeks ago, when her remains were discovered in an abandoned house in Cleveland."

"And your guy didn't do it?" asked Brenda.

Mike smiled. "He says he didn't."

"Do you believe him?"

"I think he's a lying sack of shit. But I don't know if he's lying about that. Is Amber working here?"

"Mr. Page, there are cameras everywhere in this casino. Some of them are pointed at us right now. I could lose my job if I give you information about an employee. So, I'm not going to appear as if that's what I'm doing. I will tell you that if you are here between five and midnight, you'll see Amber—unless she doesn't show up for work."

With that, Brenda shook her head and raised her hands as if she were telling Mike she couldn't discuss personnel matters. Mike nodded, took back the picture and walked toward the exit.

Gail's cell phone rang. "Hello? Gail West."

"Ms. West? It's Bree Fenner."

"Bree? What can I do for you, sweetie?"

"Have you seen the Canton Repository?"

"No. Not yet."

"Well I *have*!" Bree screamed. "I *have*!"

Gail heard a beep. Bree was gone.

ACCUSED WIFE KILLER HAD AFFAIR
by Carlton Myers

Canton—The Pluto man accused of killing his wife and dumping her body in an abandoned house had an affair that produced a child, according to sources close to the case.

Rick Fenner, 44, is charged in the 2008 death of 42-year-old Cheryl Fenner, who was missing until her remains were found March 28 in Cleveland. No cause of death has been determined, according to the Wayne County coroner Nathan Grigsby.

According to sources, Fenner met a cocktail waitress at a Cleveland night club sometime in early 2008 and began an affair that produced a son, who is now five years old and living with his grandmother. The waitress is now reportedly living in Las Vegas.

The Wayne County prosecutor's office would not comment for this story, nor would the sheriff's department. Fenner's attorney, Gail West, could not be reached for comment. Fenner did not answer our request for an interview.

Fenner is being held without bail. No trial date has been set.

"Damn!" Gail shouted at her computer. "Damn! Damn! Damn!" She grabbed her cell phone and redialed Bree.

"I guess you read it?" Bree said.

"Bree. I'm so sorry. I was waiting for the right time to tell you."

"Is it true?"

"I'm afraid so."

"Then I have a brother?"

"You do. He lives in Parma," Gail said.

"Have you met the bitch?" Bree asked.

"Her name is Amber David. The article is correct. She took off for Las Vegas a few months ago. Your coach is out there trying to find her right now. She's a drug addict who has attempted suicide at least three times in the last couple of years. We don't know if she's still using. We don't know if your mom knew anything about her."

"Anything else you'd like to share?" Bree asked.

Gail thought quickly about how much damage the whole truth might cause to Bree's relationship with her father. She decided the news about Amber David had left it in pieces too tiny to reassemble.

"There were other women. Other affairs. Three that he told us about," Gail said.

"Oh, God," said Bree, choking back tears. "Do you think he killed my mom? Do you?"

Gail tried to comfort her. "Your father says he's innocent and I have no reason to believe otherwise," she said.

"They all tried to tell me! They all tried to tell me he was no good! I didn't believe them!" Bree was wailing now. Six years of isolation had been bearable when she was certain she was right. Suddenly, every breath she took was torture.

"Bree, I wish there were something I could do to make this easier," said Gail.

"Just tell me the truth," said Bree. "Just tell me the truth!"

Gail promised to keep Bree informed. She also promised to find out how the Repository learned about Rick's affair with Amber David.

Chapter 30

MIKE HAD NEVER been to Las Vegas. His impressions were mixed. He loved the blue sky. He hated the heat. He enjoyed the mountains. He detested the pavement.

The people were interesting and energetic, but seemed trapped and pathetic. While he was certain that somewhere in the foothills families were leading normal lives, he was just as certain that the abnormal culture upon which Las Vegas was built would never truly allow it.

At 5:05 p.m., Mike walked into Binion's and shoved a twenty-dollar bill into the twenty-five-cent slot machine closest to the bar. His goal was simple: Find Amber David before the machine took the whole $20. After six spins (at seventy-five cents per spin) had produced nothing, Mike slowed his pace to one spin per minute as a means of slowing his bankroll's demise.

Twelve minutes later, down to $11, he was approached by a long-legged blonde who, unlike most of her co-workers, seemed born to wear her western-themed uniform.

"Cocktails?" she asked.

"Got anything worth nine dollars?" Mike joked.

"You're only down nine dollars? That's a win," she replied.

"Actually, I'd like to talk."

"Sorry, I'm a little busy. Try the gentleman's club, halfway down the block," she said, walking away.

"It's important, Amber," Mike called after her.

She stopped in her tracks. *Mary* was the name on her Binion's I.D. badge. "Do I know you?"

"My name is Mike Page. I'm an investigator for an attorney in Ohio. Our client is Rick Fenner."

Amber seemed disinterested. "Rick? What did he do?"

Mike thought, *how could she not know?* "He's charged with his wife's murder," he said.

"Oh, God! When did this happen?" Amber seemed genuinely surprised to hear that Cheryl Fenner had been killed.

"I'm sure you know that Cheryl disappeared back in 2008. Her remains were finally found a little over a week ago. Rick was arrested the next day."

Amber sat on the stool next to him. "His wife was dead five years?"

"Since just about when you got pregnant," said Mike. "Now he's in jail and you're in the wind. You see how it looks. Right?"

"No. Tell me how it looks," Amber said.

"All right. It looks like you're running from something, or hiding from something—or someone."

"You're on the right track," she said.

"So, tell me," said Mike.

"It's a long story and I need this job. I'm off at midnight. Be here then. We'll talk."

"Fair enough," said Mike. "I'm staying at the Nugget."

Mike hit the cash out button on his slot machine. He redeemed the $11 ticket on his way out to the oddness of Fremont Street, where he was immediately drawn to a kiosk that featured expensive-looking cheap watches that sold for between $15 and $50. Mike asked the Middle Eastern-looking attendant if he could try on a silver watch with lots of gadgets.

"Where are you from?" asked the man.

"Ohio," said Mike. "And you?"

"Israel," said the man, handing him the watch.

Mike tried it on, but the fit was too loose. As he was handing it back, he felt a hard tap on his shoulder. He turned to his left and saw a bald, well-built man in his forties who stood at least six-foot five and weighed more than two hundred fifty pounds.

"You Mike Page?" the man asked.

"Yeah," said Mike, still startled.

"You need to stay away from Amber." The man's tone was unmistakably threatening.

Mike felt reasonably safe under the Fremont Street canopy. "Can I ask who you are?"

"I'm a guy who can hurt you. That's all you need to know," said the man.

Mike definitely had no desire to fight with somebody big enough to play tight end for the Browns, but he'd traveled a long distance to find Amber.

"I just want to ask her some questions. I'm an investigator trying to save a man's life," he reasoned.

"You've been warned," said the man. "Your midnight meeting is canceled."

Mike didn't bother asking how the man knew about the meeting. He had already assumed he was Amber's new boyfriend.

"You can't assault a subpoena, pal," Mike informed him. "She talks now, or she talks later." It didn't work.

"You've been warned," said the man, who quickly dissolved into the crowd of tourists and hustlers.

As Mike lost sight of Amber's friend, he found himself standing next to a statue of Stevie Wonder positioned about fifteen feet from the entrance to the casino hotel known as "The D." It was about four feet tall, dressed in a sequined white jumpsuit and wearing oversized sunglasses with white frames. The statue stared into space with that grin unique to the blind superstar.

Near its black loafers was an open guitar case containing twenty-five or thirty one-dollar bills. Three women, two men and one person who hadn't made a decision stood watching the statue and laughing. The song, "For Once In My Life" seemed to be coming from the statue. Mike figured it had a built-in speaker. Then he realized that the music and the voice were coming from different places.

The music came from a boom box that was mostly hidden from Mike's view by the guitar case. The voice was coming from the statue, whose lips were not moving—until they did. *What?* Now Mike realized why the others were laughing. They'd seen the act. They knew the truth. Little statue Stevie wasn't a statue at all. He was real.

The song ended and the best ventriloquist/statue in the world took a deep bow and thanked his fans for their patronage. Mike pulled out the eleven dollars he'd salvaged from the slot machine and dropped the bills into the guitar case.

"God bless," said little Stevie.

Mike walked into "The D" for a few seconds of air conditioning. The temperature had reached 106 degrees in Las Vegas by 3 p.m. and didn't seem to be dropping. Within ten feet of the doorway, there were several craps and blackjack tables. Three small, square platforms divided them. On each platform, a young woman wearing a bikini and high heels danced to blaring pop music. The dancers were rough looking and heavily tattooed.

Mike tried to ignore them as he walked through the casino, but he couldn't. He felt sorry for them immediately. He wondered how cruel their lives must have been and how painful. What degree of self-hatred must they all possess? *Wow. My bulletproof reporter's vest is gone, he thought.* He did not consider that dancing at "The D" might be one of the few available paths to liberation for some of them. He wasn't getting small-minded in his old age. He was just on a different assignment.

He stepped onto an escalator leading to the second floor, where a sound nearly extinct in Las Vegas—coins dropping from the bellies of slot machines into their payout trays—was as dominating as the music had been below. "The D" had maintained some of its old-school machines for customers who actually enjoyed lugging around plastic buckets filled with nickels, dimes, quarters, half dollars or silver dollars.

He was drawn to a roar normally reserved for a craps table with a hot shooter. Half a dozen men in their early twenties were sitting around a square enclosure with clear plastic walls. They were watching five carved, wooden horses moving around a replica racetrack on pegs. Each horse traveled in its own slot at a speed that varied throughout the race. A tote board offered odds for the ten different quinella combinations. The players had thirty seconds between races to drop quarters into slots representing the quinellas of their choice.

"Eighty to one!" Screamed a young man who then tipped his bottle of Bud Light and took a long drink.

"Woo! Woo!" Yelled another, who was furiously stuffing quarters into the 1-2 quinella slot with three-to-one odds. There was one empty stool at the game. Mike shoved a quarter into the 3-4 slot with odds of ten to one. The horses started moving as the sound of pounding hooves emanated from the machine. Mike felt a rush as the number 3 horse sped to the lead, followed closely by the number 4 horse. If those two finished first and second in either order, Mike would win ten quarters. Suddenly, both of his horses slowed and were overtaken by numbers 1 and 2.

"Whoo! Whoo! Yeah!" yelled the guy who'd managed to shove fifteen quarters into the 1-2 slot in the thirty seconds allowed. Another forty-five credits loaded into the man's bank as he drained a bottle of Heineken. Mike stood to leave. As he turned, his left shoulder bumped the chest of the man who'd threatened him on Fremont Street.

"Now you're *following* me?" Mike asked.

"You got a problem with that?" asked the bald man.

"As a matter of fact, I do," said Mike. "You're like a schoolyard bully. I'm trying to do a job and you're getting in my way."

"Something you want to do about it?" asked the man, who then gave Mike a two-handed shove. Mike fell back into the horse racing game. In a split second, he processed the attack as a license to use whatever means he deemed necessary to defend himself.

At least a dozen people and several security cameras had witnessed the assault. His reaction could only be interpreted as a heat-of-the-moment act of self-preservation. With that, he faked a punch with his right hand. As the man raised an arm to block it, Mike did his best impression of Lou Groza and kicked the man in the groin with enough force to produce a sixty-yard field goal.

"Ooo!" the man screamed, dropping to his knees and rolling onto his side. Mike strolled to the escalator without looking back. No one followed him. No one aided his victim. The horses were running again.

A minute later, he entered the Golden Nugget, making sure he wasn't followed into the Rush Tower elevator. It was ten o'clock Ohio time—still five hours before his meeting with Amber. He thought a nap might do him some good—especially if the big guy came back for more.

Chapter 31

Tuesday, April 15

MIKE HADN'T DREAMED about Peggy in a couple of weeks. A friend whose wife had been dead for several years told him that her ghost had haunted his dreams for the first six months. She was constantly telling him to take out the garbage, empty the dishwasher and mow the lawn.

Eventually, she left him alone. His friend believed it took a certain amount of time for a dead wife's spirit to accept the loss of control. Peggy had never come to nag. Curiously, she paid several visits to help plan Mike's retirement. Specifically, she reminded Mike to roll her 401K from Penney's into an I.R.A. to avoid tax penalties. She wanted him to be comfortable and happy.

In life, she hounded him about his health, insisting that he maintain a vigorous exercise regimen. In death, she never mentioned his health. It made sense. Spirits have no bodies. Why would they concern themselves with matters of the flesh?

Mike awoke to five loud knocks. He scrambled to his feet. His first thought was that it was housekeeping. Then he looked at the clock on the bedside table. It was 12:30. He glanced at the window. Dark. It was 12:30 in the morning. Damn. Thirty minutes *after* his scheduled meeting with Amber. Who could it be? The boyfriend with the sore groin?

"Who's there?" Mike called.

"It's me. Amber."

Mike didn't expect to hear that. "Are you alone?"

"Yes," she said. "I'm alone."

Mike opened the door. Amber walked in with her head down. Mike started to ask what she was doing there, but his question changed when he saw her face.

"Amber? What happened?"

She stared at him with her right eye. Her left eye was swollen shut, the skin purple and red. Her lower lip was twice its normal size with a half-inch cut that was still bleeding along the edge of a forming scab.

"I was walking to my car. Some guy came up and asked where I was going. I said, "Home." He said if I ever talked to you again, he'd kill my son. Then he punched me in the face and ran off." Amber started to sob.

"Did you get a look at him?" Mike asked, grabbing a wash cloth from the bathroom shelf and soaking it with cold water.

"Tall guy. Big. Bald," she said as Mike handed her the wash cloth.

"Like six-five and two fifty? Around forty-five years old?"

"Yes," she said, dabbing her lip.

Mike was stunned. He'd been certain the big goon was Amber's boyfriend.

"He threatened me, too," said Mike. "Right after I talked to you at Binion's. He followed me and told me to stay away from you."

"Well, I don't blame you for being scared to show up for the meeting," said Amber, still crying.

Mike was slightly offended. "I wasn't scared. I took a nap and overslept. Did the guy have a limp?"

Amber thought for a few seconds. "He did kind of limp-run after he hit me. Yeah."

"Yeah, well that's because when he followed me into "The D" and shoved me into the horse race game on the second floor, I kicked him in the balls so hard they're probably still stuck in his throat. I left him writhing on the carpet."

Amber grinned and grimaced at the same time. "No wonder he was so pissed off. But who the hell was he?"

"I don't know," said Mike. "I thought he was your boyfriend at first, or at least some kind of bodyguard. Now I have no idea. At five-thirty, he told me our meeting at midnight was canceled. How did he know about our meeting?

You and I were the only people around when we spoke at Binion's. Right? And Frankly, I'd like to know how you got my room number, too."

Amber sat silent for about fifteen seconds. Then she held up a finger, as if she'd solved a mystery.

"I went outside and had a smoke and called my roommate, Chelsea. I told her about you. I told her you were coming back to talk at midnight. There were a bunch of people around. The asshole was probably listening. I got your room number from a guy I went out with a couple of times. He works at the hotel desk."

"Do you want to go to the emergency room?" Mike asked.

"I'm fine," said Amber. "I've been hit before. I could use some ice, I guess."

Mike grabbed the bucket. As he passed the elevators, one opened. A young woman stepped off. She was tall and thin, with red hair—the dark, attractive kind. Mike filled the ice bucket and walked back to room 1430. He hadn't brought a key, so he knocked.

"Who is it?" Amber asked.

"Mike."

The door swung open. The redhead stepped out of the way as he entered.

"This is Chelsea," said Amber.

Mike shook her hand. "Mike Page."

"Nice to meet you," said Chelsea.

After ten minutes of small talk, Mike learned that Amber and Chelsea had met six years before, when they were both working at The Wild Stallion. Chelsea had been a dancer. She told Mike something he already knew about Rick Fenner—that he seemed to be looking for a steady girl.

"Oh, he hit on me big time," said Chelsea. "He spent a few thousand on lap dances."

Mike asked Chelsea if Rick had ever mentioned his wife. "He said his wife left him," she said.

"He told me the same thing," said Amber, softly.

Mike definitely considered Amber a victim now, and he felt guilty for questioning Peggy's instincts about her. Still, he had a lot of questions that needed answers.

"I'm really interested in why you left Ohio, Amber," said Mike.

Amber put down the ice bag. "I left because I had no chance to make a life for my son. I left because all I thought about was suicide."

"Waitressing in Vegas is better?" Mike asked.

"I'm not doing drugs. I'm feeling better about myself. It's a start," said Amber.

"So, your goal is what?" Mike asked.

"Ideally? Make some money. Meet a man. Get married. Send for R.D. and live happily ever after."

Mike smiled. "Sounds perfect. So, can you tell me who might be paying that goon to keep me away from you?"

"Maybe somebody thinks I can clear Rick Fenner—and doesn't want that to happen," said Amber.

"Can you clear him?" Mike asked.

"I'm afraid not," she said. "But I know someone who can."

"I'm listening," said Mike.

"Last year, I tried to kill myself by over-dosing in a Penney's fitting room. One of the store managers did CPR on me and saved my life. Then she came to visit me in the hospital."

Mike wanted to interrupt, but he held back. He'd been waiting for the right time to tell Amber that Peggy was his wife—and that she had died--but this wasn't the right time.

"The cops told her about my two other suicide attempts. Peggy. Her name is Peggy something. She came to the hospital and wanted to know everything about me. I don't know if it was one of those "I saved your life, so I want to know you" things with her or not.

"Anyway, I told her that I'd been depressed about my son growing up without a father. I told her about Rick and how we met, and how he rejected me and our baby. I also mentioned that he said he'd kill me if he ever saw me again."

Mike resisted his growing urge to interrupt. Instead, he edged forward on his chair. "So why do you think Peggy can clear Rick?"

"I'm getting to that," said Amber, suddenly sprawling on the king size bed and stretching all of her long limbs at once.

Mike averted his eyes, but he'd already been treated to a memorable image of a gorgeous young woman in a cowgirl outfit. Amber sat up, fluffing her shoulder-length hair with both hands.

"When I told Peggy that Rick refused to take responsibility for the baby—and that he'd threatened to kill me. She got really pissed. She went to his house…"

"Wait!" Mike couldn't help himself. "She went to his house?"

"Drove there from Parma hospital right after I told her the story," Amber said.

Mike decided the time had come for full disclosure.

"Peggy was my wife," he said quietly.

"What? Your wife? Peggy was your *wife*? What do you mean *was*?" Amber asked.

"I mean she died of cancer last December—not long after you left Ohio."

Amber broke into tears. "Oh, God. I didn't know. I'm so sorry, Mr. Page. She was wonderful, just wonderful."

"Thanks. Yes. She certainly was," said Mike.

Amber was standing now, pacing and still crying. Chelsea grabbed her hand and pulled her onto the bed, putting an arm around her.

"Is that why you're here?" Amber asked. "Because of your wife?"

"No. No. Not at all," said Mike. "The whole thing is just a series of strange coincidences. You; Peggy; me; the coaching job in Pluto; Rick; his daughter being on my team; all of it. Just random. I'm here because I used to be an investigative reporter and Rick thought I could help him by working with his attorney.

"The only reason I knew about *you* was that after my wife died, I learned she was writing a book about her experiences working at J. C. Penney. Your story was part of it. She wrote about your overdose. She wrote about going to see you in the hospital. She wrote about talking to your mom in Parma after you took off for Vegas. She did *not* write about driving to Rick's farm."

"I'll tell you what she told me," Amber began, dabbing her eyes with a tissue. "She told me she got to Rick's place at about eight that night. When she knocked on the front door, no one answered. She said she walked around to the side door and that the window near the door was open. She heard a man and a woman arguing. She said the man accused the woman of being responsible for his wife's death. 'You killed her just as if you pulled the trigger yourself,' is what she overheard him saying."

Mike was incredulous. "What the hell? Then what?"

Amber thought for a few seconds. "That's it. She said she took off after hearing that."

Mike sighed. His thoughts raced. *My life is a never-ending series of improbable events. Five years after Cheryl Fenner disappears, my wife, while working at J. C. Penney in Parma, meets a suicidal drug addict. She gets angry when she learns that the married guy who got the drug addict pregnant won't take responsibility. She gets so angry, in fact, that she drives to the jerk's house—sixty miles away—to confront him even though he might be a cold-blooded killer. When she arrives, she overhears the guy accusing an unknown woman of being responsible for his wife's murder. Then she drives home and doesn't mention any of it to me!*

"She goes through all of that and doesn't say a word to me?" he said aloud.

Chelsea shook her head. "God, that's so random! And now she's dead, so..."

Mike smiled at Chelsea's awkward insensitivity. He finished her sentence. "So, we can't ask her any questions, but we *can* stop focusing on what she *heard* and *start* focusing on what she *didn't* hear."

"What do you mean?" Amber asked.

"Think about it," said Mike. "For Rick to have said what he said, he had to have known his wife was dead."

"You rhymed," said Amber. "And that's right. He had to have known."

"So, for at least five months before Cheryl's remains were found, her husband knew she was dead," said Mike. "And if your quote from Peggy was accurate—the part about pulling the trigger—then Rick knew she'd been shot. And if he knew she'd been shot, then he probably knew what happened from the start."

Chelsea nodded. "Which explains why he was always shopping for a girlfriend at The Wild Stallion. He knew his wife wasn't coming back." She smiled sheepishly at the others.

"Did he talk about his wife when he was with you?" Mike asked.

"Just the first time we met," said Amber. "He said Cheryl left him high and dry. Just took off one day. I had no idea she was actually a missing person."

"And you have no idea who Rick was arguing with that night?"

Amber shook her head. "None. Sorry. All I know is what Peggy told me."

Chapter 32

Wednesday, April 16

IN MIKE'S OPINION, the Vegas trip had changed everything. He called Gail and told her about Amber's revelations and about the goon who'd threatened and assaulted both of them. She told him to get on the next plane to Cleveland. He couldn't wait.

The flight home was considerably better. Mike sat in the aisle seat near the emergency exit—the seat with extra leg room. There was no middle seat. The window seat was occupied by a woman in her early twenties who never took out her ear buds and rustled only a few times before the plane landed at Hopkins.

Mike sent Gail a text after grabbing his bag from the conveyer. She'd been driving around the airport for twenty minutes to avoid a confrontation with security. The good news was that thirteen years after the 9-11 attacks, some of the paranoia had finally subsided at CLE. They were back to allowing people to park in front of the terminal to pick up arriving passengers. The bad news was that if they parked there for more than five minutes, the airport cops would write them a $35 ticket. Gail parked in front of the Southwest Airlines terminal just as Mike walked out, pulling his suitcase.

"Welcome home," said Gail through the open passenger side window.

"Thanks," said Mike, shoving his bag onto the back seat of the Mercedes. He wore navy Bermuda shorts, a white Walter Hagen golf shirt and a pair of tan boat shoes.

"Nice legs," she flirted. "Did you get some sun?"

"Oh, yes. I spent hours at the pool," he joked.

"You're lucky you didn't spend hours at the hospital," Gail said.

"Yeah," said Mike. "Very lucky."

Gail's expression grew serious. "You were pretty busy in Vegas, so I waited to tell you that Bree called me the night you left."

"Bree called *you*? What about?"

Gail handed him a clipping of the Carlton Myers article.

"Son of a bitch," said Mike. "Singer."

"Who's Singer?" asked Gail.

"The detective in Parma. The one who gave me the scoop on Amber. He must have told Myers. What an asshole! How'd she take it?"

"Not well."

"So, she knows about R.D.?"

"Yup," said Gail.

"What a fucking mess!" said Mike.

"I feel so sorry for her," said Gail. "I told her I'd keep her informed. We should meet with her soon. But I want to meet with Rick again first. He has to be confronted about what Amber said."

From the outset, Gail believed that solving the crime was the best way to defend her client. Now she was thinking that solving the crime might send her client to the death chamber.

"This is why I resisted becoming a defense attorney," she sighed.

"Lying, murdering clients?" Mike asked.

"I'll stop at lying for now," she said.

They decided Mike should go through Peggy's computer files and check for anything he might have missed. It seemed impossible that she would omit her aborted attempt to confront a complete stranger about his illegitimate child.

"I'll let you know if I find something," Mike said as he pulled his bag from the back seat.

"Get some sleep, too," said Gail.

"I will."

"Glad you're all right."

Mike smiled. "Glad you're glad."

He held the smile all the way into his kitchen, where Valentine was sound asleep near her bowl.

"Don't get up," Mike said.

It was too late to call the teenage boy he'd hired to look after the retriever while he was in Vegas, so Mike assumed she'd been fed. *It wouldn't hurt you to skip a meal anyway,* he thought. Valentine didn't wake up to chat.

Mike opened the laptop and scrolled to Peggy's first mention of Amber. He read about the overdose in the fitting room at Penney's. He skimmed to Peggy's recollection of her visit to Parma hospital. He read it carefully. There was nothing about Rick Fenner or Pluto. The next passage was unrelated:

"The staffing cutbacks are so deep now that we have no LP's (loss prevention people). So, in addition to everything else I have to do, I'm chasing shoplifters and risking my life to catch them. Imagine a major department store with no security! It would be comical, if it weren't so sad. Tonight, I watched a group of four women, all at least fifty, stuffing shopping bags with Nike clothing. They all chose different exits. I stopped one of them and radioed Clarissa in the shoe department to stop another. That woman shoved Clarissa and bolted for the parking lot. The woman I stopped kicked me in the shin, dropped her shopping bag and ran into the mall. I let her go.

In all, three large bags filled with expensive clothing left the store. We lost $2,100 in merchandise. Two LP's would have cost the company about $250 for the day. Frankly, I'm finished trying to get in the way of organized shoplifting rings— especially when they all know we're shorthanded and operating with no store security. It's dangerous and I'm not being paid enough to risk my life.

Speaking of my life, I learned a few days ago that it's going to be ending soon anyway. I have breast cancer—and my doctor says it's too far along to treat with anything but pain medication.

Tears filled Mike's eyes. He wasn't ready for that. He grabbed a napkin and blew his nose as he continued reading.

So, I'm feeling like I need to do something meaningful, but I can't imagine what that would be right now. I have no bucket list, no real regrets. I did do something dangerous the other night because I was feeling like I had nothing to lose. Funny, though, when I sensed the danger, I ran like a coward.

Mike had fought off the tears. "This is it," he said aloud. "Damn! This is it!"

I was really angry after hearing Amber's story. So, I decided to talk some sense into that son-of-a-bitch who fathered her child. I know it was stupid, but I didn't care. I drove an hour to a little town called "Pluto" in Wayne County. I found the man's farmhouse and knocked on the front door. No one answered. There were three vehicles in the driveway--a pickup, an SUV and a sedan—so, I assumed someone was home. I walked around to a side door and heard the voices of a man and a woman. I could see their shadows moving behind the curtains. It was an unusually warm November evening and the kitchen windows were cranked open. I stood out of sight and listened. They were clearly arguing. I heard the man say something about a chase and a prosecutor and something going wrong. Then, the woman said, "You can't trust anybody."

At that point, the conversation stopped. They must have moved to another room for about two minutes. I thought they might have discovered me somehow, so I started to sneak away. Then the man's voice returned.

"You killed her just like you pulled the trigger yourself," he shouted. Then I heard some glass breaking. That's when I forgot I was dying and had nothing to lose. I ran to my car as fast as I could. It was parked on the shoulder out front. I thought about calling the cops, but I thought Amber might hate me for that. The whole mess would be exposed and her son would surely suffer. What could I tell the cops anyway? That I just happened to be sneaking around outside someone's house and heard an argument that might have been about something that might have happened years ago?

When I thought about how unlikely the whole scenario would sound to anyone who wasn't there, I decided it was a sure bet the authorities would recommend a psychiatrist and send me away.

The next day, I went back to the hospital and told Amber about my adventure. She called me crazy for going there. Then she told me I must have been mistaken about what I overheard. She seemed unwilling to entertain the notion that Rick would be part of a conspiracy against his own wife. I didn't know enough about the case to have an opinion, but I know what I heard.

I told Amber I was happy that she was looking and feeling better, and that I was pleased to hear she'd be going to drug rehab later in the week. She promised to use the time to get her act together. I was thrilled to hear that!

Mike closed the laptop. He called Gail and read the passage to her.

"Wow! Your Peggy was *something*!" said Gail.

"That's an understatement," said Mike. "So, what do we do now?"

"Same plan. Confront Rick. Let's do it tomorrow morning."

"He needs to tell us who was in the house with him that night," said Mike.

"Damn straight," said Gail.

Chapter 33

Thursday, April 17

MIKE AWOKE TO roof-shaking thunder. He walked to the front room, opened the blinds and saw raindrops bouncing off the Buick. He hadn't seen hard rain like that since Georgia. He remembered the hardest rain he ever saw. It was 1988 in Savannah. He ran from the parking lot of the Holiday Inn Express to one of the hotel's side doors. She was waiting to open it.

"I'd didn't think you'd come," said Donna Parker, grabbing the lapels of his raincoat and kissing him hard on the lips. They held the kiss up the first flight of stairs on their way to room 204. Mike was not himself. He knew it. He just couldn't help it.

She was twenty-five, a reporter for a local TV station. He was twenty-eight, a reporter for the local newspaper. They met covering the story of a house fire that killed three young children and their parents. The icy exteriors most reporters maintain were no match for this sad story. Interviews with weeping firefighters close enough to hear the victims' screams, but helpless to reach them, were a bonding agent for Mike and Donna.

One thing just led to another, he thought. She was the opposite of Peggy in obvious ways—she was a tall brunette with one of those deep, sexy voices—but her personality was exactly like Peggy's. She was pushy and determined to get answers to her questions immediately.

"When can we get together?" She had asked as they sat with other reporters waiting for the fire chief's news conference.

"I think you know I'm married," Mike had responded in a whisper.

"I'm not interested in stealing you," she had whispered back.

"Not yet," he had flirted.

A few days later, they ran into each other while covering a story at city hall. Their flirtation produced the plan to meet at the Holiday Inn Express. Mike smiled as he remembered the first embrace. He remembered her smell and her hot breath on his neck. He remembered her soft fingers touching his face. He remembered wishing the night would never end. Later, he drove home devastated by his deceit and terrified about the possible consequences. It was the definition of guilt. He wished he'd never met Donna Parker.

The rain kept tapping at the window. Mike kept staring at the explosions of water on the hood of his car. He couldn't stop remembering that night with his mistress. He remembered pushing the door open with his shoulder as Donna wrapped her body around his. He remembered peeling off his wet coat and tossing it on the chair, then grabbing her and pulling her hard against his chest as she struggled to step out of her skirt.

"You know this has to end," he said.

"I know," she said. "Last time. I promise."

It was the first time—and the last time. When they parted that night, the rain was still pounding. Mike ran to his car without looking back at Donna, who was standing at the side door waiting to make a run for it. It was over.

He took a job in Atlanta three weeks later. She took a job in Houston a year later. She married an attorney and had three children.

They never even spoke again.

Mike's cell phone rang. It was Walt.

"I'm raining us out for today," he said. "I'll reschedule Austintown for tomorrow at four. It's supposed to clear up tonight. The tarps are already on. Okay?"

Mike felt relieved. He had completely forgotten about the first conference game.

"Yeah. Sounds good. I'll call Morgan." He hung up and started to dial, but decided against it. Morgan usually worked late at the pub. She was probably sleeping. He called Gail instead. She told him she'd been on the phone with Bree.

"What did you tell her?" Mike asked.

"Not much," said Gail. "Only that you found Amber in Vegas and learned some interesting things. She wanted to know more, but I told her she should hear it in person. I told her I'd get with you to arrange a time—maybe later today or tonight."

"Good," said Mike.

Bree raised her hand and asked to be excused. Her Biology teacher, Miss Jackson, nodded and told her to come up for a hall pass. Bree grabbed the pass and walked straight to the restroom. She took out her phone and re-dialed the number with the 702 area code.

"I've been waiting for your call," said the woman.

"Sorry. I had a test first period. Yes. Mr. Page found Amber in Vegas."

"Did she talk to him?"

"Yeah. But I have no details. I don't know what was said."

"But you'll find out." The woman's tone was urgent.

"I will," said Bree.

"Call as soon as you do," the woman warned. "Then I'll tell you who killed your mother."

"I will," said Bree. "I will."

Two weeks in jail had changed Rick's appearance dramatically. His complexion was chalky, his eyes bloodshot, his skin blotchy. He had gained five pounds. The smile, the smirk and the sense of well-being he exuded the last time Gail and Mike saw him were gone.

"How's Bree?" Rick asked as Mike sat on the bench to his left.

"Fine, as far as I know," said Mike. "I haven't seen her since practice Friday."

Gail stood. She wasn't in a mood for small talk. "Mike went to Vegas over the weekend, Rick."

"Oh?"

"And he found Amber. You remember Amber? Your son's mother?"

"I know who Amber is," Rick sighed.

Mike stood. "I want you to pay close attention, Rick. I'm going to tell you a little story."

Rick stared at his feet.

"My late wife managed the J. C. Penney store in Parma. Your Amber over-dosed one night in the fitting room there. My wife performed CPR on her and called an ambulance. They got to know each other after that. When Amber told her that you refused to take responsibility for your child, my wife decided to pay you a visit. She drove to your house one night last November. She told Amber that she heard a man and a woman arguing inside the house. From the conversation, she said, it was clear that you knew your wife was dead—and that you knew how she died."

"Stop! Stop!" Rick shouted. "I have no idea what you're talking about!"

Mike grabbed Rick's collar. "You're saying my wife was lying?"

Rick pulled away. He stood with his fists clenched. "Okay. Okay," he sighed. "No. She wasn't lying."

Gail moved between the men. "This twist wasn't on my radar." She stared at Rick for a few seconds. Then, she sat on the metal seat next to Mike. "Let's hear it all, Rick."

Rick looked at Mike, then at Gail. "Damn," he said, taking a seat next to Gail. "It wasn't what you think."

"Oh, come on!" Mike shouted.

"I'm just not really prepared to talk about this," Rick said.

"What the hell does that mean?" Gail bristled.

"I have to talk to Bree first," Rick insisted.

"Jesus Christ!" said Mike, reaching across Gail and trying to grab him by the neck.

Gail pushed his arm away and glared at him like a mother lion with a mis-chievous cub. "Get it done today," Gail warned. "Or get another lawyer. We'll be back tomorrow. Same time."

Gail and Mike walked in silence to the front door of the jail. When they stepped outside, Mike stopped.

"That guy lies about everything."

"Welcome to my world," said Gail.

"At what point do we start talking to the cops and the prosecutor?" Mike asked.

"We don't. Not until after we see what they have at the prelim," said Gail. "It sure would be nice to know the truth before that."

"When do we talk to Bree?" Mike asked.

"Before she talks to her father. I'm thinking right after school," said Gail. "Let's have lunch and talk about our approach."

Mike followed her to Miller's Pub. It was still raining hard as they pulled into the lot. He threw the Buick into park and grabbed his umbrella from the back seat. As he stepped onto the muddy lot, he noticed a pickup that looked familiar. He hustled to catch up with Gail.

"See that red truck?"

"Yeah."

"That's Bree's."

"Convenient," said Gail. "Let's play it by ear."

They walked inside and spotted Bree at a table with two people. She was facing the entrance; the others were facing her. Mike avoided eye contact with Bree as he and Gail slid into opposite sides of a booth about twenty feet from her table.

"Who's she with?" asked Gail.

"I can't tell," said Mike. "A woman and a man. Not kids."

"Let's leave them alone," said Gail. "If they start to leave, we'll get Bree's attention."

"I've got a better idea," said Mike, sliding out of the booth. "I'll be back. Order a cheeseburger and fries for me." He walked to the bar, where his assistant coach was waiting on customers.

"Hi, Mike," said Morgan.

"Hey coach. Ready for tomorrow?"

"Sis and I worked on her changeup last night. She's definitely ready."

Mike climbed onto a bar stool. "That's good news. What about Bree? How's she doing?"

Morgan pointed over Mike's shoulder. "She's right there. Ask her."

Mike turned and looked, then turned back with a question: "Who's she with?"

"The little one is Aunt Leti. You've met her. The man is Al Riordan. He's Leti's son-in-law. He's my uncle by marriage, I guess, but I've only met him a couple of times. I don't know much about him."

"I didn't know Cragmere had a daughter," said Mike.

"You should go over there," said Morgan.

Mike paused. He couldn't think of a down side. "Okay," he said.

Leticia Cragmere sat with a Burberry raincoat draped across her narrow shoulders. She jabbed at her salad left handed and did not look up as Mike arrived. Bree did. Her greeting was lukewarm at best.

"Coach. Hello. How was Vegas?"

Mike hesitated. "Fine. Just got back. No school?"

"Well. Yeah. But..."

"Just don't do anything to get suspended. Big game tomorrow."

"I won't," she said.

Mike addressed Cragmere first. "Ms. Cragmere? Nice to see you," he said.

"You, too, coach," said Cragmere, her mouth full of lettuce. "Rained out, huh?"

"Rained out," said Mike. "Rescheduled for tomorrow at four. Hope you can be there to root for us."

"Wouldn't miss it," she said.

Al Riordan was watching intently, waiting to be introduced. He was in his forties. Mike figured he was over six feet tall, maybe as tall as six-three. What was left of his hair was silver. His skin was tanned, as if he'd spent part of the winter in Florida or out west. Mike didn't wait for a proper introduction.

"Mike Page," he said, extending a hand. "I'm Bree's softball coach."

"Al Riordan," he said with a firm shake.

"Pleasure. What do you do Al?" Mike asked, quickly getting to the point.

Riordan hesitated. "Today? I'm Leti's lunch date," he said with a smile.

Mike wouldn't let it go. "And the rest of the time?"

"Investigations," said Riordan. "I'm a retired Mississippi State Police captain. Now I work part time for the prosecutor's office in Stark County—and I dabble in real estate."

"Pleasure to meet you," Mike said. He turned to Bree and asked if she had time for a chat after school.

"I get out at two thirty," she said. I can meet you in the cafeteria if you want."

"Sounds good," said Mike. He said his goodbyes and walked back to the bar, where Morgan was standing hands on hips.

"What'd you find out?" she asked.

"Riordan says he's a former state police captain in Mississippi," said Mike.

Morgan smiled. "Yeah. I remember hearing something like that. Looks like a cop. Doesn't he?"

"You think?" Mike asked.

"Yup. See his shoes?"

"No. You *did*?"

Morgan nodded. "When he first walked in. They're brown. They're scuffed. They have those rubber soles that cops wear so they can sneak up on people."

"How do you know so much about cops?" Mike asked.

"I've had a few run-in's. Nothing serious. Had a few dates, too." she smiled.

"I wonder why he quit the state police," Mike said.

"No clue," said Morgan. "I was away at school when he married Cousin Jennifer."

"What does Jennifer do?" Mike asked.

"Nothing," said Morgan. "She's dead. Killed in a car crash two years after they got married. She was only thirty-five or so. They were living down south, but Leti talked them into moving up here. Bought them a house and everything. Then Jenny got killed. The wreck was in the spring. I was on a softball trip to Arkansas when it happened."

"Tragic," said Mike. "Whose fault?"

"The accident? I think Riordan was driving. Claimed a deer jumped in front of the car. He swerved. Hit a telephone pole."

"Drunk?" Mike asked.

"Not as I recall," said Morgan. "He wasn't charged."

So, that explains Riordan's connection. But why is Bree at the table?"

Morgan shook her head. "That, I couldn't tell you. She walked in with Leti. Riordan met them here. That's all I know."

Mike nodded. Let's talk about Austintown later. Five-ish?"

"I'll be here 'till ten," she said.

Mike told Gail what he learned, including the family history Morgan shared.

"Cragmere. What's she up to?" Gail asked, rhetorically.

Mike answered anyway. "I wish I knew."

"Well, we've got about three hours before the meeting with Bree. Can you find out more about this Riordan character?"

"What about my burger?" Mike asked.

"Get a box from Morgan on your way out," she smiled.

"You're a tough boss," said Mike. I'll see you in the high school cafeteria at three."

"Have fun," Gail smiled, handing him the plate.

Chapter 34

FOR MIKE, THE fastest way to invade the privacy of anyone living in Ohio was by making a phone call to Jerry Baxter. They met in a courthouse hallway in 2005. Mike was writing a column for the Plain Dealer about an arson that killed nine children during a sleepover at a house in Cleveland. Jerry was an investigator for an insurance company. He was testifying in a workman's compensation case in another courtroom. He recognized Mike from his Plain Dealer photo and started a conversation.

The two found they had a lot in common, including baseball. Jerry had played outfield at Kent State in the early seventies. His freshman year was 1971, the year after four students were shot to death by national guardsmen during a protest on the KSU campus.

As a licensed P.I. and a retired Cleveland police lieutenant, Jerry had direct or indirect access to just about every relevant database on the planet. Whenever Mike needed to know the registered owner of a car, a person's address, criminal record or credit score, Jerry got it for him. He never failed and he never charged more than twenty bucks.

Mike had him on speed dial.

"Hey! Mike! What's up, pal? I hear you're coaching softball."

Mike laughed. "I don't even want to know how you knew that."

"It's all over the internet," Jerry joked. "What can I do for you?"

"I need anything you can find on a guy named Al Riordan. I don't know where he lives, but he had lunch at a bar in Pluto this afternoon. He's in his forties. Six feet two or three; maybe two-twenty or two-thirty. Says he's an investigator with the Stark County Prosecutor's Office now, but used to be a state police captain in Mississippi."

"That's a good start. All right. I'll see what I can find," said Jerry.

"Is before three o'clock asking too much?"

"Yes, but I'll get it done," said Jerry.

Mike was almost to Pluto High when the conversation ended. He realized he was still more than two hours early for the meeting with Bree, so he turned into the lot nearest the softball field and parked. The rain had stopped. The dark clouds were moving fast, revealing random patches of blue sky. He grabbed the box holding his burger and fries. He popped the trunk and grabbed a blanket. He laid it across a section of the wet bleachers and sat on it. He took a bite of the burger and shook his head. "This can't be good for me," he mumbled. He ate a couple of French fries. "Peggy would have a fit over these," he mumbled again.

"I hope that's not your regular diet," said a voice from behind him. Mike turned to see Lana. She was dressed in a yellow poodle skirt.

"No. It's not," said Mike. "What's with the fifties look?"

"I'm in the chorus for "Bye Bye Birdie. It's our spring musical. I tried out for Kim McAfee, but didn't get it."

"I don't see why not," said Mike. "You look just like Ann-Margaret."

"Yeah. Ha, ha. Very funny," said Lana. "Except for the face, legs, boobs and hair. What are you doing here?"

"Eating a burger and fries."

"Okay. And why are you doing that here?"

"Everybody has to be somewhere."

Lana folded her arms and glared at him. "Your honor, could you please instruct the witness to answer the question?"

"You're a stitch," Mike chuckled. "All right. If you must know, I've got a meeting in the cafeteria after school and I stopped to get a burger at Miller's Pub, where I also needed to speak with the bartender, who is my assistant coach, about tomorrow's game. I'm eating it here because I'm early and I wanted to see how the field handled the rain. Satisfied?"

"Why didn't you just eat it there? It seems you had time," she persisted.

"I didn't know I had time at the time," said Mike. "Satisfied?"

"Somewhat," Lana said, unfolding her arms. "Don't you want to know what *I'm* doing here?"

Mike took a big bite of his burger. "Umm. Want a bite?" he asked.

"I'll have a French fry," she said, plucking one from the box. "If you must know, I'm here because I called your cell phone, but you didn't answer. Then I called Gail West's office. The lady there said you might be with Miss West at the jail. Then I called the jail and the guy said you'd already left. Then I called Morgan and she said you were just there, but took off with a to-go lunch a few minutes ago and might be headed here. Whew! So, I waited by the music door because it faces the entrance that you'd be most likely to use if you were driving here from Miller's Pub."

Mike smiled. "I trust you have the unlimited everything plan on your phone."

"I do. So, you must be *dying* to know why I was looking for you."

"Yes. Dying," said Mike.

"Okay. Here's the thing," she began. "I don't know if it means anything or not, but I was in the stall in the little girls' room by the main office this morning and I overheard something."

"Go on," said Mike.

Lana stood and spun twice, watching her skirt twirl. "I overheard someone on her cell phone talking about you. It was Bree."

"Bree? What did you hear?"

Lana spun twice more. "She said—and I quote—'Yes. Mr. Page found Amber in Vegas.' Then the other person must have asked what happened or something because Bree said she didn't have any details, but that she would find out more today."

"Does Bree know you were there?" Mike asked.

"No. She never saw me," said Lana.

"Do you have any idea who was on the other end of that call?"

"None at all. I didn't hear anything, and Bree didn't use any names or gender-specific pronouns or anything."

Mike took another bite of his burger. "What time was it?"

"Around ten," said Lana.

"More fries?"

"Just one," she said, grabbing it from the box. "Does that mean anything?"

"Probably not," Mike lied. "But you never know. So, thanks."

"You're welcome. What time should I be here tomorrow?"

"By three is fine. Game's at four," said Mike.

"Okay," said Lana, spinning away toward the parking lot.

Mike smiled as he watched her go. He ate the last of his burger and threw the box—and what was left of the fries—into a trash barrel. He looked up at the clearing sky and smiled again. He thought Peggy might be having a great time watching his life unfold. His phone rang. He recognized Gail's number and reminded himself to take her photo so he could see her face when she called.

"Anything on Riordan yet?" Gail asked.

"Not yet. I should have it by three," said Mike. "Did you talk to Bree at the pub?"

"No. Riordan left first and Bree walked out with Cragmere a few minutes later." Mike's phone beeped. He saw Jerry Baxter's number. He did not remind himself to take Jerry's photo. "Gail? I'm getting the call about Riordan right now. I'll call you right back."

Mike answered the second call. "Jerry? Talk to me, pal."

"All right," said Jerry. "Here's what I know: Al Riordan is forty-three. He grew up in Starkville, Mississippi and went to Mississippi State. He earned a degree in Criminal Justice and joined the Mississippi Highway Patrol at the age of twenty-three. He rose to the rank of captain, but quit in 2005 with eleven years on the job after marrying a woman named Jennifer Cragmere. They moved to her home in Akron. She was killed in a single-car accident in 2007. He was driving, but wasn't charged. He found full-time work as an investigator with the Summit County prosecutor's office. He left that job in 2011. Since then, he's been doing similar work part time in Stark County, as well as some real estate speculating. No wants or warrants. Nothing shady. That's about all I can tell you."

"That's a lot. Thanks, Jerry," said Mike.

"Oh. One more thing: For what it's worth, Riordan has a twin brother named Dan. He's a cop, too—a detective with the Las Vegas P.D."

Mike thanked his friend and called Gail. "Riordan was telling the truth," he said.

"He was a cop?"

"Mississippi State Police," said Mike.

Half a dozen students sat at the table nearest the north entrance to the cafeteria. In one way or another, all were using their cell phones—three texting, two viewing YouTube videos, one talking. Mike walked to the opposite end of the room and sat at a small, round table. High on the wall above him was a long line of framed photos of Pluto's former All-State athletes. His eyes found the photo of Morgan Miller. She was smiling broadly, holding the state championship trophy in one hand and a softball in the other. Her photo was flanked by those of a wrestler and a volleyball player. Mike felt his eyebrows rise. Morgan had aged twenty years over the last eight, he thought.

He looked down just as Gail entered the cafeteria from a door some fifty feet to his right. She carried a black briefcase in her left hand. She walked with purpose, head moving slightly, eyes searching, blonde hair bouncing. Mike waved to get her attention. She saw his hand and smiled. Her smile made him smile.

"Hi. Any sign of her?" asked Gail, sitting to his right.

"Not yet. We're a few minutes early, though," Mike said calmly.

They used the time to go over their interview strategy. The plan was to begin by telling Bree everything that happened in Las Vegas. That way, she'd see the meeting as friendly and informative. Naturally, they'd have to ask what she knew about the voices Peggy had overheard at Bree's house. They'd play it by ear from there. Gail looked up at the photos. Mike looked at Gail.

"Morgan looks so young!" Gail said.

"Yeah. Well, she's been through a lot in the last eight years."

"Yeah. Me, too," Gail smiled. "And you!" she added.

"Life," Mike said. "It makes for good conversation. We should have a conversation sometime. You know, when this is over."

"Sounds like a plan," she smiled. "Look. There's our girl."

Bree walked with short steps, like she was avoiding the grooves in the tile. She stopped in the middle of the room and looked left and right. Mike waved and caught her attention.

"Hello, coach. Miss West," she said with a nod.

"Hi Bree," said Gail. "How was lunch at Miller's Pub?"

"Good. Free food is my fave."

"Should I ask what that was all about?" Mike probed.

"Only if you want to be nosey," said Bree.

"I do," said Mike.

"Well, Ms. Cragmere and Mr. Riordan, who is her son-in-law, are interested in buying our property."

Gail was surprised. "So, they're talking to *you*?"

"Mom's dead and dad's in jail, so..." Bree said with a sarcastic tone.

"Yes. Well..." Gail didn't get to finish her response.

"Let's talk about Vegas," Mike interrupted.

He immediately launched into an incredibly detailed report about his trip. Bree listened intently, reacting with wide eyes at times to the odd events. She gasped when Mike described his confrontation with the goon. She gasped, "Oh my God!" when he told her the same guy had assaulted Amber.

As Gail listened to Mike, she watched Bree's face. It was clear that Bree's attitude toward Amber had at least softened. Gail had expected interjections with the words "whore" or "bitch." Instead, Bree seemed sympathetic and understanding. Gail wasn't sure what that meant.

"Now the strange part," said Mike.

"*Now* the strange part?" Bree said.

Mike nodded and told her the story of Peggy's trip to Pluto. When he was finished, Mike asked Bree if any of it sounded familiar.

"I remember that night," she said.

"Tell us what you remember, Bree," said Gail. "Take your time."

"I guess I started it," she said. "I was mad about something unrelated. He wouldn't let me go out with my friends that night. I made a comment about him cheating on mom. Then he started yelling at me about a bunch of stuff."

"Like what?" Mike pressed.

"I don't know. Just stuff. School and boys and softball stuff," she said, looking at the floor.

"Did he say he blamed you for your mother's disappearance?" Gail asked.

"What? No! He didn't say anything like that," said Bree, still looking down.

"You're sure?" Mike asked. "Nothing like, 'You might as well have pulled the trigger yourself'?"

"Where did you get that?" Bree asked.

"Let's move on," said Gail.

"I know it wasn't my dad," Bree said, wiping her eyes.

"Do you think your dad knows who killed your mom?" Mike asked.

Bree paused. "Yes. I do. I think he knows."

Mike decided it was time to ask about the conversation Lana overheard in the bathroom. "Bree, have you told anyone about my trip to Las Vegas?"

The question caught her by surprise. "Why do you ask?"

"Hold on, Bree," Gail interrupted. "Mike? May I speak with you over here for a moment?" She motioned to an empty table about twenty feet away. Mike followed her.

"What's going on?" Gail asked.

Mike told her what Lana said she overheard in the bathroom. "I didn't get a chance to tell you," he apologized.

"Yeah. Well. All right. Let me handle it," said Gail. "We don't want her to be paranoid around her friends."

Mike agreed. They walked back to the other table and found Bree texting and smiling.

"Bree, your phone records are part of the discovery in the case against your dad," Gail lied. "So, I'll ask you again: Have you been talking to someone on the phone about this case?"

"Okay. Yes. But I don't know who it is," Bree said.

"What do you mean?" Mike asked.

"I have to go," said Bree. "I have to go."

She stood and ran from the cafeteria, leaving Gail and Mike confused and wondering when the next odd twist might be coming.

"Wow," said Gail. Any ideas on the caller?"

"We should know in an hour or so," said Mike.

"How?" Gail asked.

"Because we know what time she made the call. I'll have my friend Jerry get Bree's phone records. He'll figure it out."

"He can do that?"

Mike put his hand over hers. "He can do that."

Chapter 35

DUNCAN CHASE NEVER wanted to be a lawyer. At age twenty, he was a left-handed pitcher at Kent State University with his sights set on a big league career. His fast ball hit 95 M.P.H. on the radar gun. He won fifteen games his junior year and led the Golden Flashes to the semi-finals of the College World Series. He was drafted by the Baltimore Orioles in the second round that year and received a $500,000 signing bonus.

Two weeks after losing 2-1 in his final collegiate game, Chase was on the hill for the Frederick (Md.) Keys. He mowed down the first nine batters in his professional debut, striking out five of them. Then, after the first pitch of the fourth inning, he felt a sharp pain in his left elbow. He threw another pitch and the pain doubled. He threw one more and fell to his knees. It was over. When fortune and fame depend upon the reliability of ligaments and tendons, they are huge underdogs to survive. For every Clayton Kershaw, there are a thousand Duncan Chases living their lives disappointed that fortune and fame didn't beat the odds for them.

Chase closed the Rick Fenner file with a sigh. He didn't like the state's case at all. Sure, Fenner had legitimate motives for killing his wife. He certainly had the means and the opportunity. Scoundrel? Yes. Cheater? Yes. Killer? The assistant prosecutor tilted back in his chair. The preliminary hearing loomed. He was glad it wasn't the trial. Fenner would walk for sure.

"Paula? Can you get me Arch Kimball?"

His secretary, Paula Patterson, had celebrated her thirtieth birthday the previous week by announcing that she was pregnant with her fifth child.

"Dialing now," she said. "Kimball on two," she hollered a few seconds later.

"Tell me something good, Arch," said Chase.

"Three hundred seventeen days to retirement," said the detective.

"Congratulations," Chase smiled. "How about something on the Fenner case?"

"Nothing new," said Kimball.

"Okay. Let's meet tomorrow to go over your testimony for the prelim. What time?"

"Morning's best for me."

"Ten? My office?"

"I'll be there."

Chase hung up and shook his head. He opened the file. It should have been thicker. "Paula? Can you get me Gail West, please?"

Gail was still driving back to the office when her phone rang. She was surprised to hear from Chase. They'd been good friends as colleagues in the prosecutor's office, but hadn't spoken in more than a year.

"Dunk? Tell me you don't have the Fenner case," she said.

"Can't do it," he said. "Somebody decided I'd look handsome on TV."

Gail laughed. "Well, with the right makeup, I guess anything's possible."

Chase ignored her playful dig. "Ready for the prelim?"

She knew he was fishing for something. She just didn't know what it was. "Ready as I can be."

"Well, *I'm* not," he said. "I'm definitely not."

Gail wasn't expecting to hear that. "I hope you're not asking for help," she joked.

His tone remained serious. "Actually? I need some. Between you me, I can't figure out how they even arrested your guy, let alone how I'm supposed to prove he killed his wife."

"I almost crashed my car just now," Gail said. "You should be expressing that concern to detective Kimball. He's the one who decided Fenner was guilty five years ago."

"Don't crash," he laughed. "We're not supposed to be having this conversation, so I'm going to hang up. We'll talk soon."

"Sounds good," said Gail. She hung up smiling. One of the things she liked about Chase was that his job wasn't his whole life. He said he had made that mistake with baseball. He told her that his injury had sent him into a deep depression and that he was lucky to be alive.

He was given up for adoption at birth. His adoptive parents were poor, but they were good people who wouldn't let him quit on himself. They never left him alone to brood. They were always finding ways to keep his mind occupied in the months after his injury. Eventually, he developed a 'win some, lose some' attitude about the law.

He told Gail he'd never lose a minute of sleep over any case. Gail could hardly say the same about herself. The inability to separate her work life from her personal life had pretty much eliminated her personal life. She hadn't been on a date in two years. She hadn't even been *asked* on a date in six months. The pickings for fifty-something single women are slim by default, but adding a work obsession creates a simple equation whose sum is loneliness.

The law offices of Gail West occupied the upper level of a two-story, red brick building constructed in 1957 to house the Bolenbacher Funeral Home. Winston Bolenbacher III and his wife, Olivia, used the upper level as their living quarters. They raised four children—three boys and a girl. None followed them into the field of Mortuary Science. So, when Winston died suddenly in 2009, Olivia sold the building to an investor and moved to Florida.

Theirs had been the only funeral home serving Pluto, Austintown, Marshallville and the rest of the rural areas of Wayne County until the Wickershams opened for business in Renfro in 1988. The thirty-one-year monopoly made the Bollenbachers very wealthy. Their children, however, were common people.

Sons Mark and Rob were local farmers. Mark grew soy beans. Rob grew corn. Son Dennis was a firefighter in Marietta, down near the West Virginia border. Daughter Rhonda stayed home. She was a practicing dentist who leased an office on the building's lower level. Gail had seen her come and go, but they'd never had a conversation.

Gail parked in her space near the back entrance. She grabbed her briefcase and stepped out of her Mercedes.

"Excuse me," said a man's voice. Gail turned to see a familiar face about twenty feet behind her.

"Detective Kimball?" She closed the car door and stood still.

"Can we talk?" His tone was always serious. Gail pictured him questioning his grandchildren's playmates about their whereabouts during a broken window investigation.

"Sure. I'm listening."

"Off the record?"

"All right," said Gail.

"We know Rick Fenner didn't kill his wife."

Gail froze. She was absolutely shocked that Kimball was standing in front of her saying this. "Well, that's great news! You've arrested the real perp?"

"No. Hell no," said Kimball.

"So, what's happening?" Gail didn't like the guy, and she definitely didn't trust him. She also knew those feelings were mutual.

"I'm meeting with the prosecutor tomorrow morning. I'm going to tell him we don't like Fenner for the murder anymore. But I'm also going to tell him that Fenner's life will be in danger if he's released."

"In danger? Why?"

"I can't tell you."

"So, what are you saying? What do you want from me?" Gail asked.

Kimball summoned his most serious glare. "Waive the prelim. Ask for a trial date in July."

"July? He sits another ninety days?"

"Better alive in jail than dead on the street."

"I won't do that. I have to tell him."

"You can't," Kimball insisted.

Gail glared at him. "I can and I will! And I'm not playing this game." She stormed into the building. Kimball drove away.

Chapter 36

MIKE'S PHONE RANG as he pulled into his driveway. "Jerry. Any news?"

"Yes. Bree Fenner only had one incoming call before noon. Kids don't call much anymore. They text incessantly, but they don't call."

"Who was it?" Mike asked, impatiently.

"The number came from the 7-0-2. That's Vegas. Belongs to a Dan Riordan. Ring any bells?"

"Riordan? Dan Riordan? The twin brother. Right?"

"I'd say so," said Jerry.

"Thanks buddy," said Mike, disconnecting the call and hitting Gail's speed dial number.

"Hi, Mike. I've got some news," she said.

"I've got some, too," said Mike. "You first."

"Kimball just came to the office," said Gail. "He told me they know Rick didn't do it."

"What? That's unbelievable! Do they have a suspect?"

"He said they don't, but they want to keep Rick in jail because there's a threat on his life," she said.

"Threat? From whom?" Mike asked.

"He didn't say. He wants me to waive the prelim and ask for a July trial date. I told him no, but I'll have to talk it over with Rick. The prosecutor on the case is a friend of mine. I'll call him when I hang up with you. What's your news?"

"Bree's phone call this morning."

"Oh, yes. Did Jerry come though?" Gail asked.

"It was made from a phone registered to Dan Riordan," Mike said.

"The twin from Vegas? But it was a woman's voice," said Gail.

A Season in Pluto

"Right. So, who? And why?" asked Mike.

"Good questions," Gail said.

"In the meantime, if we let them drop the charges against Rick, it won't be any of our business anyway. Right?"

Gail paused. "Good point. You know what? Maybe Kimball's idea isn't so bad after all."

"So, what do we tell Rick?" Mike asked.

"For now, I think we only convince him that waiving the prelim is the best strategy. We'll tell Kimball and the prosecutor that we're keeping Rick in the dark about the threat on his life. You know, because we don't want him to worry."

"So, everybody's in the dark—or at least in the shade?"

"Yeah. Even us," said Gail.

Duncan Chase was driving home when his cell phone rang. "Gail? Haven't heard from you in an hour or so."

"Did you send Kimball to my office?"

"Kimball? No. Why?" Chase asked.

Gail told him about the visit.

"First I've heard any of that," said Chase. "We're meeting tomorrow to go over the evidence—or lack thereof."

"Well, my response to Kimball was that I was going to tell Rick and that I wouldn't play his game. I want you to know I've reconsidered. I'll be advising him that waiving the prelim is a *good* idea. I'm going to tell him to sit tight. I'd appreciate it if you'd tell Kimball that. I don't like talking to the guy."

Chase laughed. "Okay. Will do. What about the death threats? Did Kimball elaborate?"

"No. I was thinking you could help me out on that one," said Gail.

"I'll call you after our 10 a.m. meeting. I'll tell him I can talk you into playing along. I don't want him to know you tipped me off. I don't trust the guy," said Chase.

"You trust *me*?" Gail asked.

"No," said Chase. "But I like you."

Chapter 37

Friday, April 18

DETECTIVE ARCH KIMBALL arrived at the prosecutor's office fifteen minutes early. He wore black pants and brown wing tips. His sports jacket was purchased at a department store in 1985. It was dark brown corduroy with black elbow patches. He wore a pale-yellow button-down shirt with buttons on the cuffs. Arch was always early. His father had insisted upon it.

Bart Kimball had been a police captain in the city of Canton. He was a no-nonsense, by-the-book cop. His wife Kate was a seamstress. Together they raised Archibald and two daughters in a home that was run with great precision. Bart insisted that his children be seated at the dinner table no later than 5:55 p.m. He required that their bedrooms be kept spotless at times. Until they reached high school, their lights had to be out by 9 p.m.—and by 10 p.m. thereafter. He also required straight A's on their report cards. Bart retired in 2005 after forty-seven years on the force. He died of a heart attack a year later. Arch joked that the lack of stress had killed him.

Duncan Chase appeared in the large waiting room that served as a holding area for witnesses, cops and anyone else with an appointment to see one of the assistant prosecutors. He motioned to Kimball to follow him. He punched four buttons on a number pad, opened the door to the inner hallway and turned right. The fourth door on the left had his name on it. The two men walked past Paula's desk toward the inner office. Kimball stopped.

"Are you?" he hesitated, realizing it's always a bad idea to ask a woman if she's pregnant. Then he decided to go with his gut. "Having another one?"

"Case solved, detective," Paula smiled.

"Congratulations," said Kimball, relieved. He walked into Chase's office and sat in the black leather armchair to the right of his desk.

"Ready?" Chase asked.

"Duncan, we don't think Fenner's good for the murder," said Kimball. "It's true, his alibi didn't check out, but only because he was protecting his girlfriend—well, *one* of his girlfriends."

Chase leaned forward. "So, who did it?"

"Not sure. We've got some leads. In the meantime, we think Fenner could be a target, so I'm hoping you can keep him in jail for a little while."

"A target? What kind of target?" Chase asked.

Kimball thought for a moment. "There's been a credible threat, so we hope you can keep him locked up."

"Like how? When his attorney finds out he's not even a suspect anymore, she'll have him out in five minutes. You have to give me more."

Kimball leaned forward. "How about this?" Kimball asked, handing Chase a folded piece of white paper.

Chase read it out loud. *If the law won't take care of Rick Fenner, we will.* "Who's "we"? Any guesses?"

"Not really. Not yet," said Kimball. "But like I said, Fenner's safer in jail, so I was thinking you could talk to Ms. West and get her to waive the prelim and ask for a July trial date. By that time, we should have this whole thing wrapped up."

Chase rubbed his chin. "I'll talk to her," he said. Then he took a photo of the threatening note with his cell phone. "I'll show her this. Maybe it'll convince her."

Kimball stood up. "We're done then?"

"Go find the killer, detective," said Chase.

Chapter 38

AT 3:15 P.M., a school bus carrying the Austintown Aces pulled into the parking lot at Pluto High. Mike stared across the dugout roof as the players made their way to the field. After thirty seconds, he could read the name, "Austintown" stitched in gold across their maroon jerseys. They wore maroon pants with gold stripes down the sides, gold belts and gold pocket flaps. They also wore gold stirrups with white socks underneath. Their shoes were black Adidas with gold stripes. They looked sharp. Mike hoped they looked better than they played.

"Coach?" It was Lana, wearing a royal blue T-shirt with *Pluto Invaders Softball* on the front; her yellow poodle skirt; bobby socks; and saddle shoes.

"Lana. Cute outfit. Rehearsal after the game?"

"Yep," she said. "Just saw Jen Miller throw up. Thought you'd like to know."

"Yeah. Thanks," said Mike. "I'll check on her."

Mike left the dugout and walked up the left field line to where the girls were doing their warm-up routines. Jen Miller was stretching her legs.

"I had a teammate once who threw up before every game," said Mike. "Not on purpose. Just from being nervous. But he said it made him relax."

"I haven't been feeling well all day," said Jen. "I'm not really a puker. I've just had like a sick stomach."

"So, can you pitch? We *could* start Callie."

"Yeah. No. I'm fine," she said.

"Okay," Mike said.

Gail was torn. As an attorney, she hated having to ask her innocent client to sit in jail for another three months. As a woman, she thought Rick Fenner deserved a lot worse.

"It's our best chance to win," she said after breaking the news about waiving his preliminary hearing."

"Don't I get a vote?" Rick asked.

"Sure," she said. "I'm listening."

"I vote against another ninety days in jail."

"Your vote doesn't count. It'll go fast," Gail said, standing to leave.

Rick smiled. "How's Bree doing?"

"Good," said Gail. "First conference game today."

"Let me know how they do," he said.

The wind was blowing out. Mike kicked dirt in front of the dugout as he watched Jen warm up. She threw two drops that bounced in front of the plate and a rise over the catcher's head to the backstop. Allie ran to retrieve it. Then, she hollered, "Comin' down!" Jen finally threw one over the plate. Allie caught it and fired a laser beam to second base. Then, she jogged to the circle in time to take a short toss from first baseman Rachel McKenzie. She handed the ball to Jen and shouted, "Let's go!"

Austintown's leadoff hitter was Kelly McClain, a highly-recruited lefty slapper who posted a .735 on-base percentage as a junior. There was speculation that she would not play as a senior after accepting a scholarship from Notre Dame over the summer. No such luck for Mike.

As McClain stepped into the box, third baseman Andrea Kendall moved to within twenty feet of home plate. The game plan was to force McClain to swing the bat. She would not be allowed to bunt her way on base, at least not down the third base line. Jen's first pitch was a fast ball high and tight. McClain ran up on it with her bat cocked. She ducked to avoid getting hit in the face mask. Jen's second pitch was low and away for ball two. Her third pitch was another high fast ball that glanced off McClain's front shoulder.

"Dead ball!" the umpire yelled. McClain trotted to first. Mike hollered, "Allie!" Then he gave her the signal for a pitch out on the first pitch. Allie relayed the signal to the rest of the infield. The play is called when there's a great expectation that the base runner will attempt to steal. The pitcher throws a fast ball well outside the strike zone. The catcher stands, catches it and throws quickly to second, where the shortstop, who knew there was no chance the ball would be hit, is waiting to tag out the runner. It's a beautiful play when it works.

As Jen went into her motion, McClain coiled like a sprinter in a starting block. She stared at the yellow ball, shifting her weight to her back foot as it neared the release point from Jen's hand. Then, just as Jen let it go, McClain exploded from the base. "Runner!" yelled Darcy Lomax, sprinting to cover second. Jen's pitch hit the target; Allie's throw was perfect; Darcy caught it and swiped a tag at second. One problem: McClain wasn't there. She had stopped after three strides and was back at first, smiling.

Mike glanced at the third base coaching box. He recalled his telephone conversation with Leslie Cunningham, the Aces' young head coach. She had played college ball at Kent State. She had three older brothers who played baseball in high school and college. Her father had been a baseball coach for many years.

"Figures," Mike said aloud. Allie looked over at Mike as if to ask, *what do you want to do now?* Mike gave her the *wipe off* sign, which means no play is on. He fully expected McClain to steal on the next pitch, but she bluffed again as Jen threw a screw ball inside. Mike was surprised also that the batter wasn't even hinting she might bunt. "Ball three!" the umpire shouted as Jen's sixth pitch of the game bounced in front of the plate. Allie did well to block it, but the ball caromed up the third base line and McClain took second. "Ball four!" the umpire shouted as Jen's next pitch crossed the plate chin high.

"Time!" Mike yelled as the batter reached first.

"Time!" The ump yelled.

Mike trotted to the circle where Jen was using the side of her foot to fill the hole in front of the rubber with dirt. "Now you're in trouble," Mike smiled.

"I'm fine," Jen said calmly.

"Well that's good news," said Mike. "I'm fine, too, but I'm concerned that my pitcher hasn't thrown a strike yet and they've got two on and nobody out with three, four and five coming up. How about you?"

"How about me, what?"

"Are you concerned?" Mike asked.

"I'm fine. Just a little nervous," she said quietly.

"Okay," said Mike, patting her on the shoulder and starting back to the dugout. "Throw strikes."

Casey Johnson was the third batter in Austintown's lineup for good reason. She hit .537 as a sophomore and .580 as a junior with 28 homers and 110 RBI over the two seasons. She had committed to Ohio State at the age of 15 before playing her first high school game.

Mike yelled, "Rachel!" Then he motioned for his third baseman to move back. "Play even with the bag!" he shouted. "If you get a one-hopper, turn three!"

Mike definitely wanted the Austintown coach to hear him. He figured if she countered by giving Johnson the bunt sign, she'd be doing Pluto a big favor since Johnson was a threat to hit a three-run homer. If she ignored the strategy, at least his third baseman would be back where she could cover more ground—not mention protect herself from a vicious line drive off Johnson's bat.

Jen took her sign from Allie and threw a screw ball on the inside corner. "Strike!" yelled the umpire. Johnson stepped out of the box and stared at her coach, who was now furiously flashing signs. Allie called for a rise ball. Johnson positioned herself to bunt. Mike's jaw dropped. Rachel charged from third. Jen's pitch hit Johnson's bat letter high. A second later, the ball landed in Jen's glove on the fly. She wheeled and threw a strike to Darcy at second. Darcy stepped on the base and threw to Andrea at first. Neither base runner could get back in time. It was a triple play!

The girls ran off the field celebrating as the capacity crowd cheered wildly. Mike couldn't believe his young counterpart had given his number three hitter the bunt sign with two on and nobody out in the top of the first inning—especially since Jen hadn't even thrown a strike yet. He looked at Morgan. "Do they do that a lot?"

"Do what? She asked.

"Bunt the number three hitter with two on in the first inning."

"Yeah. They do," said Morgan.

"Dumb," said Mike.

Bree stepped up and lined the first pitch to center field for a single. Lauren bluffed a bunt on her first pitch and took a ball. Mike flashed the hit-and-run sign. Austintown pitcher Melissa Maloney was a senior with outstanding control. She averaged less than two walks every seven innings. He figured Lauren would get a good pitch to hit with a 1-0 count. Plus, even if Lauren should swing and miss, Bree was a good bet to steal the base on her own.

Maloney fired a fast ball down the middle. Bree got a good jump off first. Lauren swung and hit a grounder to the left of the pitcher, but no one was there to field it. The Aces' shortstop had run to cover second for the steal before the ball had reached the plate. Bree hit the bag at second and kept going as the ball rolled to left center field. The center fielder gloved it and fired it to third. Bree slid to the inside of the bag.

"Safe!" the umpire yelled. Just then, Lauren slid into second and the Invaders were in business. Mike called time and walked toward home plate. Darcy met him halfway.

"Nobody out. Second and third. Get a good pitch. She's got first base open, so she can be careful if she wants. Make sure you get a good one. Don't try to do too much. Just move the ball or take your walk."

"Okay, coach," said Darcy as she started toward home.

"Hey. Come here," said Mike. "Do you know why I really wanted to talk to you?"

"Why?"

"So their corner infielders have to play up a little. If their coach thinks you might squeeze, she's got to play them up. Right?"

"Right," Darcy agreed.

"Don't bunt. Get a hit."

Darcy laughed. "Okay."

Maloney pitched carefully to Darcy with first base open just as Mike suspected she would. But with a 3-1 count, Darcy hit a hard grounder between third and short. The ball tipped off the third baseman's glove and ricocheted to the left of the shortstop, spinning in the dirt near second base. Bree scored from third. Lauren had hesitated coming from second, but took off when she saw the ball coming her way.

"Come on! Come on!" Mike yelled, waving Lauren home as the second baseman scrambled to get the ball. Lauren slid home just ahead of the throw. "Safe!" yelled the umpire. Then the catcher stood and fired the ball to third as a hustling Darcy slid head first. "Safe!" yelled the other umpire. The Invaders led 2-0 with a runner at third and nobody out.

Allie was next up. Mike reminded Darcy to stay on the base and tag up on a fly ball. Maloney's first pitch was a change-up. Allie swung way too early and felt as foolish as she looked. She stepped out of the box and laughed. Mike laughed, too.

"You're on it, Allie!" Mike joked, clapping his hands.

Maloney's second pitch was a rise ball, intended to cross the plate about letter high. It was belt high. Allie swung and hit a towering fly ball to center field. Darcy stood on third waiting to tag up and score, but it wasn't necessary. The ball cleared the fence and the twenty-foot ravine behind it for a two-run homer. The Invaders led 4-0. They added two more in the first inning, three in the second inning and five in the third inning for a 14-0 lead.

Jen struggled with her control, walking six and hitting two, but she gave up only one run in the five-inning game shortened because of the ten-run rule. Mike had heard so many scary things about Austintown that a 14-1 victory seemed surreal.

"We'll try to give you a better game at our place," said Coach Cunningham, as they shook hands near home plate.

"I know you will," said Mike.

Walt McKee was standing near the dugout. "Helluva game," he said, extending a hand to Mike.

"Yeah, thanks," Mike said, shaking Walt's hand. "We got lucky in that first inning."

"Those triple plays tend to be rally killers," Walt laughed.

"And that, my friend is why you don't ask your number three hitter to bunt," Mike smiled.

"Amen," said Walt. "Looks like you've got a nice team on your hands."

"Really nice," said Mike.

"Nice game, coach," said a tall, handsome man in his fifties, extending his right hand across the top of the fence.

"Thanks," Mike said, shaking the hand.

"I'm Russ Miller, Jen's dad."

"Nice to meet you, Russ," said Mike, thinking there was a chance he'd done something that his pitcher's dad didn't like. "What'd you think?"

"I think I'm glad they bunted into a triple play," said Russ. "With their three hitter in the first inning, no less."

Mike laughed. "Where does that come from?" he asked.

"I know exactly where it comes from," said Russ. "It comes from coaching clinics run by control freaks who probably won a lot of games by scores of 2-1 or 1-0 that they could have won 10-1 or 10-0 if they hadn't killed so many of their own rallies by giving away outs with bunts."

Mike laughed again. "Exactly," he said.

"I mean, that coach today had a chance to knock Jen out in the first inning. She hadn't even thrown a strike yet! I don't think the pitch the girl bunted was even a strike," said Russ.

"It wasn't," said Mike. "It was high."

"What'd you say when you went out there?" Russ asked.

"Just asked how she was doing," said Mike. "And she said…"

"I'm fine," Russ interrupted. "I'm fine," he repeated.

"How'd you know?" Mike asked.

"She always says, 'I'm fine,' even when she isn't," Russ said. "And it's my fault, totally. I was too tough on Morgan when she was in high school. Way too tough. Jen was little, but she overheard me yelling at her sister a lot about being soft or not tough enough. So, Jen went the other way. The result is that she's as tough as they come, but she'd sooner get kicked by a bull than admit she's hurt or doesn't have her best stuff."

"So how will I know?" Mike asked.

"Use your best judgment," said Russ. "Or ask the catcher. They usually know. Of course, if Morgan's catcher had ever told the coach she didn't have her stuff, she would have fought her right on the field, so…"

Mike smiled. "Yeah, well that's the kind of player you want. And it's nice to have Morgan with us. She's a very good coach."

"Well, I appreciate you giving her the opportunity. Maybe it'll pull her out of the rut she's been digging for herself lately."

Mike watched Russ walk to the other side of the dugout, where his younger daughter was zipping her bat bag. They exchanged a few words. Then, Russ gave her a pat on the shoulder and headed for the parking lot.

I guess I'd have been like that, Mike thought.

Chapter 39

GAIL MET MIKE at his car. "I spoke with Rick. He's on board."

"Did you have to twist his arm?" Mike asked.

"Into a pretzel," Gail smiled.

"I don't blame him, I guess," Mike said.

"Neither do I," said Gail.

Mike's phone rang. "Bree? Bree, slow down. Slow down! What's wrong?" He listened for about ten seconds. "I'm on my way, Bree. I'll be right there."

"What? What?" Gail asked, impatiently.

Mike paused. His eyes turned glassy. "Somebody just ran Bree off the road."

"What? On her way to Morgan's? Is she all right?"

"She's in a ditch on Montville Road. Let's go."

"I'll drive," said Gail.

They arrived at the accident scene to find Bree sitting in the back of a Wayne County Sheriff's car in a driveway about twenty yards from her truck. A deputy was directing traffic in the twilight, having placed some orange cones and flares on the shoulder where the pickup was teetering half in and half out of the drainage ditch.

Another sheriff's car was parked at an angle near the pickup, extending a few feet onto the roadway. Mike tapped on the window. Bree opened the door and stepped out. Her face looked like some toddlers had used it for finger painting practice. The eye black she wore during the game was smeared to her jaw line. Her mascara had spread to her temples. "Are you all right?" Mike asked.

"Yeah. Fine," she said. "A van came up behind me and banged my bumper. I hit the brakes and I spun out."

"Did you see the driver?" asked Gail.

"No. It happened too fast. All I saw was a white van."

"Was there any writing on it? Like it belonged to a business?" Gail asked.

"I think so," said Bree. "But I'm not sure. It just hit me from behind and I lost control."

A tow truck arrived. The driver spoke with the deputy, then hooked up Bree's truck and yanked it out of the ditch and onto the road. He sat writing something for about thirty seconds, then drove away.

"He's taking your truck to our warehouse. We'll process it for evidence and get it back to you in a couple of days," the deputy told Bree. "You can take her home now," he said to Gail and Mike. "We've got her statement. A detective will be in touch."

"Tell Kimball she wants *him* to handle it," said Gail.

"I'll pass it along. Pop your trunk," he said.

Gail opened her trunk and the deputy deposited Bree's softball bag and school backpack. He closed the lid and waved to Gail's image in the side view mirror.

Bree sat in the back seat behind Gail. Mike turned in the passenger seat so he could see Bree's face. *Her face always told the truth*, Mike thought, *especially when her mouth was telling lies.*

"You sure you're okay?" Mike asked.

"Yeah, fine," said Bree. "Didn't hit my head or anything."

"Do you think it could have been an accident?"

"Not a chance. They would have stopped," said Bree

"Not necessarily. Not if they were drunk," said Mike.

"Yeah, well, I'm starting to think whoever killed my mom might want me dead, too," said Bree.

Mike was watching her eyes. He saw no hint of deception. She believed what she was saying.

"Bree. We know there's something you're not telling us," said Mike, hoping that would be enough to get Bree talking. It didn't work.

"What's that?" she said casually.

Mike couldn't turn back now. He was committed like a third base coach who'd just waved a runner home.

"We know you've been talking to someone from Nevada," he said

"The discovery?" she asked.

"We're trying to save your dad's life!" Gail snapped.

"So, who are you talking to from Nevada?" Mike pressed.

They were pulling into Morgan's driveway.

"I don't know," Bree said, flatly. "I really don't know."

Mike's patience was gone. "Just tell us what's going on, Bree. This is getting old."

"All right," she said. "All right!"

Gail threw the car into "park" and turned to look at Bree. "Just start from the beginning," she said.

"Okay. A woman called me like last November. She didn't identify herself. She told me my mom had been murdered. I'm like, 'Who are you? And how do you know that?' And she's like, 'It will all come out soon.' So, I start crying, and she asks me if I know about a video camera that my mom got from Uncle Jonas. I told her I didn't—and she hung up."

"But you *did* know, right?" asked Gail.

"I knew about a picture of a video camera that was in the box he left her. That's all," said Bree.

"Was that call before or after the argument at your house we talked about in the cafeteria?" Gail asked.

Bree thought for a few seconds. "Just after, I think. Yeah. Like a week or so after."

"So, let's go back to that argument, Bree," said Gail. "Tell us what your dad really said to you."

"I told you."

"No. You didn't," Mike insisted. "Someone overheard that argument. Your dad said your mom's death was your fault. Why did he say that, Bree? Why?"

"Okay! Okay!" Bree shouted. "Stop!"

"Just tell the truth, Bree," Gail urged.

"I wrote an essay."

"An essay. About what?" Gail asked.

"About what was in the box," said Bree.

"For school?" asked Mike.

"Yeah. Our teacher was on maternity leave. We had Cragmere as a sub. She told us to write an essay about something happening in our lives—so I wrote about the box."

Mike and Gail had been staring at each other since the name *Cragmere* left Bree's lips. Bree's face turned ashen. "It's Cragmere. Isn't it?" she asked.

"We think so," said Gail, calmly.

"And my dad knew?"

"He knew," said Mike. "Almost from the start."

"Tell us about the latest call from that 7-0-2 number," Gail said, handing a tissue to Bree.

"She called the night Coach Page got back from Las Vegas. She said she had evidence that proved my dad was innocent. But she wanted to know everything you learned on your trip before she'd tell me."

"So, what happened?" Mike asked.

"She called Tuesday morning during school," said Bree. "I told her I didn't know anything yet. After I talked to you guys, I called her and told her everything you told me."

"So, what was the evidence?" asked Gail.

"Beats me. The bitch hung up after she got what she wanted," said Bree.

"Are you sure it was the same person?" asked Mike.

"It was like slightly altered, electronically. But it was the same sound. Yes."

"Bree, you have to tell us if she calls back," said Gail.

"I will," said Bree, stepping out of the car and closing the door.

Gail put the car in gear. "Are you thinking what I'm thinking?"

"That a kiss would be nice right now?" Mike asked.

"Yeah, exactly," Gail said. She smiled and kissed him softly. "What do you think?"

"I think I'd like another," Mike said, leaning across with his lips puckered.

Gail obliged. "I mean about the caller."

"Oh. Yeah. Well, it's obvious. The caller is the killer," he said.

"The caller is the killer?"

"The caller is the killer," he repeated, leaning in for another soft kiss.

"Of course," said Gail. "The caller is the killer."

As they drove toward Brecksville, Mike daydreamed—but not about falling in love (which he seemed to be doing), or about the Cheryl Fenner murder case. He was game-planning for Saturday's visit to Wyoming. Forty-two hours to prepare for the team coached by the legendary Jake Moffitt wasn't much time.

"What?" He said, shaking his head.

Gail laughed. "Ha! You're cute when you're in a fog, Mr. Page."

"I must be cute most of the time," he said.

Chapter 40

Arch Kimball sat tapping a pen on the tiny plastic face mask of his Jim Brown bobble head. As he tapped, he stared at two pages of notes on his desk. In bright green capital letters at the top of one page were the words, *WHY DID CHERYL HAVE TO DIE?* Underneath that heading, Kimball had written possible motives for her murder. He had drawn a line through the first three:

1. ~~She was in Rick's way (women, insurance).~~
2. ~~One of Rick's women did it (Amber, Patti, others).~~
3. ~~She was having an affair.~~
4. She knew too much about something.
5. Someone had a grudge.

Kimball had been certain for years that Rick Fenner was guilty. Now he was just as certain that he wasn't. He blamed Fenner for refusing to take a polygraph test to help eliminate himself as a suspect. He also blamed the instincts that convinced him to break the cardinal rule of keeping an open mind.

His mind was certainly open now. He reached into one of three white cardboard boxes sitting side-by-side to the left of his desk. He grabbed a file folder labeled, "Fenner Financials." He dumped it on his desk and stared at the pile of bills, receipts and bank statements. He'd been through them all at least five times, hoping to find a clue that would lead him to the killer.

He stared at the numbers. He stared at the names of merchants and personal friends and charities. He stared and he stared some more.

"How's that Cheryl Fenner murder case coming, Arch? Any leads?"

Kimball turned to see Captain Stan Krumrie. He'd been the commanding officer of the Robbery-Homicide Division for twelve years. Kimball considered him a friend, though he hadn't been particularly supportive after Ron Parker was acquitted of murder. Instead of backing Kimball when he insisted that the jury was wrong, Krumrie ordered him to re-open the case and investigate the two people Gail West had implicated as a means of creating reasonable doubt during the trial.

Kimball spent six months turning the lives of Jack and Jo Ann Weatherby inside out, eventually proving that neither was involved in the murder of Melissa Parker. Jo Ann had been devastated by the original investigation—she learned that her husband was a cheater; she left him; she lost her job as a police dispatcher because she started drinking heavily. The second round of interrogation had been more than she could bear. She attempted suicide by swallowing a handful of sleeping pills. Eventually, she moved to California to live with her sister.

Jack had moved into a one-bedroom apartment in Shaker Heights during the trial. It was much closer to his job as a Cleveland cop. It was also a safe thirty miles or so from his ex-wife, who had become mentally unstable to say the least. Kimball's investigation confirmed Jack's affair with the late Mrs. Parker. It also revealed some other embarrassing aspects of his personal life, including the fact that he'd been arrested two years earlier for shoplifting from an adult superstore.

The charges were dropped when he agreed to pay for the merchandise. Jack had explained it away as a prank, part of a bet with two friends. The friends, both cops, confirmed his story, but the Cleveland Police Department suspended him for two weeks and disciplined the other two. Kimball was angry that he'd caused so much grief unrelated to Melissa Parker's murder.

Kimball and prosecutors were convinced that Ron Parker had stopped loving his wife long before her affair with Jack. They claimed Ron had killed her for the life insurance money. One policy he took out when they were married in 1999 paid $250,000; the other, from Key Bank, where she worked as teller, paid $50,000. He collected on both shortly after his acquittal.

"It's a son of a bitch," Kimball replied. "Six years is a long time."

Krumrie stared at the pile of papers. "Anything interesting from the state lab?"

"They gave us a probable cause of death," said Kimball. "Gunshot wound to the head."

"Probable?"

"Not enough left of her to do any more. So, yeah, that's the best they'll ever do," Kimball said.

"What about motive? Any progress?"

Kimball grabbed some papers from his desk and tossed them a foot into the air. "That's why I'm back with these financials," he said as the papers landed with a clap.

Krumrie picked up a credit card statement and stared at it. "Cheryl Benson Fenner. Who killed you, Cheryl Benson Fenner?" He wondered aloud.

Kimball smiled as Krumrie tossed the paper onto the pile and walked away. "Let me know if she answers."

Gail pushed open her front door and kicked it closed. She flipped the light switch with her left shoulder and set her brief case and three plastic grocery bags on the kitchen island. The house was a three- bedroom colonial in a Bath Township subdivision. She'd been a life-long apartment dweller, but something she read about real estate investments sent her into a buying frenzy of sorts when interest rates dipped near two percent in 2012. She bought three houses—two for half a million each in Bath; and the other for $200,000 in nearby Copley. Then, she hired a property management company and earned enough from renting two of the houses to pay the mortgages on all three.

She placed packages of ground beef and sliced cheese into the refrigerator. She tossed whole wheat bread onto the counter near the toaster. She set the rest—three cans of Campbell's chicken noodle soup, a box of Minute Rice and a bottle of Heinz ketchup—on pantry shelves. Then, she walked into the living room, flopped onto the red leather sofa and took a deep breath.

How did it come to this? How did I get to be fifty years old and completely alone? What does anyone think when they hear my name? All they CAN think is 'she's a lawyer.' Maybe some people throw in adjectives like "good" or "excellent." Maybe they call me "relentless" or "stubborn." Some perverted colleagues might use "hot" to describe me. I'm not hot. I'm pathetic and lonely and sad.

I did it to myself. Every time a man approached me, I thought the worst. I never gave anyone a chance. I let one failed relationship ruin my life. It's too late for children. It's too late to get it right.

The face of every man who'd asked her out since she graduated from law school flashed in her mind. She saw Rod Colburn, the architect with too many teeth. She saw Marty Greenberg, the corporate attorney with three ex-wives. She saw Bill Shaw, the electrician who was as close to "Mr. Right" as any man could have been. He just lacked the proper pedigree.

They all lacked something. Right? They all weren't quite good enough. Well, maybe it was you who wasn't quite good enough, Gail. Maybe it was you.

Bree wasn't in a talking mood. She sat on the sofa in her robe and slippers with a towel wrapped around her head. A few specks of eye black remained on her face even after a hard scrubbing in the shower. She answered Morgan's questions, but with as few words as possible.

"Did they offer you any kind of protection?" Morgan asked.

"Who? The sheriff's department? They're clueless," said Bree.

"Yeah. Obviously," Morgan agreed. "They arrested your dad. Right?"

Bree stared at the television. The wheel was spinning on *Wheel of Fortune.* "Right."

"Are you afraid they'll try again?" Morgan asked.

"I haven't had time to think about it," Bree replied.

"Well, I would be," said Morgan. "Do you think it's the same people who killed your mom?"

Bree turned and glared at her. "Why would you ask that?"

"I didn't mean anything," said Morgan. "I'm just, I'm just concerned. You're a sister to me now. You know?"

Bree's glare softened. "I know. I know. I'm just sick of this shit. I spent six years hoping mom was alive somewhere, trying to find herself or something. When I find out she's dead, the cops screw up my mind by arresting my dad for no reason. Now somebody's trying to kill *me*. Plus, I have to keep up my grade point and my batting average so I can get a scholarship. It's a little much," she said, starting to cry.

Morgan rushed across the room and held her close. "What can I do? Tell me."

Bree didn't answer. She kept crying until she fell asleep. Morgan sat a few minutes longer. Then, she covered her friend with a quilt.

Chapter 41

Saturday, April 19

KIMBALL'S DREAM SHOOK him awake. He called his partner, Ed Franks. "Ed. We need to go back to Fenner's house."

"What time is it? It's five o'clock!" Franks screamed, answering his own question.

"We were looking for the wrong thing," said Kimball, calmly.

"Okay." said Franks. "What are you talking about?"

"We were looking for things that might implicate Rick Fenner. We should have been looking for things that might make Cheryl Fenner a target," said Kimball.

"Don't tell me. It came to you in a dream?" Franks sighed.

"You doubt my dreams after what happened in the Jenson case?" Kimball asked.

"Come on, Arch. You dreamed the guy stashed the gun in a secret room in his basement—and we found it in his attic."

"I dreamed it was hidden in the house. You thought he tossed it in the lake," said Kimball, defiantly.

"We already went through her stuff," said Franks.

"Not really. Not *all* of it," said Kimball. "Meet me out there at eight. I'll clear it with the prosecutor."

Kimball called Chase. Chase called Gail. Gail told him to get a warrant and that she wanted to be there to supervise.

"Did you hear about Bree getting run off the road last night?" she asked.

"Kimball told me," said Chase.

"What about protection for her?"

"Come on, Gail. That's a little cloak and dagger. Don't you think?"

"No. I don't!" Gail snapped. "Her life's in danger!"

"Well, I disagree. And it's not my call anyway," said Chase.

Gail hung up on him. "Screw you, Duncan," she said to her phone.

Gail called Mike next and asked him to be at the Fenner place by eight.

"What are they looking for?" he asked.

"I'm quite sure they don't know," she said.

At eight o'clock, a marked Sheriff's car containing two uniformed deputies was positioned at the bottom of Rick Fenner's driveway. A crime scene investigation van squeezed past the patrol car and parked near the front door. Kimball and Franks followed in their unmarked brown sedan. Gail's Mercedes pulled up two minutes later—a minute before Mike's Buick. At 8:10 a.m., Kimball and Franks, Gail and Mike, and two CSI's walked into the house.

"Master bedroom first," said Kimball.

They paraded through the kitchen and living room, then down the narrow, gray-carpeted hallway which led to a small bathroom on the right and two bedrooms on the left. The double doors to the master bedroom were open at the end of the hallway.

"You guys take the closets," Kimball told the CSI's. "We'll get the drawers."

As they searched, it became clear that Rick Fenner hadn't tried to forget his wife or even to move on from the loss. The CSI's found dresses, skirts, blouses and pants on hangers. They found sweaters and T-shirts folded on shelves. They found shoes and belts and purses. They found jewelry, much of it fourteen karat gold.

In Cheryl's bureau, Kimball found socks, bras, panties and pantyhose. He turned them over with two hands, feeling for anything that might be hidden among them. There was nothing.

Franks dropped to his hands and knees and lifted the bed skirt. He extended his right arm and waved it left and then right. He felt nothing. His shirt sleeve emerged covered with dust. He moved to the end of the bed and to the opposite side of it, repeating the process. There was nothing under the bed but dust.

"Closet's clean," said Jack Ferguson, the taller of the two CSI's.

"Nothing here, either," said Franks, slapping at his dusty shirt sleeve.

"Not so fast!" shouted Rich Echols, the other CSI. "That closet had a little crawl space!" He held a rectangular metal box that was fifteen inches long, eight inches wide and about that deep. It looked like a fishing tackle box. Echols set it on the bed and flipped the latches.

"Dump it out," said Kimball.

Echols dumped it on the bed. There were two pieces of printer paper rolled and held together by a rubber band. There were five gold coins, three Polaroid photos and a black leather wallet.

"Those coins are nice," said Franks.

"Recognize the guy?" asked Mike.

"Not me," said Kimball. "Anyone?"

They all looked at the first photo and shook their heads. It showed a man, probably in his mid-seventies, standing in the woods near a cabin. The second photo showed a medicine bottle labeled, "Succinylcholine" with a syringe next to it. The third photo was a close up of a JVC video camera.

"Somebody Google that Suckin' o-lean or whatever and see what it is," said Kimball, as he grabbed the roll of papers and slid off the rubber band. His eyes widened as he read the cover page.

"It's a letter to Cheryl," he announced.

Gail moved closer and read over his shoulder. "Jonas Benson. Jonas Benson," she repeated. "Benson's drugs?"

"I'll Google him," said Ferguson.

"Cheryl Benson Fenner," said Kimball. "Pretty sure Benson was her maiden name."

"What's it say?" asked Mike. "Does it have a date?"

"It's a powerful muscle relaxer," said Echols. "They use it during throat surgery, it says. There's also a warning that it can cause cardiac arrest. It's given by injection."

"Yeah. There's a syringe in the photo," said Franks.

"Here's an article about Succinylcholine being among the more untraceable methods of inducing a heart attack," said Echols. "It says it constricts the muscles in the throat and chest so as to cause suffocation. The cause of death is then determined to be a heart attack. It says it's rarely included in toxicology testing by medical examiners."

"Just pulled an obit for Jonas Benson," said Ferguson. "Died April 30, 2008. He was seventy-eight, a pharmacist, the founder of Benson's Drugs of Pluto. Educated at The Ohio State University. Wife, Lucille preceded him in death, 2001. One child—Marine Sgt. Gordon Benson of Pluto, died in combat, Lebanon. One grandchild—Cheryl Benson Fenner of Pluto."

"Okay. So, grandpa left Cheryl this box of stuff with a letter dated April 21, 2008. Why don't you read it for us, Mr. Page?" asked Franks.

"Let's check the wallet first," said Kimball. He picked it up and unfolded it. No money in the middle. He flipped through the plastic photo holders. Empty. He shoved a finger into each credit card compartment.

"Nothing, nothing. Nothing, nothing. Nothing. Ah!" he said, pulling a gold key from the final compartment. "The key to the case!"

The others grinned. "Might be the key to the cabin," said Franks.

"Might be," Kimball agreed.

"Go ahead, Mr. Page," said Franks, nodding at the papers.

Mike read the letter slowly and clearly:

My Dear Granddaughter:

As I lie here incapacitated but for the brain that managed to diminish at a slightly slower rate than my body, I think about my long life with great pride for all I accomplished and with few regrets.

While I am gratified by the success of my business, a venture built with blood, sweat and tears beginning in 1957, it is my marriage of nearly fifty years to your grandmother and the subsequent success of our child, your father, of which I am proudest.

The fact that J. Gordon Benson became a sergeant in the United States Marine Corps, and gave his life for his country fighting in Lebanon, makes me feel I contributed more to the betterment of the world than anyone I know.

Leaving you as his legacy is equally great. You are a loving wife and mother with a heart of gold. You have given of yourself without expecting anything in return.

When I needed you, you were there. When your grandmother, rest her soul, needed you, you were there. When your mother, rest her soul, was taken ill with breast cancer, you were her rock. I could not have asked for a better person to represent the Benson name into the future.

With all of that said, the reason I am writing is simple: I am dying and likely won't make it through the month. I have consulted with my attorney and decided that selling Benson's drugs to a previously interested buyer is the best course of action. The sale price for the building, the business and everything associated with it will be $316,000. My attorney will take care of the details. As my sole heir, you will receive approximately $50,000 cash and my pickup, which is the only personal vehicle I have. What remains after attorney's fees, taxes and my final expenses will be donated to Pluto's general fund. In exchange, the public library will be named in my honor.

As you may know, I sold my house and cashed in all of my stocks and bonds several years ago to pay for medical and living expenses involving the removal of my left kidney. The business is my only asset now. If I had lived like this another two years, I would have been bankrupt, so it's just as well that I'm going soon.

I have only one item of unfinished business. Many years ago, I swore an oath that I would never reveal a secret. I have kept that promise. What happens after I'm dead, however, is of no concern to me. Still, I am not certain that the karma of the afterlife will be pleased with that conclusion. With that in mind, I have left you several items that might or might not lead you to the truth. If you do find the truth, many people's lives will be affected—and most of those effects will be negative.

I leave it up to you. Thank you, dear granddaughter. I wish you happiness always.

Jonas Benson

Mike tossed the letter onto the bed. "I think you've found what you were looking for," he said.

Mike was looking at Kimball, but Kimball didn't react. He kept staring at the items on the bed. After a few seconds, he gathered them and placed them in the tackle box.

"I think we're done here," the detective said.

"What's your next move?" asked Gail.

Kimball paused. "I'd like to re-interview your client."

"Absolutely," said Gail. "Let's do it tomorrow."

Chapter 42

Monday, April 21

BILL MILLER STOOD chatting across the bar with two of his regulars. Like him, Bruno Palucci and Gary O'Malley were Viet Nam veterans in their late sixties. Palucci owned a meat market in Renfro. O'Malley was disabled, living off his government pension. Bill poured the draft beer and they drank it—nearly every day.

Mike walked in, waved to Bill and sat in a booth.

"Beer, Mike?" Bill called.

"Yeah, why not?" Mike said. "Bud light is fine."

Bill poured the beer and delivered it. "Meeting someone?" he asked.

"Gail's on her way," Mike said.

"Menus?"

"Yup, thanks."

"Awful what happened to Bree," said Bill. "They sure it was deliberate?"

"Haven't been told anything," Mike said. "But the sheriff's department is definitely treating it that way.

"Hi, guys," said Gail, sliding into the booth opposite Mike.

Bill seemed to ignore her. "Any description on the car?"

"Bree said it was a van," said Mike.

"Any leads that you know of?" Bill asked.

"I'll have an iced tea, no sugar, Bill," Gail interrupted.

"Not really," Mike said.

"No plate number?" asked Bill.

"No. Bree said it happened too fast," said Mike.

"And a menu, Bill, if you don't mind," said Gail.

"Tell me again, Gail. I'm sorry," said Bill.

"Iced tea. No sugar. Menu. Please," she said, smiling.

Bill walked back to the bar. Mike sipped his beer. "He was asking about Bree's mishap."

"I heard," said Gail. "Seemed a little hyper about it."

"Yeah. Maybe," said Mike. "But the guy did five tours in Viet Nam. That earns him a little suspicious behavior credit in my book."

Gail changed the subject. "We have to find the attorney."

"Kimball's probably all over that right now," said Mike.

"Probably thinks Rick knows him," said Gail. "That's why he wants to talk to him."

"I'll make a call," said Mike. He Googled Benson's Drugs, then called the number.

"Benson's Drugs. Please hold," said the voice.

Gail excused herself and went to the ladies room. Bill returned with an iced tea and two menus.

"Must have scared her half to death," said Bill.

"Who?" Mike asked.

"Bree," said Bill. "Getting run off the road like that."

"Oh. Yeah. I would imagine so," said Mike. "Tuna melt on wheat for me with regular chips. Half-size grilled chicken salad with that balsamic dressing for Gail. Thanks, Bill."

"May I help you?" said the woman at the drug store counter.

Mike asked to speak with the owner. The woman went to find the store manager, who was polite but had no idea who Jonas Benson was, let alone who Benson's attorney had been. He said the store was owned by a corporation based in Cincinnati. Mike thanked him and called his friend Jerry to ask him to dig deeper.

"Any luck," Gail asked, sliding into her side of the booth.

"Benson's is owned by a corporation in Cincy," Mike said. "The manager never heard of Jonas. I've got Jerry on the case and I ordered half a grilled chicken salad with balsamic for you."

172

"I was thinking cheeseburger and fries," said Gail.

"That'll be the day," Mike smiled. He sipped his beer, reached across the table and lifted her left hand. "How'd you cut yourself?"

Gail looked down at the two-inch scratch that had barely bled. "I don't really know," she said. "I guess I didn't notice when it happened." She noticed he wasn't letting go of her hand.

"Might need stitches," he joked.

"You just want to hold my hand," she said, squeezing his.

"Guilty, your honor," Mike smiled. His phone rang. He used the hand that wasn't holding Gail's hand to answer it. He recognized the number. It was Jerry.

"That was quick," he said. "He's dead? When? I've got Gail here, Jerry. I'm putting you on speaker."

"Samuel Burkett. Attorney at law. Died six years ago. May 13, 2008. Age sixty-six," said Jerry.

"Cause?" Mike asked.

"Might have to find a relative to get that," he said. "It wasn't determined to be foul play. I know that much."

"Married? Children?"

"Wife. Dorothy. Now seventy-four. Lives up in Hinckley."

"Yeah. That's near me," said Mike.

"Son. Edward. Fifty. Lives in Enid, Oklahoma," Jerry continued. "I think that's near the Texas border, a couple of hours from Dallas. That's pretty much it."

He gave them Dorothy Burkett's street address and promised to keep digging.

"Thanks, Jerry," said Mike. "Check's in the mail."

"He died a week after Cheryl disappeared!" said Gail.

"Probably just a coincidence," Mike deadpanned.

"Let's find the wife tonight," said Gail.

"All right," said Mike. "After practice. We've got a big game tomorrow at Wyoming."

Rick hadn't heard about his daughter's accident. "What? When? Is she all right?"

"She's fine. Not a scratch. It happened last night on her way back to Morgan's after the game," said Mike.

Rick didn't seem overly concerned. He asked Kimball about witnesses and who'd be handling the investigation, but seemed to assume that a drunk driver was the culprit.

Gail was anxious to find out what Rick new about Jonas Benson and his attorney. "Did you know Cheryl's grandfather?" she asked.

"Jonas Benson. Sure. He owned Benson's Drugs," said Rick.

"Do you remember when he died?" Kimball asked.

"Yeah. I remember," said Rick. "We went to his funeral three or four days before Cheryl went missing."

"Cheryl was his only relative. Right?" asked Kimball.

"As far as I remember, that's true. He left her his pick-up—that's the truck Bree drives—and some money, maybe thirty-five grand after taxes. I think he sold the business and gave the rest of his money to the city of Pluto so they'd name the library after him."

"Do you remember anything else he might have left your wife?" Kimball asked.

"No. I don't think there was anything else. I wasn't there when the will was read. I think it was just Cheryl and the lawyer."

"What was his name?" asked Kimball.

"The lawyer? God. I can't remember," said Rick.

"If we told you we found a tackle box in your house with some items left to Cheryl by Jonas Benson would you know what we were talking about?" asked Kimball.

"A tackle box? Where?" Rick asked.

"It was in the crawl space in your bedroom closet," said Kimball.

"No. What was in it?" Rick asked.

"I'm going to show you," said Kimball. He motioned to Franks, who had transferred the contents of the box to his briefcase. Rick started with the photos.

"That's Jonas," he said. "The cabin doesn't look familiar, but he did invite us once to a time share he had in Michigan. Couldn't tell you where. What's up with these other pictures?"

"We're not sure," said Kimball. "The drug is a strong muscle relaxer capable of causing a heart attack. We're thinking the camera could be hidden somewhere. Maybe at that cabin behind him."

Rick handled one of the coins. "Not in a protective case, so I'm guessing they're nothing special. Twenty-dollar American Gold Eagles? Maybe three-fifty each right now. I've got a few myself. Paid seventy-five bucks apiece for them, years ago. This is everything?"

"That's all of it," said Franks. "Except for the letter. Ever see or hear about this?" He pulled the two-page document from his briefcase and handed it to Rick.

When Rick finished reading, he looked at Kimball. "This is why they killed her! Somebody knew about this letter! Who knew? The lawyer? The lawyer must have known!"

"The lawyer's dead," said Kimball. "The week after Cheryl disappeared."

"Jesus! How'd he die?" Rick asked.

"We're checking," said Franks.

"Then you know I didn't kill my wife. Don't you?"

Gail put her arm around Rick. "They know, Rick."

"So why am I still in here? Get me out!" he shouted.

"Rick, there have been threats on your life," said Kimball.

"On *my* life? Who?"

"We don't know," said Kimball.

Gail showed Rick the photo of the threatening note Chase had sent to her phone.

"You need to get me out of here. Now!" Rick shouted.

Kimball gave Gail a stern look. "Rick, this isn't a game. This is real. Look what happened to Bree," Gail said.

"Today!" Rick shouted even louder.

Now Gail was shouting. "It doesn't work that way! You're still charged with murder!"

"Yeah? Well maybe if you'd tell people I'm *not* a murderer, they wouldn't want me dead!"

Kimball intervened. "Give us a little more time to sort this out, Rick. We'll keep Bree safe—and you're safe here."

"So, I'm not going on trial?" Rick asked.

"No trial," said Gail.

"How long 'till I'm out?" he asked.

"Not more than a week," Kimball promised.

Chapter 43

MIKE WAS FIFTEEN minutes late for practice. The girls were playing catch and stretching in the outfield. Lana was in a panic.

"Coach! You'll notice the squad seems a little light," she said.

Mike counted nine players. "Yeah. Missing four. Where are they?"

Lana twirled and ran a few strides to the dugout, where she retrieved a notepad. "Okay. Halle, Callie and Maddie are all at a 4-H meeting. Lauren has detention."

"Why does Lauren have detention?" Mike asked, fearing the worst.

Lana smiled. "Well, I can tell you it has nothing to do with Mr. Willoughby. That's the good news."

"What's the bad news?" Mike asked.

"Yeah. How can I put this? She gave somebody the finger."

"Details, please," said Mike.

"In school."

"More," Mike demanded.

"Mr. Richter."

"The principal?"

Lana twirled. "But it wasn't that bad, coach."

Mike shook his head like he must have heard wrong. "Lauren gave the finger to the principal and it wasn't that bad?"

"Well, here's what happened. She was standing on a table in the cafeteria at lunch, and..."

"What? Why was she standing on a table?" Mike interrupted.

"I'm getting to it," said Lana. "She was announcing her candidacy for spring prom queen."

"And?"

"And some kids were shouting things—some supportive, some nasty. And she was saying something like, 'What if I told you we could have food catered by Chipotle and Pizza Hut?'"

"And?"

"And from behind her, somebody said, 'What if I told *you* to get down before you get detention?' And Lauren spun around with her middle finger pointed to the ceiling and screamed, 'I'd say *screw you!*'"

"And it was Richter?"

"Unless he has a twin," said Lana.

"What about the others? Did I know about this 4-H thing?"

"You knew."

"Damn."

Mike called the girls together. "Listen up," he began. "Halle, Callie and Maddie have 4-H, Lauren's in detention for giving Mr. Richter the finger and somebody's trying to kill Bree. But that doesn't mean we can't have a good practice.

"Yeah. It kinda does," said Jen.

Mike smiled. "We're just missing outfielders and a pitcher, so we can work on hitting and infield."

After batting practice, Mike told the girls to take their positions. "I've seen Wyoming play," he lied. "They play like a nine and under team. They bunt a lot, but they're not very good at it. When they strike out, they sprint to first even when it's obvious the ball wasn't dropped. When their faster players walk, they sprint to first, round the bag and try to steal second—especially with another runner on base.

"I don't blame them. Most of the teams they play don't field bunts very well, and their catchers aren't coached well enough to know when to throw the ball to first and when not to. Most of the teams they play have no idea how to stop them from taking an extra base on a walk. Well, we're not most teams."

Over the next forty-five minutes, they worked on defense against the bunt in every possible situation.

"Okay," Mike said. Nice work. Now I'm going to show you what to do in the rare event that our pitchers walk somebody and the batter tries to go all the way to second base." He told his catchers to throw the ball back to the pitcher right away after ball four. He told Bree to step into the baseline about halfway between first and second.

"As soon as the batter rounds first, just throw it to Bree. The runner will run right into the tag. If she stops, get her into a rundown. Now, if there's a runner at third and it's a close game, all I want you to do, Jen, is turn and fake a throw to Bree, then spin around and check the runner from third. If she goes for the fake, run at her. If you have to give up the ball early, make sure you throw it home, so that the worst-case scenario is the runner from third being safe back at third, and the hitter safe at second.

"We don't want to make a play on the batter rounding first in that situation unless we're several runs ahead because we'll probably give them that base anyway if they steal on the next pitch. Remember, we've got really good pitchers who can strike out the next batter or two, so we don't have to force anything. Mike asked the girls to name the two plays.

"How about blue and white?" Andrea suggested.

"Green Day and Fall Out Boy," said Dee.

"Pride and Prejudice," said Nikki.

"Scooby and Shaggy," said Bree.

Mike laughed. "Let's vote."

Six girls voted for Scooby and Shaggy.

"Okay," said Mike. It's Scooby when we throw to Bree and Shaggy when we fake it. The bus leaves from here at 11 a.m. Game's at one. Don't be late."

Mike walked with Morgan to the parking lot. "Is Jen ready for this?" he asked.

"I think so," said Morgan.

"She's a better fielder than Callie," said Mike. "Quicker to the ball. If we don't handle the bunts, it could be a long day."

"I'll tell her she's starting," said Morgan.

Mike's phone rang as he started the car.

"I found her," Gail said.

"You're in Hinckley?"

"Having coffee with Dorothy Burkett. Are you on your way?"

"Forty minutes," said Mike.

"See you in forty," said Gail.

Mike used the drive time to call the four players who missed practice. He reached Halle first, then Maddie, then Callie. He asked them all about the 4-H meeting and pretended to care. He told Callie that Jen was going to start in the circle and he told her why.

"I'm hoping she'll throw a no-hitter, but I'm thinking you'll be needed at some point. So, be ready."

"I will," she said, without complaining that the freshman was getting the start against the arch-rival.

Mike went over the Scooby and Shaggy plays with her before calling Lauren, who started talking without saying "hello."

"I know. I know," she said with her best apologetic voice. "I screwed up. It's my own fault. It was stupid. Am I benched?"

"Hello to you, too," said Mike. "Yes. You screwed up big time. And heck no, you're not benched. We're playing Wyoming tomorrow. I need your head on straight. The bus leaves at eleven. Be early."

"I will. Thanks!" said Lauren.

Mike hung up smiling. *I'm all for teaching life lessons about respecting authority,* he thought. *But I'm not losing to Jake Moffitt because my center fielder accidentally gave the finger to the principal. You have to have priorities.*

Pluto was a metropolis compared to the township of Hinckley, population 7,600 (give or take). It is best known for buzzards, which are actually turkey vultures. Every March 15, thousands of buzzards return from their winter homes to the Hinckley Reservation, part of the Cleveland Metroparks. At 6:30 a.m., a large (or small, depending on the weather) crowd gathers to watch the return of the buzzards. It's a sure sign that spring is just around the corner.

Hinckley became the San Juan Capistrano of the Midwest in 1957, when residents decided to commemorate the strange phenomenon. Clearly, the reservation is a perfect home for the birds with its high ledges, open fields, tall trees and fresh water. Still, the best explanations of why the buzzards choose March 15 for their return can't help but fall short.

The most prevalent legend speaks of a decision on December 24, 1818 to protect the herds by ridding the area of predatory animals. Four hundred townspeople, armed with all kinds of weapons, formed a large circle for the "Great Hunt" and forced deer, bears, foxes and other animals to the center, killing them along the way. Most of the animals were slaughtered for food and clothing. The rest, along with the butchered carcasses, were left on the snowy, frozen ground. Months later, presumably on March 15, thousands of buzzards flew in to feast on the thawing remains.

Mike had driven through Hinckley many times on the way to Brunswick, where he'd given a few hitting lessons at an indoor facility. From what he knew, Hinckley consisted of a dozen or so small businesses around the intersection of Ridge Road and Route 303, including a gas station whose prices were always at least ten cents higher than the highest prices in northeast Ohio. There were many farms (corn and soy beans, of course), a couple of public golf courses and a shooting club.

Sam and Dorothy Burkett had moved into the Ridge Road home of Dorothy's parents after her father died in 1970. They cared for Dorothy's mother there until she passed away in 1982.

Mike spotted Dorothy's address on a mailbox and turned into the driveway. The red-brick house looked too small for its three-acre lot. It was sixteen hundred square feet with two bedrooms, one and a half bathrooms and a den. Mike used the door-knocker. Gail opened it and whispered, "She's got a lot to say. Take off your shoes."

They walked a few steps into the kitchen, where Dorothy Burkett sat with her back to sliding door that led to a deck. Gail and Mike sat on the opposite side of the oak table.

"Coffee?" asked Dorothy.

"Yes. Thanks," said Mike.

"Serve yourself. Cups on the shelf, milk in the fridge, sugar on the island."

Mike grabbed a cup with the words, *Great Coffee* on it and poured until it was full.

"No milk and sugar?" asked Dorothy, whose shoulder-length silver hair was remarkably thick. Her skin was well-preserved. Mike thought she looked like Jane Mansfield might have—if she'd lived through that car accident.

"No, thanks," said Mike. "So, catch me up on what you girls have been talking about," he said to Gail.

Dorothy didn't let her speak. "I told her I wasn't satisfied with the coroner's finding that Samuel had died of a heart attack. He was diabetic, but it was under control. He had no heart problems and no family history of them. So, he dies of a heart attack?"

"How did it happen? Where was he?" Mike asked.

"In his office on Main Street in Pluto," said Dorothy. "His secretary went out to get lunch at noon. She brought him half a tuna melt and a cup of clam chowder from the diner. He ate while he did some paperwork on a divorce case. Half an hour later, the secretary found him dead."

"The secretary. Was she working for him long?" asked Gail.

"No. Six weeks," said Dorothy. "His old girl, Margie Vincent, had retired that winter. She'd been with him twenty years."

"The autopsy. Nothing suspicious?" Mike asked.

"That's what they said. Natural causes," said Dorothy, raising her eyebrows.

"Have you ever heard of Succinylcholine?" Mike asked.

"I don't think I can even pronounce it," said Dorothy. "What is it?"

"It's a strong muscle relaxer taken by injection," Mike explained. "In hospitals, they call it 'Sux.' It's used a lot in emergency medicine as a means of getting patients who need breathing tubes inserted to relax.

"The problem is that it's so strong and fast-acting that within twenty minutes, it's impossible for a patient to breathe *without* artificial ventilation. It wears off quickly, usually in five to ten minutes, but if injected outside the hospital setting, a person would surely die from a medium dose."

"And it looks like a heart attack?" asked Dorothy.

"Exactly. And it's virtually untraceable at autopsy," said Mike.

"He *was* murdered? Who then? Why?" Dorothy asked. "He had no enemies. None."

"The same person or people who murdered Cheryl Fenner," said Gail. "We don't have it solved yet, but between Mike and me and the Wayne County Sheriff's Department, it's going to happen."

Dorothy handed her cup to Mike. "Half-way with just a little milk, thanks."

Mike filled her order and poured himself another cup. "Did Sam ever discuss his clients with you?" he asked, setting her cup on the table.

"Once in a while, he did. Yes," said Dorothy.

"I ask because Jonas Benson wrote a very interesting letter to his granddaughter about a week before he died," Mike said. "In that letter, Benson revealed that he'd been keeping a secret--a secret that would change a lot of lives for the worse if discovered."

"And you want to know if Samuel discussed Mr. Benson's secret with me?" asked Dorothy.

"That's what I want to know," said Mike. "Because we're thinking that somebody was very determined to keep that secret a secret."

"Determined enough to kill my husband?" asked Dorothy.

"And Cheryl Fenner," said Gail.

"The answer is "no." This is the first I've heard of it," she said.

"Can you tell us anything your husband might have mentioned about Jonas Benson that seemed odd or unusual?" asked Gail.

"I'm trying to think," said Dorothy, sipping her coffee. "Samuel handled a lot of his business over the years. I do remember Samuel being apprehensive about taking Jonas on as a client, but that was a long time ago—back in the seventies."

"Why was he apprehensive?" Gail asked.

"Because Benson was a devious man," Dorothy said. "Samuel mentioned that he'd been investigated by the Drug Enforcement Agency for failing to maintain proper records and such. No arrests, mind you, but some shady practices."

"Anything else," Mike asked.

"He was a philanderer. I know that," she said.

Gail leaned forward. "How do you know?" she asked.

"Besides the fact that he hit on *me* once?" she smiled.

"We'd like to hear all about that," Gail smiled back. "And any other information you have about his philandering."

"We were all at a charity dinner—Samuel and I; Benson and his wife, Lucille. It was 1974. Late January. I remember because Nixon had just signed the official cease fire for the Viet Nam war and everybody was talking about it. Jonas asked me to dance. They were playing that Sinatra song, *The Way You Look Tonight*. He pulled me a little too close, you know, and he said some very, very inappropriate things."

"Is that as far as it went?" Gail asked.

"You bet it was. Yes. He got the message right then and there. But here's the strange part. I called Lucille the next day and told her about it. She said, and I quote, 'Maybe he's over his girlfriend.'"

"His girlfriend? Do you know who she was?" Gail asked.

"Yes. Her name is Leticia Cragmere."

Gail and Mike looked at each other and stepped on each other's astonished reaction.

"Leticia Cragmere?" they asked together.

"Yes. She was a married woman—married to a man named Robert Cragmere, who inherited millions when his first wife drowned a few years earlier."

"Yes, in 1971," said Gail.

"Oh, we're very familiar with Leticia Cragmere," said Mike. "She still teaches English at Pluto High."

"Really? Didn't she get that money when her husband died? When was it? In the mid-nineties, I think."

"Yeah. It was 1996," said Mike. "She got the money, but never stopped working. He died of a heart attack, by the way, at age sixty."

Gail's mind was racing so fast she could barely keep up with it. Cragmere's emotional connection to Benson was an astonishing development. Obviously, Benson was a perfect source for a lethal dose of Succinylcholine. Did Cragmere kill Wanda with it? Did she take out Robert the same way years later? What about Cheryl? What about Sam Burkett? He must have known Jonas Benson's secret. Did Sam and Cheryl die more than forty years later because of it? What about Bree? Who's trying to kill *her*? And why?

"We can't thank you enough for your help, Dorothy," she finally said, standing to leave. "We'll keep you informed."

"Please do," Dorothy said. "Please do."

Mike thanked Dorothy and followed Gail out the front door. "Should we give Kimball a call?"

"He's a detective. He'll figure it out," she said.

Mike sat in his kitchen sipping beer from a can, thankful for a moment of relaxation. Valentine lay at his feet as always. Mike opened Peggy's laptop. He found where he'd left off. Then, he scrolled to see how much remained.

"Not much left," he mumbled aloud. "She must have been pretty sick by this point."

I'll be quitting my job in a week. This attempt at a novel now morphs into a journal documenting the final thoughts of a disease victim. I guess some people leave the world without confronting the issues or the people who plagued them in life. I understand their thinking. What's the point? Right? I, however, feel compelled to leave with a clear conscience. Therefore, I hereby declare that I detest working in retail. It's true, there are small, daily joys that sometimes make it bearable. I have helped my share of old wives find the perfect gifts for their old husbands and vice versa. I have reunited lost children with their mothers. I have aided countless shoplifters in their quest to hit bottom so they could begin to rehabilitate themselves. I have made a few good friends.

Still, the overall experience is hopeless and degrading. All of us work for companies whose business model is to cut staffing and customer service to improve a bottom line they've reduced themselves by seducing their customers to shop online. All of us work for companies that conspire to make it impossible for employees to earn a decent living no matter how many hours they work, no matter how exemplary their performance might be.

The cost of insurance benefits is so high that despite being paid nearly twice what our new associates are paid, my paychecks amount to just $400 a week. No *one is living the American dream working at J. C. Penney unless they're the district manager or they're married to someone who is actually paid well for the job they do.*

Mike looked at Valentine. "That was my fault, pal," he said. "If I hadn't lost my job, she could have quit that hell hole." He kept reading.

I did meet Amber David because of my awful job. For that, and for the opportunity to help her and her son, I am eternally grateful. My emotional involvement with their plight may have been ill-advised, but it may have inadvertently solved a very cold murder case. Who knows? I sincerely hope the police can use the information I gave them to solve it. I'm glad I changed my mind and reported what I heard at the home of Rick Fenner on November 8. I hope they took me seriously.

"What? What!" Mike screamed. "She told the cops?" He closed the laptop and grabbed his cell phone. Gail answered on the first ring.

"Peggy told the cops about what she overheard at Fenner's house!"

"What? How do you know?" Gail asked.

"I just read it on her laptop," Mike said. "She wrote about how grateful she was to have met Amber and then she said she hoped the police could use the information she gave them to solve a very cold murder case."

"Kimball! That son of a bitch!" Gail shouted. "He's been sitting on this for months. Why?"

"And why didn't Peggy tell me she called the cops?" Mike asked.

"Well, she'd have been forced to give up the whole story then—and for some reason, she didn't want to," said Gail.

"I guess," said Mike. "I wonder if Kimball knows who was inside Fenner's house that night," said Mike.

"That's what I was wondering," said Gail. She made a mental note to call Duncan Chase to find out if Kimball had shared Peggy's information.

"Have him check the sheriff's department for reports involving Fenner's address around November 8, 2013, too," said Mike. "I'd do it myself, but we've got a big game, as you know."

"Oh, yeah. I'm on it. How about a victory dinner tomorrow night?" Gail asked.

"Sounds good," said Mike. "Let's hope it's a victory dinner. I'll call you when I get home."

"Okay. Good luck," said Gail.

I think she asked me out on a date, Mike thought.

Chapter 44

Tuesday, April 22

THE BUS RIDE from Pluto to Wyoming was twelve miles southwest on a two-lane road through corn, corn and more corn. It was the warmest day of the year, heading toward seventy-five degrees. Mike pulled down the window and risked a deep breath as the bus passed a dairy farm. *That was a mistake*, he thought, as the disgusting smell almost made him choke. He smiled anyway.

The Wyoming Rustlers played home games at the community park a half-mile from the high school. As the bus pulled into the parking lot, Mike noticed about a dozen SUV's and pickups in a straight line with their tailgates open. Nearby, adults and children played corn hole and threw footballs back and forth. Smoke rose from portable gas grills. The aroma of hamburgers, hot dogs, brats and chicken wings overcame the stench of cow manure, at least in this corner of the township.

"They're having a tailgate party at a Tuesday afternoon softball game," Mike mumbled to himself. "They really take this shit seriously."

By the time the Rustlers ran out for infield practice, no empty seats remained in the concrete grandstand behind home plate or the bleachers along the baselines. Visiting fans were not offered the seating section behind home plate nearest the visitors' dugout as is customary. A few Invaders' fans, dressed in royal blue, were sprinkled in the grandstand, outnumbered ten to one by fans wearing Rustlers brown. The rest of the Pluto faithful found standing room along the baselines or beyond the outfield fence.

Morgan stood between Jen and Callie as they warmed up behind the first base dugout.

"I told you guys this would be a circus," said Morgan.

"I can't believe the people!" said Callie.

"You should see it when they play on a Saturday! They have a farmers' market all day before the game. Five or six hundred people who didn't even know a game was scheduled wind up staying to watch," said Morgan.

"I think it's great," said Jen as she worked on her screw ball. "I love big crowds."

"I threw a no hitter here my senior year," said Morgan. "You never heard so many people make so little noise!"

The umpires finished checking the bats, helmets and catcher's equipment in both dugouts and called the coaches to the home plate area for a pre-game meeting. The plate umpire was sixty-something, short, bald and overweight. He introduced himself as Art Pritchard. The base umpire was thirty-something, tall, bushy-haired and thin. His name was Phil Buckley.

"Coach, good to see you," said Mike extending his hand to the legendary Jake Moffitt.

"Great day for softball," said Moffitt, giving Mike's hand a firm, but brief shake.

As Pritchard explained the ground rules, Mike stared at his counterpart. Moffitt was closing in on seventy. His face was thin and wrinkled from too much sun and not enough sunscreen. There were several red blotches on his face, including one just below the bridge of his nose from a recent skin cancer operation. Moffitt stood six feet, two inches and weighed about two hundred pounds. His stomach was flat and his arms bulged from lifting weights. He had been a star linebacker at Toledo in the sixties.

After graduating, he landed a teaching job in his home town of Wyoming. He was added to the football coaching staff to work with the linebackers and defensive backs. Eventually, he became the head coach, but after three unsuccessful seasons, he was asked to step down. He was appointed defensive coordinator for the following season, a job he held until 2000.

He agreed to take over the softball program in 1975, when the existing coach went on maternity leave and never returned. Moffitt's first team won the conference championship. Three years later, his Rustlers won the first of their three state titles.

Moffitt's formula was to involve the entire community. He created the Wyoming Girls Fast Pitch Association (WGFPA). He held tryouts for girls from seven to seventeen and appointed coaches to teach his philosophy of the game all the way up the ranks. By the time the girls reached high school, they were ready to play at a high level. His own two daughters had played in the late nineties. Both earned college scholarships and went on to become college coaches.

"Any questions?" Pritchard asked.

Mike awoke from his daydream. "No. Good luck," he said to Moffitt without offering another hand shake.

"You, too," said the legend.

Courtney Whitmer was the definition of "intimidating." She stood six feet tall and was built like a nose tackle. She wore multi-colored reflecting lenses in her white, Oakley sunglasses. She grunted like Monica Seles serving a tennis ball when she delivered her pitches, which consistently reached 63 M.P.H.

Bree stepped into the lefty batter's box, as Mike flashed a few decoy signs. Whitmer turned loose a rise ball with a monster grunt. Bree ducked as it popped into the catcher's mitt.

"Ball!" Prichard yelled.

The next pitch was a straight one down the middle. Bree was ready for it, knowing Whitmer wouldn't want to get behind 2-0. She swung and hit it solid, like a ball off the tee in her barn. It sailed over the shortstop's head and rolled between the fielders all the way to the fence. Bree stopped at second with a double, remembering a fundamental rule: Don't make the first out of an inning at third base.

The scattered Pluto fans cheered as Bree raised a fist and shouted, "Let's go!" Lauren was next. She checked Mike's signs and dug in on the left side. The Rustlers' infield prepared for a bunt. As the pitcher went into her windup, Lauren left the bat on her shoulder and stood casually in the box. The pitch sailed past her, neck high.

"Ball!" yelled the umpire.

Lauren smiled. Mike had told her that Whitmer loved throwing the rise ball on the first pitch, and that she rarely threw it for a strike. She was taking all the way. Now Lauren could count on a good pitch to hit, just as Bree had done. She looked at Mike for a sign. He touched the bill of his cap, then his left arm, then his left leg. None of that meant anything. Then, he walked toward home plate clapping his hands and yelling, "Let's go!" That was the steal sign.

As Whitmer let her next pitch go, Bree took off for third. Lauren swung and missed. The Rustlers' catcher made a perfect throw to third, but the shortstop was late getting there and was off balance. The ball hit the heel of her glove and fell to the ground.

"Safe!" hollered Buckley.

Mike reminded Bree that there were no outs. He flashed meaningless signs to Lauren. Whitmer threw the 1-1 pitch in the dirt. It skipped past the catcher and bounced off the backstop, which was less than ten feet behind the umpire. Bree stayed at third.

Whitmer's 2-1 pitch was a fast ball. Lauren swung and hit a line drive over the first baseman's head. Bree jogged home, scoring the game's first run. Lauren watched the ball as she ran to first and saw the right fielder slip as she tried to field it. She didn't hesitate around first. As she sprinted to second, Lauren looked at Mike in the third base coaching box. He was waving his right arm like a windmill.

"Come on! Come on!" he yelled.

Lauren hit the bag and turned for third. Seconds later, she dove in head first well ahead of the outfielder's throw. Mike had noticed during the Rustlers' infield practice that the right fielder had a very weak arm. Right after wondering why the coach would reveal that weakness by letting her take infield, Mike planned to exploit it as much as possible.

Mike called time out and walked toward home plate for a conference with Darcy.

"You know the drill," said Mike. "We're just putting the squeeze into their heads. She'll go with the rise again first pitch to find out if you're bunting, so you might as well bluff a bunt to get the corners charging. Then you can jump on the 1-0 pitch."

"Sounds like a plan," said Darcy.

Whitmer was kicking dirt behind the rubber and talking to herself. Giving up a run on two hits after only four pitches was a nightmare. Mike smiled as the star pitcher slammed the ball into her glove, then pulled it out and slammed it again. *That's always a good sign*, he thought.

The third baseman was already positioned nearly halfway between third and home as Darcy stepped into the right side of the batter's box. Whitmer wound up and fired a high rise ball. Darcy pivoted on the balls of her feet and squared her shoulders to the pitcher, holding an angled bat slightly extended. She pulled back the bat as the pitch sailed eye-high into the catcher's mitt.

"Ball!" shouted the umpire.

Darcy knew the next one would be fat. She dug in, ready for a fast ball down the middle. She could see the corner infielders creeping forward. Whitmer slammed the ball into her glove. She wound up and turned it loose with a loud grunt. Darcy's eyes widened as she watched it coming straight down the middle. She swung hard enough to send the ball over the fence, across the parking lot and into the duck pond--but the ball wasn't there. Whitmer had thrown a changeup. Instead of 63 M.P.H., the ball had traveled just 53 M.P.H. It reached the catcher's mitt half a second *after* Darcy finished her swing.

Gutsy pitch, Mike thought. Darcy stared at him, waiting for signs. Mike touched a few body parts, then clapped his hands and hollered, "Get a good pitch!"

Whitmer wound up and threw another changeup, this one even slower than the last. Darcy froze.

"Strike two," hollered Pritchard.

Darcy didn't look for a sign this time—not with two strikes. She dug in, determined to drive in the run. Whitmer had other ideas. She wound up and threw a high rise ball, just out of the strike zone. Darcy let it go.

"Strike three!" Pritchard yelled, as the Wyoming fans cheered wildly.

Darcy walked to the dugout, disgusted by the bad call. Allie was next. Whitmer started her off with a changeup that Pritchard called a "strike." Allie fouled off a curve ball and then struck out swinging on another changeup. As Rachel stepped into the box, Mike wasn't feeling confident about getting Lauren home.

Whitmer slammed the ball into her glove and started her windup. Rachel stood relaxed with the bat still resting on her shoulder. As Whitmer let the ball go, Rachel kept the bat on her shoulder. She didn't appear to be interested in the first pitch. Then, with the changeup floating halfway home, Rachel raised her bat, drew it back and swung. The sound was unmistakable—the barrel of the bat striking the center of the ball with the kind of speed that a clean-up hitter is supposed to have. There was never a doubt. The left fielder didn't even turn to watch it. The ball landed in the parking lot, forty feet clear of the fence. It hit the roof of a pickup and bounced off two other vehicles, setting off all three alarms.

Rachel rounded the bases with her fist in the air as the Pluto fans and the car alarms screamed. Mike gave her a fist bump as she rounded third. There was no silent treatment after this homer. The whole team, including Lana, came out to greet her at home plate.

Andrea flew out to center field to end the top of the first. Now it was Jen's turn in the circle. Mike was anxious to see how the freshman would handle the electric atmosphere and the Wyoming lineup. He was anxious, but he wasn't worried. Morgan had come back to the dugout after infield practice and told him that Jen's stuff looked unhittable.

She threw three consecutive drop balls to the leadoff hitter and struck her out swinging. She threw three consecutive changeups to the second hitter and got her out on a grounder to shortstop. She started the third hitter with a rise ball. She popped it up to Bree at second base.

By the bottom of the seventh inning, the Invaders had built their lead to 6-0, thanks to solo homers from Halle and Maria, and an RBI triple by Darcy. Jen had allowed just two hits. The Wyoming fans were restless. This was not the performance they'd expected from either team.

Jen was facing the bottom of the order. Second baseman Becky Holmstrom, batting seventh, had struck out twice on a total of seven pitches. She stood close to the plate in a crouch. Jen wound up and fired a screw ball that barely clipped Holmstrom's jersey.

"Dead ball!" yelled the umpire. "Take your base."

Holmstrom ran to first, delighted that she had avoided a third strike out. The next batter was Lee Ann Gilliam, the weak-armed right fielder. She had struck out and popped up in her two trips to the plate. Jen's first pitch was drop ball that she thought was a strike at the knees.

"Ball!" yelled Pritchard

Her next pitch was a fast ball that she thought was a strike at the letters.

"Ball!" yelled Pritchard.

Jen took the throw from Allie and walked behind the rubber. Now *she* was talking to herself.

Mike looked at Morgan. "What is it about softball pitchers talking to themselves?"

"What? You never talk to yourself?" Morgan asked.

"I guess," said Mike. "Think she's done?"

"I think she's getting squeezed by an umpire who wants to help the home team but hasn't had much of a chance," she smiled.

"Make sure Callie's ready," said Mike.

Jen's third pitch to Gilliam was in the dirt. Allie blocked it. Holmstrom stayed at first, but jogged to second after the next pitch was called "ball four" by Pritchard.

Mike bounced out of the dugout. "Time!" he yelled to the umpire, then trotted to the circle.

"What are you doing here?" Jen asked, pouting.

"I don't know. I just thought I'd see how you're doing," said Mike with a smile.

"I'm fine," said Jen.

"Well, you've pitched a really good game, but I'm concerned because you started the inning with a six nothing lead facing the bottom or the order, and the first two have reached without a hit," said Mike.

"I'm fine," said Jen.

"I'm going to let Callie finish up," said Mike. "She needs the work. He opened his hand and Jen gave him the ball and ran to the dugout. The Pluto fans clapped and whistled to let her know she'd done a great job.

Callie ran to the circle, took the ball from Mike and started warming up.

"Two on, nobody out. Number nine coming up," Mike said. "Just work on the hitter. Get this first out. Then we'll trade runs for outs if we have to. We're up six nothing."

Callie understood. She faced Emily Sommers first. Jen had struck her out twice. Callie threw a fast ball down the middle for a called strike. She threw another fast ball and Sommers swung and hit a soft, spinning liner off the end of the bat. The ball landed just out of Callie's reach and just in front of Andrea. It touched Andrea's glove and spun toward Bree, who was charging from her position between first and second. Everybody was safe.

The Rustler's crowd came alive, cheering and whistling. Some were hollering negative things at Callie. "Throw some gas on the fire, thirteen!" One man shouted, referring to Callie's jersey number.

"Tell Jen to stay ready, just in case," Mike said to Morgan. "Don't let her tighten up."

Wyoming's lead-off hitter hadn't reached base against Jen, but Leigh Meadows had dangerous speed and sneaky power. She was a senior committed to Bowling Green, where her mother had run track. Moffitt walked toward her and clapped his hands. "Our inning," he said. "Pick one out."

Callie threw a drop on the first pitch and Meadows beat it into the ground. It hopped high over Callie's head. Darcy charged it, fielded it and threw to first on the run, but Meadows was too fast. It was 6-1 and the bases were still loaded with nobody out.

"Any thoughts?" Mike said to Morgan.

"Yeah. Let *me* pitch," she smiled.

"Come on, Callie!" Mike yelled. "Get an out!"

Sara Briscoe was next. She had one of the two hits off Jen, a liner over third base for a lead-off double in the fourth inning. She stepped into the lefty batter's box and took Callie's first pitch low for a ball. She worked the count to 3-1 before taking a strike on the outside corner.

"One more, Callie!" Bree hollered.

"You got this, Callie!" yelled Andrea.

The 3-2 pitch hit the same spot as the 3-1 pitch, but Pritchard yelled, "Ball four!" Callie was visibly upset by the call. She kicked the dirt in front of the rubber as another runner crossed the plate. Now it was 6-2 with the bases loaded, nobody out and the Rustlers' number three, four and five hitters coming up.

Mike paced. Callie had faced two batters who'd hit the ball a total of forty feet, and a third who was handed a gift walk by a hometown umpire. *I should have left Jen out there*, he thought. *What the heck was I thinking? She said she was fine.*

Briana DeVries was next. The Rustlers' best hitter had walked and singled off Jen. Now she had a chance to make it a close game. Callie threw a drop and DeVries swung and missed. Callie threw a rise and DeVries fouled it straight back. Callie's 0-2 pitch was a curve that missed the outside corner by a few inches. Her 1-2 pitch was a drop in the dirt. Allie blocked it to save a run. The 2-2 pitch was a rise that missed high.

Allie called for a changeup. Callie nodded. She wound up let it fly with the same arm speed as her previous pitches, only this ball floated home at least ten miles per hour slower. DeVries was fooled so badly that she couldn't manage a swing. Allie caught the ball and yelled, "Yeah!"

"Ball four!" shouted Pritchard.

"What?" Callie yelled.

"No way!" Allie screamed.

Mike jumped out of the dugout. "Come on! That was dead center!" he screamed.

Morgan grabbed the back of his shirt and pulled him back to the top step. "Easy," she said.

Now it was 6-3, bases loaded and nobody out. Maria Gonzalez, the Rustlers' cleanup hitter was next, representing the go-ahead run. If she hit her sixth homer of the young season, the Rustlers would be on top after trailing 6-0.

Morgan motioned to Allie that she wanted her to set up inside on Gonzalez. She called for a drop ball. Callie threw a good one, down and inside. The big hitter couldn't extend her arms. She fouled it on the ground toward her dugout. Allie called for the same pitch. Callie threw another good one. Gonzalez let it go.

"Ball!" shouted Pritchard.

"Nice pitch, Callie," Mike yelled. "This friggin' guy is starting to piss me off," Mike said to Morgan.

"She'll get out of it," said Morgan.

"Not if they keep taking pitches," said Mike. "He'll walk the whole team around."

Allie called for another drop inside. Gonzalez swung hard and hit a bullet on one hop to Rachel at third. It was a perfect home-to-first double play ball, but Rachel bobbled it. She picked it up just in time to step on third for an out, but another run scored to make it 6-4 with runners at first and second and one out.

Marti Wilson was next. She had struck out both times against Jen. "Jen struck her out twice," Morgan said.

"You think I should bring her back?" Mike asked.

"I would," said Morgan.

"Time!" Mike yelled.

He walked to the circle. "Good job," he said to Callie. "Jen struck this girl out twice. I'm going to let her go for three."

Callie ran to the dugout as the Pluto fans cheered her performance.

"Throw strikes," Mike said to Jen as she began warming up.

Jen said nothing. Mike walked off the field and spotted Russ Miller leaning on the fence down the right field line. He wondered what Russ was thinking. *He's probably wondering why I took Jen out in the first place*, Mike thought. *He's the one who said I'd have to guess at what 'I'm fine' really meant. It's his damn fault.*

Wilson stepped into the box on the right side. Jen wound up and blew a fast ball right by her.

"Strike one!" hollered Pritchard as Wilson swung and missed.

"Atta girl, Jen. Tough to call that one a ball!" Mike yelled.

"Easy now," Morgan said.

Jen wound up and fired another fast ball. This time Wilson did something no one expected. She shortened up on the bat and laid down a bunt to the left of the circle. It was too far out for Allie and too far left for Rachel. Jen took three quick steps and grabbed the slow roller with her right hand. She planted her right foot in the dirt and twisted her hips toward first, throwing the ball as hard as she could. Andrea anchored her left foot to the base and stretched as far as she could toward the ball. She caught it just before Wilson's right foot hit the base.

"Out!" yelled Buckley, as the Wyoming fans booed in protest.

"Yeah! Good call!" yelled Mike. Nice play, Jen!"

Now it was 6-4 with runners at second and third and two outs. The number six hitter, third baseman Gabby Duncan was next in the order. Mike turned to Morgan.

"Holmstrom's on deck. Jen struck her out twice before she hit her on the shirt last time up. If we walk Duncan, we've got a force at every base. What do *you* think?" he asked.

"Works for me," Morgan said.

Mike yelled to Allie, "Put her on!"

Allie held her right arm straight out and caught Jen's first pitch two feet off the plate. She did the same for the second pitch as Duncan stood with her bat on her shoulder. Jen aimed the third pitch for the same place, but she held the ball a bit too long and the pitch sailed over Allie's head. Briscoe broke from third and slid home with the fifth run. DeVries ran to third. She was now the tying run, just sixty feet away.

"Might as well try to strike her out now," said Mike.

"I like her chances better against Holmstrom," Morgan said.

"All right. Yeah. Let's finish the walk," he said.

"Don't forget the play," said Morgan.

"Scooby!" Mike hollered. "Scooby!" he repeated.

"Scooby!" Bree yelled.

"Scooby!" Jen yelled, as she wound up and threw a fast ball outside.

"Ball four!" yelled Pritchard.

Duncan tossed the bat toward the third base dugout and sprinted to first base. Allie threw the ball back to Jen, who turned around in time to see Duncan round the bag at full speed. Jen didn't hesitate. She fired a strike to Bree, who was moving into the baseline between first and second. At the same time, DeVries bolted from third, heading home with the potential tying run.

Duncan saw Bree catch the ball and slammed on the brakes, sliding to a stop flat on her back about ten feet from the Invaders' second baseman. Bree looked up and saw DeVries just a few strides from the plate. Bree took one more step and dove head-long at the fallen base runner. Her outstretched glove slammed into Duncan's helmet, knocking it off her head just before DeVries slid across the plate.

"She's out!" yelled Buckley.

"Run scores!" screamed the legendary Jake Moffitt.

"No run! Game over!" yelled Pritchard.

"Yes!" Mike hollered, running to the foul line to give high fives to Jen, Bree and the rest of the team.

Moffitt argued the call for about three minutes as the Wyoming fans booed and called Pritchard names like "blind man" and "Mr. Magoo." The girls lined up to shake hands. Mike and Morgan went with them.

Mike patted the arguing Moffitt on the shoulder as he walked by. "Nice game, coach," he said.

Moffitt ignored him and kept pointing at the ground. "You blew it, Art. Plain and simple!" he yelled.

"It wasn't even close," Mike said to Morgan as they walked back to the first base dugout.

"It was pretty close," Morgan said. "Let's get out of here before Moffitt makes him change it."

Mike laughed. "He's a legend and a dick."

Chapter 45

MIKE HONKED HIS horn as he pulled into Gail's driveway. Then he thought, *what a jerk! This is a date! Get out and go to the door!* It was too late. She was ready, watching from the front window. He jumped out of the car just as Gail stepped outside.

"Sorry about honking," said Mike. "That was dumb."

Gail laughed. "It's fine. Hey! I heard you won the big game!"

"Yeah. We made it too close. Blew a six nothing lead in the last inning and held on six to five," said Mike, as he pulled open the passenger door.

"The story's already online," said Gail. "It said you took out your starting pitcher in the last inning and it backfired."

"Oh, come on! Really?" said Mike. "That's not fair!"

"Well, you need a thick skin to coach in the big time, my dear." She gave him a peck on the cheek before ducking into the Buick.

Mike closed her door and stood still for a few seconds—just long enough to realize that he hadn't felt the same exhilaration since his first kiss with Donna Parker. Only this time it was guilt-free.

"I spoke with Duncan Chase this morning," Gail said.

"And?"

"Nothing from Kimball about the thing at Fenner's house last November. Then, he called the sheriff's department and had the records checked."

"And?"

"No report," said Gail.

"Wow. What does *that* mean?" Mike asked.

"Well, assuming Peggy made that call, it means the person who took it never filed a report, or that somebody—possibly Kimball—deleted it from the system."

"And there's no way to learn the truth," said Mike.

"Not until this whole thing unravels," said Gail. "If Kimball's dirty, he's dangerous—and we don't want him thinking we're onto him."

"This is so nuts," said Mike. "Italian?"

"Perfect," said Gail.

They chose a place in the Canton suburbs called *Paulino's*. It was located on the south end of a strip mall that included a Giant Eagle grocery store; a Sprint phone center; a Chinese buffet; a PNC bank branch and a Radio Shack. The front window had a dark tint on both sides. It was impossible to look through it and recognize anyone.

There were five booths on the right, eight tables on the left. Swinging doors at the back of the room led to the kitchen. Mike and Gail were shown to the second table from the front. A candle was already burning. They decided on a mid-priced bottle of Merlot.

"So how do we run down old man Benson's clues?" Gail asked.

"Sure you want to?" Mike asked.

"We could wait for Kimball to do it," said Gail. "But people might die."

"Good point. Very good point," said Mike. "I thought you'd feel that way. I snapped photos of everything in the box. Jerry's on the case already. He's trying to find the cabin."

The wine arrived. The waiter opened the bottle and filled Mike's glass halfway. Mike held up the glass and stared at it for a few seconds, then sipped the Merlot and declared it acceptable. The waiter filled their glasses and walked away.

"To the sneakiest man I know," Gail said, raising her glass.

Mike touched her glass with his. "Are you talking to me?"

She took a drink. "And the cutest."

"I like that better," said Mike.

They ate slowly and without mentioning the Fenner case. Mike wanted to hear her story from the beginning. She described herself as a curious child, one who used reading as an escape. She had loved the Nancy Drew mysteries and classic novels with strong female characters, such as Jane Eyre. She read biographies of famous women by the dozen. She enjoyed old movies starring Bette Davis, Katherine Hepburn, Lauren Bacall and Debbie Reynolds. Her favorite singers were Patsy Cline, Judy Collins and Celine Dion. Her favorite color? Red.

When she wasn't reading or watching movies, she was riding the horse she nick-named Pistol—not because he was high-spirited, but because her father's favorite basketball player was Pistol Pete Maravich. Pistol was a quarter horse who'd run a handful of losing races at county fairs in Ohio and West Virginia under the name of "Otis The Great."

His five 330-yard efforts resulted in finishes of 8th, 7th, 8th, 6th and 7th, beaten a total of 33 lengths. When a quarter horse is losing $2,000 claiming races by an average of six lengths, he needs to consider life as a pet.

Gail's father had been a partner in an Akron law firm. One of his clients owned a ranch about fifteen miles from Wooster. When Walter West mentioned that his fifteen-year-old daughter wanted a horse for her birthday, the rancher suggested a trade for his services. West figured he paid about eight hundred dollars for "Otis the Great," who turned out to be quite proficient at negotiating shorter distances like those in rodeo barrel racing. Gail won some ribbons while in high school and later at regional competitions. She actually considered a career on the professional rodeo circuit, but talked herself out of it.

"The risk wasn't worth the reward," she said. "High expenses, low prize money and ridiculous insurance rates. I realized you either have to be independently wealthy or have a desire to be destitute. Neither one fit me."

Mike laughed. "So, you gave it up just like that?"

"Cold turkey at eighteen. Went to Michigan. Here I am."

They had reached the bottom third of the wine bottle. Mike split the rest between them. Gail had started a couple of times to mention the tragic loss of her parents, but the words never reached her lips. Mike's questions were coming too fast.

"You said you came close to getting married?"

"At law school. We were engaged. He met somebody else, broke it off with me and married her instead. It all happened within about sixty days."

"That's very sad," said Mike, taking a drink. "I'm sorry."

"Don't be. They divorced after three years," said Gail. "He remarried and divorced again before age thirty. I have no idea what happened to him after that—and I don't really care. It hurt then. It doesn't hurt now. I probably dodged a bullet."

"It's been a long time since then," said Mike. "There haven't been any other bullets?"

"Sadly, no," she said, gulping the last of her wine. "We're opposites, you know. Relationship history-wise."

"I guess that's true. I married my high school sweetheart and made it all the way to 'death us do part," Mike said, draining his glass.

"What's wrong with that?" asked Gail.

"Nothing," he said. "And everything. I know what I had. I'll never know what I missed."

Gail threw her head back and laughed a little louder than seemed appropriate for the setting.

"What's so funny?" Mike asked.

"What you said. I was thinking about how pathetic my life has been. What I *had* was emptiness. What I *missed* was probably worse. I haven't even had an opportunity to regret something. Now *that's* funny!"

Mike reached across the table and squeezed her hand. "I am formally offering you an opportunity to regret something."

Gail squeezed back. "I accept."

Chapter 46

Wednesday, April 23

BREE WOKE FROM a sound sleep and fumbled for her phone. It was 6:30—too early to be a friend.

"Hello?"

"How are you feeling?" The voice asked. "I heard you had an accident."

"What do you want?!" Bree screamed.

"I know who killed your mother," said the voice.

"Then tell me!"

"It was me," said the voice.

"Who are you? Where are you?" Bree shouted.

The call disconnected. "Damn! Damn!" she yelled, punching her pillow.

Gail had been awake half an hour, alternately staring at the ceiling and at her handsome guest. She grabbed her phone from the night stand after one ring and saw Bree's name and number on the display.

"Bree. Hi. What can I do for you?"

"That woman just called again."

"What did she say?" Gail asked. She gave Mike a nudge and pointed to her phone. "It's Bree," she whispered.

"She said, 'I know who killed your mom.' When I asked, 'Who?' she said *she* did. Then she hung up."

"She said *she* did?"

"Yes."

"Was it the same 702 number?" Gail asked.

"Yes," Bree said.

"What about the voice? Same voice?" asked Gail.

"I don't know. It was quick. It wasn't a great connection. I don't know."

"Okay. Let's keep it between us for now."

Gail set her phone on the night table and turned to see a man in her bed for the first time in years.

"Good morning," she said, placing a soft kiss on his cheek.

"Good morning to you," said Mike.

"Maybe we should talk about this," said Gail.

"What?" asked Mike.

"This," she said pointing at him and then at herself.

"Oh! This!" he said, pointing at her and then at himself. "Maybe we shouldn't."

The smell of coffee and bacon led Bree to the kitchen. Morgan sat reading the Akron Beacon Journal sports section.

"You got your name in the paper," she said as Bree sat across from her.

"Me? What's it say?"

Morgan held up the paper. "It says, 'Speedy lead-off hitter Bree Fenner doubled and stole third before Wyoming hurler Courtney Whitmer could settle into the circle. Fenner scored on center fielder Lauren Phillips' single. Phillips ran all the way to third when the Rustlers' right fielder slipped while trying to field the ball.'"

"Is that all?" Bree asked.

"No. There's more," said Morgan.

"Read, sister! Read!" Bree encouraged.

"Okay, it's talking about the seventh inning. It says 'A wild pitch brought home the fifth run and sent the potential tying run to third base. Then, the Invaders completed the intentional walk to Gabby Duncan, but Duncan didn't stop at first base. She sprinted around the bag and headed for second, hoping either to steal the base or draw a throw that might score the tying run from third.

"'The plan backfired when freshman pitcher Jen Miller threw the ball to Fenner, who had run into the baseline between first and second. Duncan fell trying to get back to first, and Fenner dove and tagged her on the head a fraction of a second before Briana DeVries slid home.

"Wow! There's even a quote from you, Bree!" said Morgan. "You say, 'We worked on that play in practice, just in case. It sure paid off.' Woo! Nice! Want some breakfast?"

"Sure. Scrambled eggs and bacon would be great," said Bree.

"Comin' up," said Morgan.

They ate and talked about softball. Bree didn't mention the phone call.

Chapter 47

Thursday, April 24

THE STRANGE SPRING heat wave in Las Vegas was as stubborn as an old woman playing nickel slots—ten consecutive days above 105 degrees. Amber waited for the bus outside Binion's. It was noon. The bus was late and she was exhausted. She'd been on her feet fourteen hours. She touched the top of her head. Her blonde hair felt like it was about to ignite. Finally, the bus arrived. She stepped on and swiped her pass as the driver, a morbidly obese black woman in her fifties, started barking directions and instructions for the dozen or so tourists bound for the strip.

Amber sat near the front and pressed the side of her face into the window. She closed her eyes as the breeze from the air conditioning enveloped her body. *Riding the city bus is one of the few bargains Vegas offers,* she thought. *It's a fifty-dollar cab ride from Binion's to Caesars, but you can make the trip on the RTC for two bucks.* In a land of deception, the bus was an island of honesty. It was exactly what it appeared to be—transportation for tourists and poor people.

Her bungalow looked like every other four-room dwelling on the treeless streets near Las Vegas Boulevard—like a Monopoly house, only dull yellow. The glorious feeling of kicking off her shoes after a long night of running cocktails gave it the feeling of "home." The rest of the time it was a one-star motel, complete with low-rent neighbors.

"How you doin' baby?" asked the skinny, forty-something, tattoo-covered refugee from the Aryan Nation wing at Lompoc who lived next door.

"Tired, Bobby," said Amber. "Long damn night."

"I'll keep the noise down over here," he said.

"Thanks," said Amber, as she unlocked her door. "Have a good one."

The tiny house was dark, quiet and very warm. The window unit air conditioner wasn't running. Amber turned it on. She sniffed the air and smelled something that wasn't her scent or Chelsea's. *Chelsea's working days at The Four Queens,* she thought. She sniffed again and tossed her purse on the kitchen chair. Suddenly, the scent grew stronger. She felt pressure on her right arm and some sort of material—a towel or a cloth—against her face. Everything went black.

Mike woke up in his own bed. He checked his phone for the time, 9:07 a. m. There was one missed call notification. It was Jerry's number. He called him.

"Mike. I think I found the cabin," said Jerry.

"That's great! How?"

"The old-fashioned way. Back in the day, Sundays were busy for drug stores. People would stop after church and get a paper and whatever else they might need. All the other stores were closed. In a little place like Pluto, traditions die hard. Benson's was busy yesterday.

"So, I just hung around and started conversations with some of the older customers. After an hour, I met a man named Spivey, who said he was a good friend of Jonas Benson years ago. We got to talking and I showed him the photo you sent to my phone. I asked if he had any idea where the cabin was."

"And?"

"Twin Lake, Michigan," said Jerry. "Spivey said Benson went up there every summer to fish for lake trout, perch and bass."

"I've been up there," said Mike. It's on the way to Ludington."

"Yeah. West side. Near the big lake. Six hours or so."

"We don't have a game until next week. You up for a trip?" Mike asked.

"What about Gail?"

"I think this is a guy thing," said Mike.

"You think there could be trouble up there?" asked Jerry.

"I think there could be competition. And I don't know if we're ahead or behind," said Mike.

"The cops?" asked Jerry.

"And others," said Mike.

"Let's go today," said Jerry.

"If we leave soon, we'll get through Ann Arbor before rush hour."

"I'll pick you up," said Jerry.

Kimball's voice wasn't the one Gail wanted to hear. It had been eighteen hours since she'd seen or heard from Mike. She missed him.

"Hello?"

"It's Kimball. I wanted to let you know we caught the person who threatened Rick Fenner."

"Oh, that's great! Who is it?" Gail asked.

"Somebody you know," said Kimball.

"Who?"

"His daughter," said Kimball.

"What? No! Bree? Come on," said Gail.

"She left a print on the paper and a piece of hair in the envelope. The lab just got around to it."

"Oh, Jesus. Did you arrest her?"

"Debating it," said Kimball. "It's serious, yet the time table says she did it a few days after finding out her dad was accused of killing her mom, and that he was *definitely* a liar and a cheat."

"Does Chase know?" Gail asked.

"Yeah. He's leaning toward a stern lecture."

"I think you should deliver it. You're intimidating," said Gail.

"Arrange it for me?" asked Kimball.

"Yes. I'll do that," said Gail. "I'll shoot for tomorrow."

"Sounds good," said Kimball.

"Any luck with the Benson box from the house?"

Kimball hesitated. "We're working on it," he said.

Gail took that to mean, *none of your damn business*. "I'll call you after I talk to Bree," she said.

Gail's phone rang again. This time it made her smile. "Hi there!" she said.

"Good morning!" said Mike. "I have some news. Jerry called. He found the cabin."

"Where?"

"Michigan."

"Specifically?"

"Twin Lake," said Mike. "It's a little town about twenty minutes north of Muskegon. Western Michigan. We're leaving soon."

"You and Jerry?" asked Gail.

"Yup. Driving. Six hours or so," said Mike.

"Do you need me?" asked Gail.

"Desperately," said Mike.

"Sweet man," said Gail. "I have some news, too. Kimball just called. He says Bree is the one who threatened Rick's life."

"You're kidding!"

"The lab matched a print and a hair," said Gail. "But they're not going to charge her. Kimball wants to yell at her, though. I'm arranging it."

"Have fun with that," said Mike.

"Please be careful up there," said Gail.

"We will," he promised.

"Oh. I've got a hearing on the docket tomorrow. Rick's getting out," said Gail.

Chapter 48

THE TRIP COVERED approximately three hundred fifty miles. The route from Cleveland included Toledo, Ann Arbor, Lansing, Grand Rapids and Muskegon. They left I-96 West for U.S. 31 North as they entered Muskegon. They took the M-20 cutoff as they left North Muskegon. Holton Road led them into the tiny, unincorporated resort town of Twin Lake. Jerry followed GPS directions down a dirt road to a cottage about forty yards from the shore of West Lake.

"This is it," said Jerry.

"Are you sure," Mike asked.

A green mini-van was parked near the cottage. Jerry put his palm on the hood. It was hot.

"Somebody's home," he said.

Mike knocked on the door. In a few seconds, a child opened it. She was four or five.

"My mommy's in the kitchen putting the groceries away," she said without being asked a question.

Mike smiled. "Could you tell her there's a Mr. Page at the door and he'd like to speak to her?"

"Okay," she said.

A few seconds later, a young woman wearing sunglasses and a baseball cap appeared. "Hi. May I help you?"

"I'm Mike Page and this is my colleague, Jerry Baxter. Ever hear of a man named Jonas Benson?"

"Benson? No. It doesn't sound familiar," said the woman.

"He's the man in this photo," said Mike, holding up his phone.

"Never met him," she said. "But I do remember that photo."

"You've seen it before? When?" Jerry asked.

"Years ago," said the woman. "Before my little girl was born, so it had to be two thousand six or seven. A man knocked on the door just like you did. He said this house had been a timeshare for the guy in the picture."

"We're investigators from Ohio, working for a defense attorney. Actually, the man is dead. We need to find the cabin in the photo."

The woman nodded. "I'll tell you the same thing I told the other guy: It looks like one of the cabins at the Blue Lake Fine Arts Camp, or maybe Camp Douglass, which was an old YMCA camp just down the road. It closed in the nineties, but it's still there."

"Where is it?" Mike asked.

"Just turn right when you get back to the road. You'll see the sign in a mile or so."

Like everything else in Twin Lake, Camp Douglass was carved from thick forest. April brought a light green contrast to the dark green pines. The oak, hickory, birch, maple, ash and other native trees were sprouting. The setting sun flashed through the branches and briefly blinded Jerry as he turned into the camp.

"Mess hall," said Mike, pointing at the long, one-story building on the far side of an unpaved parking area cleared for about a hundred vehicles. "I just Googled Camp Douglass. Founded in 1931. Non-profit YMCA camp based in Oak Park, Illinois. Closed in '96."

"Ah, yes," said Jerry. "Your standard summer dumpsite for suburban Chicago youngsters for sixty-five years."

"You're a cynical man," Mike laughed. "We're talking swimming, canoeing, archery, arts and crafts and more. Not to mention the opportunity to form new friendships that could last a lifetime. It was a child's paradise."

"You sound like a brochure," said Jerry.

"And so much better than sitting home all summer listening to their soon-to-be divorced parents piss and moan about their awful lives—and taking most of the blame," said Mike.

"And *I'm* the cynical one?" Jerry asked.

"Or watching their already-divorced parents pawing their new squeezes," Mike continued.

"Which is enough to make any kid want to run away to a camp in Twin Lake, Michigan," said Jerry. "Okay, good point. It was *indeed* a paradise."

They parked in front of the mess hall. Mike put the photo of Benson and the cabin on the screen of his phone.

"Let's go for a walk," he said. "We've got an hour of light left."

They started east toward the only cabin in sight. It was dark brown and slightly elevated with three wooden steps leading to a small porch.

"Probably some kind of administration building," said Mike.

Jerry pointed to a small sign on the porch railing just a few feet from Mike. *NURSE*.

Mike laughed. "Okay, well a nurse is an administrator. In any case, it's not the right cabin."

"It looks like the lake is down that path," said Jerry. "Do you know how I know that?"

Mike smiled as his friend pointed to another sign that read, *LAKE*. "You know how I know you're about to get your ass kicked?"

Jerry laughed. "Let's go that way," he said, pointing west.

They followed a path that the years had narrowed with weeds in some places and rendered nearly impassable with fallen tree limbs in others.

"There," said Mike, pointing to a small cabin covered in dull, chipped orange paint. A sign near the front door read, *ERIE*. Jerry turned the knob. It opened to a single room with four sets of steel bunk beds without mattresses, one in each corner. That was all, except cobwebs and some piles of glass shards from four broken windows, two on each side of the room.

"Campers' cabins," said Jerry.

Mike looked at the photo. "Right size, but wrong color. Don't you think?" he asked.

"Yup. We're looking for brown," said Jerry. "And look by his shoulder. Maybe that's a letter from the sign by the front door. I'd say an "S.""

Mike stared at the photo. Yeah, that could be the top of an "S," for sure. Let's go look."

Twenty-five yards down the path they spotted two more cabins. The first was red.

"Apache," said Mike. "Nope," he said, looking at the photo to make sure.

The second was green.

"Huron," said Jerry. "Not our tribe."

They walked twenty-five yards and spotted another pair. "Chippewa," said Mike. "Blue."

"Ah, now we're talkin'," said Jerry. "Iroquois!" He jogged to the brown cabin and stood at the front left corner facing Mike.

"I think we have a winner!" Mike announced, holding up the photo. That's the "s" all right."

Jerry turned the knob. The door was stuck. He turned it again and kicked the bottom. It swung open and banged against the wall.

"No bunks," said Mike.

"No nothin'," said Jerry.

Mike glanced around the room, his eyes scanning the walls for hiding places. Nothing. They walked outside and looked over every inch of the cabin. Still nothing.

"Let's look at the photo again," said Jerry.

Mike put it on his phone screen. There was no doubt they'd found the right cabin. The "s" over Benson's shoulder matched the "s" in Iroquois perfectly.

"Somebody beat us to it," said Mike. "That's the only thing I can think of."

"Well, they've had six years, theoretically," said Jerry.

"True. Let's get some sleep and come back out in the morning," said Mike.

"I'm for that," said his friend.

Chapter 49

Friday April 25

AMBER AWOKE WITH her face buried in a pillow without a case, on a twin bed without sheets. A green, wool army blanket lay on the floor—kicked off in the night. The room was ten by twelve. The walls were bare, covered with white primer paint. A gray metal nightstand with a reading lamp was the only piece of furniture. The floor was carpeted—dirty, reddish brown shag. There was a rusty sink and a filthy toilet in the corner to the right of a closed door. She stood up woozy.

"Where the hell *am* I?" she wondered aloud. "What happened?"

She staggered a few steps to the door. She turned the knob. Locked. She kicked the bottom. It didn't move.

"Hello?" she called. No response. She moved to the window. A black shade was drawn to a dusty ledge. She gave it a tug. The sun blinded her. *It must be morning. God. Where am I?*

The view was nothing familiar—an alley and the back of a one-story building, maybe a liquor store, maybe a fast food restaurant. She assumed she was still in Vegas. She felt the pockets of her jeans. No phone. No keys. No money. *Who did this? Why?*

Mike and Jerry checked out of their rooms at the Starlight Motel in Dalton Township at 8 a.m. They grabbed bananas, Danish and coffee in the lobby and drove back to Camp Douglass for another look at *Iroquois*.

As the mess hall came into view, Mike spotted a black SUV parked on the right side of the lot near the path they'd taken the evening before.

"Company," said Mike.

"Yeah. It's a rental," said Jerry as they rolled closer.

"How can you tell?" Mike asked.

"Plate frame says "Avis." There's a barcode on the front passenger window," said Jerry.

"That's why you're the detective," said Mike.

They saw no one as they walked past Erie, Apache and Huron, but as they rounded the bend, two men came into view. It looked like they had just walked out of Iroquois.

"Detective Franks and CSI Ferguson, Wayne County S.O.," said Mike.

"Friendly?" asked Jerry.

"As far as I know," said Mike. "Let's find out what *they* know, and not tell them what *we* know."

"Wait. Fill me in on what *we* know," Jerry said.

"We know we don't know anything," said Mike.

"Okay, that's what I thought," said Jerry.

Franks spotted Mike and Jerry as he began a conversation on his cell phone. He recognized Mike and waved. Ferguson walked up and shook Mike's hand.

"This is my private eye pal, Jerry Baxter," Mike said.

"Good to meet you. I'm Jack Ferguson. Wayne County CSI."

Franks finished his call. "Just getting here? Or making a second trip?" Franks asked, extending a hand to Mike.

Mike introduced Jerry. Then he said, "If I told you we were here last night, you might think we found something."

Franks laughed. "Well, did you?"

"We found what you found," said Mike. "Zip."

"It's definitely the right place," Ferguson said.

"It matches the photo," Mike agreed.

"Yeah. It does," said Franks. "We've been here since six. We're leaving. We'll see you back in Ohio."

"We'll be right behind you," said Mike.

The law enforcement crew walked up the path and disappeared. Mike stood still, staring at the cabin. He walked all the way around it, then sat on a tree stump to the left of it and stared some more.

"Are you ready to go?" Jerry asked.

"There!" Mike said, pointing to the woods south of Iroquois.

Jerry followed his finger. "What?"

Mike showed him the photo on his phone screen. "We've been looking at the cabin," he said. "Look to the right of the cabin."

"The reddish thing on the tree?" asked Jerry.

"Yeah. That reddish thing is a cedar nesting box, probably for bluebirds," said Mike. "Maybe some kind of project for campers back in the day."

"It's definitely big enough," said Jerry.

The box was about eighteen inches high and twelve inches deep. It was attached to an oak tree by a wire loop hung on a nail about seven feet off the ground.

"The front panel should be loose. There's usually a shelf or two inside," said Mike, as he reached up and grabbed the bottom. He gave it a jerk, but it didn't move.

"That's funny," he said. He stood on his tip-toes and peered over the ledge on the bottom of the bird house.

"Look at this, Jerry. There's a key lock," said Mike.

"A key lock on a bird house? That *is* funny," said Jerry.

"We need to catch those cops!" Mike shouted.

"Why a bluebird box?" Jerry asked, as they jogged to the car.

"They're prolific bug eaters," said Mike, breathing hard. "Spiders, flies, dragonflies, caterpillars, sod grubs, moths, crickets, worms, beetles, grasshoppers, apple maggots, corn borers and alfalfa beetles—just to name a few. And that's always a good thing when you're living in the woods."

"Why do you know that?" Jerry asked.

"They're still here," said Mike, pointing at the SUV that was just beginning to back out of its parking place. They waved their arms and attracted Franks' attention.

"Did you find something?" Franks asked.

"Did you bring the box from Fenner's house?" Mike asked.

"Yes. We've got it," said Franks.

Mike told them about the key lock on the bluebird house and they all hustled back down the path together.

Amber jumped back from the door as she heard the lock turn.

"You!" Amber shouted as the bald man opened the door and walked toward her.

"Why did you kidnap me?"

The bald man grabbed her and threw her on the bed. Amber screamed and curled into a ball.

"Shut up!" he yelled. "You've got one chance to get out of this alive! So, listen carefully! I'm going to ask you a simple question. Give the wrong answer and I'll hurt you. Give the wrong answer twice and I'll kill you. Do you understand?

Amber was shaking. "Yes," she said.

"Remember," he said. "I'm going to hurt you if you give the wrong answer. "Do you understand that?"

"Yes!" she screamed.

"Do—You—Understand?" He shouted, kneeling over her on the bed.

"Yes!" she screamed as loud as she could.

"Where is the camera?"

"What camera?"

"Wrong answer, sweetheart!" He grabbed a handful of her blonde hair. He pulled it hard and slapped her face with the back of his hand. "You get one more chance! Then you die! Where's the video camera?"

"Okay! Okay!" Amber screamed. "I'll get it for you!"

"Where is it?!" He slapped her again, even harder.

"It's at the casino! In my locker!" she screamed.

He punched her in the shoulder. "You've got five minutes to clean up. Then we're going to Binion's."

Gail and Bree walked out of the Sheriff's office smiling. Bree was happy that she'd been let off the hook for threatening her father's life. Gail was happy that Kimball had followed the script, though she was still a bit surprised at herself for collaborating with *him* on anything. Kimball, she conceded, had played his role well, lecturing Bree in his toughest voice, laying out the life of misery she faced if sent to prison for the next five years. Still, Gail knew she'd never trust him—*once a liar and a cheat, always a liar and a cheat,* she told herself.

Chapter 50

Jean Swanson told her grandson to sit still while she answered the door. The man flashed a badge and identified himself as Mark Lawrence, an investigator from Wayne County.

"May I ask you a few questions, ma'am? It's about the Cheryl Fenner case. Are you familiar with it?"

"Yes. Of course, I am," said Jean. "The victim's husband is my grandson's father, as I'm sure you know."

The investigator's phone rang. "Yes. Yes, I am. Sure, I'd be happy to." He handed his phone to Jean. "Someone wants to speak with you," he said.

"Hello? Amber? What? Yes. Mr. Lawrence is here," she said. "All right. Sure."

Jean gave the phone back to its owner and asked if he wanted coffee.

"Sure. That would be very nice of you," he said.

The bald man handed his keys and a ten-dollar bill to a parking attendant at the Golden Nugget. He took Amber's arm and walked her through the casino to an exit that faced Binion's.

"If you say a word to anyone, your son and your mother are dead. My partner will stay with them until he hears from me that I have the camera and the tape. Do you understand?"

"Yes. I understand. Please don't let him hurt my son," she said.

"Just get the camera," said the bald man as they entered Binion's from East Fremont Street. "I'll wait in the cafe."

Amber hurried past the cashier's window to the door marked, *Employees Only*. She walked to the ladies dressing room, used the combination, 6-24-21 on locker number 17 and opened it. She reached to the top shelf and felt all the way back. Her hand found the camera and pulled it down.

She sat on the bench in front of the locker and stared at the JVC. She turned it on, ejected the tape and dropped it into her shirt pocket.

She was terrified, her heart beating as fast as her feelings of dread were multiplying. Her plan had unraveled months before when Rick refused to pay her for the camera after she'd stolen it and run off to Vegas. Her dreams had already dissolved into the fog of a strange and sad reality. Saving her son and her mother were all she had left. She had to do that, at least.

She walked into the cafe and sat at the counter next to the bald man. "Here's the camera," she said, setting it next to his coffee cup. "You get the tape when you call off your partner and I'm sure my son is all right."

He glared like he was about to rip out her throat. Then he smiled. "Fair enough," he said. He dialed a number with a 330 area code. "I have the package. You can go," he said.

Amber ordered coffee. "We'll wait a few minutes. I'll call my mother. If your guy is gone, I'll give you the tape."

"I'll play it your way, sweetheart," said the bald man. "But if I don't get the tape, my brother goes back to kill them both."

"Your brother?" Amber asked. "You kidnap and murder as a family? How nice."

"Make your call," said the bald man.

Amber's mother said the man had asked a few questions about Rick Fenner. Nothing new. She said she didn't know why he'd come. Amber thought to herself: *No, she certainly didn't.*

"Here," said Amber, reaching into her bra for the tape.

"Thanks," said the man, standing to leave. "If it's not the real deal, I'll find you. You know I will."

Amber exhaled as he walked away. She sat for fifteen minutes just breathing and thinking about how close she and her son and her mother had come to losing their lives. She thought: *How absolutely bizarre is it that six months ago I was a suicidal drug addict? How could my feelings about life, love, family and the future change so dramatically in such a short time? It was Peggy. It was all Peggy. The trip she made to Rick's house last November was the most caring thing anyone had ever done for me. I thanked her, but not enough—not nearly enough.*

The conversation Peggy overheard changed everything. I was in the hospital feeling sorry for myself. Rick had been coming to visit his son once a week and dropping off money, but he didn't want us. He definitely didn't want me. That's why I wanted to die. Peggy breathed life into me. She convinced me that I was worth something. Whatever happens now, even if it's all wrong, I know I'll survive.

The bald man's phone rang as the valet handed him his keys.

"Do you have it?" asked his brother.

"Camera and tape," he said.

"Great. We'll be there at noon tomorrow."

Rick shook Gail's hand.

"Thanks again for getting me out," he said as he stepped from her Mercedes.

"Remember," she said. "Just because you're out of jail, doesn't mean you're off the radar. If Kimball comes around or tries to talk to you or Bree, I suggest you remind him that you're represented by counsel."

"I will," said Rick, as he disappeared through the side door of his house.

Gail drove away feeling empty. She had done her job well. Rick was free and apparently eliminated as a murder suspect, but there was no closure, no victory. Gail loved winning. She hated losing. This felt like a loss.

The other three stared up at the western red cedar box as Franks shoved the gold key into the lock, turned it to the right and pulled. Only he could see inside as the front of the box lifted to reveal a single shelf dividing it into two sections. The upper section was empty, but the lower wasn't.

"Got something," Franks declared. He closed the box, turned the key back to center and removed it. "Syringe."

"The one in the picture," said Mike.

"Sealed in a plastic bag. Maybe with a nice fat print on it," said CSI Ferguson, smiling.

"That Jonas Benson! What a strange, crazy old fart!" Mike shouted.

"I hope he's smiling," said Franks.

It felt good to be home. Jail wasn't on Rick's list of favorite places. It was damp and lonely and smelled alternately of chemicals and sweat. It was always either too loud or too quiet. It gave him a headache that throbbed from the first day to the last. He rarely slept through the night.

His house smelled good. Six years later, it held the scent of his wife's perfume; six years later, he swallowed hard when he thought about why she died. He walked into the bedroom and fell onto the king size mattress. "Ah!" he exhaled. In a few seconds, he was asleep.

Chapter 51

Saturday, April 26

DAN RIORDAN'S PHONE rang.

"It's Al. We're in 1623 at the Stratosphere."

"I'll be there in ten minutes," Dan said.

The door was open when he arrived. The bald man walked in to find his brother, Al, and Leticia Cragmere eating hamburgers.

"How was your flight?" asked Dan.

"Cut the chit chat," Cragmere mumbled with her mouth full. "Let's see the tape."

Al gave his brother a hug. "She's been an absolute bitch all the way here," he whispered. He set the camera on the TV stand and started the tape.

Jonas Benson sat in a high-backed chair. He was framed by two black and white photographs on blue wall. The photo to his right showed him as a young pharmacist standing outside his drug store. The other showed him standing at the counter inside the store. It was a much older man who stared blankly at the camera lens for a few seconds before offering the confession that he hoped would save his soul.

My name is Jonas Benson. I'm making this recording because I'm about to die and there's something I cannot take with me to the grave, even though I promised I would.

"Son of a bitch," said Cragmere. "Little son of a bitch."

In 1971, my business was struggling. Some of it was my fault; some of it wasn't. Regardless of the reasons, I was desperate for money to stay afloat and could not acquire the necessary capital through conventional means. I came very close to part-nering with some Cleveland mobsters. While I was considering that unpleasant path, I met a young woman named Leticia Ramsey. She was a school teacher, about twenty-five years old and very attractive. She came into my pharmacy asking for cold medicine.

I was thirty-five, with a wife and a son who was in high school. Like I said, my business was failing. She sat at the lunch counter and ordered coffee and a tuna sandwich. We talked about the cold weather. It was February 6th, a Saturday. Apollo 14 had landed on the moon the day before and the astronauts were still up there. She told me how fascinating the children she taught found the whole concept of space exploration.

Her eyes were bright and full of life, yet she seemed very troubled--almost as troubled as I was. She stayed only thirty or forty minutes, just long enough to eat her lunch, and just long enough to make me feel a polarizing connection to her. I'm sure it had much to do with the hopelessness I was feeling in both my personal and professional lives. The imminent failure of my business had been taking a serious toll on my marriage.

Cragmere sat motionless, glaring at the camera, hypnotized. Her son-in-law and his brother sat together on the edge of the opposite queen size bed equally transfixed.

My wife and I had stopped being intimate, which included talking about anything except our money troubles. Leti came back a few days later. We talked again about current events and such, but eventually the conversation turned to more personal things.

I emptied my heart and soul to her, as she did to me. She told me that she was desperately in love with a married man named Robert Cragmere. His wife was the former Wanda Shaw, heiress to the Shaw Department Stores fortune. I can't say I was happy to hear that her heart belonged to another. Still, being able to do anything to make her happy was enough for me. So, when she came to me in April and asked if I would help her to ease the pain of her dying father, I told her I would.

She said a doctor had told her that Succinylcholine, a powerful muscle relaxer used in surgery, would put him out of his misery quickly, painlessly and without any chance of detection. I explained to her that giving her the drug would be illegal and highly unethical. She offered me twenty-five thousand dollars, enough to solve my financial problems and to pay for the expansion that would produce the comfortable life I led from then until now. I gave her a syringe with a strong dose. A few days later, her father drowned in a fishing accident.

She came to me crying and told me she had injected the drug into him as he sat on the pier in Cleveland. He fell into the water and apparently breathed just long enough that his lungs filled with water before the drug stopped his heart. The medical examiner ruled it an accidental drowning. No trace of the drug was uncovered.

Two months later, on a Friday afternoon, I received a phone call from Leti. She sounded desperate. She wanted another dose of Succinylcholine. She told me she'd pay another twenty-five thousand if I could deliver it that night. I asked her why she needed it, but she wouldn't tell me. It didn't matter. I was greedy, just plain greedy.

I brought another syringe with a dose of Succinylcholine to her apartment. She opened the door long enough to take it from me and to promise a cash delivery the following Monday morning. My wife and son were both away that weekend. I had time, so I decided to follow her.

She left her apartment about thirty minutes later and drove straight to Bob and Wanda's mansion. I waited in my Delta 88 about forty yards from the driveway on East Main Street. I was prepared to wait all night, but she was in and out in less than twenty minutes.

She drove a Pontiac Catalina, blue-green, 1965 or '66. She cruised through town traveling just under the speed limit. Then, she turned onto a dirt road. Within thirty seconds, I saw her left arm extend as if she were signaling a turn. I saw something fall from her hand. If she had tossed it just ten feet, it would have disappeared into the corn field. Instead, she simply dropped it onto the road. I was following maybe two hundred feet behind her. I stopped and easily found what she had dropped. It was one of the syringes I'd given her. It was empty, but for a few drops of the drug. I handled the syringe carefully, making sure I didn't smear any possible finger prints. When I returned home, I placed it into a plastic bag.

"Good luck with that," Cragmere smirked.

Early the next morning Bob Cragmere found his wealthy, drunkard of a wife, floating face down in their swimming pool. The medical examiner ruled her death an accidental drowning. Leti walked into the store the next Monday with a manila envelope containing $25,000.

We spoke for a moment, but not about Wanda's death, not about anything related to our business together. Leti didn't come around again until March, 1972, when she delivered an invitation to her wedding. She married Bob Cragmere that June, just about a year after she killed Wanda. I didn't go. How could I, when I knew what she'd done with my assistance?

Something happened between Bob and Leti in 1974. She left him for a time— about six months. Part of it had to do with their inability to have a child. Leti had two miscarriages. Another part of it had to do with the guilt they felt over killing Wanda. Getting away with it didn't mean it was all right. I know all of this because she came into the pharmacy one afternoon and poured out her heart.

We grew very close after that. In fact, we had an affair that lasted about six months. There was never any thought on either of our parts that it would turn into something permanent. For her, the money meant too much. After all, she had killed for it. For me, the possibility of becoming her next victim was just too frightening.

"Asshole!" Cragmere yelled at the camera.

They reconciled not long after we ended our affair. Less than a year later, Leticia's only child was born. We never spoke again, even after Bob's death of a heart attack in 1996. I do not believe there was any foul play with Bob. I think she truly loved him.

In any event, if you're watching this, then you've found the camera inside the cabin named "Iroquois" at the old Camp Douglass site. You may or may not have found the syringe. If it is meant to be, then it is meant to be.

My conscience is clear, at last.

Cragmere tossed the last of her burger back into its paper carton, then stood and slammed the carton into the garbage can.

"I'm not worried about the syringe," she said.

Franks and Ferguson made it back to the sheriff's office by dark. Kimball was waiting. They processed the syringe for prints and DNA. When they were satisfied the syringe was safe in the evidence room, Franks and Kimball drove to the prosecutor's office to meet with Duncan Chase. They brought the tackle box.

"So, you've got the syringe, but not the camera?" asked Chase.

"Right," said Franks. "We can't be sure there *is* a camera. We're assuming."

"And others are assuming the same?" asked Chase.

"Mike Page and his private eye pal beat us up there by a day," said Franks. "They were looking for the camera, too."

"Are you sure they didn't find it?" asked Chase.

"Well, they said they didn't. Actually, they're the ones who spotted a lock on the bird house and told us about it. That's how we found the syringe," said Franks.

"Yeah. Some detective you are," Kimball grinned.

"So, the little key in the wallet fit the bird house lock?" asked Chase.

"Right," said Franks.

"But what do we have?" asked Chase. "What does the syringe mean? And what does it have to do with Cheryl Fenner's murder?"

"Well, the camera is the key," said Kimball. "There has to be a video that incriminates someone for something."

"It can't be about Cheryl Fenner. Benson died first," said Chase.

"We'll know when we find it," said Franks.

"I hope you do," said Chase. "Because right now, we're at square one. Let me know if you learn anything from the syringe."

Rick's phone rang. "Amber?"

"Yes."

"What the hell do *you* want?" Rick asked.

"I was kidnapped. He forced me to give him the camera and tape," she said. "They threatened to kill R.D. if I didn't give it up."

"Who? Who are *they*?" Rick asked.

"It was the same guy who attacked me when Mike Page was out here—a big bald dude in his forties."

"Attacked you? What happened?" Rick asked.

"He punched me in the face and told me not to talk to Page," said Amber.

"And you did it anyway, of course."

"Uh. Yeah," she said. "I wanted to live. You should have made a copy of that tape, by the way."

"Yeah," said Rick. "That would have been smart."

"Do you think I'm in any danger now?" Amber asked.

"I doubt it," said Rick. "Seems like they've got what they want."

"I'm sorry I took the camera," said Amber.

"No, you're not. You're just sorry I wouldn't buy it back from you," said Rick.

"You can't blame a girl for tryin' baby," Amber said.

"I can't?" said Rick. "When's the last time you saw our son?"

"God. Not since I got here. But I talk to him all the time. He's fine with my mom." she said.

"I hope so," said Rick, just before hitting the disconnect button.

Chapter 52

SHE WAS BORN Leticia Beatrice Ramsey on January 14, 1944, in Canton, Ohio. Her parents, Harold and Elizabeth, were elementary school teachers in the area. Harold was a principal for twenty-five years. He was drafted to the army in 1943, but classified 4-F because of deafness in his left ear. He was later diagnosed with Multiple Sclerosis and suffered with it until his death by drowning at age 55 in 1971.

Elizabeth was a concert violinist who gave lessons and played in the local symphony orchestra and for musical theatre productions. She died of pneumonia in 1969 at the age of fifty.

Leticia followed in her mother's footsteps, becoming an excellent violinist and a school teacher. She attended the University of Akron for a year before transferring to Otterbein College near Columbus, where she finished her bachelor's degree in English and earned a Master's in Classical Music.

Her mother's death was devastating. Leticia had idolized her. She had dreamed of teaching in the same school and playing in the same symphony. There was no gaining revenge against the sudden illness that took Elizabeth Ramsey. Leticia was left to curse God and damn the stars. She lost her faith; she lost her humanity; she lost her conscience.

"What do you want to do with it?" asked her son-in-law.

"Eject the tape," said Cragmere.

Al Riordan pushed the switch on the bottom of the camera and opened the compartment. He handed her the tape. Cragmere reached under the plastic flap and yanked a foot of it free. She handed it back to Al and said, "Take it into the

bathroom and burn it. Then go out and take care of your loose ends." He nodded. Seconds later, Cragmere smelled smoke and smiled.

Walt was on the telephone when Mike walked into the sports office.

"Sure, I do," he said. "They're *that* good. All right. Thanks. No problem.
Anytime."

Mike tossed his jacket on the sofa near the door as Walt hung up the
phone.

"Hi, Walt. What's happening?"

"Just got off the phone with The Repository. They've got us ranked number one in the region," said Walt.

"What sport?" Mike asked.

"Softball!" said Walt.

"You're kidding. We've only played three games," said Mike.

"Yeah, well, they had Austintown ranked number five and Wyoming number one at the beginning of the season. We beat 'em both, so..."

"So maybe they didn't know what they were talking about at the beginning
of the season," Mike laughed.

"Obviously," said Walt. "We weren't even on the radar. How's Jen Miller
doing, by the way?"

"No issues at all," said Mike. "Met her dad the other day. Seems like a
good guy."

"Maybe he learned something from the whole Morgan thing," said Walt.

"I'm sure he did," said Mike.

"How about Bree? Do you really think they ran her off the road on
purpose?"

"Not sure," said Mike. "The sheriff's department's handling it. She's doing
all right."

"Keep me posted?"

"Will do," said Mike, grabbing his mail and walking out.

Gail called as soon as Mike reached the parking lot on his way to the softball field.

"I just heard from Rick," she said. "He wants to meet with us after your game. He says it's important."

"Any details?" Mike asked.

"No. Just said he wants to meet. Miller's Pub. Seven o'clock."

"All right. I'll see you then."

"Good luck today," she said.

Franks wasn't happy. He tossed a folder onto Kimball's desk. "Lab says no prints on the syringe. No contents left to I.D. If anything had been there, it evaporated over the years. We're talking 1971 here. So much for that."

"We need that tape," said Kimball. "Are you sure you didn't overlook something in Michigan?"

"If we did, all four of us overlooked it," said Franks.

"Well, we're all missing something," said Kimball. "We just have to figure out what the hell it is."

"Oh. I almost forgot," said Franks, tossing another folder toward his partner. "Coroner's finding. Cheryl Fenner's most likely C.O.D. Gunshot wound to the head."

Morgan was hung over. She grabbed the side of the pitching screen and took a deep breath, fighting back the urge to vomit. Her usual pinpoint control as a batting practice pitcher was gone.

"Something above the ankle would be nice!" Allie hollered from the box.

Morgan threw the next one at her head. Allie ducked. It banged off the backstop. "How's that? Better?"

"Okay! Okay! In the dirt is fine!" Allie yelled, half-amused, half-terrified.

Mike had arrived just as Morgan let go of the high hard one. He laughed at the banter. It was exactly what he missed most about playing ball; however, when Morgan dropped to her knees after the next pitch, no one was laughing.

Mike ran to the circle as she wretched and vomited.

"Tell me you're not pregnant," said Mike.

"Not funny," said Morgan with a groan.

"Gin?" Mike asked.

"Jack Daniels," said Morgan.

"What happened?" Mike asked. "What brought this on?"

"Grandpa sold the pub," she said. "He told me last night. He sold it right out from under me. It was supposed to be mine."

"Who bought it?" Mike asked.

"Riordan," she said.

"Cragmere's son-in-law?"

"Yeah. Grandpa's been talking about retiring to Florida for years. I guess he decided it was time," she said.

"I'm sorry, Morgan. Does your dad know?"

"He knows. He's pissed, too," she said.

"Go sit down," said Mike. "I'll finish up."

Mike pitched to the last few hitters knowing his arm, shoulder, back and legs would ache in the morning. As it turned out, his 45-MPH stuff was faster than the pitcher from Walnut Grove would throw.

The Invaders scored eight runs in the bottom of the first inning and another seven in the second. They won 22-0 in a game stopped by the "mercy" rule after four and a half innings. Allie pitched a one-hitter. Morgan sat in the dugout with her eyes closed for most of the game.

"Gail and I are meeting Bree's dad for dinner at the pub tonight," said Mike as he and Morgan walked to the parking lot. "Maybe I'll have a conversation with Bill."

"It's a free country," said Morgan. "But it's a done deal."

The cool window felt good. Cragmere pressed her face into it a little harder as she curled up in her first-class seat. Vegas had been too hot and too cold and never just right. She stared at the mountains as the plane taxied for takeoff. Where had the time gone? Where had that young girl gone—the one with the wide eyes? The one who could feel every emotion? The one who knew how to love? She closed her eyes as the plane lifted off the runway. She fell asleep as the civilized desert disappeared.

It was a dark drive to 1084 W. Main St.—no street lights for the final three miles. The farmer's market sign was the final illumination, unless you count the occasional flash of a crescent moon determined to duck behind thick rain clouds. Brown, yellow and orange leaves from oaks and maples swirled around the headlights of her Pontiac like they were following at thirty-five miles per hour. Leticia drove through the open, iron, gate and parked to the right of her boyfriend's black Mercedes 380 SL convertible.

She wore a white, silk, short-sleeve blouse, blue jeans and black shoes with square, three-inch heels. It was nearly eighty degrees in mid-October, more like an August night except for the wind and the falling leaves. She strode confidently to the back of the secluded three-story Victorian house that Wanda Shaw's father, Maynard, had renovated in the fifties and willed to her. It had been built in 1889 by his father, Oscar, whose first business was a feed store and blacksmith shop.

As Leticia climbed the brick steps that led to the patio and pool, she pulled the syringe from her bag. She could hear soft, rhythmic splashes when she reached the platform. She stood for a moment watching the woman in the pool pulling water with her arms and kicking her feet with her legs close together. She was an excellent swimmer by any account. As Leticia walked slowly toward the pool, the woman turned on her back and craned her neck to shout at someone standing on the balcony.

"That's ten! Two more and you lose!" She said, turning over to bury her face in the water just before plunging into a flip turn. The man did not speak or move. Leticia crept cautiously, making sure she wasn't seen. Wanda swam two more lengths and grabbed the near edge of the pool exhausted, but exhilarated.

"I win!" she exclaimed, her eyes scanning the balcony. "Hey! Where are you? Robert?"

Just then, Leticia sprung from the darkness, syringe in hand. She stabbed Wanda in the neck and depressed the plunger. Wanda screamed and tried to swim away from her attacker. She was gasping, her muscles seizing as she reached the center of the pool. Then she sank like she'd been caught in an undertow.

Leticia took apart the syringe and rinsed it thoroughly in the pool. She put it together and returned it to her bag. She did not glance at the man on the balcony as she walked to her car and drove away. She took a brief detour down a dirt road and dropped the syringe out of the window. It was done.

The plane jerked her awake as it cleared the Rockies. The window was cold now and she shivered. Maybe it was the dream that made her shiver. There was no shaking the dream.

Mike arrived at Miller's Pub half an hour early. He sat at the bar and waited for Bill.

"Coach Page. Good to see you. What'll you have?"

"Bud Light and some information," said Mike.

Bill poured the draft and set the glass on a napkin. "What's your question?"

"Morgan says you've sold the place. True?"

"True. It was time," said Bill.

"What about Morgan?" Mike asked.

"She'll have her job as long as she wants it," said Bill. "But this place shouldn't be her future. She'll be better off somewhere else—coaching in college, maybe."

Mike was surprised by Bill's logic. For some reason, he expected an odd explanation, maybe even something sinister.

"I can't argue with that," Mike said. "In fact, I agree with you. I think she'd turn into an old woman with a drinking problem if she owned this place."

"Exactly," said Bill. "The fastest way to become an old drunk is to start off as a young drunk."

"Why Al Riordan?" Mike asked.

"Why not?" said Bill. "He wants to try something new. Leti has his back. He'll pay Morgan well and let her manage the place if she wants. It's all good."

"You've got a place to go in Florida?"

"Looking," said Bill. "Hoping to move at the end of summer."

"Well, congratulations," said Mike. "I'm happy for you."

Mike sat sipping his beer for a few minutes. The pre-game show for the Cleveland Indians game was on every television. Apparently, Bill had deemed the NBA playoffs irrelevant because the Cavaliers were not involved. In fact, they hadn't made the playoffs since LeBron James escaped to Miami in 2010. Like most Cavaliers' fans, Bill had no desire to watch LeBron make another title run with the Heat.

"Hey, coach!" said a forty-something man with a pronounced belly. "I'm Nikki's dad. Tom LoPresti."

"Mike Page. Nice to meet you," said Mike, fearing the worst, but hoping Tom wasn't the kind of parent who'd complain about his daughter's lack of playing time.

"You're off to a great start," said Tom. "How's Nikki doing?"

Well, that was a little subtler than I expected, Mike thought. "Nikki is great," he said. "She does everything we ask and she has a terrific attitude."

"Oh. That's good to hear," said Tom. "I was wondering because she hasn't been playing much."

Still subtle, Mike thought. *But he finally got around to telling me I should be playing his daughter more.* "Thanks for your support," Mike said, refusing to take the bait. "Excuse me." He grabbed his beer and walked toward Gail, who had just settled into a booth.

"Good timing," Mike said, sliding in next to her. "I missed you, by the way."

Gail smiled. "Oh, you did? I'm blushing. I'm too old to blush," she said. "I missed you, too."

Rick Fenner hadn't been to a restaurant of any kind in weeks. The aroma of steaks, burgers, onion rings and French fries was overwhelming.

"Wow! This place smells great! I'll have one of everything," he said, sliding into the booth.

"Was the jail food pretty bad?" Mike asked.

"Worse than bad," said Rick. "Worse than bad." He ordered a steak and a Budweiser. Mike and Gail ordered grilled chicken salads.

"This is still under the lawyer-client privilege thing. Right?" asked Rick.

"Absolutely," said Gail. Mike is bound by it, too."

"All right," said Rick. "First of all, you're going to be angered, I'm sure, to learn that I haven't been honest."

"Angered? Yes. Surprised? No," said Mike.

"Okay. I deserved that," said Rick. "What I'm about to tell you is the truth, the whole truth and nothing but the truth." The beer arrived and Rick took a long drink. Mike did the same.

Gail sipped her white wine. "We're all ears," she said.

Rick took another long drink. "Amber was kidnapped yesterday in Las Vegas. The man who did it was the bald guy you ran into when you were there, Mike. His name is Dan Riordan and he's the twin brother of Leticia Cragmere's son-in-law, Al Riordan. He forced her to give him the video camera in Jonas Benson's photo..."

"Wait," said Gail. "How did Amber get the camera? And how did Al Riordan know she had it?"

"Both good questions," said Rick. "I was getting there. Riordan knew she had the camera because I told Cragmere—anonymously. Amber stole the camera from me right before she took off to Vegas." He paused to gulp his beer. "Questions?"

Gail beat Mike to the punch. "Why did you tell Cragmere?"

"To trap her," said Rick. "She killed my wife."

"Wait. Wait. Wait. I think you need to start at the beginning," said Gail. "Like from the day your wife received the box from Jonas Benson's lawyer."

"We looked through that box together," said Rick.

"You told the cops you didn't even know about the box!" Mike interrupted.

"Yeah, well. Do you want to hear this or not?" Rick bristled.

"Go ahead, Rick," said Gail, shooting Mike a look that said, 'cool it,'"

"After reading the letter, Cheryl thought we should sell the gold coins and stick the box in the crawl space. She wanted nothing to do with grandpa's dying declaration game.

"But I couldn't let it lie. I found an old email from Jonas inviting us to his timeshare in Twin Lake. The very next day, I drove to Michigan. There was a lady living at the address. She didn't know Jonas, but she gave me some ideas about where the cabin in the photo might be. I went to Camp Douglass, which was on the same lake, West Lake. I found the cabin and I and found the camera. It was in a box taped under a bench by the door.

"I watched the video, then drove back to Pluto and hid the camera in the barn..."

"Wait." said Gail. "Tell us what was on the tape."

"It was Jonas sitting in front of a camera. He said his business had been failing when he met Cragmere. She offered him twenty-five thousand dollars for an untraceable drug so she could put her sick father out of his misery. Then she paid him another twenty-five thousand for another dose to kill Wanda Shaw, though I don't think Benson knew what she was going to do with the second dose when he sold it to her."

The waitress arrived. Rick started eating almost before the plate hit the table.

"Did your wife see the tape?" Mike asked.

"No. Like I said, I hid it in the barn. Two days later, she was gone."

"Why didn't you show her right away?" Mike asked.

Rick mumbled with his mouth full of fries. "She didn't want me to go in the first place. She didn't want us to be involved."

"So why didn't Cragmere kill you, too," asked Gail.

"Another good question," said Rick. "I don't know. I really don't. She could have. But I wasn't sure the old bitch was in on it. I wasn't sure Cheryl hadn't just walked out on me."

"With a daughter in sixth grade?" asked Gail.

"Well, let's see," said Rick. "I had a pregnant girlfriend; I was having an affair with two other women; and Cheryl was using the word divorce in almost every sentence. So, yeah, even with a daughter in sixth grade."

"Father of the year," Mike muttered.

Rick shoved some food into his mouth. "Plus, I was thinking about black-mailing Cragmere, knowing I'd need some off-the-books money if Cheryl de-cided to file."

"But you didn't blackmail her?" asked Gail.

"Well, yeah. I tried," said Rick.

"Maybe you should start from the *very* beginning," said Gail. "Like from the day your wife disappeared."

"All right," he said, cutting a large piece of steak and devouring it. "Here goes: The cops had to wait twenty-four hours to start looking into Cheryl's disappearance. But I started that afternoon.

"When I got home, I could tell things had been moved in the house. Someone had definitely searched our bedroom. I thought of Jonas Benson's video right away. I tried to convince myself that it was too weird, too far-fetched to think that Cragmere had come looking for the box and decided to kidnap or kill Cheryl to get it.

"But after a week passed without any word from Cheryl, it seemed plausible. No. It seemed likely. I thought about spilling the whole story to Kimball, but he was so focused on me as the only possible suspect, I decided it might do more harm than good—even if I showed him the video.

"So, I ran a little bluff on Cragmere. I wrote her a letter using words cut from newspaper headlines, you know, like you see in the movies. It said something like, 'I know you're responsible for the disappearance of Cheryl Fenner and the murder of Wanda Shaw. You can buy the evidence and my silence for two million dollars.'"

"Two million?" Mike asked. "That's a *big* bluff."

"I wanted her to believe I was serious," Rick said.

"Right. And what if Cheryl had still been alive at that point?" Mike asked.

"I'm not saying it was a brilliant plan," said Rick. "I'm just telling you what I did."

"Fair enough," said Gail. "Continue."

"I threatened to turn my evidence over to the cops if she didn't call a certain phone number at exactly 2 p.m. on a certain date. It was a pay phone at the Akron-Canton airport, and I was sitting near that phone at the designated time. It rang at 2 p.m. on the nose."

"And?" Gail asked, twirling her arms like a basketball official making a traveling call.

"And I just let it ring," said Rick. "That was the end of it."

"You never spoke with Cragmere again?" Mike asked.

"That's correct," said Rick. "Until this week, when I made that anonymous call to tell her that Amber had the tape."

"And what, exactly, were you trying to accomplish by doing that?" Gail asked.

Rick paused. "I plead the fifth," he said.

"You thought they'd kill her! Didn't you?" Mike shouted.

Rick stood and glared at Mike. "She stole the camera and tried to sell it back to me. Then, she threatened to give it to Cragmere and tell her I was working with the cops. On top of that, her mother hasn't let me near my son. So, yeah, I don't have a lot of affection for the bitch!"

"You went from a two-million-dollar blackmail scheme to giving away the video and hoping Amber might be murdered?" Gail asked.

"Basically," Rick said.

"Absolute scum," Mike said, glaring at Rick.

"How do you know Amber was kidnapped?" Gail asked.

"She called," said Rick.

"She called?" asked Gail.

"Yes," said Rick. "She wanted me to know she was all right."

"How did you leave it with her?" asked Gail.

"She apologized for stealing the camera in the first place. She wanted to know if I thought she was in danger. I told her I didn't think so. That was it," said Rick.

"So, you lied—for like the hundredth time." said Mike.

"Yeah," Rick nodded. "I guess I did."

Chapter 53

Monday, April 28

KIMBALL SLAMMED THE lieutenant's door and walked to his desk muttering. No one in the office stared or even glanced his way. That particular noise was no more conspicuous to them than the honks of Canada geese.

"No trip to Vegas," Kimball said, as Franks finished a call.

"What was his reason?" Franks asked.

"The usual. Not in the budget," said Kimball.

"Shit's getting old," said Franks.

Kimball's phone rang. "Kimball. Yeah. When? How? Has her mother been notified? Who's handling it? You got a number for him? Got it. Thanks."

Franks could see that his partner was stunned. "Who was that?" he asked.

"Vegas P.D. Amber David. She's dead," said Kimball.

"When? How?" Franks asked.

"Somebody found her in a dumpster this morning. Strangled," said Kimball.

"Shit! Guess we'd better tell the lieutenant," said Franks.

"Yeah," said Kimball. "I know what he'll say. 'No point in going out there to question a corpse. Was there?'"

"What about Page and Gail West?" Franks asked.

"Call West," said Kimball. "Find out what she knows."

An investigator from the Clark County Coroner's office zipped the body bag. Then he ducked under the police tape. He shook hands with two detectives who had just interviewed the sanitation worker who'd discovered the body two hours earlier.

"Dan, Glenn, good to see you," said Marty Paulson. The three men had been meeting at homicide scenes for almost a decade.

"You, too, pal. What's it been? A week?" Glenn Woodward was forty-two. He had grown up in Vegas and graduated from UNLV. He was a slight man, standing about 5'9" and weighing something less than 150 pounds. His father was a retired Vegas cop. His mother was a LVPD dispatcher with forty-six years on the job. He wore a beige straw hat; a white short-sleeve shirt; and a thin black tie. His linen pants were light gray. His shoes were darker gray canvass loafers. He looked like a wise guy in a movie set in 1950s Vegas. He knew it and he liked it.

Dan Riordan took no fashion cues from his partner. He wore a 4XL red, gold and white Hawaiian shirt; tan khakis; and black Wing Tips. He had sprayed his bald head with 50 SPF Copper Tone, making sure the tips of his pointy ears were well covered before exiting the car. Riordan had moved to Vegas from Mississippi shortly after his twin brother, Al, had married an Ohio girl and moved to Ohio with her.

"Didn't get much from the garbage man, Marty," said Riordan. "Let us know what you come up with. We'll do our thing."

"I'll call ya," said the investigator.

The killer or killers had left Amber's purse in the dumpster. Her credit cards and money—if there had been any—were gone, but her driver's license and casino I.D. remained in her wallet. There had been no immediate sign of sexual assault, so it was either a robbery and murder, or a murder made to look like a robbery—unless it was something weird.

Riordan looked at his partner. "Binion's or her apartment?"

"You hungry?" asked Woodward."

"I'm kinda craving greasy sausage and hash browns," said Riordan. "I didn't get breakfast."

"Can you get the gambler's special at this hour?"

"Oh yeah," said Riordan.

"Okay. Binion's it is," said Woodward.

Gail had learned to handle tragic news the hard way. In 2003, her parents were killed in car accidents three months apart. Neither was driving. In 2005, her only sibling, Ron, died of a heart attack at the age of forty-seven. In 2010, a twelve-year-old girl—her key witness in a murder trial—was killed on the court-house steps by a bolt of lightning.

Her expression barely changed when Franks told her about Amber. She thanked him and said she didn't have anything to add. She ended the call and turned to Rick.

"You got your wish."

"What wish?" Rick asked.

"That was detective Franks. Vegas P.D. called him this morning. Amber David is dead. Strangled. A garbage man found her in a dumpster."

"Oh, God. No!" Rick shouted.

Mike put his head in his hands. "Jesus!" he said.

"Cragmere! That old bitch!" Rick screamed.

"Don't even start," said Mike. "You might as well have killed Amber yourself."

"That sounds familiar," said Gail. "What you just said. Like what your wife overheard the night she went to this guy's house. Right?"

Mike nodded. "That's what she heard."

"You know what, Rick? I think you lied about that, too," said Gail. "I think the male voice Peggy heard *was* yours."

Mike hit the table with his fist. "The whole truth and nothing but the truth, Rick!"

"Okay. You're right. I lied…"

"There's a shocker," Mike interrupted.

"It was me," Rick continued. "And I was talking to Bree."

"And Bree lied," Gail interjected.

"She was missing her mother, I guess. And she just went off about how it was my fault about Cheryl. She was right, of course. She just didn't know why. So, I told her the whole story about Jonas Benson's box and how Cragmere found out about it."

"So, Bree knows about the video," said Gail.

"Yeah. She knows," said Rick.

"How did Cragmere find out about the box?" Mike asked.

"That's the part your wife overheard," said Rick. "I was angry and I told Bree it was *her* fault. I said she might as well have fired the gun herself. It was pure, stupid coincidence, actually. Bree's regular English teacher was a woman named Alice Ross. She went out on maternity leave toward the end of the school year.

"Cragmere was one of the teachers who took her place from time to time. She assigned an essay. Bree wrote about Benson's box. Cragmere read it. Then, she must have sent people to search the house. Cheryl probably got in the way. So, they killed her."

Gail sighed. "So, you had the whole thing figured out right away, but instead of telling the cops, you tried to make a profit?"

"I didn't know she was dead right away," said Rick.

"When *did* you know?" asked Mike.

"Officially? When they found her remains. Unofficially? I'd say about a week after she disappeared. That asshole Kimball started accusing me. He said there had been no activity on Cheryl's credit cards; no withdrawals from her bank account; no calls from her cell phone. He'd say things like, 'She's dead and you did it. Where'd you hide the gun?'"

"Why the hell didn't you tell him what you knew?" Mike asked.

"I couldn't risk him turning it around on me and charging me with extortion or something," said Rick. What if Cragmere had a recording of my call? I screwed it up. I know."

Gail stood and drank some water. "Let's wrap this up. I have calls to make," she declared. "Get the bill, Mike. Keep the receipt. My advice to you, Rick, is to keep away from your son and his grandmother for a couple of days." She walked out, leaving the two men dazed.

"I think she's disgusted and just a bit pissed off," said Mike.

"Yeah," said Rick. "You want a beer?"

Mike walked out glaring at him.

"I guess that's a 'no,'" Rick mumbled to himself.

Chapter 54

GAIL WAS NEITHER disgusted *nor* pissed off. As she drove away, she voice dialed Duncan Chase.

"We need to talk," she said.

"Yeah. I just heard about Amber David. Where are you," asked Chase.

"Pluto. Just leaving Miller's," said Gail. "It's about more than Amber David."

They agreed to meet at the Olive Garden in Fairlawn. It was nearly thirty miles for Gail, but it gave her time to call Mike.

"Did you hear what I heard?" she asked.

"When?" Mike asked.

"Is Rick still with you?"

"No. He left. I'm just settling up with the waitress. Did I hear what?"

"When Rick was talking about Kimball hounding him. Remember what he said? He said Kimball asked him where he hid the gun."

"Yeah. I heard that," said Mike. "So how did Kimball know Cheryl had been shot?"

"Exactly," said Gail. "I'm on my way to meet Duncan Chase."

"Tell me what you're thinking," Mike said.

"I'm thinking there's no doubt in my mind now. That son of a bitch Kimball is dirty."

"Let me know what Chase has to say," Mike said.

"I will," said Gail.

Dan Riordan tossed his napkin onto a white plate that held remnants of egg yolk, hash browns and wheat toast. He sipped his third cup of coffee and caught the attention of the waitress. "He's got it," he said, pointing across the table at Woodward.

Woodward looked at the check, handed the waitress $16.00 and told her to keep the change.

"Thanks, boys," said the sixty-something woman.

The detectives quickly found Amber's supervisor, who checked her time card for Wednesday into Thursday. They interviewed several co-workers. None said they saw anything unusual during her shift. None said they heard her mention any kind of trouble in the last week.

They spent the next two hours in the security office watching video recorded by various cameras during Amber's shift. They saw nothing that could be considered a clue.

They found the RTC driver from Amber's trip home. Emmaline Parker told them she remembered Amber as one of her regular passengers and assured them that she had travelled alone and that she wasn't hassled or followed.

"She's the only one who gets off at her stop, usually," said the driver. "I would have noticed if something wasn't right."

Confident they'd eliminated Binion's, Fremont Street and the city bus as locations where Amber could have been accosted or abducted, the detectives agreed to meet at Amber's apartment in an hour.

Gail had no idea how Duncan Chase would react to her conspiracy theory. During the drive, she rehearsed telling him, trying to hide her general feeling of disdain for Kimball. Her friendship with Chase had been mothballed after she left the prosecutor's office. Once a trusted confidant and mentor, Gail had all but disappeared from his life. Still, he'd shown no signs of resentment during their recent conversations. *Why would he?* She thought. *He has a life.*

She found him in a booth drinking Shiraz.

"I ordered you a white Zinfandel," said Chase.

"Perfect," said Gail, sliding in opposite the deputy prosecutor. "Tough day?"

"All my tough days are behind me," Chase smiled. "What's on your mind?"

The waitress brought her wine. Gail held the glass with two hands as she leaned forward and began in a voice that was just above a whisper.

"I think Kimball's dirty. I think he's on Leticia Cragmere's payroll."

"What? What payroll?" Chase laughed.

"Rick Fenner said something tonight," she began.

"Rick Fenner the professional liar?" Chase interrupted. "Sorry. Go ahead."

Gail ignored his comment and his apology. "We all know that Kimball targeted Rick as his wife's killer from the beginning. I'm not saying he didn't have good reason to suspect she was dead. He did. I'm not saying he didn't have good reason to believe Rick wanted her dead..."

"So, what's your point, counselor?" Chase interrupted, sipping his wine.

"Here's my point, Mr. Prosecutor," said Gail. "Tonight, Rick mentioned that during one of his harassing tirades just after Cheryl disappeared, Kimball said something like, 'She's dead and you did it. Where'd you hide the gun?' To my knowledge, the probable cause of death wasn't determined to be a gunshot wound until very recently."

Chase grabbed his menu as the waitress arrived. "Anything?" he asked Gail.

"Nothing for me," Gail said to the waitress.

Chase pointed to a menu item and asked for bleu cheese dressing with his salad. "Maybe he was guessing," he said.

"He wasn't guessing, Dunk. He knew. He knew she'd been shot. And he knew it wasn't Rick Fenner who did it. That means he went after the wrong person to protect the right person."

"That's a giant leap, Gail," Chase warned. "Speaking as a prosecutor, we need proof. All I've heard is conjecture so far."

"More like simple math," she smiled. "I think at the very least it's time to scrutinize every move he makes."

"I can certainly do that. Do you think Kimball had anything to do with Amber David's murder?" asked Chase.

"Maybe. Or maybe somebody just beat him to it," said Gail.

Chapter 55

VALENTINE RUSTLED AND snorted. She raised her pale-yellow chin just long enough to see or smell her master's presence in the kitchen, then lowered it to the cool tile.

Mike sat waiting for Gail's call. He wanted to hear about her conversation with Chase. He wanted to hear her voice. He scrolled to the last pages of Peggy's unfinished memoir.

> *I can't bring myself to think about the end—the end of my existence on this planet, the end of this person who has always been. I can't bring myself to think about whether something else awaits. No one knows for sure. No one will ever know for sure.*
>
> *I think I've done well here. I wasn't given some things that most women have--the ability to bear children being the most obvious. I was given some things most women don't have, including a wonderful, understanding husband who accepted me as I am and asked very little in return for his devotion. I don't feel cheated. I don't feel special. I feel satisfied. I was a good person. I was a good wife. Do I wish I had been a better person and a better wife? Who wouldn't? Maybe if I had been, my husband wouldn't have felt the need to cheat on me when we lived in Georgia.*

An icy shock rushed from Mike's brain through his spine. *She knew! Shit! She knew!* He kept reading.

> *On the other hand, I think some things are just bound to happen. Fate throws people together in situations that test their character and reveal their flaws. If we were all*

248

flawless, it would be a dull world. I didn't marry Mike believing he was flawless. He may have believed I was flawless—for a little while. I did a few things he doesn't know about, and that he never will know about. I'm not flawless.

The shock returned, and this time his whole body shivered. *What was she talking about? Did she have an affair, too? Was it about Amber? What else could it be? Some cruel revenge thing, knowing I'd have to wonder until the day I die?*

Mike scrolled to read more, but there was no more. That was all she wrote. He closed the laptop and cried.

Riordan and Woodward arrived at Amber's bungalow within seconds of each other in their personal vehicles. Riordan drove a 2014 black Cadillac Escalade. Woodward drove a 2007 white Ford Taurus. They nodded at the uniformed police officer who'd been guarding the front door since before midnight.

"We've got it now. Thanks," said Woodward.

The officer radioed his partner, who'd been guarding the back door. "We're clear," he said.

"Touch anything?" Riordan asked the officer.

"No," he said.

"Try the door?"

"Nope. Just ran the tape from pole to pole and stood behind it all night," said the officer.

"Anybody show up?" Riordan asked.

"Just the neighbor. He asked what was going on. I told him I didn't know. I was just here to make sure no one crossed the line."

"He home now?" asked Woodward.

"Didn't see him leave," said the officer.

"Anything else?" Riordan asked.

"No. That's it."

The detective turned the knob on the front door with a gloved hand. It opened. He raised his eyebrows at his partner. With two steps each, they were standing in the middle of the front room. They saw obvious signs of a struggle. Two *Glamour* magazines lay open on the hardwood floor. One of the two couch cushions was out of place, jammed between the dark brown, cloth couch and the coffee table.

"Anybody home?" Crime Scene Investigator Carl Brodie and his partner, Jennifer Breakstone, were there to search for finger prints, blood, weapons— anything that could help the detectives answer the who, what, when, where, why and how of Amber David's murder.

"We're in here!" Woodward called, sarcastically, from five feet away.

"Looks like it might have happened here, huh?" said Breakstone.

"You tell us," said Riordan.

The CSI's went to work. The detectives went to interview the neighbors. Woodward walked outside, turned left and knocked on Bobby Galbraith's door. Galbraith's name was written on Woodward's note pad, along with notes on his arrest record.

"What the hell happened?" Galbraith asked. Woodward stared at the neighbor's tattoos. They seemed to have been randomly applied. None was particularly interesting or menacing, except the swastika on the left side of his neck.

"Where'd you do your time?" asked Woodward.

"I'd say your mother's house, but you don't look like you ever had one," said Galbraith.

"Funny," said Woodward. "Maybe we should just violate your parole so you can try your jokes on the general population at Ely."

"If you knew, why'd you ask?" said Galbraith.

"When's the last time you saw Amber David?" Woodward asked.

"What happened to her?" Galbraith asked.

"Just answer the question. Okay, Bobby?"

Woodward had done this interview hundreds of times. Galbraith's eyes would tell him if he knew anything about Amber's death.

"Thursday afternoon. Early. Right out there," said Bobby. "She just got home. Said she worked all night and was going to sleep. I told her I'd keep the noise down. She said, 'Thanks, Bobby.' Never saw her again. Now tell me what's going on, man."

Woodward believed him. "She's dead, Bobby."

"Oh, God!" Galbraith put his hands over his face. "How?"

"We don't have the report yet," Woodward said. "A trash guy found her in a dumpster yesterday morning. You sure you didn't see or hear anything Thursday night? Maybe late, like around midnight?"

"No, man. Nothin'. I'd help if I could. She's a good kid," said Galbraith. "She *was* a good kid. Damn. I can't believe she's gone."

"Any enemies? Any trouble recently around here?" asked Woodward.

"Nothing with Amber," he said. "She never had anybody over that I saw. Chelsea either. They were quiet. Is Chelsea all right?"

"We don't know," said Woodward, handing him a business card. "If she shows up, tell her to give me a call."

Riordan had completed his interview with Amber's other neighbor. He was back inside the tiny house chatting with the CSI's by the time Woodward returned.

"Anything?" Riordan asked his partner.

"Zip," said Woodward. "He's a burnout on parole, but he's not involved. Yours?"

"Old Mrs. Larch? Eighty-six. Can't hear. Goes to bed at seven. Nada."

"How are you guys doing?" Riordan asked the CSI's.

Brodie was crouched over the coffee table. "Getting some prints, some hair and other stuff. No way to know how long any of it has been here"

"So, you've got nothing?" asked Riordan.

"Yeah," said Brodie.

"Let us know if that changes," said Woodward. "We're out."

The detectives walked to their cars. "Meet you back at the ranch," said Woodward.

Bree sat with five teammates at the royal blue picnic table behind the press box. They all wore white uniform tops and royal blue pants. They ate sack lunches and talked and texted and posted photos on Instagram and Facebook. As their feet fidgeted, the metal spikes on their shoes scraped the concrete. The picture was every bit as representative of Pluto as a corn field—a dateless image, except for the phones.

"He looks like the guy on *Survivor*," said Rachel, staring at an Instagram photo posted by a classmate.

"Which guy?" Andrea asked.

"Which *Survivor*? Maria asked.

"The one on that island," said Rachel.

"They're all on an island," laughed Maddie.

"No, they're not," said Halle. "Sometimes they're in a jungle; sometimes they're in a desert."

"They should have one in Pluto," said Lauren.

"No one would win," laughed Bree. "But he does look like that guy. Same eyes."

Bree had gathered her friends three hours before game time for the sole purpose of being silly. She wanted to talk about things that didn't matter. She wanted to talk about things that could never be a matter of life and death. She wanted to be eighteen or seventeen or sixteen. She wanted to be any of the years she'd skipped to become an adult too soon.

"Lauren, what's the difference between Mr. Willoughby and a bucket of cow shit?" Bree asked.

"I don't know," Lauren smiled.

"The bucket," said Bree.

"Funny," said Lauren. "That sounds like something my dad would say, right before he'd say, 'get me another brewski.'"

"Yeah, and my dad would be right there with him," Bree laughed.

"How is your dad, Bree?" Andrea asked.

Bree didn't want to talk about her dad. "He's out. That's a good thing. I really haven't talked to him much. I'm still staying at Morgan's."

"Are you going home soon?" asked Maddie.

"I guess," said Bree. "I'm not in a big hurry."

They all knew about the murder of Amber David, but none dared ask about it, or about her stepbrother—at least until Lana joined the group.

"Bree! Oh, God, Bree! I just heard about Amber David's murder! I'm so sorry!" Lana hugged her friend and started to cry.

"Lana, stop!" Bree said. "I don't want to talk about that."

"Yeah. We're trying to have some fun here," said Maddie.

Lana wiped her eyes. "Sorry. Okay? I just couldn't believe it. You know. I just couldn't believe that happened to someone I know."

"You didn't know her, Lana," said Bree. "*I* didn't even know her."

"I knew *of* her," said Lana.

"Yeah, well, you knew of Andy Griffith, too, but you didn't cry when he passed away," said Bree.

"Says who?" asked Lana. "In fact, I did cry and then I screamed bloody murder when the Oscars left him off the "in memoriam" reel."

"I give up," said Bree, throwing her hands in the air.

"As well you should," Lana smiled.

Chapter 56

CRAGMERE SHUFFLED TO her classroom, arms loaded with yellow folders containing corrected assignments from her Advanced Placement Creative Writing class. Her reputation as a meticulous and stingy grader was well-deserved. In the five years she'd been teaching the course, only a handful of students had earned an "A." There were no "A's" earned for this particular assignment—an essay on the final chapter of "One Flew Over the Cuckoo's Nest."

The door to room 117 was open wide. Cragmere hesitated as she crossed the threshold. She had locked the door after sixth period, as always. She looked left and right as she walked to the back of the room. Nothing seemed amiss. She sat at her desk and placed the folders in the wire basket at the top right corner. Just as she opened a text book, she heard a scraping sound coming from the front of the room. She looked up and saw the left side of the large bookcase moving forward. Before she could gasp, Rick Fenner emerged from behind it.

"I dropped a quarter. It rolled back there," he said.

"When did you get out?" asked Cragmere.

"While you were in Vegas murdering Amber David," said Rick.

"It sucks being mother to a child of yours. And now that I've destroyed the tape, it might not suck so bad being me," Cragmere smiled.

"We'll see about that," said Rick. "Got a DVD player in that laptop?"

"I do," said Cragmere.

Rick pulled a disc from his jacket pocket. "Play this," he said, walking to the desk and handing it to her.

Cragmere put the disc in the drive. A second after she hit the "play" button, she knew what it was. "So, you made a copy," she said. "Congratulations on not being as dumb as you look."

"I made several," said Rick. "The rest are well hidden and guaranteed to be delivered to the prosecutor's office if anything happens to me or anyone in my family—ever."

Cragmere ejected the disc and handed it to him. "So, the whore died for nothing. Pity."

"You're damn smug for somebody who's one phone call away from death row!" said Rick.

"I've got a class in five minutes." Cragmere snapped. "If there's nothing else, please take your ass out of here."

Rick leaned over the front of the desk, resting on his elbows. "There *is* something else," he said. "I'd like to know who ran my daughter off the road last week."

Cragmere glared at him. "It wasn't me."

Mike wanted Jen in the circle against Division I powerhouse North Canton Hoover. He didn't think Callie threw hard enough to get past the middle of Vikings order. He didn't tell her that. He told her he needed her to shut the door if Jen got into trouble. She asked why it couldn't be the other way around. He said it was just one of those tough decisions coaches have to make. Five minutes into the game, he'd be second-guessing himself.

Jen walked the first batter, hit the second batter and gave up a two-run double to the third batter. The fourth batter lined a single to right field, putting runners at first and third with nobody out. Mike walked to the circle for a conference.

"These girls are good," he said. "They've won three state championships in a row. So, they don't need your help. Don't walk people and don't hit people. Now suck it up and get us out of the inning." Mike didn't require a response from the freshman and she didn't offer one.

The next batter hit a one-one rise ball over the scoreboard to make it 5-0. Mike turned to Morgan, who shrugged and said, "I'm guessing you didn't tell her to throw it down the middle with nothing on it."

"Nope," said Mike.

Jen struck out the next three batters and stomped to the dugout with her head down. The Invaders failed to score in their first four at bats. Jen gave up a single run in the top of the fifth on a walk, a double and a wild pitch. Mike brought in Callie, who struck out the number nine hitter (something Jen had already done twice) to end the inning.

"I liked that move," said Morgan, as Mike started toward the third base coaching box.

"Which?" Mike asked.

"Letting Callie strike out the nine hitter so she could gain confidence for the next inning," said Morgan.

"Oh, yeah. That," said Mike, who smiled because he had actually pulled Jen in anger over the walk and the wild pitch.

The Invaders came alive in their half of the fifth inning. Maddie walked. Bree beat out a roller to shortstop. Lauren walked to load the bases. Darcy singled to right field, scoring Maddie and Bree. Allie walked. Rachael doubled to left, scoring Lauren and Darcy. Andrea flew out to center field, scoring Allie. Halle bunted to the right of the circle. The pitcher threw her out, but Rachael scored to tie the game 6-6.

Then, something amazing happened. Bree came up for the second time in the inning and smacked a home run over the center field fence. It was the first homer of her life at any level. After all, she was a slapper—a singles hitter. She always ran at the ball as she swung, just trying to hit it on the ground and beat the throw to first. Occasionally, she'd hit a line drive into an outfield gap for a double or triple, but home runs were not part of her game.

Bree ran too fast around the bases, forgetting to break into a trot to milk the moment. She jumped on home plate as her teammates mobbed her. Morgan greeted her housemate in the dugout with a hug.

"I can't believe you just did that!" Morgan shouted.

"Me either," Bree sighed. "Wow. That felt so good!"

After Lauren ended the inning with a grounder to third base,

Mike called a meeting on the foul line. "Hey. Hey! Listen!" he shouted. "We've made a great comeback. But this is a championship team we're playing. They're not going to quit. We need six more outs. Callie, you've got to throw strikes. Don't walk anybody. Let's play some defense! Let's win this thing!"

The girls ran onto the field looking as determined as Mike had ever seen them. Callie faced the top of the Hoover order in the sixth. She got the first two hitters to ground out to Darcy at short. The third batter smoked a line drive just inside the right field line. Halle gloved it on one hop, whirled and threw a strike to Darcy, who slapped a tag on the batter as she slid into second base.

"Out!" yelled the umpire. The home crowd erupted as the Invaders ran off the field pumping their fists.

"Let's get some runs!" shouted Bree.

As Mike took his place in the coaching box, he saw something he loved: Jen Miller was patting Callie on the back, congratulating her.

The Invaders added an insurance run in the bottom of the sixth when Maria led off with a double to right center, Maddie laid down a sacrifice bunt and Bree blooped a double that dropped between two diving fielders near the left field line.

Mike's team had overcome a 6-0 deficit to lead, 8-6 as they took the field for the top of the seventh inning. The lead-off hitter was Emma Jarvis, who had nine home runs in her team's first eight games. She was an imposing player, standing just over six feet tall with a thick, muscular build.

Callie wasn't going to risk walking Jarvis with a two-run lead. She threw the first pitch down the middle at the knees. Jarvis took it for a strike. Callie fired the second pitch under Jarvis' chin. The clean-up hitter ducked out of the way and lost her balance, falling onto her backside.

Callie's third pitch was a curve ball that started over the middle of the plate. Jarvis swung and missed as the pitch broke out of the strike zone. The next pitch was high and tight again. This time, Jarvis backed away without going down. Callie's 2-2 pitch was shocker—a change-up that turned the big hitter into a statue.

"Strike three!" yelled the umpire, as the crowd roared and Callie pounded her fist into her glove.

The next batter popped up the first pitch. Andrea made the catch, reaching above the roof of the first base dugout and scraping her elbow in the process.

"Two down! Tall is good!" She yelled with a smile.

The next batter took a strike. Then, she hit the 0-1 pitch back to Callie on one hop. Callie squeezed the ball in her glove, ran a few strides toward first base and underhanded it to Andrea for the final out. The entire team ran to congratulate Callie as the fans cheered like they hadn't since Morgan was in the circle.

Mike stayed in the dugout and watched his players celebrate. They had become a team during this game, he thought. They had truly become a team.

Chapter 57

"GLENN WOODWARD?"

"This is Detective Woodward."

"My name is Randy Green. I'm the security chief at the Golden Nugget."

"What can I do for you, Randy?" Woodward asked.

"It's what I can do for you," said Green.

"How so?"

"You're working a murder case? Girl in a dumpster?"

"Right."

"I've got her on video the day before she died."

"She worked at Binion's," said Woodward. "That wouldn't be unusual."

"It's who she's with that's unusual," said Green.

"Who?"

"You need to see for yourself. And come alone."

"Why?"

"Just come alone and don't tell anyone why," said Green.

"I'm on my way," said Woodward.

Gail parked her Mercedes next to Mike's Buick. She smiled watching him talking and laughing with his players as they left the field. She guessed they won.

"Good game?" she asked, getting out of the car to greet him.

"Amazing game," said Mike. "We were hopelessly behind and came back to win anyway."

Gail hugged him. "Congratulations! I wish I could have seen it."

"Busy day?" asked Mike.

"Annoying court appearances. Annoying clients. I miss representing in-nocent people," she sighed.

"What about Fenner?" Mike asked.

"Fenner is filth," said Gail.

"Why, Ms. West! That seems a bit harsh," Mike joked. "Perhaps your client is simply misguided."

"He's misguided, all right," said Gail. "Because his moral compass points at his crotch."

"Mine seems to point at you," said Mike.

"Your crotch?" asked Gail, smiling.

Mike laughed. "That, too."

Woodward stared at the far-left screen on the bank of monitors in the Golden Nugget's security office.

"Here it comes," said Green.

The video was remarkably clear, certainly not what the detective expect-ed. It showed a man and a woman from the back walking briskly through the Golden Nugget's casino area. The man had a firm grip on the woman's left elbow. Just as they reached the end of the bar near the race and sports book, a second camera showed them from the front.

Woodward felt a rush of emotions. Shock, anger, betrayal and disgust flowed from his brain to his fists, which pounded the table in front of him.

Green paused the video and zoomed to the faces.

"As you can see on the time code, this was Monday at around 11:30 a.m. Binion's cameras picked them up across the way."

"We only had them check Sunday," said Woodward. "I had no reason to have them check Monday, too."

"Your partner figured no one ever would, I guess," said Green.

"How many people know about this?" Woodward asked.

"Me and Arnie Bates at Binion's. He's got his video cued and he's waiting for us," said Green.

"Let's go," said Woodward.

As they walked across Fremont Street, Woodward considered his next move. He decided Riordan had to be arrested before he found out anyone was onto him. He called Major Crimes Command and asked for Captain Hooks, who'd been his boss for three years. To say the least, Hooks wasn't a fan of Dan Riordan. The two had clashed constantly, mostly over Riordan's cavalier attitude about following proper procedure. "By the Book Hooks," as he was known, had recently threatened to go after Riordan's shield after a "call girl" complained that Riordan had slapped her around and threatened to arrest her if she didn't give up the phone number of a client.

The hooker couldn't provide visual evidence of the slapping incident, but after Riordan had pumped her client for information, the client backed the hooker's claim. He told Internal Affairs that Riordan must have done some terrible things to her because she was ordinarily a very discreet prostitute.

Woodward remembered having a laugh with Riordan after hearing the client's glowing review of the prostitute's character. Hooks didn't see the humor. He threw Riordan under the proverbial bus, calling him a "loose cannon" capable of anything. The department wound up reaching "an understanding" with the woman, then suspended Riordan for three days without pay.

"Captain?"

"Yeah. What's up, Woodward?"

"I'm downtown. I just looked at surveillance from the Nugget showing Dan Riordan walking through the casino with our murder victim Monday around noon."

"Wait. What?" the captain interrupted. "Monday? Why?"

"Nothing good," said Woodward. "I'm on my way to Binion's, where the security chief has more video cued. I think you should locate Riordan and detain him."

"All right," said Hooks. "Let me know what you see at Binion's."

Arnie Bates greeted Woodward and Green at the entrance to the security office.

"I've got it ready for you," said Bates.

"Let it roll," said Woodward.

The video showed Riordan walking with Amber through the casino to the kitchen entrance. Later, Woodward watched as Amber handed the camcorder to Riordan. A few seconds later, Amber could be seen on her cell phone. When the call was complete, she reached down her blouse and pulled out an object.

"Can you zoom in on that?" Woodward asked.

Bates punched a couple of buttons on his console.

"It's a cassette," said Woodward. "From the camcorder, probably."

He watched Amber hand the cassette to Riordan. He watched Riordan point a finger at her before walking out of Binion's café.

"Is that it?" asked Woodward.

"That's it," said Bates.

"What now?" Green asked.

"Make copies of your stuff. I'll send someone to pick it up tomorrow. Is that enough time?" Woodward asked.

"Plenty," said Bates.

Chapter 58

CHASE DECIDED TO follow up on Gail's suspicions. He called Kimball's boss.

"This is Capn' Krumrie. What can I do for you?"

"It's Duncan Chase at the prosecutor's office. I'm going over the Cheryl Fenner case files and I have a question for you," said Chase.

"That's Detective Kimball's case. Have you spoken to him?"

"I have. I want to speak with you," said Chase.

"Okay, shoot," said Krumrie.

"I'd like to know if you've noticed anything unusual or suspicious about the way the case has been investigated."

"Why? Have you?" Krumrie answered.

"I asked you first," said Chase.

"Well, that's a pretty broad question," said Krumrie. "It covers more than six years. Be more specific."

If Chase were conducting a loyalty check, then Krumrie had passed. He definitely had Kimball's back.

"Last November, a woman named Peggy Page called the Sheriff's department and reported something she overheard while standing outside Rick Fenner's house. To her, it sounded like a man said he knew that Cheryl Fenner had been shot and that she was dead. This was several months before the remains were discovered, as you know. I'm wondering if you could try to find a record of that call, or a report someone took—anything in writing."

"You've asked Kimball about this?" asked Krumrie.

"He said he never heard of it," said Chase.

"You don't believe him? Krumrie asked.

"I'm not saying that," Chase said.

"What are you saying?" asked Krumrie.

"I need to find out whether I've got a lying witness, a lying cop or a failure in the administrative process—all of which could be exploited by a sharp defense attorney, should this case ever reach that point," said Chase.

"Well, I don't know about your witness, but I know about the cop," said Krumrie in an irritated tone.

"Will you check it out?" asked Chase.

"I'd be happy to," said Krumrie. "Anything else?"

"No, thanks," said Chase. "Let me know as soon as possible."

"Of course," said Krumrie.

Hooks wasn't happy. He called Woodward into his office and told him to close the door.

"Where the hell is he?" Hooks demanded.

"You don't have him?" Woodward was stunned.

"He didn't show up here, so I sent some people to his apartment. There isn't much left there," said Hooks. "It goes without saying that if you tipped him, I'll have your shield and your ass."

"I wouldn't do that," said Woodward. "He's at least a kidnapper and most likely a murderer. He needs to be caught."

"We'll get the son-of-a-bitch," said Hooks.

Woodward's phone rang as he walked out of the office. It was Jane Bell, a young detective Hooks had assigned to replace Riordan on the David murder investigation. As he answered, he saw Bell walking toward him.

"Hello? Oh. Hello, Bell."

Bell shoved her phone into the back pocket of her blue jeans.

"I've got Amber David's phone records. That call she made on the Binion's video? It was to her mother."

"Her mother? Why would she be calling her mother with Riordan sitting there?"

"Why speculate? Let's ask mom," said Bell.

"I like it. You want to do the honors?" asked Woodward.

They called Jean Swanson together from the conference room.

"All I know is a guy named Lawrence, his last name was Lawrence, told me he was working on the Cheryl Fenner case and wanted to ask me a couple of questions," she said.

"Did he show you a badge?" asked Woodward.

"Wayne County Sheriff's Department," said Swanson.

"So, when you spoke with Amber, did she seem under duress at all?" asked Bell.

"Not really," said Swanson. "She asked if R.D. was all right. I told her he was fine. I mentioned that the investigator was there and that he just wanted to ask a few questions. That's about it."

"Would you recognize the investigator if you saw him again?" asked Woodward.

"I'm sure I would," said Swanson.

"Could you give us a description, please?" asked Bell.

"Certainly," said Swanson. "He was in his forties. Bald. Blue eyes. Broad shoulders. Maybe two hundred twenty-five pounds. He had pointy ears, too."

Bell and Woodward looked at each other in shock, but for different reasons. Bell thought she'd heard a detailed description of Detective Dan Riordan of the Las Vegas Police Department. Woodward was certain the man in Swanson's house that day was Riordan's twin brother, Al.

Woodward held his index finger to his lips. He didn't want his new partner to give Swanson more information than she needed.

"I'll text you our cell phone numbers. If you think of anything else that might help, please give one of us a call," said Woodward.

"I will," said Swanson.

"And if you hear from Lawrence again, call right away."

Bell was perplexed. "She described Riordan. But that's impossible."

Woodward smiled. "She described Riordan's twin brother."

"He has a twin?"

"Identical. And a former Mississippi State Trooper who'd be quite capable of posing as a detective."

"What the hell were they up to?" asked Bell.

"That's what we have to find out," said Woodward.

After Bell went back to her computer, Woodward went back to see Hooks.

"I think I should take a trip to Ohio," he said.

"What's in Ohio?" asked the Captain.

"Riordan's twin brother. I think he was in it up to his ears," said Woodward.

"Go tomorrow then," said Hooks.

Chapter 59

DAN RIORDAN CHECKED the rearview mirror. Nothing but dust had followed his Escalade to the meeting point in the desert near Barstow. He was worried that he might have missed a call, but removing the battery from his cell phone before leaving Las Vegas was a necessary precaution. He knew it would be a few hours at most before his hasty departure was discovered.

He was early. The orange sun wouldn't melt into the horizon for an hour. He turned toward an acre of mangled cars and pickups. *Action Salvage.* A gray, 1987 Camaro and a new-looking tow truck were parked side by side in front of a wooden shack. Riordan parked next to the Camaro and walked toward the shack. The door opened before he reached it.

"Riordan. Long time no see." Buddy Grabowski shook his hand. "Come on in."

"The plane should be here in half an hour," Riordan said, skipping pleasantries and settling into a leather recliner to the right of door.

"Want a beer?" Grabowski asked, opening a waist-high refrigerator that held nothing but Budweiser long necks.

"Absolutely," said Riordan. "Thanks."

Grabowski was forty-two. He stood six feet tall and weighed more than two hundred fifty pounds. A good deal of his weight was concentrated in his belly, the natural result of extreme beer and snack food consumption over decades. He wore a black Route 66 T-shirt and tan cargo shorts.

They'd met two years earlier when Riordan was investigating a series of auto thefts on the Vegas Strip. Grabowski's cousin was one of the ring leaders.

He offered Grabowski a piece of the action to look the other way while he and his partners conducted their business at the salvage yard. When Riordan and Woodward uncovered the operation, they gave Grabowski a choice: Go to jail, or testify against the others. The detectives had never seen a weasel turn into a rat so quickly.

"Got a letter from my cousin yesterday," said Grabowski.

"Yeah?"

"Read the first line," he said, handing it to Riordan.

"'Dear Dipshit,'" Riordan smiled. "'You're dead in five years, forty-seven days and six hours.' How does he know exactly when he'll get out on parole?"

"Good question. But I ain't scared." Grabowski swung open a metal cabinet.

Riordan counted three assault rifles, half a dozen hand guns and two shotguns. "Looks like you're ready for him," he laughed, taking a long drink.

"Damn straight," said Grabowski.

They both looked toward the window as they heard a roaring sound. Lights flashed in the dirty glass as they stood up and walked outside. The Lear Jet landed behind the junkyard with a few jumps and bumps as it shredded prickly pear and cholla cactus, shooting debris back at the cabin.

"Ah! God damn!" Grabowski shouted. He reached down and pulled a cactus needle from his calf. He wiped a bead of blood from the wound with his middle finger and pointed it at the plane. "Fucker!" he shouted.

Riordan opened the rear hatch of the Escalade and pulled out a suitcase and two duffel bags, handing one to the still-cursing Grabowski.

"Let's go," he said.

They walked toward the plane as it rolled to a stop about a quarter mile into the desert.

"Got the keys?" asked Grabowski.

"Here," said Riordan, tossing them to Grabowski's free hand. "Pink slip's in the glove box."

Grabowski caught the keys and stuffed them into his front right pocket. The Escalade was his payment for facilitating the getaway.

The plane turned and taxied toward them. When it stopped again, an air stair lowered and a man wearing blue jeans, a plain white T-shirt and a straw cowboy hat walked down it. Riordan noticed that the man wore a shoulder holster that held what appeared to be a .38 caliber revolver.

"Mr. Riordan? We'll be ready for you to board in a quick little minute," said the cowboy, with a considerable southern twang. "I'll get those bags."

The cowboy grabbed the suitcase with one hand and the two duffels with the other. He walked up the stairs and disappeared for about ten seconds. When he reappeared, he stood on the top step long enough for a glance in all directions. Then he started down again, quickly.

Riordan's eyes fixed on the cowboy's shoulder holster. It was empty. It took three seconds for the cowboy to reach the desert floor. In that time, Riordan's brain processed the sight of the empty holster; made his eyes spot the .38 in the cowboy's right hand; sensed danger; told him to reach for his own gun; and to scream as the cowboy raised his arm and pointed the gun at his head.

Grabowski froze, praying the cowboy's assignment had ended when Riordan hit the ground. Another flash from the .38 was the last thing Grabowski saw. He never heard the shot that killed him. The cowboy emptied their pockets, stuffing their cash, wallets and keys into his own. He lifted Riordan's body to his shoulders and carried him up the stairs. He did the same with Grabowski's body. He brought down a push broom and a bucket of water and made all signs of foul play disappear. The desert wind would soon take care of the footprints and the tracks made by landing gear. He walked to the Escalade and started it. He drove it behind a pile of wrecked cars and got out. He wiped the steering wheel and the door handle with a cloth.

The pilot had never shut down the Lear's engines. In a quick little minute, the cowboy and the jet were gone.

Chapter 60

Saturday, April 24

THE WEATHER FORECAST for Northeast Ohio included a seventy percent chance of severe thunderstorms. Mike awoke from a nightmare about Peggy. She was walking on the treadmill in their basement and screaming his name. He was standing right next to her, but she couldn't see or hear him. No matter what he did or said, he couldn't get her attention. She just kept screaming his name.

"Mike? Mike?" The voice came from the bathroom. It wasn't Peggy's voice. Mike rolled out of bed. He could hear the shower running.

"Yeah. Hey. Good morning," he said, opening the door. Gail stood in the walk-in shower with her back to him. Water streamed through her blonde hair, down her narrow back, round bottom and long, muscular legs.

"I don't see any shampoo," she called.

"Sorry," said Mike, grabbing a plastic bottle of Suave from the shelf above the towel rack. He pulled open the glass door and touched her right hand with the bottle. She grabbed it without turning.

"Ah! The good stuff!" she laughed.

"Dollar store," said Mike, taking a longer look at her body before closing the door. He felt uncomfortable that he was so comfortable with Gail after such a short time. Was it guilt? He decided it wasn't. He decided he just wasn't used to being in love.

"I'll make some breakfast," said Mike. "Eggs over easy?"

"I'll eat whatever you make," she said, rubbing shampoo into her hair and turning to give him a frontal view.

And I'll do whatever you say, he thought, turning to leave and dragging his eyes behind him.

The bell rang. Cragmere dismissed her third-period class, reminding her students that their essays on responsible citizenship were due next Tuesday. She closed the door and dialed her son-in-law.

"Where the hell have you been? I've been calling for two days!"

"Lying low," said Al Riordan. "I think the cops know it was me at Jean Swanson's house."

"How?" asked Cragmere

"They're not stupid. One phone call and they know there's no Mark Lawrence at the Wayne County Sheriff's Department."

"It doesn't matter. You're leaving tomorrow morning. Seven sharp. You'll meet the jet at Akron-Canton. I'll send a car to pick you up at six," she said.

"Did Dan get there all right?"

"You'll be with him by supper time," she said.

Woodward pulled his suitcase from the conveyor and rolled it outside.

"Detective? I'm Arch Kimball."

"Yeah. Glenn Woodward," he said, shaking Kimball's hand. "Good to meet you."

They drove straight from Cleveland International to Parma. In less than fifteen minutes, Jean Swanson was pouring coffee for them at her kitchen table.

"Is this the man who called himself Mark Lawrence?" Kimball asked, handing her a photo of Al Riordan.

"That's him," said Swanson, sipping her coffee from a Disney World mug.

"His real name is Riordan. Al Riordan," said Woodward. "While he was here with you, his twin brother was with your daughter in Las Vegas. They were after a video tape that she had taken from Rick Fenner right before she moved out there."

"They killed her for it?" Swanson asked, her eyes welling with tears.

"They killed her because she knew what was on it," said Kimball.

Swanson dabbed her eyes with a tissue. "Doesn't Fenner know?"

Kimball shook his head. "I'm sure he does. But he's got a lawyer. He's not talking."

The detectives promised to keep in touch. Armed with a positive I.D., they had enough to arrest Riordan for impersonating a police officer at the very least.

"What's next?" asked Woodward.

"Let's get you settled. You're at the Fairfield Inn, about three miles from the office. We'll eat. I'll do the paperwork. We'll pick up Riordan tomorrow," said Kimball.

"Yeah. On his way to church," Woodward joked. His phone rang as they drove away. "Woodward," he answered. He listened for about thirty seconds. "Positive I.D? Really? Jesus. Yeah. We're picking up his brother in the morning. Okay. I'll let you know."

"What was that?" asked Kimball.

"Hikers found my partner Dan Riordan's body in the mountains by Lake Mead. In a bag."

"C.O.D?" Kimball asked.

"Gunshot wound to the head," said Woodward.

"One case closed. Another case open," said Kimball.

"Yeah," said Woodward.

Mike heard a loud rumble of thunder and walked to the front window. Rain was blowing hard against the glass, slapping it. "Look at this, Gail!" he called.

Gail had just finished loading the dishwasher. She hurried from the kitchen.

"Oh my God!" she screamed. Just as she reached the window, the basketball hoop from the driveway across the street—the stand, the pole, the backboard and rim—flew end over end into Mike's front yard, bouncing once and hitting the concrete porch with a loud clank.

"Jesus! Let's get to the basement!" Mike yelled, grabbing her hand and pulling her to the door. As they hurried down the wooden steps, they heard a loud, crashing noise. The whole house shook.

"A tree just hit us, I think," said Mike, shouting over the thunder.

272

"Or a bus," said Gail, nervously.

They heard a roar—like a train. The house shook again.

They tried the television near the treadmill. Nothing. Debris peppered the basement windows. They heard three loud bangs, like shotgun blasts.

"Wires?" Mike supposed.

"Hope we're not on fire," said Gail.

"I just want it to blow by," said Mike.

"Yeah."

Fifty-two miles south and eleven miles east, the swath of severe storms aimed itself at a small town trying desperately to hide behind its less-than-knee-high corn fields. Pluto's only hope was that Fate would change its fickle mind in a big hurry.

Cragmere's cat cowered in the corner of the laundry room. Cragmere stared at the sky and smiled.

"That's a big storm coming, Cordelia Cragmere," she said.

It was Cragmere's custom to use the cat's full name. She liked the sound of it. Alliteration had been one of Shakespeare's greatest tools, she would tell her students. Naming her cat after King Lear's ill-fated daughter seemed "purr-fect," she would tell them with a smile, hoping they'd warm to her sense of humor. The Calico lifted her nose and sniffed. Its ears pricked and twitched.

"Big storm," said Cragmere. "Big storm."

Mike and Gail held hands as they ascended the basement stairs. They hadn't heard a sound in more than five minutes. Whatever it was—severe thunderstorm or tornado—had moved on. It was time to check the damage.

Mike pushed open the door leading to the kitchen. He felt a breeze as he stepped onto the white tile floor. Then, he felt something strike the side of his face—not hard enough to knock him down.

"Shit!" he yelled, grabbing the inch-thick branch and holding it so they could make it through the doorway.

"Oh, my God!" said Gail.

A maple tree had crashed through the wall where the kitchen sink and dishwasher had been. Two squirrels chased each other from the living room to the tree trunk. They scurried across it, leaping through the open space and onto the roof of a 1985 Cadillac before disappearing from sight.

"Oh my God!" said Mike.

"Whose car is that?" asked Gail.

"Mine now," Mike joked. "Let's go."

He led the way to the front door. It was there, but it was lying flat in the entry way, as if a SWAT team had paid a visit with a battering ram. A black lamppost protruded from the dining room window, the top of it extending across the wooden porch swing like a crude reading light. They stepped onto the porch, speechless. Their eyes scanned the yard and the block. Mike counted uprooted trees—maple, oak, cedar and fir. His mind stopped the count at seventeen, but there were more, many more.

"Look at the trees," he said, calmly. "Look at the friggin' trees."

"I know," said Gail, awestruck. "And the cars. Just look at the cars!"

Mike's Buick seemed untouched by the storm, but at least a dozen vehicles littered front yards and tree lawns in a variety of unnatural positions. A red Jeep Wrangler lay on its top in the boxwoods at the front of the house across the street. A silver Toyota pickup was parked on its side by Mike's mailbox.

"There's mine!" Gail screamed, as they stepped across limbs and telephone wires intertwined on the lawn. Gail's Mercedes was a hundred feet away, standing on its back end like a begging dog.

"How could that happen?" she asked.

"Tornado," said Mike. "The real thing."

They stood in silence for nearly a minute. The whole world had changed. All the things that meant something in their lives had dissolved into a frozen moment. What they wanted; what they needed; what they struggled to hold; what they fought to be free of—none of it mattered measured against simple survival.

"I thought we were goners," Mike finally said, grabbing her hand.

"Yeah. Me, too," said Gail. "And guess what? I was all right with it."

"What?"

"I was thinking it would have been okay to die next to you," she said.

Mike squeezed her hand. "I thought the same thing."

Pluto's severe weather warning system consisted of a fire truck rolling slowly through town, its wailing siren intermittently interrupted by an advisory from a bullhorn.

"Plutonians, take cover! Plutonians, take cover! A tornado has already struck parts of Northeast Ohio, causing heavy damage and possible loss of life. The storm is headed this way and will arrive within the half-hour. Take cover immediately! Repeat: Take cover immediately!"

Cragmere watched from a basement window as the truck continued east on Main Street. The sound of the siren had melted into distant thunder by the time she turned to see Cordelia in full stride. The cat skidded to a stop on the tile floor in the bathroom, then walked the final few steps to the space behind the toilet and curled into a tight ball.

A few miles away, Rick Fenner secured the barn door after parking Bree's truck between the batting practice hay bales and the empty horse stall that served as a storage area. He had insisted that Bree hurry home after hearing news reports about a tornado touching down to the northwest. Rain started in drips as he walked toward the house. By the time he reached the side porch, it was pouring.

"Bree! I put your truck in the barn!" Rick called to his daughter.

"Thanks, dad!" Bree called back from her bedroom. "It's starting to pour outside!"

Rick opened the door halfway. "I know. That storm is heading our way for sure. I'll let you know if we need to run to the basement."

Bree smiled. Her father had always been a bad weather hypochondriac. She remembered many hours spent huddled in the basement, listening to Rick's paranoid histrionics. Cheryl would beg him not speak of impending doom, but he would always persist.

When the storms passed without causing damage—as they always did—Rick would say something like, "Better safe than sorry." Then he'd make a joke about how God couldn't find Pluto on the map. Cheryl was never amused. Her reaction was consistent. She'd hold a twenty-four-hour grudge that included the "silent treatment" and a kitchen strike.

Despite her father's insensitivity, Bree would always take his side, lobbying for his early release from the proverbial dog house. Her pleadings were incredibly ineffective. Cheryl wasn't much for compromise—about anything.

Bree's memories lasted just long enough to fill the space between her father's past odd behavior and his present odd behavior.

"Bree! Let's go! Basement! Now!" Rick hollered.

Bree jumped off her bed and opened the door. Rick was already walking quickly toward the kitchen. "Let's go!" he shouted, without turning.

"Okay! Okay!" his dutiful daughter yelled. "I'm Coming!"

The fire engine shook. Eighteen tons of pumper had always felt like a fortress to Charlie Fordyce. He'd been driving pumpers or much heavier ladder trucks for forty years, but never feared that one would tip over. He jammed on the brakes and jumped to the pavement just as a huge oak limb crashed through the windshield. He ran clear of the truck, thinking himself lucky, but the same fierce wind that had snapped and hurled the limb was now lifting him like he'd been kidnapped by a magic carpet.

There was actually time to think as he sailed toward the giant vanilla ice cream cone on the Dairy Freeze sign—five full seconds. So, he thought about his wife, his two grown daughters, his four grandchildren and his life of service as a firefighter—twenty-five years in Canton and twenty more as a volunteer in Pluto. He thought of those things as he flew screaming toward the sign that was illuminated by constant flashes of lightning.

He barely felt the impact.

Rick and Bree stopped discussing the Invaders' batting order when they felt the house shake. They heard low squealing noises—first a few, then a symphony.

"Nails!" Rick had to shout to be heard from two feet away.

"The house is coming apart!" Bree shouted back.

The next thirty seconds were the definition of fear. Rick grabbed two pillows and pulled his daughter to the floor.

"Stay against the wall and cover your head!" He screamed.

Bree closed her eyes and held the pillow tight to her head, the right side of her face buried in the plush carpet, the tip of her nose touching the wall. Rick covered her with his body and held his pillow tight to the left side of his face.

The house shook again. They felt a rush of wet, cold air. They heard wood snapping and glass shattering. They heard whizzing sounds—hundreds of small objects propelled like bullets by a killer tornado. Bree couldn't scream. She could barely breathe.

Cragmere couldn't coax Cordelia from behind the toilet. There had been a couple of loud thuds as the storm passed, and she was anxious to check for damage. The cat didn't care. The cat was a cat.

"Very well. I'll go it alone," Cragmere called as she ascended the stairs.

She opened the front door and saw two sixty-foot oak trees lying side by side a few feet from the porch. They had fallen from opposite ends of the property. Cragmere smiled.

"Not possible," she smirked, staring at the giant roots and breathing the aroma of fresh soil.

If Leticia Cragmere loved anything in life, it was the randomness of it. She would laugh about being stung by a bee, rear-ended in traffic or drenched in a sudden downpour. "Who wants a scripted life?" she would ask her students whenever some unexpected tragedy became the topic of classroom discussion. "Random good things; random bad things—they're what assures us this isn't some John Ford movie we're starring in," she'd say. "For better or worse, they make life worth living."

She stepped over or around at least a dozen downed limbs on the way to the other end of the property. "At times like these, it does no good to wonder why your number wasn't called," she said aloud.

The back of the house had stopped all kinds of debris. There were men's shirts and pants stuck to the second-story windows. There were toys and tools and books and blankets lining the base of the facade like inventory at a yard sale. It seemed there was at least one of everything that might be part of any household, including a furnace and a kitchen sink.

Bree hadn't moved or made a noise in more than two minutes. It seemed like two hours. She slowly opened her eyes and turned her face. The pillow fell to the floor, and her father's hand fell with it.

"I think it's over," she said. She tried to stand, but her father's weight kept her pinned to the carpet. "Dad? It's over," Bree repeated, twisting a little to look at him. Rick didn't respond. She twisted a little more. Then she pried herself free.

"Dad?"

Rick's mouth and eyes were open. He did not respond.

"Dad!" she shouted, shaking him with a hand on each shoulder. "Dad!" she screamed. Then she saw it—the metallic green, blood-stained bowling ball. It sat a just a few feet away. She touched the blood. It was wet. She grabbed his shoulders again, turning him onto his stomach. The right side of his head was covered in blood. He was dead.

"Oh God! Oh God!" she screamed. "Help! Somebody help!"

Cragmere's cell phone rang. She listened for about fifteen seconds. "I understand. Thanks for the information," she said. She tapped the disconnect button. Then, she dialed her son-in-law.

"Change of plan," she said before he could say 'hello.'

"I assume the tornado missed you," said Al Riordan.

Cragmere ignored the small talk. "You're leaving tonight," she said. "A car will pick you up in an hour."

"What's the hurry?" Riordan asked.

"Can't risk the storm damage delaying flights," she said.

"All right," said Riordan. "I'll be ready."

Cragmere hung up without saying 'goodbye.' She walked into the house and called Cordelia. The cat was still cowering in the basement.

Chapter 61

ARCH KIMBALL DROVE around a fallen tree and pulled into the parking lot of the Fairfield Inn. His colleague from Las Vegas was waiting outside.

"Helluva storm!" said Woodward, stepping into Kimball's unmarked county sedan.

"Yeah. Trees down everywhere," said Kimball. "And the radio says some houses were leveled."

"Anybody killed?" asked Woodward.

"Probably," said Kimball. "It's hard to believe there wouldn't be."

"Any idea who tipped you off about Riordan skipping town?" Woodward asked.

Kimball turned onto northbound I-77. It was a twenty-minute trip to Riordan's apartment in Akron. "Nope. Anonymous call to dispatch. A woman. All she said was, 'Tell Kimball that Riordan's leaving the country tonight.'"

"Airport covered?" asked Woodward.

"We're all over Akron-Canton and Hopkins," said Kimball. He tries to fly—he's caught."

"Maybe they're still shut down from the storm," said Woodward.

"We'll know in a bit," said Kimball.

Riordan saw headlights. He grabbed his suitcase and computer bag and set them near the door. Then he turned off the TV and walked into the bathroom to empty his bladder for the flight to Buenos Aires. He heard a knock. He zipped his fly and walked toward the door.

"Yeah. I'm coming," he called. He opened the door and reached down with his left hand to pull out the handle on the suitcase. A man in a cowboy hat stood in front of him.

"Evnin' Mr. Riordan," said the man.

"Here. You take the big one," said Riordan, offering the handle.

"Change of plan," said the cowboy, extending his left leg and kicking Riordan in the chest with enough force to send him tumbling into the living room. Riordan landed with a groan, his back to the cowboy, who had pulled a knife from his jacket pocket. "Time to join your brother," said the assassin.

He knelt and grabbed for the ex-cop's hair to expose his neck for the kill.

Bang!

The cowboy dropped the knife and fell back. A small hole between his eyes oozed blood. Riordan shook off the blow to his chest and rubbed his forehead, which had struck the coffee table when he fell. He pocketed the .25 caliber pistol that was in his right hand when he answered the door. He dragged the cowboy's body into the bathroom. He went back to get the straw hat and tossed it into the tub. Then, he turned the lock on the inside of the knob and pulled the door shut.

"I'll be long gone by the time you get ripe," he said aloud. He paused for a moment when he realized that the cowboy had killed his brother. The confession confirmed what he suspected when he hadn't heard from his twin in nearly two days. The brothers had spoken at least once every day of their lives. Nothing but Dan's demise would have kept him from communicating.

Al covered the blood stain with a newspaper, gathered his bags and locked the door behind him. The cowboy's limousine still purred in the parking lot. Al got in and drove. Destination: To be determined.

Kimball merged onto Route 8 near the University of Akron campus and took the first exit. "A few blocks and we're there," he said.

"It doesn't look like the storm came this way," said Woodward.

"No. No tree limbs," said Kimball.

"What's the plan if he doesn't answer the door," Woodward asked.

"The manager's on board. She'll let us in," Kimball said, waiting three seconds at a stop sign. He drove slowly, even for the residential neighborhood, stopping at every stop sign just long enough to annoy his passenger. Finally, he pulled into the parking lot of the two-story, eight-unit apartment building. "B-3," he said, slowing to a stop. Woodward had already jumped out and was waiting impatiently on the tree lawn.

They took the elevator to the second floor. Woodward found Riordan's door first. He looked at Kimball, who nodded. Woodward knocked four times. No answer. He knocked again and hollered, "Al Riordan! Police!" No response.

Kimball called the manager. "We need to get in," he said. "Yes. Right now. Thank you."

Riordan drove north on I-77 to the Ohio Turnpike. He set the cruise control at 75 m.p.h. after choosing the westbound route toward Toledo. From there it would be a short trip to Detroit and the bridge into Windsor, Ontario. *I can disappear in Canada*, he thought. He reached for his computer bag on the passenger seat. He unzipped it and felt for the manila envelope he'd stuffed with $20,000 cash for his escape to South America. It was there. He smiled. *Loose ends don't always get tied.*

The manager stepped back after opening the door. Kimball walked inside slowly, his service revolver drawn and aimed into the living room. Woodward followed, his weapon ready as well. He stepped on the newspaper that covered the blood stain, but didn't look down. There were no signs of life.

"Bedroom's clear," Kimball announced.

"Bathroom?" Woodward asked, nodding at the closed door.

They stood on either side of it as Kimball reached for the knob and turned it. Locked.

"Come on out, Riordan!" Kimball yelled.

"Don't make it worse, Riordan!" Woodward added. No response.

"Here we go," said Kimball, raising his right leg. He kicked the door just below the knob. It popped open.

"Jesus!" said Woodward.

Kimball crouched over the cowboy's body. "One in the forehead. Neat. Very neat," he said.

"Except it's not Al Riordan," said Woodward.

"Yeah," said Kimball, checking his pockets for identification. "So, who is he?"

Gail's phone rang. "Hello? Bree? Bree, slow down," she said. "Bree, tell me what happened." She listened for a few seconds and the color left her face. "Are you sure? Did you call 9-1-1? Of course. Of course. All right. We're heading your way."

Mike put some pressure on the gas pedal. "What happened?"

"Rick Fenner is dead," Gail said blankly.

"Oh my God! In the storm?" Mike asked.

"Yeah. They were in the basement. He was protecting Bree—lying on top of her—as the tornado hit," said Gail.

"God. The first decent thing the man ever did got him killed," said Mike.

"Karma's a bitch," said Gail.

Riordan had changed his mind about Canada by the time he reached Toledo. *Of course, they'll have the border covered.* He merged onto U.S. 23 and headed for Ann Arbor. Plan "B" became hiding out somewhere along Lake Michigan—maybe Silver Lake or Hart or Pentwater. Summer was approaching. Tourists raise no suspicion in tourist towns. *That's the smart thing to do.*

The cowboy was bagged as a "John Doe" and sent to the morgue. Woodward found two residents who saw a man wearing a cowboy hat exit a stretch limo and walk into Riordan's building. Neither remembered the license plate number.

"Now what?" asked Woodward.

"We wait," said Kimball. "We've got the bases covered—the airports, the borders. I've got every law enforcement agency within five hundred miles looking for limos now. He'll turn up. You could head home in the morning if you want."

That plan appealed to the cop from Vegas, who'd had more than his fill of nasty Midwest weather during his only day in Ohio. "I was thinking the same thing," Woodward said.

Chapter 62

BREE SAT ON the tailgate of her pickup. Her face was blank. She closed her eyes for a few seconds. She re-opened them, hoping the scene would revert to what it was before the storm—but nothing changed. Mike slowed the Buick to a crawl as he maneuvered it around tree limbs, two-by-fours, shingles and other debris. Bree's truck appeared to be unscathed. Illuminated by the lights from three sheriff's cars and a fire engine, it sat in a pile of rubble that used to be the garage. Bree's black batting tee stood in the same place it had always stood, now surrounded by splintered wood and hay ripped from the bales.

Bree stared at the medical examiner's van. It was parked on one of the few portions of pavement not covered by pieces of the house or by tree limbs. She had watched two men shove her father's body into the back of it just a few minutes earlier.

Her eyes moved to the exposed foundation of her home, now a ruin. Her whole life was unrecognizable.

Mike reached Bree first and hugged her without speaking. "Bree, I'm so sorry," he said.

"Thank you," she replied.

"Bree, sweetie. I don't know what to say," Gail began. "Tell us what we can do."

"My dad. He told me something when the tornado was ripping the house apart," she said.

Gail squeezed her hand. "What did he tell you, Bree? What did he tell you?"

"He told me he loved me. Then, he told me that Morgan's grandfather has a friend who drives a white van. He's a meat distributor," she said, wiping a tear from her cheek. "He said Mr. Miller can't be trusted. Morgan either."

"Did he say why?" Gail asked.

"No. No. He just blurted it out while all the crap was flying around. I was too scared to really pay attention. The next thing I knew, he was…" She didn't finish the sentence.

Gail put her arm around Bree. Then, she looked at Mike.

"Morgan?" she asked, as if her ears had deceived her.

"No," said Mike, shaking his head. "No. No. That doesn't make sense. Not Morgan."

"Actually, it makes perfect sense," said Gail.

Bree jumped off the tailgate. "Morgan said something to me once. She said anybody who crosses her Aunt Leti might not live to regret it. Maybe she didn't have a choice."

"There's one way to find out," said Gail.

Riordan took the I-96 fork toward Lansing. He switched on the wipers as drops gathered on the windshield. He glanced at the dashboard. The low fuel light was flashing. He maneuvered the limo to the right lane and took the first exit. He veered right at the end of the ramp, drove about a quarter mile and turned into a truck stop. He parked at pump number six, locked the limo and walked toward the building. He kept his eyes moving, but there were too many people to scrutinize them all.

He walked into the men's room. He could see that two of the urinals were occupied. He turned and watched two men enter—one white, one black. The black man was overweight and in his thirties. He wore an orange Cleveland Browns sweatshirt and blue jeans. The white man was tall and thin. He appeared to be at least sixty, but the bucket hat that matched his long, tan raincoat concealed most of his face. Riordan kept an eye on the white man until he disappeared into a stall. Then, he washed his hands, walked to the front counter and handed the clerk $50.

"Pump six, please," he said.

"Fifty on six," said the clerk. "You're all set."

Riordan hurried back to the limo and started pumping gas. He kept his eyes moving, watching every car and truck that pulled into the lot. More than three hours had passed since Cragmere's hitman had come to call. Surely somebody was on his trail by now. Both Cragmere *and* the cops? Probably.

A black BMW rolled up to pump number five, stopping a few feet from the limo's rear bumper. The engine stopped, but the headlights stayed on. Riordan squinted. He couldn't see the driver. He kept staring and squinting, expecting someone to emerge. He glanced at the pump. Eleven gallons—just over half full. His eyes turned back to the BMW. The headlights went out. Still no driver. Through the tinted windshield, he saw movement, but no form. The glare from the flood lights on the roof above the pumps didn't help. He noticed the car had no license plate. He looked at the pump. Fifteen gallons. *Slowest damn pump in the world,* he thought. He turned back to the BMW. Still no driver. He thought about walking to the door and tapping on the window. *Everything all right?* He would ask.

Then he felt pain—sharp pain, excruciating pain—in the right side of his neck and down his spine. He fell to his knees. His brain never processed the event. His face hit the cold concrete. He was dead. The pump clicked. The limo's tank was finally full. The BMW's headlights stayed off when its engine started. A man wearing a long, tan raincoat and matching bucket hat entered the sedan through the front passenger door just before it sped from the lot into the darkness.

Gail and Mike approached Morgan's front door together. Mike knocked. No answer. Gail peeked through the kitchen window. No sign of life.

"The pub?" Mike asked.

"Let's go," said Gail.

They arrived five minutes later to learn that Miller's Pub had been turned into a staging area for emergency services personnel and the media. Red Cross volunteers were interviewing locals whose homes had been damaged by the tornado. The pub's kitchen was churning out soup and sandwiches. Temporary lighting in the parking lot made it look more like a carnival midway than a restaurant.

Gail and Mike wandered through the maze of people for the next half hour, but didn't find Morgan or anyone who'd seen her. They didn't find Morgan's grandfather, either.

"No. Not since early this afternoon," said Sandi Stahl, the pub's business manager. "I hope they're all right."

"I'm sure they are," said Gail.

Kimball's phone rang while he was waiting in the drive thru lane at Arby's.

"Where? Any witnesses? What exit? All right. I'm on my way." He looked at his recent calls and found Woodward's number. He'd dropped him back at the Fairfield Inn half an hour before.

"Woodward? It's Kimball."

"Yeah. I just booked my return flight for 11 a.m."

"You might want to un-book it," said Kimball.

"Why? What happened?"

"They just found our guy."

"Where?" asked Woodward.

"Around Brighton, Michigan. Somebody stabbed him while he was gassing up the limo at a truck stop," said Kimball.

"Get the hell out of here!" said Woodward. "Was it a robbery? Did they catch the guy?"

"The video shows a tall figure in a raincoat and hat approaching Riordan from behind and sticking a knife in his neck. Riordan never saw it coming. Then, the killer jumped into a BMW that was parked at the next pump."

"Plate number?" Asked Woodward.

"They're working on it," said Kimball. "Nothing so far."

"That's just too strange," said Woodward.

Cragmere's brown eyes brightened. "That's good news. That's *very* good news. Keep me informed," she said, setting her phone on the kitchen table. She sipped black tea from a china cup and stared at Cordelia. The cat was perched on the window sill with her eyes half closed. "That tornado interrupted your nap. Poor kitty."

Sunday, April 25

Investigators from the Michigan State Police and the Livingston County Sheriff's Department had closed Crown Brothers truck stop minutes after Al Riordan was murdered. Still, the scene had been compromised by well-meaning witnesses and others who had rushed to his aid. They fought to keep him breathing with CPR until paramedics arrived. In doing so, they likely contaminated any evidence the killer left behind, though there couldn't have been much. No weapon was found. Riordan didn't struggle; he didn't even see his attacker. The driver of the BMW never left that vehicle, which had no front plate. The rear plate had been altered in such a way that it couldn't be read. One witness said it looked like a strip of black tape was covering the numbers.

A BMW matching the getaway car's description was stopped near Grand Rapids about two hours later, but the occupant had an alibi and was not detained. Two more black BMW's were pulled over on U.S. 23 South. One was near Ann Arbor, one near Sylvania. Same result. Were there two crews involved? Had they switched vehicles?

Woodward crouched over the body. The medical examiner showed him the wound in the right side of Riordan's neck, surmising that the killer was a professional.

"Carotid Artery," said the M.E. "It carries oxygenated blood to the brain. He probably used a combat knife—something big. We could match it to a particular model if it came to that."

Woodward thanked him and walked about twenty yards to the front of the building, where Kimball stood with a group of cops from the local agencies.

"Well, I've been briefed," said Kimball. "Looks like a perfect crime in a crowded place with working surveillance cameras."

"I thought there was no such thing as a perfect crime," said Woodward. "What about the limo?"

"Reported stolen in Barberton two weeks ago," said Kimball. "Belonged to a one-man, one-car business. The guy said it was boosted from his driveway overnight."

"So that's a dead end," said Woodward. "Maybe when we I.D. the cowboy in the bathroom the whole thing will unravel."

"Yeah? That guy might not even have fingerprints," said Kimball.

Woodward laughed. "Wouldn't be surprised."

Chapter 63

THE WHITE VAN took the right fork on I-75 in Toledo toward Dayton. Bill Miller glanced at his sleeping granddaughter. He always knew something like this might happen. He knew from that day in 1970 when his sister, Leticia, picked him up at the bus station. He'd just flown from Viet Nam to Camp Pendelton, CA, to Cleveland. At a time when Viet Nam veterans were rarely greeted with anything but disdain, Bill enjoyed a wonderful welcome home party attended by half the town of Pluto.

Then, within a week, Leticia purchased property and hired a builder so Bill could own his own business—Miller's Pub. It was beyond his dreams. Still, he knew there would come a day of reciprocation. *Leticia never did anything for nothing.* He shook Morgan awake.

"How much did she promise you?" he asked.

"Half a million," Morgan said without looking at him.

"You can start over somewhere else."

"I thought I was starting over here," she said.

"Plans change," said Bill.

They rode in silence to the cutoff for highway 224 near Tiffin University. A few miles later, when the last lights of civilization disappeared, Bill pulled onto the right shoulder.

"Sit tight," he said. He opened the tailgate and grabbed a spade and a large plastic garbage bag. He walked into the field of shin-high corn and dug a hole too deep for a harvester or planting machine to disturb. He buried the raincoat, hat and knife. Then he walked backwards to the van, scraping over his footprints with the shovel.

Morgan had fallen asleep. Bill put the van in gear and drove at the speed limit all the way to the parking lot of Palucci Meats in Canton.

"Time to wake up, Morgan," Bill said, nudging her.

"Are we home?" She asked, rubbing her eyes.

"We're back at Palucci's. Let's go."

They locked the van and drove away in Morgan's Focus.

Duncan Chase had just poured his first cup of coffee when his cell phone rang. "Chase here."

"My name is Montrose," said the caller. "You gave me this number back when Rick Fenner was arrested for his wife's murder."

"I remember. What can I do for you?"

"I just heard he was killed in the tornado," she said.

"Yes. Sad," said Chase.

"As you know, we had an affair a long time ago," she began. "I'm calling because I have something he gave me back then.

He said to give it to the prosecutor's office if anything happened to him."

"What is it?" Chase asked.

"It's a padded, manila envelope," she said. "I never opened it. I can drop it off this morning."

"I'll be there at nine," said the prosecutor.

Cragmere sat in her living room watching the local news on television. She was hoping to hear about a man found shot to death in Akron; or another man who'd been murdered in Michigan. Instead, the coverage was all about tornado damage. Then, she heard news that would change everything. A reporter was standing in a pile of debris, pointing to the foundation of a farm house.

"This home in Pluto is among six leveled in a square-mile section of Wayne County. The owner, identified as Richard Fenner, was killed by flying debris while protecting his daughter in the basement. Eighteen-year-old Bree Fenner, who plays second base on Pluto High School's top-ranked softball team, told authorities that her father saved her life.

This is not the first tragedy this family has suffered. In 2008, you might recall, Bree's mother, Cheryl, went missing. Just a few weeks ago, after six years, her remains were discovered in an abandoned house in Cleveland. Investigators say they've determined that Cheryl Fenner was murdered—shot to death. And Richard Fenner was actually arrested in the case last month, but he was released for lack of evidence last week."

The reporter's voice trailed. Cragmere grabbed her cell phone. She dialed Bill Miller.

"Have you seen the news?"

"I'm just waking up," said Bill. "It was a late night."

"Fenner's dead."

"Fenner? How?"

"In the tornado. It leveled his house," said Cragmere.

"The copies?" asked Bill.

Cragmere sipped her black tea and stared through the large bay window at the fallen tree. *Won't have to call the landscaper*, she thought. *Won't be around that long.* Her focus pulled back to the square panes. She had always kept them spotless. A speck of dirt or a fingerprint would send her scrambling for Windex. *Disgusting*, she thought as she scanned the nine squares of glass that looked like mosaics of shredded leaves and bark chips.

"No clue," she said. "No clue how many copies. No clue what he did with them. I must say I wasn't concerned. I never expected to outlive the man."

"So, what now?" asked Bill.

Cragmere paused, tapping her fingers on the coffee table. "I might be able to buy some time."

"I mean what about Morgan and me?" Bill asked.

"What *about* Morgan and you? Keep your mouths shut and you'll be fine. They don't have anything on either of you," she said.

Chapter 64

KIMBALL READ FROM the notes he'd taken over the phone. "His name was Gregory Michael Morrison," said Kimball. "Born July 20, 1981 in Tye, Texas, just outside of Abilene. Attended Hardin-Simmons for two years before enlisting in the United States Army in October of 2001—just after the nine-eleven attacks.

"Purple Heart, Bronze Star. Three tours in Iraq. Honorably discharged in 2010. The guy was a hero."

"So how does a guy like that get dead in Akron, Ohio?" Woodward wondered aloud.

Kimball shook his head. "There's nothing much on his sheet after discharge. Worked some odd jobs. Collected his disability," said Kimball. "Not married. Parents dead. One sibling—a sister in Austin. She's a high school gym teacher."

"He was a ghost," said Woodward.

"Most mercenaries are," said Kimball.

"A hitter?" asked Woodward.

"You think it's a coincidence that both Riordan twins got whacked within 24 hours?"

"You think Morrison killed Dan Riordan in Nevada, and then jetted to Ohio to kill his brother?" Woodward asked.

"That's exactly what I think," said Kimball. "But Al got the jump on him."

"Okay. *Then* what happened?" asked Woodward. "How does Al end up dead at a truck stop in Michigan?"

Kimball paused. "O-B-D. Let's check it."

They walked toward the limo and ducked under the yellow crime scene tape. It was threatening to rain. So, the CSI's had decided to process the outside of the car at the scene. A technician was dusting the driver's side window for prints.

"Have you looked at the onboard diagnostics port?" Kimball asked.

"Not yet," said the man. "Be my guest."

Kimball put on a pair of latex gloves and reached under the steering column. "Bingo," he said, holding a small, plastic box in his palm. "GPS tracker. Gold Star Technologies. Seventy-nine bucks and a twenty- dollar monthly subscription."

Woodward's eyes brightened. "Let's give Gold Star a jingle. Shall we?"

"They'll want a subpoena. I'll call Chase," said Kimball.

It was 12:30 p.m. Mike knocked on Morgan's door. Gail stood behind him.

"Who is it?" Morgan called.

"Mike Page and Gail West," Mike said.

The door opened. Morgan was dressed in a number 32 Cleveland Browns jersey and slippers.

"Coach? Gail? Come in. What's going on?"

"Late night?" asked Mike.

"Yeah. Some friends had storm damage. I was out with them," she said, rubbing her eyes.

"We were looking for you. Did you hear about Rick Fenner?" Gail asked.

"I heard," said Morgan. "Terrible. I feel so sorry for Bree."

"Have you talked to her," Mike asked.

"No. Not yet," said Morgan, walking into her bedroom.

Mike turned to Gail. "Are *you* going to ask her, or am *I*?"

"You do it," she said.

Morgan walked back into the kitchen wearing a Kent State T-shirt and blue jeans.

"Coffee anyone?" she asked.

"No, thanks," said Gail.

"Morgan. I want to ask you what you think about something," said Mike.

"Shoot," said Morgan.

"Before he died, Rick Fenner said something to Bree," Mike began. "He said your grandfather's meat supplier drives a white van—like the one that ran her truck off the road."

"He thought grandpa's meat guy tried to kill Bree?" Morgan asked, holding her arms out, palms up.

"Not exactly," said Mike. "What he said was that he thought Bill was being paid by his sister, Leticia, to frighten Bree as a means of intimidating her father."

Gail glanced at Mike, impressed by his creative interpretation of what Bree had told them.

"Wait. What? That sounds crazy to me," said Morgan, expressionless. "Why would Leti want to intimidate Rick Fenner?"

"I think you know," said Mike.

Morgan held her face in her hands. She wanted to run for her car. She wanted to disappear. *How much does Mike know?* She wondered. *How much do the cops know?*

"What do you think *you* know?" Morgan finally blurted, hoping to turn the tables.

Mike studied her for a few seconds. He was committed to going for the home run. Anything less than a confession would be a loss.

"Your aunt has killed two people by herself, and she has ordered the murders of at least two others," he said. "It's only a matter of time before she's arrested. I'm not sure what you know or if you've become entangled in it somehow, but if you're smart, you'll get ahead of it."

Gail nodded in agreement. "We'll help you, Morgan. And you're going to need help if you've played any role at all."

Tears streamed down Morgan's face. All the demons she'd been battling since age sixteen had gathered in the same room. She had nowhere left to run. *Morgan Miller,* she thought, *has never known one thing about herself—except that she was weak.*

"I drove the car last night," she said.

Chapter 65

"Do you want to see what's on it?" Chase asked.

"No," said Grace. "I don't."

He thanked her and closed his office door. He held the envelope in both hands and squeezed slightly with his fingers to feel the shape of the contents like a child with a present two days before Christmas. Then, he bent the silver prongs, slipped a finger under the flap and slid it across. He reached inside the envelope and pulled out a single DVD which was tucked into a square, white envelope.

"Ah, the confessions of a tormented druggist," he said aloud. He pulled open the top left drawer of his desk and set the disc on top of two identical discs delivered earlier in the week by Patti Grant and Lisa Workman.

Paula buzzed his phone. "Detective Kimball on two," she said.

"Yeah, Arch. What's happening? Sure. Let me write it down. Gold Star Tech? Got it. Yeah. Good. No. No. I'll take care of it. Just give me the plate number. Okay. I'll let you know. Yeah. You guys get some sleep. Call me tonight and I'll have it for you."

Chase Googled Gold Star Technologies. He called the 800 number, identified himself and asked for a supervisor.

"Do I need a subpoena?"

"Eventually," said the man. "But, I'll trust you to send it along. "What's your fax?"

Chase gave him the number and waited for the paperwork. A cover sheet and a single information page arrived in less than two minutes.

"Surprise, surprise," he said aloud. "Leti."

Morgan held the ends of her hair in each hand like someone trying to pull on a winter hat. She stared at the floor as she spoke. "Grandpa called at about six o'clock and said to meet him at Palucci's. He didn't say why," she began.

This might be more than just a home run, Mike thought. *It might be a grand slam.* He had no idea.

"He showed up in a black BMW I'd never seen before and he told me to get in and drive," she continued. "We went to I-77 north and then to the turnpike west. His phone rang every twenty minutes or so. Aunt Leti was giving directions. We drove into Michigan and headed toward Lansing.

"Somewhere past Ann Arbor, we spotted a limo on the highway and followed it for a while. We kept following when it pulled off to gas up at a truck stop. Grandpa told me to drop him off by the door of the building and then park at the pump behind the limo.

"I sat there for a few minutes. Then, I saw Al Riordan pumping gas into the limo. He was staring right at me, but I don't think he could see through the tinted windshield.

"Then, I saw grandpa. He was wearing a raincoat and a hat pulled down so far I could barely see his face. He walked up to Riordan, stabbed him, got back in the car and told me to drive."

Gail let out a gasp. She grabbed Mike's hand and released it just as fast. Morgan kept talking.

"Grandpa called Leti as soon as we got back on the highway. He told me to get off after a few miles. We drove to an intersection on a country road. A white van pulled next to us. Grandpa told me to get out of the BMW and get into the van.

"The BMW took off. We stopped in a corn field at some point and Grandpa got out. I assume he buried his clothing and the knife. The next thing I knew, we were back at Palucci's parking lot. I guess I fell asleep. We switched into my car. I dropped Grandpa off and I drove home and went to bed."

Gail and Mike were stunned. Neither said a word for fifteen seconds. Morgan let go of her hair and slumped to the floor.

"We have to call the authorities," said Gail.

"No!" Morgan shouted. "Please! No! I can't do that to Grandpa. He's been too good to me."

"Morgan, Listen! You're as culpable under the law as he is," said Gail. "They *will* figure it out. It's just a matter of when. Get ahead of it. We can help you."

"It's the only way," Mike said.

Cragmere's phone rang.

"Chase?"

"Yeah. Good news and bad news."

"Give me the good," she said.

"I now have three copies of the video in my desk drawer– delivered by Rick Fenner's ex-lovers."

"What's the bad?"

"Kimball's getting closer. He found your tracker in the limo. He asked me to trace the ownership. Your name is all over it—as you know."

"I guess my next move is pretty clear then," Cragmere said.

"You disappear or you get arrested," said Chase.

"How much time do I have?" asked Cragmere.

"Not much. A few hours. I can stall, but not for very long," said Chase."

"Do your best, kid."

"I will," said Chase. "And thanks for everything, Leti. I hope it works out."

Chapter 66

KIMBALL PULLED INTO the right lane and set the cruise control at 68 M.P.H. after entering the Ohio Turnpike in Toledo. They'd slept six hours at the Holiday Inn Express about two miles from the murder scene. It was 5 p.m. Woodward yawned and looked at his watch.

"Should we try the prosecutor?" he asked.

Kimball checked his side view mirror as a UPS truck pulling two trailers passed him from the center lane. Then, he put his phone to his ear.

"Calling him now," he said, as another large truck stormed past.

Kimball put his phone on speaker when Chase answered.

"Chase? Kimball. Any word on that tracker?"

"I put in the call," Chase said. "They said they'll get back to me. I told them to put a rush on it."

"Good," said Kimball. "We're headed back. Call me when you get it."

"Will do," said Chase.

After an hour of convincing, Morgan agreed to meet Gail at her office in the morning. They would craft a statement in which Morgan would admit her involvement in the murder of Al Riordan—key evidence in the case that could send both her grandfather and her Great Aunt Leti to the death chamber. Then, Gail would call her friend Duncan Chase.

Two people who'd heard and seen just about everything in their respective careers walked out of Morgan Miller's condo in a state of shock. Mike pointed the Buick toward Bath.

"I hope my house is still there," she said.

"And if it isn't?" asked Mike.

"I'll have to move in with you," she smiled.

"Hmm. Not sure which way I'm rooting," said Mike.

"Me either," she said.

Twenty-five minutes later, Gail pulled off I-77 at Ghent Road. Broken branches and twigs crunched beneath the Lucerne's tires and rattled off its frame for the next half mile.

"We'll know in a few seconds," she said.

"Damn!" Mike shouted, as the undamaged house came into view. "Looks like I still live alone."

Monday, April 26

Cragmere held a hand in front of her eyes. The sun was a bad sign. She'd fallen asleep when she should have been packing.

"What the hell time is it?" she wondered aloud. The grandfather clock in the hallway chimed nine times. Chase would have to give her up soon. She called her brother.

"Are you ready?"

"I'm ready," said Bill.

"I'll pick you up in a cab in one hour," said Cragmere.

Kimball met Woodward at the Fairfield Inn.

"I've been calling the prosecutor for the last half hour. His secretary says he's not in yet."

"He's what? Ten minutes away? Let's bring him a coffee," said Woodward.

"Good idea," said Kimball.

Morgan was waiting when Gail and Mike arrived at Gail's office. They all walked up the back stairs. Gail logged into a desktop computer and told Morgan to write her statement.

"Just write what happened," she said. "We'll refine it together when you're done."

Gail called Chase's cell phone.

"Gail? Hi. What's up?" he answered.

"I assume you've heard about Rick Fenner," she said.

"Yes. Tragic," said Chase.

"And Al Riordan?"

"Not so tragic," said Chase. "Stabbed at a truck stop in Michigan, from what I hear. What's your interest?"

"I have a new client," said Gail. "This client might have information on the Riordan murder."

"Shit, Gail. Have you called the prosecutor up there?" Chase asked.

"Not yet. We're putting a statement together," said Gail. "You'll want to read it."

"Why? The Cheryl Fenner case?"

"And more," said Gail.

"When can I have it?" Chase asked.

"I'll meet you for lunch at Miller's Pub to talk about it. They're serving again. The red cross moved to middle school gym."

"Twelve-thirty?"

"Fine," Gail agreed.

Paula buzzed Chase's office phone. "You have visitors."

"Who?"

"Detectives Kimball and Woodward," she announced.

"Fine. Send them in," said Chase.

"Good morning," said Kimball, plopping into a chair in front of the prosecutor's desk. "This is detective Glenn Woodward from Las Vegas."

"Glenn. A pleasure," said Chase, shaking hands with him. "By the way, I have the fax from Gold Star." He handed two sheets of paper to Kimball, who studied them for about ten seconds.

"Cragmere." he said, calmly. Then, as he was handing it to Woodward, he pulled it back and studied it for another few seconds before finally releasing it to his colleague.

Woodward nodded and smiled. "This should help us answer a few questions," he said.

"It already has," Kimball said. "We'll take it from here, counselor."

Chapter 67

THE CAB DRIVER pulled to the curb outside Pluto High's main lobby. Cragmere stepped out. She wore a tight, black, leather skirt hemmed a few inches above the knee; black tights; a white blouse; and black pumps with three-inch heels. She walked quickly down the hallway to her classroom. She acknowledged with a slight smile those who greeted her, but she didn't stop to chat. When she reached the room, she used a key to open the top desk drawer.

She lifted three file folders and some loose papers. A small jewelry box rested at the bottom of the drawer. She placed it inside her purse, closed the drawer and retraced her steps to the cab without speaking to anyone.

She gave Bill Miller's address to the driver. Less than ten minutes later, they were parked in her brother's driveway. They waited a few minutes before Cragmere sent the driver to knock on the front door. He stood there a minute. No one answered. Cragmere dialed her brother's cell phone. No answer. The driver came back.

"I looked through the window, ma'am. I think someone's sleeping in the chair."

A chill ran up Cragmere's spine. She hurried to the house, her heels clattering, her ankles threatening to collapse. She reached the door and started pounding.

"Bill? Bill!" she shouted. No answer. She moved to the window and pressed her nose to it, cupping her hands near her temples. He was in the chair, his right arm dangling over the side. On the floor, under his right hand, she saw his Colt .45. She stared for a few seconds—just long enough to consider the possible consequences of delaying her departure. Then, she ran back to the cab.

"He's not coming," she said. "Akron-Canton airport. Let's go."

No one answered Cragmere's door.

"I'll call for an A.P.B.," said Kimball.

"Closest airport?" asked Woodward.

"Akron-Canton," said Kimball. "Let's go fast."

"I'll drive," said Woodward.

Cragmere's phone rang.

"Where are you?" Chase asked.

"Almost to Akron-Canton," said Cragmere.

"I gave you up fifteen minutes ago. They'll have it covered."

"Damn it!" said Cragmere. "All right. Thanks for letting me know."

"Of course," said Chase.

"You've done well," she said. "I'm glad you came to me back then."

"Me, too," said Chase. "Good luck, Leti."

Cragmere tapped the back of the driver's headrest. "Change of plan. Head north on seventy-seven. Take the turnpike east."

"Okay," said the driver. "Where we goin'?"

"Not far," she said.

Cragmere looked out the window. She thought about the day Duncan Chase called her for help. He told her his arm was shot. He told her he was broke. He told her he had nowhere to turn. She remembered asking him what he wanted to do with the rest of his life. He said he wasn't sure there was going to be a "rest" of his life. She remembered the sadness in his voice. *How could someone so young and bright and healthy be so defeated?*

Three days later, Chase found a package from UPS in his locker. It contained $150,000 cash and a brief note: *Your contract with the Frederick Keys has been sold to the law school of your choice. Failure is not an option. Good luck!*

Morgan hit the print button. Her statement covered two pages, double spaced. She explained that her Great Aunt, Leticia Cragmere, had promised to give her

$500,000 to drive Bill Miller on an errand he was running for her. She said she had no idea that Miller was on a mission to murder Al Riordan. She said she did not know the motive for Riordan's murder.

She explained that once she realized what had happened, she was too frightened to do anything except what she was told to do by her grandfather. Once free of his reach she immediately contacted her attorney, Gail West, who advised her to contact authorities.

"We'll leave for the pub in an hour. The prosecutor is meeting us there," said Gail. "Just relax, Morgan."

As Woodward turned into the airport, Kimball received a call from its administrator.

"All right. Yeah. That's very good. Keep in touch," he said. "No sign of her," he said to Woodward. "But they've got everything covered."

"Next move?" Woodward asked.

"I want you to look at something," Kimball said, pulling the Gold Star fax from his briefcase. "Take a look at what time this came over."

"It says 9:25 a.m.," Woodward said.

"Yeah. My phone says that's less than fifteen minutes after my initial call."

"And when you called him back later, he said he hadn't heard anything yet," said Woodward.

"My phone says it was 5:12 p.m.," said Kimball. "That means he lied. He had that fax for almost eight hours and still said he was waiting for a call."

"Then, he sat on it all night. So, he gave us the information twenty-four hours late. Do you think his secretary just didn't tell him about it?" asked Woodward.

"Paula? Not a chance," said Kimball. Let's try Miller's Pub. I'm a little hungry anyway."

Bree's paternal grandmother was alive, but suffering from dementia and living in a senior center near Chicago. She knew of no other family members. The night of the tornado, Bree accepted an offer to stay with Lauren's family.

Lauren's dad, Marty Phillips, had a sister who married into the Wickersham family. She immediately called Marty to extend an offer of free funeral arrangements for Bree's father. The funeral was scheduled for the coming Saturday.

With the high school closed because of storm damage, Bree's friends were free to hang out with her. Bree, Lauren and Darcy walked into Miller's Pub at 12:15 p.m. They sat in a booth and ordered soft drinks, burgers and fries.

"Has anybody talked to Coach Mike about practice or games or anything?" Darcy asked.

Bree put her hand on Lauren's arm. She could see that her pal was about to jump on Darcy for even thinking about softball.

"He'll let us know," Bree said. "I still want to play. I don't know about you guys."

They all agreed they did.

Cragmere tapped the back of the driver's headrest. "Pull over right here," she ordered.

"Here?"

"Right here!" she insisted.

"All right," said the driver. "You got it."

He pulled to the turnpike shoulder about halfway across the bridge over the Cuyahoga Valley National Park. Cragmere stepped out of the car, tapped on his window and dangled a wad of cash in front of his face.

"I'll pay you a thousand dollars to do me a favor," she said.

"Name it," said the driver.

She reached into her purse and pulled out the jewelry box. "Swear on your family that you won't open this box."

"All right. I swear," said the driver, a white man in his thirties, who sported multiple arm tattoos, all with a military motif. He was slight, looking more like a punk band guitar player than a soldier—except that his hair was buzzed ultra-short. He wore an orange Cleveland Browns T-shirt, blue jeans and combat boots.

"What else?" he asked.

Cragmere stared into his brown eyes. "I want you to drive back to Pluto and find Miller's Pub. There's a woman who works there named Morgan

Miller. Tall, blonde, attractive. If she's not there, someone will know how to find her. Give her the box. Give it to her personally. Don't hand it off to somebody else."

"Is that all?" asked the driver.

"Don't mention any of this to anyone," she said. "Don't mention that you drove me here. Don't mention that I gave you the box."

"Okay. Got it," said the man. "Drive to Pluto; find Miller's Pub; give the box to no one but Morgan Miller; and forget that we ever met."

"Perfect," said Cragmere, handing the cash and the box to the driver. "I trust you. Now drive away. Oh. Tell Morgan I love her."

"Who are you?" the driver asked.

"She'll know," said Cragmere.

Gail, Morgan and Mike arrived at the pub only a minute before Kimball and Woodward. They chose a booth near the back door. The detectives sat at the bar. Neither group saw the other.

Bree and her teammates did not see their coach, but Bree spotted Kimball right way. In her mind now, he was a friend. He could have ended her dream of playing softball in college by filing felony charges against her. Instead, he told her he was sorry for the way he treated her father for so many years. Instead, he gave her another chance. She slid out of the booth to greet him.

"Bree? I'm so sorry," said Kimball.

"Thank you," said Bree.

"This is detective Woodward from Las Vegas," he said.

Bree shook Woodward's hand. "I'm sorry for your loss," he said.

"Thank you," said Bree, reaching into her purse and pulling out a manila envelope. "Oh. My father left this with a note for me to give it to the prosecutor if anything happened to him. Can I trust you to deliver it? I think it has to do with my mom's case."

"Absolutely," said Kimball. "Have you seen what's inside?"

"No. I found it in my bureau drawer." said Bree. "The note just said, 'Get this to the county prosecutor if anything happens to me'."

"Speak of the devil," said Kimball, nodding at the entrance.

Duncan Chase wore a navy, pinstripe suit, white shirt and red tie. He scanned the room and quickly spotted Gail's blonde hair. He didn't see Kimball, who gave Bree a hug and promised to deliver the package.

As Bree rejoined her friends, Kimball's eyes followed Chase. He watched him shake hands with Mike Page and hug Gail West. He knew that Morgan Miller worked at the pub and that her grandfather owned it. He knew she was Mike's assistant coach. Still, Kimball found it odd that Morgan was part of that group, shaking hands with Chase as he sat opposite her and next to Mike.

"I wonder what's going on there," Kimball said to Woodward. As he spoke, a man in his thirties wearing an orange Cleveland Browns shirt stepped between them.

"I'm looking for Morgan Miller," the man declared to the bartender.

"Over there," said Janice Williams, who'd been working part-time at the pub for two years. "The younger of the blondes by the back door."

"Thanks," said the man.

Kimball watched him walk to Morgan. He seemed to whisper something. Morgan stood and led him to the back door as the others stared with puzzled looks on their faces. Morgan returned to the group a few minutes later holding a square jewelry box.

"A gift from a friend," she said, placing the box into her purse.

Kimball's phone rang. "Kimball. Yeah. Just now? Shit! What's the address?" he asked, pulling out his pen. "His granddaughter is thirty feet from me. All right. All right. I'll tell her. Yeah. And we'll bring her with us. Yeah."

"What?" Woodward asked.

"A neighbor just found Bill Miller dead. Apparent suicide."

"Shot? Hanged?" Woodward asked.

"Shot," said Kimball.

"What was *that* all about?" Gail asked.

Morgan took a deep breath. "I think I need to excuse myself."

"Morgan. What happened? Who *was* that guy?" Mike asked.

Morgan shook her head. "It's personal. I can't say right now."

Chase was first to spot Kimball and Woodward as they approached. "Detectives. Small world," said Chase.

Kimball nodded at Chase. "Sorry to intrude, but I need to speak with Morgan. There's been some tragic news."

"What news? You can tell them, too," said Morgan.

"It's your grandfather," said Kimball. "I'm sorry. He's dead."

Morgan put her hands to her face and started sobbing. "No! No! How?" she asked.

"A neighbor found him. Gunshot wound to the head," said Kimball. "Apparently, self-inflicted."

Kimball looked at Gail. "We'd like her to come with us to the house," he said.

"We'll all follow, if that's okay," Gail said.

"Fine," Kimball said.

Chapter 68

THE WAYNE COUNTY CSI unit was already processing the scene when Kimball, Woodward and Chase entered Bill Miller's house.

"Arch? Good to see ya," said Larry Heimler, who had just finished placing plastic bags over Bill Miller's hands. "Looks like he ate it."

"Anything to suggest he didn't?" Kimball asked.

"Not that I see," said Heimler. Then, he pointed to a plastic bag containing a piece of computer paper. "Unless you can determine that his hand-written suicide note was written by someone else."

Kimball picked up the bag and read the note.

To Whom It May Concern:

I'm too old and too tired to run. I wouldn't do well in prison. I leave this life with few regrets. I served my country, though I never agreed with its position on Viet Nam. I lived a long time with haunting memories of atrocities I committed there in the name of freedom. I paid my taxes. I paid my debts.

I won't dwell on the circumstances that led to this moment. I will say only that I was certain my fate was sealed, and that it would not be pleasant.

I confess to the murder of Al Riordan. I acted alone, except for the help of two people who had no idea what I was going to do. I paid one person to drive me to the truck stop and another to meet me at a particular location to exchange vehicles. Neither had knowledge of my intentions with regard to Riordan.

I killed Riordan because my sister, Leticia Cragmere, ordered me to do it. She had sent a hitman to murder him in his apartment, but Riordan got away in the hitman's limo. Riordan did not know that Leticia had placed a tracking device inside the vehicle. That's how she was able to direct me to the truck stop in Michigan. You might wonder why she would be willing to kill her own son-in-law. I can tell you that she always blamed Al for the accident that killed her daughter. She kept him around to do her dirty work, but she always planned to have him killed.

She was also angry with Al for raping and murdering Cheryl Fenner when she sent him to search for Jonas Benson's confession video. Leticia told me that Al broke into the house, thinking no one was home. When he started tossing the master bedroom, he heard the shower running. He opened the bathroom door and saw Cheryl. When she screamed, he punched her and dragged her to the bedroom. Then, he put her in the trunk of his car and drove her somewhere and put a bullet in her head.

I will also reveal what I know to be true about the deaths of Dan Riordan and Amber David. Dan Riordan was murdered by the same hitman who attempted to kill his brother, Al. I only knew the hitman as "The Cowboy." He was paid by my sister, Leticia Cragmere, to eliminate both Riordan brothers after the murder of Amber David. Al Riordan actually killed David during a trip to Las Vegas that he took with Leticia.

Lastly, I will tell you that I have no official will, but I bequeath all of my possessions, including the pub, to my granddaughter, Morgan Miller. I am sure she will be generous to her sister.

Good bye,
Bill Miller

Kimball handed the bagged letter to Woodward, who was examining the bagged Colt .45.

"You might want to read this," Kimball said. "Give it to Chase when you're done. I'll be outside."

Kimball had been called to at least a dozen suicide scenes in his long career. They all had one thing in common: A victim who had left a life of certain misery behind. He walked out to find Morgan standing just inside the yellow police tape with Gail and Mike.

"He shot himself. And he left a long note."

Morgan's knees went limp. Her reaction was half shock at the loss of her grandfather, and half fear that his note had implicated her in a murder.

"Why?" she asked. "What did the note say?"

Kimball paused. "I can't discuss specifics right now. We have to complete the process. There's no foul play here, but your grandfather may not have been the person you thought he was. He confessed to some things that would have sent him to prison for life—or even to death row. I'm sorry."

Morgan sobbed. Mike put his arm around her. Gail took a step closer to Kimball.

"Is there anything else we should know?" Gail asked.

"No. Not really," Kimball said. "We already had an A.P.B. out on Leticia Cragmere—and Miller's suicide note places her in the middle of at least four murders.

Gail tried to list them. "The Riordans, Amber David and..."

"And Cheryl Fenner," said Kimball.

"God. Who would have thought that little old woman was capable of such evil?" Gail said, turning her back on Morgan and Mike. "Any mention of Morgan in the note, she whispered."

"He left her the pub," Kimball said, matter-of-factly. "He left her everything, actually, and instructed her to share with her sister. That's about it," said Kimball.

"All right. Well, we'll leave you to it," said Gail, turning to the others. "Let's go back to my office," she said, taking Morgan by the arm. She glanced at Mike and moved her eyebrows up and down with a quick grin. As they reached the Buick, which was parked at the curb some fifty feet east of the house, Gail spotted Chase. He was standing by the front door, scanning the property, probably looking for her.

Two minutes into the drive, Gail's phone rang.

"May I help you?" She answered formally.

"Is something wrong?" he asked.

"Not at all," Gail lied. "Just headed back to the office. Morgan broke down when Kimball came out to give her the news," said Gail.

"What about our meeting? Did your new client ever show up?" asked Chase.

Gail had no idea that Chase didn't know Morgan was the new client. *That's right*, she thought. *I never did say it was Morgan. Chase probably thought Morgan was working and just came to the table to say 'hello.'*

"No. We took off before he got there. This stuff is more important. We can back-burner that meeting until next week sometime."

"Sounds good," said Chase. "Let me know."

"I will," said Gail. She ended the call and turned to Mike. "Timing is everything."

Mike smiled and put his hand over hers. He thought about the past two months of his life—about feeling completely empty and lost before taking the coaching job in Pluto; about feeling reborn the first time he met Gail West. The timing had been impossibly perfect.

"I'll say."

Chapter 69

CHASE STOOD NEAR the police tape and answered a call from his counterpart in Livingston County, Michigan. He provided a synopsis of Bill Miller's suicide note.

"So, let's review," said Deputy Prosecutor Rodney Carrol. "Riordan was killed by your suicide victim, Bill Miller; you don't know who Miller's accomplices were, but he claimed in his suicide note that they were both ignorant of what he was planning to do."

"That's pretty much it—as it pertains to your jurisdiction," said Chase.

"Nice doin' business," said Carrol. "I figure I'm third in line when Cragmere gets caught. Keep me posted, though, huh?"

"You got it," said Chase.

Morgan held the jewelry box in her left hand. "Here goes," she said. Gail and Mike sat watching from the edge of their seats on the office couch as Morgan lifted the top to reveal three round plastic cases, each containing a gold coin measuring 1.3 inches in diameter. On the face of the coins was Lady Liberty holding a torch in one hand and an olive branch in the other. The date, 1933, was engraved below the olive branch. On the other side, a bald eagle in flight was centered below the words, *UNITED STATES OF AMERICA TWENTY DOLLARS*.

"Could the coins in Benson's box have been a clue about these?" Gail asked.

"I wonder. Let's see what they're worth first," said Mike.

Morgan handed the box to Mike. He moved to a desktop computer and started typing. He tapped a key. He tapped another key. Then, he started scrolling and reading, glancing occasionally at the coins.

"What did you find?" Morgan asked.

"If these are what I think they are..." Mike said, pausing for several seconds, unintentionally building suspense.

"What?" Morgan asked.

"The real McCoy," said Mike. "Nineteen thirty-three double eagles."

"What are they worth?" Gail asked.

"A lot," said Mike. "But they happen to be illegal to possess."

"That's never good," said Gail.

"About half a million were minted in March of thirty-three, but because of the Great Depression, F.D.R. stopped their circulation and ordered them melted into bullion. It says a few were stolen, probably by a cashier at Fort Knox. The government thought it had an accurate count of the missing coins and managed to get them back. But, it looks like a jeweler in Philadelphia—a guy named Israel Switt—acquired a number of them. It says the government took them back, but who knows how many he actually had?"

"So, how much are they worth?" Gail persisted.

"Looks like the King of Egypt paid seven and a half million for one!" said Mike. "But, like I said, they're not legal to possess."

"Neither is cocaine," said Morgan.

Mike smiled. Gail didn't. She walked over to the computer and picked up the coins, holding one in each hand, examining them for a few seconds before setting them on the table near Mike's right arm. Then, she picked up the jewelry box, which measured six-by-six inches. She snapped it closed and ran the fingers of her right hand across the blue velvet. She re-opened it. She held it closer to her face. Then, she slipped a finger nail down the side of the padded bottom of the box and lifted the bottom to reveal a space about half an inch deep, like a secret compartment.

"Ah. What's this?" she said, lifting a folded piece of paper about the size of a post-it. She read the note aloud: *"Wait six months and call 215-555-2424. Speak only to Marvin Switt."*

"That's Philly," said Mike. "Maybe he's Israel Switt's son?"

"Or grandson," said Gail. "Either way, Cragmere must know him well."

"Maybe Cragmere and Marvin have had this planned," said Mike.

"Kinda seems like it," said Gail.

"So, what do we do?" Morgan asked.

"You're free to do what you want with the coins," said Gail. "It's up to you. Obviously, you risk prosecution if you try to sell them. Either way, you can't go wrong by storing them in a safety deposit box at your bank for six months while you make a decision.

"As far as your statement, I don't see a reason to come forward with it now that your grandfather is gone—especially since his suicide note doesn't implicate you."

Morgan started crying. "He was such a good man. I can't believe this has happened. It's surreal."

Mike nodded, but thought, *except for the fact that Bill Miller was a cold-blooded murderer, she's right.*

Cragmere looked down at the police car passing in the right lane of the eastbound Ohio Turnpike. *If only he knew,* she thought.

"I can't thank you enough for picking us up," she said to the trucker. "How far to Philly?"

"A little over four hundred miles," said the man, who appeared to be in his late thirties. "About eight hours including stops."

"And you can drop us at 30th Street Station?"

"No problem," he said. "That seat goes all the way back. Set your cat carrier next to me. Have a nap. We'll stop for dinner in a few hours."

"Thanks," said Cragmere. "It's been a long day for us already."

Arch Kimball stared at his wrinkled hands. They were too small for a man of his size—and the skin seemed too soft. Nothing on his life's resume spoke of manual labor, but his gruff manor almost required huge, calloused paws. His mind flashed to his high school days when buddies would tease him, mentioning myths about correlations between hand size and penis size. He grimaced, at the thought, but it seemed to his colleagues that he'd been assessing their chances of collaring Cragmere.

"I'm afraid she's long gone," he lamented to Woodward and Franks as the three detectives walked through Cragmere's front door.

"Didn't even lock the place," said Franks.

"Yeah. She knew she'd never be back," said Woodward.

"And that we'd be coming with a warrant anyway," said Kimball.

"I'm surprised she didn't leave us a pan of brownies," Woodward joked.

A team of CSI's joined the detectives for five hours. They searched for evidence linking Cragmere to the murders of Al Riordan, Dan Riordan, Amber David and Cheryl Fenner. What they found was enough to convict her of being a well-educated widow who enjoyed reading, sewing and caring for her cat.

On the walls of all thirteen rooms, they saw framed photos of her parents, her daughter, her dead husband and her cat. In the drawers, cupboards, closets and cubbies they found nothing that oozed evil, nothing that revealed her black heart. It was all normal. It was all Pluto—very, very Pluto.

At 10 p.m., Kimball sat alone at his home computer. He loaded Bree's DVD and sipped his neat Jack Daniels. He smiled as Jonas Benson told the tale that revealed Leticia Cragmere as a monster. When it ended, he dialed Duncan Chase.

"Fenner made a copy of the Jonas Benson video. I just watched it," said Kimball.

"Where'd you get it?" asked Chase.

"His daughter, this afternoon at Miller's pub," said Kimball. "She asked me to give it to you."

"Guess you didn't," said Chase.

"I wanted to see it first," said Kimball. "Something told me it might be my only chance."

"What's that supposed to mean?" Chase asked.

"I saw the time on the fax from Gold Star," said Kimball.

"So?"

"So, I know you were stalling," Kimball pressed.

"Stalling? Why would I do that?" asked Chase.

"I wondered the same thing," said Kimball. "So, I gave my boss, Captain Krumrie, a little busy work. I asked him to look for a connection between you and Leticia Cragmere. He was happy to help because he greatly resented your recent insinuation that I might have hidden some evidence in the Cheryl Fenner case six years ago. And guess what? Krumrie found out you threw a few pitches for Cragmere's minor league baseball team in Maryland!"

"That's great police work. What's your point?" Chase asked.

"Here's my point: Ninety days after you hurt your arm and retired from baseball, you were attending law school at Georgetown. And no less than five former teammates, plus your manager, confirmed that the money to pay for it came from Leticia Cragmere."

"Again, I ask: What's your point?" said Chase.

"I got a warrant to search your office this afternoon. While you and I were at Bill Miller's house, my partner was going through your desk drawers," said Kimball. "And guess what he found? Three copies of the Jonas Benson video!"

"Yeah. So? Those videos were dropped off this morning. I just forgot to mention it. I didn't watch them," said Chase.

"Two of the videos were dropped off this morning," said Kimball. "I ran into Lisa Workman yesterday—one of Rick Fenner's former lovers—and she mentioned dropping something off at your office five days ago. Since that video is enough to bring Cragmere in for questioning in at least two homicides, you're under arrest for obstruction of justice."

"What do you mean, I'm under arrest?" Chase bristled.

"Oh. There's one more thing, Mr. Chase," said Kimball. "That phone call you asked my boss to run down? He found it. Turns out Stark County took the call. It was from a woman named Peggy Page. She might have been a bit confused about what she overheard that night, but she did use the words "prosecutor" and "Chase" when she tried to describe the conversation inside the Fenner house. The two people involved in that conversation were Rick and Bree Fenner. Rick was killed in the tornado, but I asked Bree what she remembered about that argument. Guess what she said?"

"I assure you I have no idea," said Chase.

"She said her father was telling her that you were Cragmere's right hand man."

"Her father the liar, you mean?" Chase cracked.

"Just another rock in a mountain of evidence, Chase," said Kimball. Get a good lawyer, pal."

Kimball smiled as he heard commotion on the other end of the phone. Franks and Krumrie had been waiting in Chase's outer office. Kimball was talking to Chase and texting Franks at the same time—telling him to go in and put handcuffs on the assistant prosecutor.

"What the hell's going on?" Chase shouted.

"We've got your phone records!" Kimball shouted. "You'll have to explain three calls from Cragmere in the past two days, including one this morning!"

Chase disconnected the call just before his hands went behind his back in cuffs.

Kimball laughed out loud. "Son of a bitch," he mumbled.

Shortly after 9 p.m., Leticia Cragmere, with Cordelia's pet carrier in one hand and a small suitcase in the other, strolled into Philadelphia's 30th street station. She sat on a wooden bench and waited until a man in his forties approached and introduced himself.

"I'm Marvin Switt," said the man, who wore a black jogging suit. "We have to go."

Switt took her suitcase and led her to a black BMW. He drove on surface streets to South Philly, where he found a southbound I-95 ramp.

"Remember, my granddaughter will contact you in six months about the coins," said Cragmere.

"I have buyers," said Switt. "She'll get the money in cash—minus my fee, of course."

In a few minutes, Switt exited the highway and turned into the Philadelphia International Airport.

"Is the plane waiting?" asked Cragmere.

"See for yourself," said Switt, pointing to a Learjet 24 on the general aviation tarmac. "Fueled and ready."

He drove straight to it. The pilot and flight attendant stood near the airstair. Switt put the BMW in park and walked around to open Cragmere's door, but she was already out. She handed him an envelope, pulled her suitcase and cat carrier from the back seat and hustled up the airstair into the jet.

Switt opened the envelope and smiled as he watched the jet taxi into position for takeoff. "Easiest twenty-five grand I'll ever make," he said aloud.

A minute later, the Learjet's lights were fading into the southern sky. Cragmere sat close to a window, her gaze glued to the disappearing landscape—her last look at North America. *Fifty years*, she thought. Fifty years had come and gone since the decision that redefined her life. She had done what circumstances required. No. Not true. She had done what made her happy. She had done what gave her pleasure. She had done anything but the *right* thing since the night she stabbed Wanda Shaw with that needle. She'd spent decades scheming to protect her freedom at any cost—and the cost had been higher than her worst fears could conjure. *When the prison has no walls, where do you run to escape?*

She stared at the crooked fingers pressed against the window. She never stopped wearing her wedding ring. It represented the last time she felt anything that wasn't a lie.

Her phone rang. She didn't recognize the number. She waited to see if the caller would leave a message. A minute later, the message notification sounded.

Leticia? My name is Gail West. I'm an attorney and a former prosecutor. I'm also a friend of your great niece, Morgan Miller and of Duncan Chase. I wanted you to know that Duncan has been arrested. I'm not sure of the charges yet. I also want you to know that Morgan could face charges as well for her role in the murder of Al Riordan. I do think there's a way to help both of them avoid jail time and go on to lead happy and fulfilling lives without criminal records. I know I could help them. Could you call me? Please? Thank you.

Tears rolled down Cragmere's cheeks. She wiped them with backs of her wrinkled hands. Then, she stood and walked toward the cockpit.

"May I help you, ma'am?" The flight attendant asked.

"I want to speak with the pilot," Cragmere demanded.

Chapter 70

KIMBALL SHOOK HANDS with Woodward, who was returning to Vegas empty handed, but with all of his cases solved, if not settled.

"Funny how things work out sometimes," said Woodward as he pulled his bag from the back seat. "I hope you catch the old lady."

Kimball smiled. "She's got money and a nice head start thanks to Duncan Chase, who *is* going to jail if I have anything to say about it. But something tells me she'll turn up."

"You'd be able to retire a happy man," said Woodward, turning and waving goodbye as he headed to his gate.

Retire happy? Sure, thought Kimball. *Sure. I will.*

Kimball's drive from the airport in Berea to the Sheriff's department in Wooster covered fifty-seven miles. About twenty-five minutes into it, his phone rang. It was Franks.

"Where are you?" His partner asked.

"Let's see, I-71 South, just passing those truck stops in Lodi," said Kimball.

"I assume you're sitting?" asked Franks.

"Yeah. I try not to drive standing up. It's bad for my back," said Kimball. "What's up?"

"Gail West is on her way here."

"And?"

"She says our suspect wants to cut a deal," said Franks.

"Our suspect? Who?" Kimball asked.

"Cragmere," said Franks.

"You're shitting me!" Kimball shouted.

"Nope. I'll see you in thirty," said Franks.

Kimball hung up and put some pressure on the gas pedal. In a second, he was going ten miles per hour above the speed limit.

Mike turned onto Highway 30. He looked at Gail and smiled. "I can't believe this. No. I guess I can—after all the other crazy shit—I guess I can. Nothing is out of the realm. Is it?"

Gail smiled back. "Nope. That's for sure. Speaking of unbelievable—I still can't believe she called me back."

"And that the 7-0-2 number Bree gave us was actually one of Cragmere's phones," said Mike.

"And that you thought it might be—and told me to leave the message!" said Gail.

"Yeah. Well, shucks, it was nothing'," Mike smiled.

"You know what? You're a special man," said Gail.

"Inspired by a special woman," said Mike.

Wednesday, April 30

Kimball wasn't happy with the deal. "Chase needs to do time," he argued. "Who knows how much he helped that woman over the years?"

Krumrie shook his head. "Come on, Arch. If you were the prosecutor, you'd have done the same damn thing. Cragmere confessed to seven murders! Besides, if it weren't for Cragmere's affection for Chase, she'd be long gone."

"Yeah. Okay. Let's just go ahead and give Chase credit for the collar," said Kimball.

Krumrie laughed. "How many days to retirement, Arch?"

"Too many," said Kimball, managing a smile.

Two days after Rick Fenner's funeral, Bree was back at second base for the Invaders, as they crushed Marshallville, 7-0. She had two hits and drove in two runs, playing through tears at times. Rachel hit a three-run homer; Allie hit a two-run homer; and Jen threw a two-hitter as the team raised its record to 6-0.

The Pluto girls maintained their number one state ranking by winning another 21 straight games, including the district and regional championships.

Bree signed a letter of intent to attend The Ohio State University on a softball scholarship. Callie signed with Notre Dame College. Allie signed with Tiffin University.

On Friday, May 30, the Invaders won the state semi-final game over perennial Division III powerhouse Carroll Bloom-Carroll, 1-0. Callie threw the shutout. Bree scored the winning run in the seventh inning, racing home on a wild pitch after she singled and then stole second and third.

That same day, Gail appeared with Leticia Cragmere inside the Wayne County Courthouse in Wooster. Also in attendance were nine television crews, as well as a herd of radio and print reporters who snapped photos and shot video with their multi-use cameras.

Cragmere calmly accepted responsibility for the deaths of her father; Wanda Shaw; Samuel Burkett; Cheryl Fenner; Amber David; Dan Riordan; and Al Riordan. In all, she pleaded guilty to one hundred thirty-seven felonies. Gail listened to every word of Cragmere's allocution, but the end of it left her in tears:

"We all need forgiveness. We all make mistakes. But, when your heart turns so dark that your soul disappears, you feel nothing for the hearts and souls of others. I still don't. There is no forgiveness on Earth for that."

Superior Court Judge John Fairbanks sentenced Cragmere to three hundred twenty-eight years in prison. Her plea agreement had taken the death penalty off the table. It also included breaks for Morgan Miller and Duncan Chase. No charges were ever filed against Morgan. Chase's charges were reduced to misdemeanors. He kept his law license, but lost his job at the Wayne County Prosecutor's Office.

Chapter 71

Saturday, May 31

MIKE WANTED TO wave at Gail, but decided it would be inappropriate behavior for a coach during a tense moment of a state championship game. So, he smiled. Then, he turned to his team and began his strategy speech.

"Listen up. There's one out. Runners at first and third. We're up one run. All kinds of things can happen. Jen could strike out the next two batters and we'll be the champs. That's what I'm rooting for." They all laughed as he patted his freshman pitcher on the shoulder.

"But that won't be easy. They've got their two best hitters coming up. Outfield? Play extra deep. The go-ahead run is at first base. Nothing over your heads unless it leaves the yard. Hit the cutoff. If they hit a fly ball and it's even medium deep, throw the ball to second base. That's the go ahead run at first. Keep her off second. We'll take our chances with a tie. We can win it in the bottom half of the inning.

"Infield? If they try to steal second, we'll trade a run for an out. Let's throw her out at second. The runner at first is slow. Just throw her out. If she stops and gets into a rundown, tag her. Don't throw home. It'll kill their rally. We'll win it in the bottom half.

"Corners? Play extra close. Take away the squeeze. If they pop up the bunt and you catch it, don't hurry your throw to third or first. Take your time, or just hold the ball. We'll get the next batter.

"Middle infield? Play half way and cheat toward the middle. You're fast, Bree. If her hands tip off the bunt, you'll beat her to first even if you're standing on second. But I want you to be at second for the double play if we get a one-hopper to short.

"Darcy? If you *do* get that one-hopper, turn the double play. Don't go home—no matter how many people are screaming, 'Home!' And if they get a bunt down, cover third—not second. Jen and the corners are either going home or to first if they field it. Cover third, so the runner from first can't just keep going to third."

Mike looked at each one of them. He knew they understood. They'd been on the same page since the first game of the season, even with only a week practice. He looked at his pitcher last.

"That's a lot of complicated stuff," he said. "That's why you should just strike out the next two batters. No pressure, though."

Jen laughed. "Yeah. No pressure. Thanks." She grabbed the resin bag, tossed it up and caught it in her right palm. She kicked some dirt near the back of the circle and slammed the yellow ball into her mitt.

That's when it hit him. This strange, wonderful, awful, invigorating, resurrecting slice of life was about to end. Win or lose, it would end. There could be no next year in Pluto—not for Mike. He loved a great story. He needed a great story—and this great story had been told—except for this, its final chapter.

Jen wound up and fired a drop ball on the outside corner. "Strike!" the umpire shouted. Mike was focused now. His stomach churned. Not because his team was in a jam in the seventh inning of the state championship game, but because he realized, just then, that the outcome actually mattered.

Sure, he had wanted to beat Jake Moffitt. The guy was an ass. Yes, he had enjoyed the prestige of knocking off North Canton Hoover. But, those were just softball games in corn fields. They were band aids for his lacerated life—distractions. This was not that. This was part of him—and it was the first thing that was part of him that was never part of Peggy. He could feel himself letting go. He was moving past his grief.

"Atta girl, Jen!" He shouted. "On your toes out there infield!"

Jen took a deep breath. Mike took a deeper one as his pitcher turned loose a knee-high changeup over the outer half of the plate. The batter swung and hit a hard line drive to center field. Lauren ran two steps to her left and dove. The ball hit the web of her glove and stuck. The runner at third had made a mistake. Instead of staying on the base to tag up after the ball was either caught or dropped, she bolted for the plate when it was hit. When she realized Lauren had made a miraculous catch, the runner sprinted back to third, tagged up and still tried to score the tying run. Lauren jumped to her feet and threw a strike on the fly to Allie. The runner stopped and tried to make it back to third, but Allie ran her down and tagged her for the final out.

The Pluto girls threw their gloves into the air and ran to the pitcher's circle to celebrate. After a few minutes, they shook hands with the girls from Warren. Then, Mike accepted the championship trophy as parents and other supporters snapped photos. Everybody gave Lauren a hug or a high five.

"That was one amazing catch," said Mr. Willoughby, holding his open hand in the air.

Lauren smiled and slapped his hand. "Thanks, Mr. Willoughby," she said.

Gail found Mike in the crowd and gave him a hug and a kiss. "You don't mind, do you?" She asked.

"Only that you stopped," he smiled.

Walt ran up and gave Mike a bigger, cologne-drenched hug. "You did it! You did it! I knew you could do it!" The athletic director shouted. "And you can do it next year, too! You're only losing a couple of players!"

Mike wiggled away from Walt's embrace. Sometime between his last trip to the circle and Lauren's heroic catch and throw, his decision about next year was made—and it was final. He would not try to become the next Jake Moffitt. He would not spend the rest of his days teaching girls how to play softball. He would never call Pluto "home."

"I think we've revived the program," said the grinning coach.

An hour later, Mike stepped off the team bus and said goodbye to each of his players with a hug. He hugged Lana last.

"Thanks, Lana. Just for being you. It's been a lot of fun."

"Thanks for giving me a chance, coach," Lana said.

Mike walked toward the softball field. He held his hand up to shield the setting sun. When he reached home plate, he stared at the scoreboard and the flag pole.

"Won't be long, we'll have another championship flag up there, coach," said Lana, who'd followed him to the field.

Mike turned, surprised to see her. "I kind of wanted to be alone, Lana."

"Yeah. I thought so," she said. "But I also thought that every time I think I want to be alone, I really don't, so I figured I'd follow you to keep you company."

"You think too much," said Mike.

"Never heard that before," she joked. Lana felt a hand on her shoulder.

"I'll take it from here, Lana," said Gail. She stood beside Mike in the batter's box and held his hand. "Are you sure you want to walk away from this?"

Mike turned and held her face in his hands. "No." He said blankly. "I might run."

"Can I go with you?" She asked.

Mike bolted toward the parking lot. "If you can keep up," he called.

Epilogue

Friday, May 8, 2015

MORGAN RETURNED TO the top step of the dugout after a quick chat with her baby sister. Jen had told her she was fine even though she'd just walked the bases loaded with a four-run lead in the top of the fifth inning.

"What did she say?" asked Lana, as she updated the score book.

"She said she's fine," said Morgan, gripping the green hand rail.

"Personally, I'm shocked by her response," Lana smiled. "Are you certain you didn't misunderstand?"

Morgan laughed. "Quite."

Jen struck out the next three batters and the Invaders went on to beat Jake Moffitt's Rustlers, 5-0. The Pluto winning streak over two seasons had reached 41 games. They'd beaten the legendary coach four in a row.

"Mike would have loved this one," said Walt, as he walked with Morgan to the parking lot.

"Yeah, he wasn't a big Moffitt fan," she laughed.

"Have you heard from him lately?" Walt asked. "I know the minor league season starts pretty late."

"This morning," said Morgan. "He called from Orlando to wish us good luck against Wyoming. He said his team doesn't start playing until mid-June. It's the rookie league, so a lot of the kids are still playing college ball. He's the hitting instructor, and he'll coach third base during games."

"What about Gail?" Walt asked.

"She's great," said Morgan. "Oh, yeah. Mike said they're going to have an announcement soon."

Walt clapped his pudgy hands. "That's fabulous! I knew it! When?"

"He said sometime after Gail wraps up her current case. She's defending a guy accused of killing his wife."

Walt smiled. "Same shit, different city."

Morgan laughed. "Coming for free food at the pub?"

"Wouldn't miss it for all the gold in Fort Knox," said Walt.

Morgan thought about her safe deposit box and smiled. "Nor would I," she said. "Nor would I."

67237235R00186

Made in the USA
Middletown, DE
20 March 2018